A secret library of magical books . . .
Two sisters tasked with its protection . . .

◆◆◆◆◆◆◆◆◆◆◆◆◆◆◆◆◆◆◆◆◆◆◆◆◆◆◆◆◆◆◆◆◆◆◆

"Törzs's debut novel features a wonderfully realized and atmospheric world and a plot filled with unexpected twists. . . . Törzs does a fantastic job creating a gripping and suspenseful story that keeps readers on their toes and wanting more. Fans of *Ninth House* by Leigh Bardugo and *The Night Circus* by Erin Morgenstern will love this magic- and suspense-filled novel."

—*Library Journal* (starred review)

"Spellbinding. . . . Unraveling the twisty mysteries that connect Nicholas to the Kalotay sisters and dismantling the dark constraints on their lives keep both characters and readers guessing throughout. Meanwhile, threads of hope and love keep the grimly gorgeous worldbuilding from growing too dark. Törzs's lyrical, idiosyncratic prose (at one point, the sky is described as 'so pale it seemed infected') elevates proceedings. This is a must-read."

—*Publishers Weekly* (starred review)

"A mysterious tale of familial memories and secrets that grip and hold. . . . Törzs carries the reader along with her telescopic descriptions and heartwarming character relationships. . . . It's all very *Practical Magic* in a way that felt comforting to read. There is such a tight knot of mystery at the center of all the bonding, queer love, familial reconciliations, and death. . . . Memories and the past loom heavy in *Ink Blood Sister Scribe*, but not in a way that weighs a reader down. Törzs's prose is evocative and compelling, creating a masterful literary fantasy of magic, family, and books."

—*Lightspeed*

"Sometimes I wonder whether creatives are reaching a point where all the possible ways that magic and its uses can be explored have already been explored. And then I read books like Emma Törzs's debut novel, *Ink Blood Sister Scribe*, and I realize that nope, there is definitely still scope for new and imaginative and twisty magics. . . . Törzs creates believable characters and, even more than that, deeply relatable family situations. . . . This is an immensely enjoyable debut, and I look forward to more."

—*Locus*

"Confident and powerful. . . . An enchanting book about enchanted books."

—*Bustle*

"Atmospheric suspense and old-school mystery twists."
—Goodreads, "Readers' 54 Most Anticipated Books of Summer"

"Secret libraries and mysterious portals, deadly jeopardy and blood magic . . . no boxes go unticked in this fabulous page-turner, a searing debut about two sisters with very different powers. . . . Much rests on the disciplined goriness of the rituals, but it's the emotional twists that hold us spellbound as the action takes us to Antarctica, Vermont, Manhattan, and an English country mansion—invisible of course."
—*Daily Mail*

"This debut novel is an absolute delight, weaving a convincing occult underground into real-world settings, with engaging characters and a compelling storyline sure to make it a lasting favorite with fantasy readers of all stripes."
—*The Guardian*

"Skillfully plotted, character-driven debut. . . . Gorgeous but not over-written prose balances violent scenes, depictions of coercive abuse, and the crafting of books written in blood. The characters, sheltered in different ways, show nuanced growth emotionally and in their relationships. Törzs expertly crafts a character-driven conclusion that keeps readers in suspense but isn't rushed, drawing out the why and the how, even if readers already know the who. *Ink Blood Sister Scribe* will speak directly to fans of Alix E. Harrow, Seanan McGuire—and magical libraries."
—Suzanne Krohn, *Shelf Awareness*

EMMA
TÖRZS

WILLIAM MORROW
An Imprint of HarperCollinsPublishers

INK

BLOOD

SISTER

SCRIBE

A NOVEL

INK BLOOD SISTER SCRIBE. Copyright © 2023 by Emma Törzs. All rights reserved. Printed in the United States of America. No part of this book may be used or reproduced in any manner whatsoever without written permission except in the case of brief quotations embodied in critical articles and reviews. For information, address HarperCollins Publishers, 195 Broadway, New York, NY 10007.

HarperCollins books may be purchased for educational, business, or sales promotional use. For information, please email the Special Markets Department at SPsales@harpercollins.com.

A hardcover edition of this book was published in 2023 by William Morrow, an imprint of HarperCollins Publishers.

FIRST WILLIAM MORROW PAPERBACK EDITION PUBLISHED 2024.

Designed by Elina Cohen

Title page arrowroot image courtesy of Shutterstock / SvetaKhlivna

The Library of Congress has catalogued a previous edition as follows:

Names: Törzs, Emma, 1987– author.
Title: Ink blood sister scribe : a novel / Emma Törzs.
Description: First edition. | New York, NY : William Morrow, an imprint of
  Harper Collins Publishers, [2023]
Identifiers: LCCN 2023004470 (print) | LCCN 2023004471 (ebook) | ISBN
  9780063253469 (hardcover) | ISBN 9780063253483 (ebook)
Subjects: LCSH: Rare books—Fiction. | Magic—Fiction. | Family
  secrets—Fiction. | LCGFT: Fantasy fiction. | Novels.
Classification: LCC PS3620.O698 I65 2023 (print) | LCC PS3620.O698
  (ebook) | DDC 813/.6—dc23/eng/20230206
LC record available at https://lccn.loc.gov/2023004470
LC ebook record available at https://lccn.loc.gov/2023004471

ISBN 978-0-06-325347-6 (pbk.)

24 25 26 27 28 LBC 5 4 3 2 1

For Jesse, my magic sister

Abe Kalotay died in his front yard in late February, beneath a sky so pale it seemed infected. There was a wintery wet snowbite to the still air and the sprawled-open pages of the book at his side had grown slightly damp by the time his daughter Joanna came home and found his body lying in the grass by their long dirt driveway.

Abe was on his back, eyes half-opened to that gray sky, mouth slack and his tongue drying blue, one of his hands with its quick-bitten nails draped across his stomach. The other hand was resting on the book, forefinger still pressed to the page as if holding his place. A last smudge of vivid red was slowly fading into the paper and Abe himself was mushroom-white and oddly shriveled. It was an image Joanna already knew she'd have to fight against forever, to keep it from supplanting the twenty-four years' worth of living memories that had, in the space of seconds, become more precious to her than anything else in the world. She didn't make a sound when she saw him, only sank to her knees, and began to shake.

Later, she would think he'd probably come outside because he'd realized what the book was doing and had been struggling to reach the road before he bled out; either to flag down a passing driver to call an ambulance, or to spare Joanna from having to heave his body into the bed of her truck and take him up their driveway and past the boundaries of their wards. But at the time she didn't question why he was outside.

She only questioned why he'd brought a book along with him.

She had not yet understood that it was the book itself that had killed him; she only understood that its presence was a rupture in one of his cardinal rules, a rule Joanna herself had not yet dreamed of breaking—though she would, eventually. But even more inconceivable than her father letting a book outside the safety of their home was the fact that it was a book Joanna did not recognize. She had spent her entire life caring for their collection and knew every book within it as intimately as one would know a family member, yet the one lying at her father's side was completely unfamiliar in both appearance and in sound. Their other books hummed like summer bees. This book throbbed like unspent thunder and when she opened the cover the handwritten words swam in front of her eyes, rearranging themselves every time a letter nearly became clear. In progress; unreadable.

The note Abe had tucked between the pages was perfectly legible, however, despite the shakiness of the hand. He'd used his left. His right had been fixed in place as the book drank.

Joanna, he had written. *I'm sorry. Don't let your mother in. Keep this book safe and away from your blood. I love you so much. Tell Esther*

It ended there, without punctuation. Joanna would never know if he'd meant to write more or if he only wanted her to pass on a final message of love to the daughter he hadn't seen in years. But kneeling there on the cold dirt, with the book in her hands, she didn't have the wherewithal to think about any of this yet.

She could only stare at Abe's lifeless body, try to breathe, and prepare herself for the next steps.

PART ONE

MIRROR
MAGIC

1

Esther couldn't get over the blue of the sunlit sky.

It was a variated blue, almost white where it met the snowy horizon but deepening as Esther's eye followed it upward: from robin's egg to cerulean to a calm, luminous azure. Beneath it the Antarctic ice was blindingly bright, and the scattered outbuildings Esther could see from her narrow dorm window drew stripes of indigo shadow on the white ruts of the road. Everything gleamed. It was eight o'clock in the evening and not discernibly darker than it had been at eight o'clock that morning.

"Excuse me," Pearl said, and hip-checked Esther to one side so she could fit a piece of custom-cut cardboard in the window frame. Esther fell backward onto her unmade bed and propped herself on her elbows, watching Pearl lean over the tiny, cluttered desk to reach the glass.

"If you'd told me two weeks ago I'd block the sun as soon as it came up, I would have laughed you off the station," Esther said.

Pearl ripped the tape with her teeth. "Well, two weeks ago you were sleeping through the night. Never say the dark did nothing for you." She applied the last strip and added, "Or me."

"Thank you, darkness, and thank you, Pearl," Esther said. Though she had indeed been sleeping badly since the sun had reappeared after six months of winter, it was still somewhat dispiriting to watch the light and the distant mountains vanish, plunging her back into the realities of her cell-like room: the bed with its rumpled purple sheets lit by the baleful overhead bulb, the scuffed tile floors, and the plywood desk piled high with scattered papers, most of them notes on the Mexican novel Esther was translating for fun. The novel itself was on top of her dresser, safely out of range of the collection of half-full water glasses leaving rings on the notebook paper.

Pearl sat opposite Esther at the foot of the bed and said, "So. Are you ready to face the unwashed masses?"

In response, Esther threw an arm over her eyes and groaned.

Esther and Pearl had spent the past winter as two of just thirty others holding down the small South Pole station, but November had ushered in the summer season and over the past few days, small roaring cargo planes had disgorged nearly a hundred new people into the station's hallways. Now scientists and astronomers filled the dorms, the galley, the gym, the upper workrooms; strangers who ate all the late-night cookies and booted up long-sleeping computers and asked constant, anxious questions about what time of day the internet satellite went up.

Esther had imagined she'd be happy to see all these new faces. She had always been a natural extrovert, not the typical candidate to be locked away on the ice in a research station that much resembled her tiny rural high school. She'd lived in Minneapolis for the year before she'd come here to the Antarctic, and her friends there had reacted with honest horror when she'd told them she'd accepted a job at the Pole station as an electrician for the winter season. Everybody knew someone who knew someone who'd tried it, loathed it, and flown home early to escape the crushing isolation. But Esther hadn't been worried.

She'd figured Antarctica couldn't be that much worse than the isolated, extreme conditions in which she had grown up. It'd be good money, it'd be an adventure—and most importantly, it would be completely inaccessible to most every other person on the planet.

Sometime over the long winter, however, Esther's extroversion had started to atrophy and with it the mask of good cheer she usually donned each morning along with her uniform. Now she gazed up at the ceiling, industrial white like the industrial white walls and industrial white hallways and her industrial white coworkers.

"Have I actually been an introvert this whole time?" she said. "All these years, have I been fooling myself? The real extroverts are out there like hell yeah, fresh meat, nonstop party, bangtown USA."

"Bangtown Antarctic Treaty International Territory," Pearl corrected. Pearl was Australian with dual citizenship.

"Right," said Esther. "That."

Pearl got to her knees and crawled down the length of the bed toward Esther. "I imagine," she said, "that six months of unwanted celibacy plus a planeful of new faces could make an extrovert of anyone."

"Mmm," Esther said. "So you're saying I've become an introvert through the sheer power of . . ."

"My amazing body, yes, obviously," said Pearl, whose lips were now trailing along the sensitive shell of Esther's ear.

Esther reached up and helped herself to a handful of Pearl's blond hair, which somehow always looked sunkissed despite the utter lack of sun. *Australians.* So indefatigably beachy and up-for-it. She wove her fingers through those tangled strands and tugged Pearl down to kiss her, feeling her smile against her mouth as Esther pulled her closer.

For the past decade, since she was eighteen, Esther had moved every November—moved cities, states, countries. She made friends and lovers breezily, picking them up like other people picked up takeout and going through them as quickly. Everybody liked her, and like many well-liked people, she worried that if people *really* got to know her, if they managed to penetrate that glancing shield of likability, they wouldn't actually like her one bit. This was a benefit of never staying in one place.

The other, vastly more important benefit: not being found.

Esther slipped a hand beneath the hem of Pearl's sweater, fingers finding the smooth dip of her waist as Pearl nudged one of her long legs between Esther's thighs. But even as she moved her hips in friction-seeking instinct, her father's long-ago words began to echo unbidden in her head—a cold glass of water thrown in the face of her subconscious.

"November 2 by eleven o'clock p.m., Eastern Standard Time," Abe had said on the last day she'd seen him, ten years ago at their home in

Vermont. "Wherever you are, you must leave on November 2 and keep moving for twenty-four hours, or the people who killed your mother will come for you, too."

The summer season had officially begun a couple days ago: November 5. Three days after Esther, according to her father's urgent edict, should have been long gone.

But she wasn't. She was still here.

Abe had been dead two years now, and for the first time since she'd started running a decade before, Esther had a reason to stay. A reason that was warm and solid and currently kissing her neck.

Technically, Esther had first met Pearl at the Christchurch airport, as part of a big group of workers waiting for their flight into the Antarctic. They'd both been hidden in the many layers required to board the plane—wool hat, huge orange parka, gloves, clompy insulated boots, dark-lensed goggles pushed up on their heads—and Esther had gotten only the briefest impression of sparkly eyes and a full-throated laugh before the group was ushered onto the plane and she and Pearl were seated on opposite ends of the cargo hold.

Because of their different duties and different schedules, their paths hadn't really crossed again until the end of the first month, when Esther had hung a sign in the gym looking for sparring buddies. *Boxing, Muy Thai, BJJ, MMA, Krav Maga, let's fight! :) :) :)* She'd added the smiley faces to counteract the aggression of "fight," but had immediately regretted it when another electrician—an obnoxiously tall white guy from Washington who insisted everyone call him "J-Dog"—saw it and began giving her endless shit.

"The Smiley Face Killer!" he'd crow when she walked into their shift meeting. If they crossed paths in the galley at lunch, he'd pretend to cower. "You gonna hit me over the head with that big ol' smile?" But the final straw came when he started loudly telling everyone about his black belt in karate, and how he'd love to find a sparring partner who was "really serious about the sport."

Honestly, he gave Esther no choice. After a week of this, he approached her one day in the galley and planted himself in her path so she couldn't get to the pizza, grinning at her so widely she could see his molars.

"What are you doing," she said.

"Fighting you!" he said.

"No," she said, and put down her tray. "*This* is fighting me."

A few minutes later she had J-Dog on the floor in a headlock, one of his arms trapped in her hold, the other swatting at her face, his long legs kicking ineffectually at the tiled floor as onlookers hooted and cheered. "Not gonna let you go until you smile," she said, and he whimpered, pulling his lips up in a forced approximation of his earlier grin. As soon as she released him, he bounced to his feet, brushing himself off and saying, "Not cool, dude, not cool!"

When Esther turned back toward her abandoned lunch tray, suppressing her own very real smile, she found herself face to face—give or take a few inches—with Pearl. Shucked from her plane layers, Pearl was tall and tough, with a pile of sun-streaked hair wadded into a precarious knot that seemed in danger of sliding off her head. Her brown eyes were as sparkling as Esther remembered. More so, because now they were sparkling right at Esther.

"That was the most magical thing I have ever seen," Pearl said, and rested a slender, long-fingered hand on Esther's arm. "You wouldn't consider giving lessons, would you?"

Pearl was terrible at self-defense. She had no killer instinct and always second-guessed herself, pulling her punches and dropping her kicks and making herself laugh so hard she went weak in Esther's grip. Within three lessons, the "training sessions" had turned into make-out sessions, and they'd moved from the gym to the bedroom. The first time they'd slept together, Pearl had asked, hitching her hips as Esther began to slide her jeans down, "Have you ever been with a woman before?"

Esther looked up from between Pearl's legs, affronted. "Yes, plenty! Why?"

"Calm down, Don Juan," Pearl said, laughing. "I'm not questioning your technique. You just seem a little nervous."

This was when Esther had realized she might be in trouble. Because not only was it true, she *was* nervous, butterfly-stomached in a way she hadn't felt for years . . . but Pearl had noticed. Had read it somehow on Esther's well-trained face or in her well-trained body. Esther wasn't used to people seeing what she didn't want them to see, and the way Pearl looked at her, *saw* her, was unsettling. In response, she'd given Pearl her most confident, reassuring smile, then set her teeth very gently to the inside of Pearl's bare thigh, which had been enough of a distraction that the conversation ended there. But even then, at the very start, she had suspected how difficult Pearl might be to leave.

Now, a whole season later, thinking about this—about leaving, about staying, about the lasting echo of her father's warning—had the unfortunate effect of breaking her current mood. She rolled Pearl over onto her side and carefully ended the kiss, lying back against the pillows, and Pearl settled against Esther's shoulder.

"I'm going to get so drunk tonight," said Pearl.

"Before or after we play?"

"Before, after, during."

"Me too," Esther decided.

Esther and Pearl were in a Pat Benatar cover band that was scheduled to play at the party that evening. The whole long winter they'd been practicing and putting on shows exclusively for the same wearily supportive thirty-five people, and by this point it was like playing the recorder in front of a parent whose pride couldn't outweigh how tired they were of hearing "Hot Cross Buns." Performing for new ears and eyes felt as nerve-racking as climbing the stage of Madison Square Garden.

"We should drink water in preparation," Pearl said, "so we don't end up puking like beakers."

She fetched them two glasses and Esther sat up on her elbows so she didn't spill it all over herself as she gulped it. This was the driest place she'd ever been, every last bit of moisture in the air frozen into ice. It was easy to get dehydrated.

"Do you think the scientists drink so much because they're making up for all the years they spent studying?" Esther said.

"No," said Pearl without hesitation. She herself worked with the carpenters. "Nerds are always absolute party freaks. I used to go to these kink nights in Sydney and it was all surgeons, engineers, orthodontists. Did you know that people who're into BDSM have notably higher IQs than their vanilla counterparts?"

"I don't think that's a testable hypothesis."

Pearl grinned. She had unusually sharp canine teeth in an otherwise soft mouth, an incongruity that did funny things to Esther's blood flow. "Can you imagine the variables?"

"I'd like to," Esther said, "but not right now. We need to get a move on."

Pearl glanced at her watch and jumped. "Shit! You're right."

They'd been holed up in this hole of a bedroom since dinner a few hours ago, and Esther stood to stretch before jamming her socked feet into her boots.

"God, I'm so glad you agreed to stay on," Pearl said. "I can't imagine facing this without you."

Esther wanted to answer but found she couldn't quite look at the woman in front of her, this person she liked more than she'd liked anyone else in a very long time. She felt a tight longing spread through her chest; not desire, but something even more familiar, something that was always with her. It was that she *missed* Pearl despite her presence. An anticipation of missing, like her emotions hadn't yet caught up to the idea that this time was different, this time she was staying.

Her father's paranoia had begun to hiss again in her ear, telling her to go, telling her she was making an abominable, selfish mistake; that she was putting Pearl in danger, and Pearl was still looking at her, face open and affectionate but starting to shutter a little at Esther's lack of response.

"I'm glad, too," Esther said. She had practice around Pearl now and could trust her own face not to betray any of her sudden, melancholy mood, and she watched Pearl relax beneath her smile. "Come get me when you're dressed," she added. "We can fortify with a shot."

Pearl raised her hand, those long fingers wrapped around the stem of an imaginary glass. "Here's to the crowd. May they love us."

THE CROWD LOVED THEM. ALL FOUR MEMBERS OF THE BAND TOOK their practice sessions very seriously and had even managed to come up with passable eighties hair band costumes: black jeans, leather jackets. Esther and Pearl had both teased their hair to great heights, though it would've been more convincing with hairspray, which no one on base had. They looked good and they sounded good, and they were aided by the fact that by the time they plugged in their amps and started playing, everyone was well on their way to wasted and willing to cheer.

Esther was the backup singer and bassist, and her throat was raw, fingers sore by the time they finished "Hell Is for Children" and ended their set. The party was in the galley, which by day resembled a high school cafeteria, complete with the long gray plastic tables that had been pushed up against the walls to free up floor space, and even without the overhead fluorescents and a set of flashing red and purple party lights turned on, there was a distinct middle school vibe that made Esther feel young and silly in a pleasantly immature kind of way. The band had played at the front of the room beneath a web of white fairy lights, and once their set was over, pop music started piping through the new speakers Esther herself had rigged in the corners of the room some months ago.

The large, tiled floor was packed with people milling around, most of them unfamiliar to both Esther and to one another, and more sat in the row of chairs that blocked off the swinging gates leading behind the buffet-style hot bar to the darkened, stainless-steel kitchen. Esther noticed that the new summer crew looked amazingly sunned and healthy compared to their Antarctically pale colleagues. The new smells, too, were overwhelming in their variation. When you lived with the same people, eating the same foods, breathing the same recycled air, you started to smell the same, too—even to a nose as keen as Esther's. These people were, quite literally, a breath of fresh air.

And a breath of something else.

Esther was midconversation with a new carpenter from Colorado named Trev, a man Pearl had described as "eager to please," when suddenly she raised her head like a hunting dog, nostrils flaring.

"Are you wearing cologne?" she asked. She'd caught something under the booze-and-plastic smell of the party, something that made her think, jarringly, of home.

"No," Trev said, smiling in amusement as she leaned over shamelessly and sniffed his neck.

"Hmm," she said.

"Maybe it's my deodorant," he said. "Cedar. Manly."

"It does smell nice," she said. "But no, I thought—well, never mind." They were closer now than they had been, and Trev's friendly eyes had become openly flirtatious, clearly taking her neck-sniffing as a declaration of interest. Esther took a step back. Even if she weren't taken, he looked like the kind of man who probably owned a lot of recreational outdoor equipment and wanted to teach her how to use it. However, she admired the controlled way he moved his body; it reminded her of the trainers she'd met at the martial arts gyms she'd been frequenting for years.

She opened her mouth to say something flirty, because she didn't want to rust, after all, but then her sensitive nose caught that other scent, the one that had distracted her a moment ago. God, what *was* it? It put her right back in her childhood kitchen; she could see the bulbous green inefficient fridge, the dents and dings of the maple cabinets, the feel of warped linoleum beneath her feet. Vegetable but not a vegetable, almost spicy, and it smelled *fresh,* which wasn't common around these parts. Rosemary? Chrysanthemum? Cabbage?

Yarrow.

The answer came to her, words tumbling back to her throat from where they had been perched on the tip of her tongue. Yarrow, achillea, milfoil, plumajillo.

"Excuse me," Esther said, eschewing social decorum, and turned away from the confused carpenter. She pushed past a cluster of people comparing tattoos by the cereal nook and ducked through the hanging blue streamers someone had taped, seemingly at random, to the ceiling, taking short breaths through her nose. She was tracking the unmistakable scent of the herb, the smell of her childhood, but she knew it was pointless even as she strained for it. It was already a memory again, supplanted by the aroma of pizza and beer and bodies.

She stood in the middle of the room, surrounded by music and chattering strangers, stunned by how strongly the fragrance had hit her heart. Was someone wearing it as a perfume? If so she wanted to put her arms around them and bury her face in their skin. Usually, Esther kept loss at arm's length; she didn't think about all the people she'd left behind over the years, she didn't think about any of the places she'd called home, and aside from the postcards she sent her sister and stepmother once a month, she didn't think about her family. It was a constant, tiring action, this not-thinking, like keeping a muscle flexed at all times. But the scent of yarrow had unflexed that stern muscle and with its relaxation came a cousin to the same sadness that had poured over her in Pearl's doorway earlier.

Pearl herself was across the room, face flushed, her teased hair tangled like she'd just stepped off the back of someone's motorcycle or out of someone's bed. She was wearing a dark purple lipstick that made her eyes look berry-bright and talking to a woman who was nearly as tall as she was. Esther charged toward them, intent on pulling herself out of this mood as quickly as she'd fallen into it.

"Tequila," she said to Pearl.

"This is Esther," Pearl said to the woman she'd been talking to. "Electrician. Esther, this is Abby in maintenance, she lived in Australia last year!"

Abby and Pearl were giggling at each other, cheerfully drunk. Pearl poured all three of them a shot, then poured Esther an extra after she'd gasped down the first. Already she was feeling better, shaking off the malaise that had been clawing at her throat. She was a person made for the present, not the past. She couldn't afford to forget that.

The party had done its job in starting to wipe away the over-winters' protective isolationism, and soon enough there was dancing, more drinking, a weird game that involved shouting the names of birds, even more drinking. A beaker, predictably, puked. Pearl and Abby spent some time screaming happily in one another's faces about someone they somehow knew in common from Sydney, someone who had a really bad dog, and then Pearl dragged Esther onto the makeshift dance floor and wrapped her long, leggy body around Esther's shorter one. The music was deep and pulsing and soon they were grinding like they were in a real club and not in a little heated box on a vast stretch of ice, many thousands of miles away from anything that might be called civilization.

Esther pushed Pearl's hair off her sweaty face and tried not to think about her family or her father's warnings or about the days that had ticked by since November 2. She focused instead on the present, on the thump of the bass and the feel of Pearl's body against hers. She thought, *I wish I could do this forever.*

But there was no "forever" where bodies were concerned, and eventually she had to pee.

In contrast to the noisy clamor of the party, the bathroom down the hall was almost eerily silent when Esther banged through the door and fumbled with her jeans. The sound of urine echoed loudly in the stainless-steel bowl and she could hear her own drunken breath, heavy from dancing, raspy from talking. The flush was a roar. At the sink, she paused in front of the mirror. With one finger she smoothed back a dark eyebrow, batted her eyelashes at herself, wound a few locks of hair around her finger to give her loose curls more definition. Then she stopped. Squinted.

There was a series of small marks along the mirror's perimeter, brownish red smears that sat atop the glass. They were symmetrical but not identical, one at each corner, a swipe as if with a paintbrush or thumb. She leaned close, examining, and wet a piece of paper towel to rub them off. The towel did nothing, not even when she added soap, her heart climbing into her throat. She tried to scratch the marks off. They didn't budge.

She stepped back so quickly she nearly fell.

A person didn't grow up like Esther had without recognizing the sight of dried blood, much less a pattern of it that could not be removed, and no one could grow up like she had without recognizing what that bloody pattern might imply. The smell of yarrow returned to her, though whether it was in her mind or here in the bathroom she wasn't certain.

Blood. Herbs.

Somebody here had a book.

Somebody here was doing magic.

"No," Esther said aloud. She was drunk, she was paranoid, she'd been locked in a cement box for six months and now she was seeing things.

She was also stepping away from the mirror, eyes still locked on her own terrified face, scared to turn her back on the glass. When she bumped up against the bathroom door, she whirled around and slammed through it, then ran down the narrow hallway toward the gym. The cardio room was so bright it seemed to buzz, the equipment standing in mechanical rows on the padded gray floor and the green walls making everything appear sickly pale. There was a couple making out on one of the weight benches, and they squawked in alarm as Esther crashed past them and into the gym's white, single-stalled bathroom.

The same reddish-brown marks were on the mirror, the same pattern. They were on the mirror in the bathroom by the rec room, too, and the one by the laboratory, and the one by the kitchen. Esther stumbled to her bedroom, heart in her throat, but thank god her own mirror was untouched. Probably just the public mirrors had been marked—a small comfort. She couldn't smash every mirror in the station without calling attention to herself or getting in trouble.

Esther locked the door behind her, standing in front of her mirror with her hands on the top of her low dresser, leaning her weight on the wood so she could think. Clearly this was some kind of mirror magic, but she was too freaked-out and drunk to recall what that might entail. One of her family's books could turn a mirror into a kind of mood ring, the glass reflecting a person's true emotions for an hour or so, and then there was that mirror in Snow White, the one that told the evil queen about the fairest in the land . . . but was that kind of magic just fairy-tale shit, or was it real life?

She needed sobriety, clarity. She hung her head and steadied her breath. On the dresser, bracketed between her hands, sat the novel she was translating from Spanish to English, and she stared at its familiar green cover, at the decorative border and stylized sketch of a dark doorway beneath the title. *La Ruta Nos Aportó Otro Paso Natural* by Alejandra Gil, 1937. As far as Esther had been able to find, this novel was Gil's first and only publication—and it was also the only thing Esther owned that had belonged to her mother, Isabel.

Inside the cover was a tightly controlled cursive note; a translation of the title, in Esther's mother's perfect hand. "Remember," her mother had written to herself in English: "The path provides the natural next step."

Esther's stepmother, Cecily, had given her this novel when she was eighteen, the day before she'd left home forever, and at the time Esther had needed the translation. Spanish should have been her mother tongue, but Isabel had died when Esther was too young for language, and so it was only her mother's tongue. But it was the Spanish title she'd gotten tattooed across her collarbones several months later: "la ruta nos aportó" on the right, "otro paso natural" on the left. A palindrome and thus readable in the mirror.

The party felt like it had been hours ago, though the sweat from dancing was still drying on Esther's skin. She had stripped down to only a black tank top; now she was shivering. In the glass, she could see the words of her tattoo around the straps of her shirt. When she'd first gotten the ink, she had just fled her home and family and been feeling adrift and frightened in a world that suddenly lacked any kind of structure, so the mere suggestion of a path, much less a natural next step, had been infinitely soothing to her. But now that she was nearing thirty, spoke excellent Spanish, and most importantly had actually read the novel, she understood that Gil's title was not meant to be soothing at all. Rather, it spoke of a kind of preordained movement, a socially constructed pathway that forced people, particularly women, into a series of steps they'd been tricked into believing they'd chosen for themselves.

These days the words struck her as a rallying cry: not to follow the path, but to veer from it. In fact, this very phrase had helped her make the decision to ignore her father's long-ago orders and stay in Antarctica for the summer season.

A decision she was now terrified she might come to regret.

"Leave every year on November 2," he had said, "or the people who killed your mother will come for you, too. And not only you, Esther. They'll come for your sister."

For these past ten years, she had listened, she had obeyed. Every November 1 she had packed up her things and every November 2 she had started moving, sometimes driving for that long day and night, sometimes taking a series of buses, planes, trains, not sleeping. From Vancouver to Mexico City. From Paris to Berlin. From Minneapolis to Antarctica. Every year, like clockwork, except this year. This year she had ignored his warning. This year she had stayed.

And now it was November 5, the station was filled with strangers, and one of them had brought a book.

2

The cat was back.

Joanna could hear him scratching at the front door, a plaintive sound like branches skidding across a roof. It was five in the evening and already growing dim, the sliver of sky outside her kitchen window fading from white to a smudgy charcoal gray. The weatherman on the radio that morning had said it might snow and she'd been hoping for it all day; she loved the first snow of the season, when all the faded browns of the sleeping earth were awakened into a new kind of aliveness, everything coarse made suddenly delicate, everything solid turned lacy and insubstantial. Magic that didn't need words to enact itself year after year.

The cat scratched again, and Joanna's heart lurched. She'd seen him stalking around her dead garden last week, a young blocky-headed tomcat, skinny and striped, and she'd put out a bowl of tuna one night and a bowl of sardines the next and now he had grown bold. But she couldn't attend to him right now: the stove was lit, herbs were charring in a pot, and her hands were covered in blood.

That last was her fault. She'd cut too deeply into the back of her left hand and instead of a trickle she'd gotten a flood. Even after she'd measured out the half ounce she needed, her hand bled sluggishly through the bandages, and it hurt more than she'd anticipated. It would be worth it if this worked—but this was her thirty-seventh attempt since she'd begun trying a year and a half ago, and so far, all she had to show for her troubles was a growing collection of thin white scars on her hands. She had no real expectations that now would be any different.

Still, she had to try. She *wanted* to try.

Tonight, she was experimenting with the new moon, after the last few full moons had yielded no results—not even when she'd had a flash of what she thought was genius and managed to gather a whole half cup of menstrual blood. She had been so hopeful that might be the key. According to her admittedly surface-level research, peripheral blood was nearly indistinguishable from menstrual blood, forensically speaking, and she'd only ever managed to have three of her many books analyzed anyway—so it was absolutely possible the tests that had listed "blood" as the main ingredient of the ink had misled her in terms of where that blood may have come from.

But no. The book she'd written with her period blood was as ineffectual as all the others she'd attempted.

As ineffectual as she knew this one would be.

Still, hope and curiosity kept her at the stove, powdering the blackened herbs in a grinder and then mixing them with the blood from her hand, an egg yolk, a pinch of gum arabic, and honey. The result was a thick, dark paste that would write beautifully when mixed with water, but likely do nothing else. She kept her third ear pricked for any sound that might suggest the ink was more than just a homemade pigment, listening for the bodily hum that ran like syrup through her veins whenever she was near a book . . . but the ink stayed black and silent.

She had planned to write the book tonight, copying the text of one of the smaller spells in her collection, a ten-page sixteenth-century Persian incantation that was now faded but had once called up a fire that blazed without burning for roughly ten minutes. "The egg-cooker," her father had called it jokingly. But looking down at the quiet paste, her hand still stinging, she knew instinctively that the act of writing would be pointless.

Blinking back tears of frustration, she left the mess on the stove and moved across the kitchen, the green-and-white seventies linoleum buckling here and there beneath her feet. The floor always brought her father's voice to her mind, deep and cheerful and so terribly missed; "Gonna retile this soon," a sentence repeated so often it had taken on the cadence of ritual, but he hadn't retiled it and no one ever would. She opened a can of tuna to scrape into a bowl, but when she stepped out onto the porch, shivering in the snow-scented air, the cat was nowhere.

It was full night now, no moon to light the sky, but the cloud cover sent down a distilled, silvery gleam that caught in the finger-bone branches of the birch trees lining her cleared yard. Among the pearly birches, the spruce and pine were little more than rustling shadows that dissolved into the darkness of the forest beyond. Joanna squinted through the trees, searching for movement, but other than a faint breeze the night was still.

Disappointment welled in her, black as the blood ink cooling in its cup, and she shook it off with a laugh. What was she doing, anyhow? Trying to lure a wild animal to her door and then what—invite him in? Offer him a bed by the fire, stroke his soft fur, talk to him, make him her friend?

Yes.

She put the bowl of tuna down on the top step and went back into the house.

Joanna had been born in this house and had lived here all her life; first with her whole family, and then, after her sister ran away and her mother moved out soon after, with just her father. For eight years it had been only Joanna and Abe, and ever since Abe's death two years ago, it had been only Joanna. The house was an old Victorian, too big for one, its formerly white paint now a stained old-tooth gray, the wooden trim aged from gingerbread elegance to stale exhaustion. Even the steep arches of the roof and windows had dulled, like overused knives. The door creaked on its hinges as she swung it closed.

Inside, it was as quiet as the forest. It always was. The dark wood of the front hall gave way to the artificial brightness of the kitchen, tinged faintly amber from the glass shade of the hanging overhead light, and the window above the sink—which during the day looked out over Joanna's herb garden—was a murky black mirror. Joanna felt herself unintentionally matching her footsteps to the quiet around her, soft, like she was trying not to disturb her own empty home.

More and more this ever-present silence felt like a function of the wards Joanna had lived behind all her life; another kind of invisible bubble that cut her off from the rest of the world, protective, stifling. For the first year after Abe died, she'd imagined him around every corner, had heard his voice as she cooked dinner ("Spaghetti again? You're gonna turn into a noodle"), practiced pop songs on the piano ("Fiona Apple, now *there's* a voice"), or sat on the porch with the watercolors he'd bought her ("You get this talent from your mother, I couldn't draw a polar bear in a snowstorm"). But little by little even his imaginary voice had faded and now she had to work to conjure it in her mind.

Sometimes Joanna couldn't help but try to imagine someone else in the house with her, a mutable dream-figure of a man, tall and strong and kind. She'd read a lifetime's worth of romance novels and had no trouble picturing the physical possibilities: his mouth on her neck, his broad shoulders crowding her against a wall, his hands hiking her skirts up around her waist. Not that she wore skirts, but the closet of her sexual subconscious was full of petticoats. It was the other parts of the fantasy that gave her trouble. The parts where she attempted to imagine anyone besides her family in this house with her. It stretched her imagination just to envision the little striped cat at her heels, though she was getting better at it. She could almost see him now, leaping onto the white-tiled tabletop to bat at one of the sprigs of dried herbs that hung in the window.

Her father had been allergic to most animal dander, but even now she couldn't bring herself to get a pet, though as a child she had wept for one. Her older sister had caught frogs for her, trapped garter snakes, collected jars of snails, but it hadn't been the same. She'd wanted something soft that could accept and return her love. Now there was something painful about the idea of letting an animal inside and making Abe's own home inhospitable to him, or to whatever wisp of his spirit remained.

If one believed in spirits, which Joanna did not. Of the hundreds of handwritten books her father had gathered, books that when read aloud could do everything from tune a piano to bring rainclouds in a drought, none held spells to speak with ghosts or otherwise reach into the realm of death. That had to have been the first thing any early writers would have tried—whoever they were, however they'd written.

"It's not for us to ask how," her father had said, over and over. "We're here to protect the books, to give them a home, to respect them—not to interrogate them."

But how could Joanna not wonder?

Especially after one of the books Abe had protected all his life turned on him.

It had only taken her six months after Abe's death to break one of his most rigid rules and bring three books—though all of them with faded ink, the spells used up—outside the protective wards of her home and to a conservation lab in Boston. Even to conservationists who didn't know the truth of what they were seeing, the books were objects of fascination, ancient and rare, and Joanna had donated all three in return for access to their lab reports once the DNA and protein samples had been analyzed.

If she could finally learn how they'd been written, perhaps she'd understand why and how her father had been killed by one. And if she learned how they'd been written, well, it stood to reason she'd then be able to write them herself—didn't it?

Apparently not.

The lab results had thrilled and frightened her in turn, though in retrospect she thought she should've suspected. The magic within the books needed blood and herbs to activate, after all, so it made sense the ink itself was based in the same. But it cast a terrifying light on some of her longer books. How much blood was in those pages? And whose?

She spread plastic wrap over her bowl of ink paste then rebandaged her hand, which had finally stopped bleeding. With the stove off, the kitchen was chilly, so she made herself a cup of tea and took it into the living room. Only one lamp was on, the tall one with the green fringed shade, and in the low greenish light the room looked even more cluttered and nest-like than usual: wool blankets piled on the faded red couch, abandoned half-drunk mugs of tea mingled with books on the floor-to-ceiling shelves, and sweaters tangled in the shiny black legs of the piano in the corner, their arms outstretched across the threadbare Persian rug. The woodstove, which Abe had installed in the brick enclosure where a fireplace had once been, glowed with warmth. Joanna felt, not unpleasantly, like a mouse returning to her den.

She had been sleeping down here by the stove since mid-October, trying to conserve heat. The tall narrow windows with their warped panes were already sealed tight in plastic, and she'd nailed thick army blankets to the ceiling and walls of the stairwell, to cut off the downstairs from the drafty upstairs—the latter of which would remain unheated and untouched until March. Functionally, her world had been reduced to four rooms: kitchen, dining room, living room, bathroom. And the basement, of course. She'd started this habit the winter her father had died and found it economical not only in terms of propane and wood, but comfort. One person didn't need a whole cold, dark house.

She fed the stove and checked the dusty face of the grandfather clock ticking by the cracked leather armchair—it was six forty-five, which meant she had fifteen minutes before the wards needed to be set, so she sat at the coffee table with a notebook and pen to make a list of errands for tomorrow's foray into town.

The list was short.

Post office.

Buy bread and see Mom at store.

Check email at library.

Like a pet, the internet was something she would have liked to welcome into her home, but the wards scrambled most kinds of communicative technology—phones fritzed, wires crossed, and so on. The radio worked, and so did walkie-talkies, which was how the family had communicated when the house had held them all, before Esther, and then Cecily, had left. The soundtrack of Joanna's childhood was her sister's enthusiastic voice in her ear, "Esther for Joanna! Do you copy! Roger that! Over and out!"

She looked again at the clock. It was time.

Back to the kitchen, where she took the little silver knife out of the drying rack. She didn't look at the refrigerator as she passed it on her way to the basement, but she could see its colorful face from the corner of her eye, postcards magneted to every available surface. One for every month her sister had been gone. Ten years' worth. Soon there'd be another. Each month Joanna collected Esther's card from the post office and each month she told herself not to put it up, but she could not stop herself from adding to the collection on the fridge, even though she hadn't talked to Esther since their father had died.

Esther had an email address, though she seemed to check it rarely, and after Abe's death it had taken Joanna five separate variations of *Esther, we have to talk,* before Esther had written back with a phone number. Joanna had gone to her mother's house outside town and called from Cecily's kitchen floor, one hand pressed to the cool tile and her mother's cell phone pressed to her ear. When Joanna told her what had happened, Esther had sobbed instantly and noisily, her cries raggedly vocalized, her breath phlegmy in her throat; so exactly the way she'd cried as a little girl that briefly Joanna had felt close to her.

Then she'd asked Esther to come home.

Begged her, actually. Screamed at her, frenzied with grief, while Esther had wept, repeating *I can't, I can't, I can't,* until Cecily had prized the cell phone from Joanna's hand and stepped away to speak to Esther herself, voice low and soothing.

Joanna had tried to forgive her sister for leaving in the first place, for vanishing with no explanation, but she could never forgive her for this: for refusing to come back when Joanna had needed her the most, when she was the only person alive who'd be able to read the book that had killed their father, the only one who could have offered Joanna answers. The only one who could have offered comfort.

Joanna had never reached out to her again.

Nevertheless, the postcards kept coming, one for Cecily and one for Joanna, faithful as the moon.

A skyline bright with an old neon sign for Gold Medal Flour: "Dear Jo, Here in Minnesota, everyone's got a sauna in their backyard. I think Vermont should get on this train. Your Northern blood will thank you. Love, your sweating sister, Esther."

A reproduction of *The Two Fridas,* the painter's dual hearts connected by delicate, bloodied veins: "Querida Jo, si quieres entender este postal en total, tendrés que aprender español. I'm here in Mexico City, bungling verb conjugations and failing at finding any information on my mother's family. Un beso muy fuerte de tu hermana errante, Esther."

The last one had penguins. "Dear Jo, Did you know that the word 'Arctic' comes from the Greek word for bears? *Antarctic* means *no* bears. So remember not to picture me among polar bears, if you ever picture me at all. Love, your freezing sister, Esther."

How many nights had Joanna spent sleeplessly staring at these postcards, rereading words she already knew by heart? How many hours had she spent at the library or on her mother's computer, looking up all these faraway sights she would never see? She was an expert in every place her sister had been. An expert in mountains she'd never climb, seas she'd never swim, cities whose streets she'd never walk.

She didn't bother turning on the light when she tugged open the basement door. Even without years of sense-memory to guide her feet, the growing golden hum would lead her. In the black she made her way down the creaky wooden steps into the mold-fragrant dampness, moving past the pale shape of the washing machine to where the tarp was stretched across the floor, held down by cement blocks, the trapdoor waiting beneath it. She pulled it open with a yawn of old wood and descended the second set of steps.

The hum filled her head.

At the bottom stair she paused to feel along the cement wall for the light switch, and an instant later the short hall was illuminated. The door to the collection was made of bare steel with vinyl weather-stripping at the bottom and a deadbolt above the handle. The key, strung with red ribbon, hung from a nail to Joanna's left, and she turned it in the lock with a familiar clunk.

It took her a moment, as always, to acclimate to the roar that surged in her mind's ears, a sound she had attempted to describe to her sister and mother more than once but never could. Like being filled with golden bees that were all actually one bee, which was actually a field of shining wheat rustling beneath a blazing sun. It was a sound but not a sound. It was in her ears but it was in her head. It was like tasting a feeling and the feeling was power.

"Seems uncomfortable," Esther had said.

It was.

It was also magnificent.

The door closed behind Joanna and she leaned against it, eyes shut, waiting until the sound was less physically overwhelming. Then she turned on the overhead light. It was warm down here, always 66 degrees Fahrenheit with 45 percent humidity—this was where all her electricity and gas went. At the front of the square room—what Abe had called "the business end," although no actual business had ever been conducted—sat a small stainless-steel sink, several behemoth filing cabinets, a towering set of oak shelves that held jars and jars of herbs, and a vast walnut desk they'd found at an estate sale in Burlington many years ago.

The rest of the room was filled with the books themselves.

There were five wooden bookshelves, each over six feet wide and taller than Joanna, each fitted with airtight glass doors. They sat in rows on an old red wool carpet, a replacement for another red carpet that Joanna's mother had burned a decade earlier, though Joanna didn't like to think about that day. Taped at the end of each shelf, like a Dewey Decimal plaque, was a list of which books could be found on which shelf and in what order.

Some of the larger folios lay flat but most books were held in bookstands, and Joanna dusted them every morning with a paintbrush and examined them for signs of damage, for silverfish, bookworms, and mice, though the basement was airtight and pests hadn't been a problem for years. She had been doing this since her father had first tested her talents at five years old.

The books were roughly organized by approximate date, though they were all old. The oldest in Joanna's collection was circa 1100 and the newest from 1730. She didn't know what had been lost in the past few centuries: Was it the knowledge of how to write the books, or the magic that had once filled them? This was a question that had plagued her since she was a child, a question to which Abe had always claimed not only ignorance, but incuriosity.

It's not for us to ask how.

Abe seemed to think protection was at odds with knowledge, as if they could not properly protect the books if they knew too much about them. This belief—in silence, in ignorance—extended through the books and into other aspects of his life, particularly where his daughters were concerned. Keeping them in the dark, he seemed to believe, was tantamount to keeping them safe.

"It's a trauma response," Esther had said once to Joanna, with that annoying air of superior wisdom she'd adopted in adolescence. "He thinks if he talks about bad things that have happened, more bad things will happen."

This sanguine analysis came after the many less-than-sanguine years Esther had spent begging to know more about her mother, Isabel, about whose death Abe would only ever share the same scant details: how he had come home one day to their apartment in Mexico City to find Esther screaming in her crib, all their books gone, and Isabel shot dead on the floor.

Isabel had been murdered, Abe said, by people who viewed the books as a commodity, like diamonds or oil—products to be bought and sold and killed for rather than a phenomenon to be guarded. Such people had been around as long as books had been around, and, like so many who dealt in commodities, book-hunters often took advantage of unrest and oppression in order to profit. Abe knew this better than most. His own paternal grandparents had possessed the same ability to hear magic that Abe had passed on to Joanna, and they'd owned a small theater in Budapest that was renowned for its incredible stage effects—actors passing through solid objects, set pieces floating with no visible wires, curtains engulfed in smokeless flame . . . Until 1939, when they were raided under the auspices of a law limiting the number of Jewish actors allowed in a theater.

Both husband and wife disappeared in the raid. So did all the books that had made their impossible special effects possible. All save for the few volumes the Kalotays had kept hidden in their home; volumes that made it to the United States with Joanna's grandfather when he came over on a container ship in 1940 to live with an uncle in New York. Three books, secreted away in the false bottom of a trunk.

These three books still sat behind glass in Joanna's basement, hard-won family heirlooms—and evidence of the danger in using magic too openly.

According to Abe, anyway. According to Cecily, the danger hadn't been in using magic; the danger had been in living under a fascist regime. The stolen books, she maintained, were simply more Nazi spoils of war, more precious things they felt entitled to, like paintings, jewelry, gold fillings, lives. It was true that Abe had a frustrating tendency to blame historical atrocity on an underlying hunt for books: once, when Esther brought home *The Crucible* in the eighth grade, he'd tried to suggest that the Salem witch trials may have been orchestrated by book-hunters, which had agitated Cecily nearly to tears.

"That's the kind of logic bigots thrive on," Cecily had said. "It makes it seem like the accusations were true, that the people killed for witchcraft were, in fact, practicing magic. But no: hatred and fear, that's all it was. That's all it ever is. Think of the lies told about the Jewish people, lies about blood ritual and human sacrifice . . . Hatred, fear, and the desire for control. Call it what it is, Abe."

However, given both the family history and what had happened to Esther's mother, Joanna supposed she couldn't blame her father for his paranoia. It was a wonder he'd kept collecting after Isabel's death, building the library back up until Joanna's bookshelves now held two hundred and twenty-eight magical volumes.

Two hundred and twenty-nine, if you counted the brown leather book Abe had borne with him into the front yard when he died.

Joanna did not.

That book was an outlier in nearly every way. All books required blood to activate, but that one hadn't simply accepted her father's blood—it had sucked him dry. And it was the thickest book she'd ever seen, its pages crammed with text, which meant it had been written with so much blood it made her own blood run cold. She was also relatively certain that the thread binding the pages together was hair. Human. It was also one of only two books in their collection that was, to use her father's words, "in progress"—a book whose spell was still ongoing.

Joanna did not know what the book did, because she could not read it. The only clear image was a small gold embossment of a book on the back cover. The words themselves eluded her eyes, they swam and darted like the colors in a kaleidoscope. This was what books in progress looked like to anyone but the reader, though Esther could have read it. Could have but wouldn't. A book in progress couldn't be destroyed, either: torn or burned or drowned. Only the person who'd first read the spell could end it. By choice—or by death.

Books in progress sounded subtly different from a resting book, too, the hum more a swarm, and this book, the one her father had hidden for years and then carried with him to his death, sounded the strangest of all. It was deep like a rotting tooth.

When Abe had first died, she'd assumed the book was new to him, recently acquired. And, raised in the shadow of his paranoia, she'd assumed, too, that his death had not been accidental. It seemed certain that someone had given him that book on purpose; someone had killed him so they could take his books for themselves. The same fate that had met Isabel, and Joanna's great-grandparents.

Her father had gathered their collection several different ways: by combing used bookstores and estate sales, attending rare books conventions, regularly ordering huge lots of antique books on eBay and hoping the boxes would arrive buzzing, and buying directly from people who knew what they were selling. He had kept detailed records of each transaction and in the days after his death Joanna had scrutinized every note he'd taken, looking for suspects—but then she had found a different record. A notebook she'd never seen before, hidden beneath his socks in his top dresser drawer.

It was an old composition notebook, the pages yellowed, and the dates went back twenty-seven years. Abe had been keeping this notebook since before she was born. There weren't many entries, perhaps one or two per year, but as she read, it became very clear that the book in progress was not new to Abe at all.

Unbeknownst to Joanna, he'd had it her entire life, and for her entire life had been attempting to destroy it. He'd soaked it in turpentine and lit it on fire; he'd taken a chainsaw to it; he'd doused it in bleach. His last entry, made the day before he died, read, *Curious what will happen if I add my own blood to the mix. Will it negate or interrupt the spell? Worth a try tomorrow.*

Abe had been attempting to end whatever spell had been ongoing between the book's pages. Instead, the book had ended him.

Now it lived atop the desk at the front of the rooms and Joanna took care never to touch it with her bare hands. Nor did she let it come too close to her book of wards, which were too precious to sully.

(Abe's voice in her head, quizzing her as he'd done when she was young: "Not a book, technically. What do we call these early manuscripts?"

A codex. *Semantics, Dad.*

Precision of language, Jo.)

The book of wards—codex of wards—was in Latin, and despite its small size was the most powerful and rare in their collection; not only for what the book could do, which was considerable, but because unlike any of the others, whose ink eventually faded and with it the magic, the ink of the wards could be recharged. The codex had belonged to Isabel and at the time of her death had been in storage with a hundred other books, untouched by whoever had killed her. Three days after she died, Abe had packed up his daughter and driven without stopping across the border, across the continent, to his family's old home in Vermont. That night he'd used the wards for the first time and had not let them drop for the rest of his life. Nor would Joanna.

She went to the sink and washed her hands thoroughly, then held them for a long while beneath the hot air of the electric dryer, until she felt every last remaining speck of moisture wick from them. Then she went to the herb cabinet and put a pinch of dried yarrow and vervain into a small bowl, which she brought back to the desk.

Herbs and plants were not strictly necessary to read the spells—blood alone would suffice—but they enhanced all magical effects, strengthening potency and increasing duration. There was never a single "correct" answer, but rather many possible factors, and Joanna had memorized everything from innate magical properties (vervain for protection, datura for knowledge and communication, belladonna for illusion) to physical correspondence (delicate herbs for delicate magic) to geographic specificity (chamomile for Polish spells, chincho for Peruvian). This last was helpful only if Joanna knew roughly where a book had come from, and yarrow was one of her most-used herbs because it was circumboreal and grew widely across the world.

She set the yarrow and vervain aside for now, picked up the tiny, leatherbound, fifteen-page codex, and spread it out on wooden support wings Abe had made. She let it fall carefully open. Silver knife in hand, she considered reopening her cut from earlier, but that would hurt unnecessarily, so she went to the usual spot on her finger and poked with the sharp tip until a drop of blood welled obediently to the surface. It was the brightest color in the room, more alive than even the body it had just quit. She held her bloody finger over the powdered herbs and let the bright red slide down her skin. Then she dipped her bleeding finger to the mixture and pressed the cut to the codex itself.

Unlike most books, which simply absorbed the drop of blood they were offered, the wards drank. As soon as she'd touched her finger to the page it began greedily swallowing her blood, her finger stinging with slight suction as if a tiny mouth was latched on, and the ink grew brighter, blacker, fiercer on the linen page. She'd been setting these wards all her life and had always found that suction comforting, but after Abe had died, she'd been terrified for months that the wards would turn on her, as that other book had on her father. They never did, though, and by now she was used to it again. As she fed the words, the Latin—a language she didn't speak well—began to re-form beneath her eyes into something she understood. She took a slow, measured breath, and began to read.

"May the Word all-powerful grant unto this home a silence born of silence, and may the silence arouse to the heavens a flight of angels that none with ill intent shall see, for as the sky closes itself tight with a mantle of clouds so now shall angels obscure this home from the seeking eyes of the wicked world. Let life make dark the herbs and the life make dark these words, which make the Word . . ."

On and on she read, fifteen pages of angels and wings and malicious gazes, until the last sentence rang out and with a rustle like a million sweeping feathers, Joanna felt the wards reassert themselves. A slight popping sensation sounded in her already-buzzing ears, as if the seal around the house was hermetic in science as well as etymology and magic. The house was again, as ever, unmappable, untraceable. Nobody with ill intent could find her.

In fact, nobody at all could find her. The wards—set each night at the same hour—made certain of that, circling the boundary of her property so that her driveway and the house beyond it were essentially invisible to anyone whose blood wasn't in the warding book. It was an invisibility not only of the eyes but also of the senses and the mind: the location of the property could not even be thought about, much less sought and found. The people in town had known Abe and Joanna for almost three decades, yet if asked where the two of them lived, a blurry look would come over the neighbors' faces and they'd shrug, smiling, baffled. "Up the mountain?" they'd suggest. Or sometimes, "Down the mountain?"

Not even Joanna's mother could locate her if she came looking; not since she'd moved out and stopped adding her own blood to the wards each night. If Cecily wanted to visit, Joanna would have to go and get her and drive her in, which Abe had made her swear she would never do.

This promise, at least, she hadn't broken.

Only Esther, whom magic had never been able to touch, would have been able to find the house if she tried. Only Esther could come right up to the front door and push it open and call Joanna's name.

But Esther wouldn't.

The wards reasserted, Joanna slid the codex back into its protective case. She stood from the desk and set things in order, then she turned off the light and closed the door. Behind her the books hummed, resonant and sweet and safe in their underground home.

3

The following morning, the bowl of tuna on the porch had been licked clean. Joanna pulled on her red wool hunter's coat and drank her morning coffee outside on the front steps, shivering, looking into the trees and hoping to see a glimpse of dark fur before she went into town.

The day was cold but damp, the humidity lending a sense of false warmth to the air; the kind of weather that reminded her of the day she'd found her father dead in the yard, but she was practiced now at pushing past that memory and focused instead on the familiar landscape. Her red truck was a bright slash of color against the frost-pitted mud of the driveway, and in the distance, the green flanks of the mountain went blue as they climbed into the mist. Everything smelled metallic and mouthy like pine needles and coming winter.

A flicker of motion caught her eye at the edge of the tree line, but it was only a squirrel skittering across the top of the old wooden swing set. When she and Esther were kids their parents had kept the front yard diligently mowed and cleared, but over the years the forest had encroached and now the weathered yellow plastic of the swing seats was mostly obscured by brush and bramble.

Joanna had a sudden, vivid sense-memory of sitting on those swings, her whole body engaged: wind catching her hair, fists tight around the ropes as she leaned back with all her weight, legs outstretched, toes pointed, Esther on the swing beside her shouting, "Kick the sky!"

On her seventh birthday, as a gift, her father had let her read a spell that gave her the ability to float down from moderate heights, and she'd spent the entire hour of the spell's duration on those swings, pumping as high as she could and then leaping off and drifting to the ground as light as a blown dandelion. Cecily and Abe had watched from the porch, eating Joanna's birthday cake and laughing, and ten-year-old Esther had swung beside her the whole time cheering her on. If she'd been jealous, she hadn't shown it.

Usually, their parents were careful to only give their daughters magic that Esther could enjoy, too, magic of the environment or of physical objects: the floating spell had been an anomaly. Perhaps in compensation, the girls had woken just days later in their shared room to find their mother sitting in the chair by Esther's bed, and their father cross-legged on the rag rug at her feet with a blue cloth-bound book in his hands.

Joanna had recognized it immediately. It was the book that had brought her parents together, the one Cecily had sold to Abe at an antiquarian expo in Boston a year or so after he and Esther had moved from Mexico to Vermont. It was an oft-repeated story in their family: how Abe's attention had been caught as much by the pretty Belgian woman manning a booth of used books as by the little blue book she'd priced at only seven dollars, not knowing how its magic hummed in Abe's head; and how, though Cecily had been drawn to the way Abe's bushy-eyebrowed intensity contrasted with his easy, roaring laughter, she'd been just as interested by the two-year-old child on his hip, who laughed every time he laughed, throwing back her small head of dark curls in imitation of grown-up good humor.

"I fell in love with you first," Cecily always said to Esther. "Your father was a bonus."

That morning after Joanna's seventh birthday, when Joanna and Esther woke, Abe was already on the last page of the spell, the air ringing with his resonant voice as the girls sat up in their beds. They'd been told what the blue book did but had never seen it read, and Esther had let out a shriek of delight as the first vines began to twine up the walls, brilliant green and sprouting fat, quick-swelling buds that just as quickly burst into velvet-petaled flowers.

The blooms were pink as sunset and as large as Joanna's head and smelled so sweet they brought tears to her eyes. Cecily leaned forward in her chair to loop her arms around Abe's shoulders and Esther was standing on her bed, but Joanna remained perfectly still, watching the vines and their enormous blossoms cover the ceiling and fill the room with their incredible scent—like caramelized roses and the sharp pith of an orange. Even after the petals had withered and fallen and the vines had shriveled up, the whole house smelled sweet for days.

The memory was so strong Joanna could almost catch that scent now, a hint of something rich and flourishing rising from the cold, hibernating earth. Books like that little blue one, that served no purpose but beauty, were rare. Cecily had taken it with her when she'd left Abe many years later, along with a few others: a spell that mended broken objects, a spell that coaxed perfect spheres of juicy red tomatoes from any living plant, a spell to trap someone within an invisible barrier.

Joanna thought it was hypocritical for her to keep them, considering how vehemently—how violently—she'd opposed the collection at the end, but still she was comforted by the thought that Cecily's resentment for the books could not completely outweigh the awestruck love she'd once had for them.

Joanna left her now-empty coffee mug on the top step of the porch and turned from the swings toward her father's old red truck.

She took the long way into town, eschewing the county highway and following the pine-fringed road that snaked alongside the green river. After Esther had gotten her license, she used to take Joanna out in this truck on weekends, just to drive, to listen to music, to talk, both of them chattier and more open when their eyes were facing forward. And once Esther had left, when Abe was still alive and Joanna wasn't solely responsible for the evening wards, she had gone on long solo drives fairly often, seeking volumes to add to their collection—sniffing around rural estate sales, picking through cluttered shelves in small-town bookstores, looking for handwritten, synonymically repetitive books that had been miscategorized as historical diaries or ledgers. Listening, always, for the rare susurration of magic. In the grand tradition of Americana, she still associated the car with a heady sense of movement-based freedom, and when she was behind the wheel, she felt a kind of wild optimism, a sense that maybe her life was her own and at any moment she could take a sudden unexpected turn.

When she pictured a map, however, it was always as a network of veins with her house as the heart. She may be swept away from time to time, might feel as if she were moving outward, but inexorably she would be drawn back, a closed cycle and not an open path.

Not for the first time she wondered how Esther conceptualized the world. How did she think of the little patch of earth where she'd lived—happily, Joanna had believed at the time—for eighteen years? Until Esther had left with no warning, there had been few secrets between them, especially not in this truck, but Joanna hadn't known her sister was planning to leave any more than she knew the reason she'd left. Nor could she imagine how Esther felt when she thought about home—if she even thought of Vermont as her home anymore. If she even thought of home at all.

THE TOWN, SUCH AS IT WAS, WAS DESCRIBED OPTIMISTICALLY IN TOUR-ist brochures as "quaint," which in this case meant the old buildings were all crumbling brick or painted white clapboard, with hand-lettered wooden signs that swung in the wind. A single-lane bridge spanned the rocky little moonstone river, laced now with ice at its edges, and separated the two blocks that constituted the town center, known colloquially as "the old town" and "the new town."

The old town held the hardware store, the glass-fronted post office, and the bar and grill with its saloon-style entrance. It also boasted the "town green," which was a square of grassy riverbank with a stone bench and an American flag. Across the bridge, the new town targeted ski tourists with a moose-and-butterfly-themed coffee shop and an outdoor outfitters on one side of the street, and Cecily's general store and the used book shop on the other.

Joanna parked in the old town in front of the post office, her truck hiccuping to a stop behind a Subaru so rusty she could see through its chassis to the engine. The small front room with the rows of metal P.O. boxes was empty, but Joanna's was not. There were two postcards sitting inside. Her heart immediately stepped up its rhythm, but she waited until she was back outside and sitting on the cold stone bench of the town green before she let herself look at them, at the handwriting that was as familiar to her as her sister's voice had once been.

The card addressed to her was of a night sky shot through with strokes of green light, "Aurora Australis" written in curly script at the bottom.

Dear Jo, I've decided to stick around the station for another season. It's summer, which means the sun never sets. There are no trees here to bloom and I miss them, and you. Love, your hardworking sister, Esther.

Cecily's was similar, as it often was. Another scene of the Southern Lights, though this sky was pinker and the font squarer.

Dear Mom, I'm going to stay another season here in the snow. I like the people and the work, though the food leaves something to be desired. I miss maple syrup—and I miss you. Love, Esther.

Joanna stared at her sister's writing until it started to blur. *I miss you.* The words and their saccharine lie made her stomach clench. If Esther truly missed them, she could come home and see them, but she didn't. Wouldn't.

She rose from the bench, wishing she had the fortitude to throw the postcards in the trash. Instead she put them carefully in her coat pocket and started across the narrow bridge, disturbing a cluster of crows who'd perched on the metal railing. They flapped away with a fading chorus of reproachful caws, and a feather drifted to her feet, oil-slick black against the concrete.

Where the old town was mostly white clapboard, the new town's few buildings were squared brick. She stopped in the book shop out of habit, first to listen for the potential hum of magic (nothing), then to stand at the counter and browse the stack of historical romances that Madge, the owner, had set aside for her. Madge was seventy-three, skinny, and energetic, and despite the fact that she'd spent much of her youth in the lesbian separatist movement, she was a self-professed "sucker" for the almost eye-rollingly heterosexual romance novels Joanna loved, where taciturn dukes had their icy hearts melted by the fiery charms of anachronistically feminist women.

"This one was excellent," Madge said, tapping a cover that depicted a thick-haired man on horseback, his billowy white shirt unbuttoned nearly to his navel. "And I actually learned a lot about yellow fever."

Joanna bought it. She'd tried modern romances but nothing post-1900 did anything for her, perhaps because she herself lived a sort of pre-1900 life, albeit with the blessings of indoor plumbing. It was hard to imagine wearing lace underwear and "sexting," but easy to imagine wearing lots of complicated layers and rolling around in front of a fireplace.

Not that she'd ever managed anything like that. Her only (partnered) sexual experiences so far had been with the boys at the parties Esther had dragged her to during her early high school years. These make outs and sloppy-fingered fumblings hadn't required anything of her beyond her willingness in the moment, and to seek out something real seemed pointless. There was no way to explain herself—no way to really know another person, or to let them know her—without explaining about the books. And that, she could not do.

Her mother's store was in the same long brick building as the book shop, and Joanna glanced down the street at its awning, then paused by a parked truck to peer into the side mirror. Her mother tended to worry less if things looked good on the outside, but the best Joanna could manage now was to undo her long, fraying braid and shake her hair out around her shoulders. It was thick and slightly wavy, the light brown of buckwheat honey, and began immediately to float with static around her wool-clad shoulders. She considered putting on the green hat Cecily always said brought out the hazel in her eyes and decided against it; right now, she thought it would probably bring out the dark circles beneath them instead. She tried on a smile and abandoned it instantly. Her own dimples jolted her whenever she saw them. They made her look like Esther.

Bells jingled as Joanna pushed her way into the general store. As always, it smelled of incense and vitamins, a back-of-your-throat chalky smell that Joanna did not necessarily like but found herself missing when she was away from it. It was the scent of Cecily herself, potent, warm, healthy. Cecily had worked here through Joanna's childhood and been promoted to manager a few years after she left Abe, and though it had started as a bulk health food co-op, it was gradually coming to resemble something closer to the kind of New Agey tchotchke stores one saw in the wealthier New England tourist towns: crystals and tarot cards infringing on the bins of organic oats; astrology workshops in addition to fermentation classes; "spiritual herb blends" taking over the looseleaf tea aisle.

There was one customer Joanna could see when she came in, an unfamiliar man looking at alpaca mittens, probably a tourist though it wasn't quite ski season. Cecily herself was up by the vegetable cooler, carefully misting the parsley and cilantro with a spritzer full of water. Like Joanna she was tall, though unlike Joanna she had excellent posture and looked her height. She had high flat cheekbones and still spoke with the traces of a Germanic accent, though she hadn't lived in Belgium in over forty years.

"My little baby!" she cried when she saw her daughter, and dropped the spritzer next to the broccoli so she could throw her arms around her.

The customer glanced up from the mittens to look askance at Joanna, who did not much resemble anyone's baby, little or otherwise. Joanna didn't mind his raised brows; she'd left embarrassment behind about ten thousand endearments ago. She hugged her mother back and then disentangled herself, letting Cecily reach for a lock of her hair so she could tut over the split ends.

"I could trim this for you in five seconds," Cecily declared. "Four!" Then she gasped. "My love, what happened to your hand?"

"Oh, nothing—I cut it opening a can."

"Did you clean it well?"

"Yes, I'm fine. Here, I picked up Esther's postcards."

Cecily's expression didn't change, but she turned away to pick up the spritzer and apply herself again to the vegetables. "Where is she now? Somewhere sunny with palm trees? In Barcelona, eating walnuts?"

"Do people eat a lot of walnuts in Barcelona?"

"I did when I was there," Cecily said, "but that was the eighties for you."

Joanna let this go. "No," she said, "she's not in Barcelona. She's staying at the station."

Cecily whirled mid-mist and caught the edge of Joanna's coat with the spray. "What? What station?"

"The same station she's been at for the past year," Joanna said, startled by her mother's reaction.

"In Antarctica?"

"Yes, where else?"

"No, you must have misread," Cecily said. "Let me see."

"Ready when you are," the customer called from the counter.

Cecily hesitated, then shoved the spray bottle into Joanna's hands and hurried to the front, narrowly avoiding a collision with a spinning rack of essential oils. Joanna followed more slowly. Usually Cecily was all salesperson charm, *did you find what you were looking for, have you seen our new goat's milk moisturizer,* but now she packed the mittens and rang the man up without so much as a smile, as if impatient for him to leave. When he did, the door chimes ringing in his wake, Cecily put out a hand.

"The postcards, baby."

Joanna gave them to her and Cecily set both on the countertop, murmuring to herself as she read first one, then the other. She pushed her sleek hair behind her ears, shook her head, and read them again, as if looking for something she'd missed.

"What is it?" Joanna said. Her mother looked more agitated than Joanna had seen her in years, and she felt a pulse of answering fear in her own chest, though she didn't know what there was to be worried about. "What's wrong?"

"She knows better," Cecily said, "she knows better than to stay, she needs to—" She broke off, choking. Joanna willed herself still as Cecily turned her head and coughed harshly into her shoulder, a long-standing cough that had at first worried Joanna greatly. Now, though, she suspected it was put on. It only tended to crop up when they were talking about Esther or other things Cecily didn't wish to discuss. Finally, Cecily caught her breath and stood with her eyes closed, hands on the postcards.

"What's upsetting you?" Joanna said, and when Cecily didn't answer, "Is it that she's so far away? She's always far away. Antarctica, Barcelona, it's all the same distance, really."

"It's so remote," Cecily said, and touched her throat. "Maybe that's good? Maybe that's a good thing." She seemed to compose herself, shaking back her shoulders and smiling at Joanna. "What if I come over for dinner tonight, hmm? I'll bring a lasagna, a bottle of wine, I'll cut your hair on the porch like when you were a little girl . . ."

Joanna felt a sour knot form in her throat. "Mom," she said. "Don't."

"Joanna, you look at me like I'm asking to slit your throat instead of come to your house. Which used to be *my* house, by the way. This is silly, can't you see that?"

What Joanna saw was the note her father had scrawled in his last moments of life. *Don't let your mother in.* It was the most difficult request he'd ever made of her and the one that had cost her the most to uphold, especially in the months following his death when she was alone in that big, echoing house, crying into her own arms instead of her mother's.

Her mother, who was mere miles away, who would've been there within minutes had Joanna invited her.

But Cecily had given up her right to an invitation ten years ago, a week after Esther had left, when Joanna had woken to the muffled sounds of screaming. It was her father, his normally rumbling baritone raised to a timbre she'd never heard from him before, rage mixed with real terror, and she had stumbled out of bed and down the stairs, following the sound until she stopped in the back hallway, her heart pounding. Her parents were in the basement with the books—and from the doorway she'd smelled the unmistakable acrid burn of smoke.

She'd raced down to find a tearstained and defiant Cecily standing over Abe, who had been on his knees in front of their wards, pouring water frantically over the fire that was still burning scorch marks onto the rug between the aisles. The fire had been carefully built, several logs and a triangle of kindling arced over the small codex and then doused in gasoline, but though the rug and floor beneath it were scorched, the wards themselves were untouched by fire or water. They'd been saved by their own in-progress, indestructible state, but some of the surrounding books were not so lucky—between smoke damage and burned paper, many were ruined beyond saving. It was obvious that while Cecily's main aim had been the wards, she was glad for any destruction she'd managed to cause, and when she turned to see Joanna standing horrified in the doorway, there was no trace of regret on her face.

"Your father has made it clear that he cares more for these books than he does for his family," Cecily had said. "I can't go on like this. I'm leaving. Please come with me, Joanna, please. There's a whole world out there for you."

Abe had looked up from the fire he'd only just managed to put out, one of the ruined books cradled in his hands like a broken bird. With a sharp-edged clarity born of shock, Joanna zeroed in on the blackened edges of the book's pages, the curled and blistered leather cover, the melting glue of the spine. It was a book she knew well, the book that had once sent her soaring from a yellow swing into a perfect blue sky. Her eyes moved to her father's face, bleak with a devastation she felt in her bones. When she looked back at her mother, Cecily had tears running down her cheeks. She had already known it wasn't a question which parent Joanna would choose.

Now, in the store, Cecily's eyes were dry though her face was defiant.

"I can't let you in," Joanna said. "You know I can't. I won't."

Cecily pushed away from the counter, blinking rapidly. "You are a prisoner, Joanna. A prisoner of your own paranoia, just like your father. I can see it in your face, I can see the bars, and it is breaking my heart."

Joanna looked away. She was too tired for this today.

"The books ruled Abe," Cecily said, reaching for her, "but they don't have to rule you. You can walk away, out into the world, you can have a real life—"

"This *is* my real life," Joanna said. "And I'm not a prisoner, I'm *choosing* this—just like you choose to stay here in this town even though you could do anything, go anywhere, even though I've told you a million times I don't mind if you leave. If I'm chained to the books, well, you're chained to me. So we're both making choices here. I respect yours, why can't you respect mine?"

Cecily's expression, which had been fierce and righteous, suddenly sagged, and she rubbed her hands up and down her face, smudging the red lipstick she never left the house without.

"You're right, Joanna," she said, sounding almost formal. "I'm sorry. It's your life."

"Yes," Joanna said, unsure if she was being placated or not, but wanting the fight to be over either way. "Thank you."

"I love you," Cecily said, gripping her hand, and Joanna squeezed back.

"I love you, too." For some reason, saying this made her tired and sad, because it was true.

Cecily fixed her lipstick with an unerring finger, wiping away the traces of red she'd smudged onto her chin. "Will you come over for lunch tomorrow, honey? I'll bake a loaf of sourdough and we'll have that carrot soup you like."

A compromise. "All right," she said.

"One? Two?"

The wards had to be set each night at seven, but that left plenty of time. "Two," she said. "Maybe I'll even let you cut my hair."

She took her postcard from the counter and Cecily tracked it with her eyes as it disappeared into her pocket. One last hug, and Joanna was free.

HOME, SHE WENT INTO THE BASEMENT AND FILLED A TWIST OF ALUMI-num foil with catnip, wolfsbane, and chickweed, then took a book down from the shelves. It was from the 1600s and written in French, and Jo-anna remembered when Abe had first brought it home—she was ten. She'd pored over it with a dictionary so they'd understand what the spell might do before they tested it aloud. The ink was fading but it still had a few uses left and Joanna brought it upstairs, snagging the silver knife from its ever-present place by the sink, then went back outside.

She walked from her porch, away from the long driveway and into the trees. There was a flat rock a few yards in and she sat down upon it, the cold stone biting through the legs of her black jeans. She opened the tinfoil, pricked her finger, and dipped the bloody tip into the herbs, then opened the book on her lap. She pressed her bloodied finger to its page, waited for the French to assemble itself into a language she understood, and began to read.

"Let my voice carry wherever the wind is blowing, and let them hear me and come calmly . . ."

This book was long and powerful—it took nearly half an hour to read it through. As she read, she could feel the energy around her begin to change, eerie and specific, the sensation of hair rising on a limb she hadn't even known she had. The hum and swarm of the spell enveloped her and the sounds of the forest around her began to flicker and magnify in reaction to her voice; the crows were louder, the wind vocal in the trees, her own heartbeat like a rhythm.

For those thirty minutes she read with her eyes locked on the page, all her senses alert to the changing sounds around her, but her gaze focused entirely on the words. She heard the crunch of leaves and the break of twigs as feet moved through the forest toward her, heard branches snap, heard the slow, hot sound of breathing, but she didn't look up. If she did, the spell would break and she would have to begin again. Her voice stayed strong and she didn't rush when she reached the final page, just let the words fall from her tongue and ring out into the cold air like struck glass.

She closed the book. Only then did she look up.

Animals stood all around her. They were as still as pieces on a chess-board waiting for a hand to come down and move them. Several deer were posed like statues, long-legged and luxuriantly winter-furred, pulses beating in the velvet skin of their necks. A bear sat on her huge furry black haunches with her wet nostrils flaring in and out, head-sized paws docile on the leaves. A russet moose, so big he was frightening, and so close Joanna could see the fuzz coating his antlers, licked his lips with a delicate pink tongue. A ragged coyote scratched slowly and uncaringly behind a tufted ear. The trees were heavy with quiet birds sitting bauble-like on their branches. There was one fox and uncountable squirrels.

But no little striped cat.

Joanna pushed down her disappointment, unfolded her limbs, and went down among the animals.

This was the very first book her father had let her read aloud on her own, when she was ten years old, and even now she felt the same over-whelming wonder and awe she'd felt as a child. The book had been meant, Abe explained, as a hunting spell, a way to quickly and easily cut down meat before the animals drifted back to wherever they'd been, but the family would never use it that way.

The bear twitched her ear as she stroked a hand down her face and chest, the fur so thick and soft it was almost sticky. She peeled back one lip and ran her fingers over the exposed yellow teeth, smelling musk and sour apples. The bear looked at her with small, shining black eyes, not without curiosity but with a total absence of either distress or intent. She cupped the knobby bone on the top of the bear's skull, sank her fingers deep into the tacky fur. She put both her hands in the ruff around her neck.

Being this close to such an animal was electrifying in a whole-body sense: her fingertips fizzing, her heart surging, her head staticky with joy. The deer let her put her arms around their necks and press her cheek into their warm fur. The moose didn't move away as she stood on her tiptoes to touch his antlers, just sighed a hot blast of gamey breath onto her face. A tiny rabbit sat in her palms, nose twitching, whole body vibrating with the beat of the heart.

In the house, surrounded by the remnants of her father's life, books buzzing beneath her feet, she sometimes felt so alone she worried she might vanish like the ink in an overused book. But here, with wildlife all around her and magic sweet in the air like good cider, she felt her lines and colors returning, her edges darkening, her core filled in.

She cupped her hands around the coyote's beautiful face and stared into those beautiful eyes, which stared right back, the pale green of the last changing leaf. How many other people could say they'd done such a thing? How many people had wielded this kind of power?

How dare she ever long for a different life?

4

Despite outward appearances, Esther was a creature of routine. In this way, if no other, she was very much her father's daughter, and she'd learned over the years that adaptability was in and of itself a routine that could be learned. Establishing habits was something she did automatically, and here at the station she lived by a regimentation that would have surprised her friends and colleagues had they made note of it. Every morning she took herself through the same paces: she woke at the same exact time, put on her clothes in the same exact order, and used the same exact stall in the shared bathroom, even lingering by the sinks pretending to fuss with her hair if her preferred stall was occupied. She had oatmeal every morning for breakfast, and every morning, as she measured out her tablespoon of brown sugar, she compared it unfavorably to the oatmeal of her childhood, swimming in thick pools of maple syrup.

This morning was the same as all the others, except anxiety made her oatmeal taste like glue and looking into the blood-marked mirrors above the sinks felt like staring into the eye of fucking Sauron. Plus, she was hungover. All around her, colleagues new and old were chatting to one another or staring with frustration into open laptops, trying in vain to get a connection good enough to call their families or send an email.

It had been two years since Esther had heard any of her family members' voices. When Esther hadn't come home after her father died, Joanna had sworn not to speak to her again, and though she knew her stepmother, Cecily, would have loved to hear from her, she found it was easier to think of her family as out of reach.

All that mattered was that Joanna was safe behind the wards.

The man who'd flirted with Esther the night before, the Coloradan carpenter, slid into a seat across from her, his plate piled so high she would've teased him about it had she been in any mood for teasing. He grinned at her through a mouthful of reconstituted eggs.

"Hey," he said. "Esther, right?"

"Hi," she said. "And you're—Trevor."

"Trev," he corrected. "So, what's on the docket for you today?"

Well, Trev, I'm going to spend the morning in a nausea-inducing hungover panic until my sense of steely resolve takes over and I can start figuring out who the hell brought a book to the base and whether they want to kill me or not.

"Not sure yet," she said, letting her spoon fall into her barely touched oatmeal. "About to head to the shop to get my assignment. In fact, I should get going."

"Oh," he said, looking disappointed before rallying a smile. "Yeah. Cool. See you around?"

She managed what she hoped was a friendly smile. As she loaded her plates onto the conveyer belt into the kitchen, she caught sight of the exuberant blond of Pearl's hair in line for food, and what had been a falsely pleasant expression on her face instantly was real. Pearl saw her, too, and made a beeline for her.

"There you are!" she said. "I was worried, where'd you go last night?"

"I overdid it," Esther said, guilty for the lie. "Got the spins, took myself to bed."

"Oh," Pearl said. "You should've told me. I would've taken care of you."

"It wasn't a cute look," Esther said.

"And this is?" Pearl said, gesturing to their matching coveralls.

"On you?" Esther said. "One hundred percent yes."

Pearl shook her head. "Anyway, are you feeling better?"

"Much. May I recommend water? Gallons of it."

"Noted." Pearl leaned forward to kiss her, and Esther—too aware of the clink of forks on plates, the chatter, the watching eyes—jerked away before she could stop herself. Even as she pulled her head back, she knew it was a mistake, hurt spreading like a bruise across Pearl's face.

"Sorry," Esther said, "sorry, I—I still feel gross from last night."

Even at the best of times, Esther wasn't comfortable with public affection, though not because she was embarrassed. It was the open declaration of feeling that frightened her. Open feeling was a vulnerability that was easily exploited, and even now someone might be observing, planning.

"Okay," Pearl said, her voice uncharacteristically flat. She took a step back and Esther immediately regretted the distance. "Well. See you at dinner?"

"At dinner," Esther echoed, chest hollow. She paused in the doorway to watch Pearl make her way through the galley, stopping once or twice to chat. The mechanic, Abby, had taken Esther's own vacated seat next to Trev and she waved Pearl down, Trev nodding his head at her in welcome.

Esther left the room.

It was minus ten Fahrenheit that morning and the wind was brutal on the walk from the dorms to the electrical shop, the snow so dry it squeaked beneath her boots. She had to squint against the powerful glare of the sun as it glinted off the white ground and the walls of the squat outbuildings, and she knew Pearl would be wearing her enormous pink knock-off Ray-Bans to protect her hungover vision, looking like a cross between a 1970s supermodel and a car mechanic. If there was a more appealing aesthetic, Esther hadn't encountered it yet.

She should have accepted that kiss.

The electrical shop was in a dome-roofed building that was little more than a glorified supply closet, packed with so much equipment Esther's jaw had dropped when she'd first seen it. Wires and cords of every thickness and color coiled around wall-mounted spools, and the walls themselves were lined with towering cabinets full of coax connectors, splicing connectors and cable ties, and pegboards displaying every kind of plier known to man.

Today, the shop was also packed with people, the morning meeting full of unfamiliar faces she'd normally have been quite interested in looking at, but she was so spaced-out it seemed like only minutes later that she'd gotten her assignment and was back out in that freezing wind, headed to one of the labs to replace some wiring.

It was easy work but uncomfortable, hours spent wedged below a subfloor, much of it on her belly and back drilling a set of holes above and below, cold because she'd stripped out of her coveralls to her jeans for better mobility. Normally she wasn't claustrophobic, but today the smallness of the space got to her, how there'd be nowhere to go if someone trapped her in, and the job took her longer than usual because she kept popping back out into the open space of the lab to warm her hands or get a level or change a drill bit, or just sit there, reassuring herself.

She wished the work was more complicated, so it would distract her from the rotisserie of her thoughts. Thinking about books, about magic, was inextricable from thinking about her family—especially about her sister, living alone in that drafty house with only her books for company. Every time Esther's mind drifted, it drifted in one of two directions: fear, or Joanna, and oftentimes the two paths crossed.

Her very first memory was the day Joanna was born, when Esther was three. This was also the day she'd learned—or at least absorbed—the truth that Cecily wasn't her biological mother, that she'd been born to a different woman entirely, and that woman was dead. She didn't know for sure whether she truly remembered this day or only remembered the story of it—but whether the memories were fabricated or not, Esther had them.

Jo had been born at home in their downstairs bathroom, in the enormous cast-iron clawfoot tub because Cecily said a Pisces should enter the world in water. Abe had spent nine months studying midwifery and delivered her himself, not only because Cecily wanted a home birth but also because Abe's paranoia wouldn't allow for the hospital. Not that Esther had known this at the time.

What she remembered from that day: the buttery taste of the cookies Abe had made to distract her; the sight of a floating cloud of red from between Cecily's submerged legs; the sound of Cecily screaming louder than Esther had known a person could. And her father's voice, answering one question and raising many more, "No, honey, *your* mother had you in a hospital." Then Joanna, crumpled and pink like a cast-off Band-Aid but with perfect tiny human hands and perfect, luminous human eyes.

Later, as the sisters grew, Esther hyperfocused on their differences, but as a little kid she'd been far more hypnotized by their sameness. They both loved chewing lemon peels and watermelon rinds, loved pictures of goats but not actual goats, loved putting sand in their hair so they could scratch it out later, loved watching their parents slow-dance in the living room to Motown records. They loved the sound of wind, the sound of breaking ice, the sound of coyotes calling on the mountain.

They disliked zippers, ham, the word "milk," flute music, the gurgling sound of the refrigerator, Cecily's long weekends away, Abe's insistence on regular chess matches, and days with no clouds. They disliked the boxes of books that came to their door daily or were lugged home by their father, disliked their dusty lonesome smell and how they consumed Abe's attention. They disliked when their parents closed the bedroom door and fought in whispers. They hated the phrase "half sister." There had been no *half* about it.

Not until the day Esther was nine and Joanna nearly six, when Abe had sat Joanna down in the living room, Cecily hovering over his shoulder with a reassuring face but a fretful air she couldn't tamp down. Joanna had been perched on the couch in front of the coffee table, and on the coffee table were seven books. The books, like most books their father concerned himself with, were very old.

"We're just trying something out," Abe said, which was not unexpected; he was always trying things out.

Only days before, he'd put a book in Esther's hands, a very old one with a soft leather cover and pages like dried leaves, and asked her, "Can you rip this up?" She'd stared at him suspiciously, thinking it must be a trick—how many times had he told her to be careful with the books, and now he wanted her to ruin one? "Go on," he'd said. So she'd given it her all, yet despite how fragile the paper had felt between her fingers, she hadn't been able to tear a single page. She hadn't even managed to make a crease. Under her father's watchful eye, she had tried to light it on fire, then tried to wreck it in water to no avail; it remained perfectly intact. Abe had been frustrated, but not with her, and she'd enjoyed his attention.

So she said, "Can I try, too?"

"Not this time, honey," he said. "You know my important books, the books that make things happen—you know how they don't work on you?"

Yes, Esther knew.

"Well, that's special. It's something special only to you. I'm checking to see if there's something special in Joanna, too."

"You're already special," Cecily said to Joanna, who'd looked alarmed at this.

"Of course," Abe said, "of course. You're both amazing little earthlings." (They'd been in the throes of an obsession with aliens at the time.) "Now, Jo." He crouched before her, his beard bristling with restrained excitement. "See these books? I want you to tell me if there's anything unusual about any of them."

Joanna accepted this task with her usual solemnity. A second later she said, "This one is very ugly."

Abe looked at the book she was pointing at, a hardbound in stained brown cloth that was a lot thicker than the others. Esther could tell her father was disappointed, but she herself felt a twinge of gladness. Whatever test was happening, she wanted Joanna to fail. It was a new feeling, and it didn't feel good.

"Okay," he said. "That's fair. I agree. Anything else?"

Joanna shook her head and Abe sat back, sighing. Cecily looked deeply relieved. But a second later Joanna said, "Except one of them sounds funny."

The mood in the room changed instantly. Abe sat fully upright, incredibly alert, and Cecily sucked in a sharp breath. Both were focused completely on Joanna.

"What's it sound like, honey?" Abe said.

"Buzzy," said Joanna. She shrugged, a gesture she'd learned recently and repeated any chance she got. "Buzzy with glitter in it. And it tastes like . . . pancakes."

"Which book sounds buzzy?" Abe said. He was on the verge of shouting, which meant he was getting excited. He rarely shouted in anger.

"That one," Joanna said, poking the thinnest of the bunch, bound in tattered red leather. "Can I have Thin Mints?"

"No!" Abe shouted, thrilled. "Thin Mints are for after dinner! Ah, I knew it! I knew it!" He pulled Joanna into his arms, kissing the top of her head again and again, exuberant in a way Esther had never seen. She looked at Cecily, wanting to understand what was happening, but Cecily was staring at Joanna, a hand at her throat, tears in her eyes. She looked so sad Esther was frightened.

"Mommy," she said. "What's happening?"

But whatever it was, it didn't include Esther. Cecily kept staring at Joanna and Abe, Joanna delighted by the attention if bewildered at its cause, and Abe radiant with happiness.

On that day, Esther stopped focusing on sameness and started to notice difference.

She didn't understand that, then, of course. Didn't know she'd just lived a turning point in her life, a line drawn between her sister, who could not only read magic but also hear it, and Esther herself, who could not. It was a line that became a wall as time passed, a stone wall like the ones that snaked through the forests around her childhood Vermont home, relics from a time before the trees had reclaimed the fields and the walls were divisions between properties, between families.

Looking back, it was silly that she'd never put two and two together. The wards were magic; Esther was immune to magic; Esther was immune to the wards. But until her father had spelled it out for her when she was eighteen, she hadn't fully understood the ramifications.

As long as she was living in the house, the wards couldn't protect anyone, not Abe, not Cecily . . . not Joanna. Anyone who wanted to find Esther's family had only to find Esther.

Esther sighed. She wasn't a person given to introspection or nostalgia—or rather, any natural tendency she might have had toward such things had been stamped out years ago. They didn't serve a life like hers. But today she was positively wallowing.

Normally she treated a bad mood with socialization or sex, but the blood-marks marring all the communal mirrors had made her far too suspicious to seek out company, and she couldn't find Pearl. So after work ended for the day she made her way back to her room and set to remembering everything she could about mirror magic.

There were two kinds she knew of, two that her family had in their collection: magic that impacted one mirror, and magic that connected two. Single-mirror magic, which could alter the reflection a person saw in the glass and probably do other things Esther didn't know about, required only one person to read the spell, only one to activate it with their blood. Double-mirror spells, however, required two people: one at either mirror. Then they could be used for communication, like a kind of esoteric video call, and to pass things back and forth.

Not *living* things, however. She remembered now—and wished she didn't—an afternoon her father and sister had spent experimenting with groundhogs. Joanna had ended up crying, and Esther had overheard Abe saying to Cecily, sounding mildly traumatized himself, "They effed up all our cucumbers, but no creature deserves *that*."

Otherwise, she didn't know much. After all, to Esther magic was irrelevant. Her blood was singularly useless in activating spells and magic had no effect on her whatsoever. As a kid she'd been fascinated by her family's work—what kid wouldn't be?—but as the years had passed, she'd turned decisively away from books and blood and spellwork, and toward the tangibles: things she could touch, see, manipulate, fix. Magic felt like a dreary extension of the world itself, a world of people seeking, holding, and losing power she herself could never access.

She stretched out flat on her bed and hurled her pen at the ceiling, then caught it when it came back down. It had left a tiny, almost imperceptible black dot, which joined all the other tiny dots from all the other times she'd thrown all her other pens. A creature of habit, indeed.

One single person with a book way out here would be remarkable but it did not necessarily have to be alarming. Two people, however, two people in separate places operating two sets of mirrors that functioned in tandem . . .

That would suggest intention. A reason. A plan.

Esther had tried to wipe away the blood and it hadn't come off. So, whatever the spell was, it was still in progress. Which meant if there *was* someone watching on the other end, they'd have seen Esther notice.

They would know *she* knew.

Her bedroom door suddenly rattled and caught, and she sat up so quickly she felt her heart in her ears. The fluorescent brightness of her room reasserted itself, as if she'd been somewhere dim, and she stood, automatically assuming a stance she'd perfected after years of training in martial arts gyms.

"Hello?" she called.

"It's me," Pearl called back, and immediately Esther's pulse reacted to the familiar voice and settled. She opened the door and Pearl smiled down at her. "Want to head to dinner?"

Esther had lost track of time. "Oh, yes, let me get my sweater."

Pearl milled around the stamp-sized room while Esther tugged on her red wool sweater, pulling her hair out from its collar in a staticky tangle. She didn't know much about her mother, Isabel, but from the one photograph she'd seen she'd had beautiful, straight, shiny hair. It seemed unfair that of all the traits Esther could've gotten from her father, like, oh, the ability to hear magic, she'd instead inherited his frizz-prone curls and lactose intolerance.

"How goes the translation?" Pearl said, picking up the Gil novel from Esther's nightstand and peering at one of the colored Post-it Notes.

"Amateur as ever," said Esther.

Pearl threw herself down on the bed. "I looked that book up," she said. "Did you know it's worth, like, thousands of dollars?"

"Yeah," Esther said. "It could've been my college fund, if I'd gone to college."

As soon as she'd said this, she wished she could take it back; she knew college was a tender spot for Pearl, even if she wouldn't admit it. Pearl only said, breezy as ever, "Oh, higher education is overrated."

Esther reached down to squeeze her socked foot. Pearl's parents had split up when she was a baby and both were heavy drinkers, but while her American father had barely been around, her mother had determinedly held things together for her daughter as best she could. She'd worked for twenty years as a receptionist in the same Sydney dental office, saved money for Pearl to go to university, and only drank in the evenings. Esther knew Pearl had spent many mornings tiptoeing around her mother's passed-out form, usually on the couch but sometimes on the floor, cleaning up the bottles and sticky spills of booze from the night before so her mother wouldn't wake up and weep from shame at the mess she'd made.

They'd been very close, and when Pearl had gone overseas to study in California, Pearl's mother had missed her terribly. Without someone else to care for, someone for whom to perform the stability she'd valiantly maintained for so long, what control she'd had over her drinking quickly eroded. Pearl had come home the summer after her freshman year to find her mother in such a sharp decline that she'd stayed in Sydney and hadn't ever returned to her studies, even after her mother died six years later. For Pearl, college was synonymous with a bone-deep, grieving guilt, whereas for Esther it was just another bitter bead in her rosary of missed opportunities.

"Where'd you find this book, anyway?" Pearl asked now, turning the pages with great care.

Esther could have told Pearl the truth without revealing any other truths. A gift from her stepmother, who'd found it in the attic; there was nothing strange about that. But speaking about her family wasn't something she did, not even when she might have liked to, though even as she answered, she felt a queasy jolt at the unevenness of it. Pearl freely offered up all the joys and ugliness of her own past, and in return, Esther gave her lies.

"A used bookstore in Mexico City," she lied.

"Read me a passage?" said Pearl. "In English, I mean. Your translation."

Esther flushed. "No, it's not any good."

"I'm not interested in good," Pearl said, and reached out a hand to stroke the only part of Esther she could reach from her position, her knee. A dirty trick. Pearl knew that Esther was more amenable to saying yes to things when she was being touched. "Please? One paragraph?"

"If you really want," Esther said, because at least maybe she could give Pearl this, and Pearl adjusted herself on the bed, sitting against the wall and looking attentive. Esther went over to her ancient, bulky laptop and let it grumble itself awake, then perched at her desk and scrolled through the document. "It's bad," she warned Pearl again. "My Spanish isn't perfect and I'm no writer."

"I'm your adoring fan," said Pearl. "I'll be proud no matter what."

Esther cleared her throat self-consciously and read.

"After the mirror you gave me broke, Doña Marcela demanded it be covered. No one knows how the glass first shattered but she's convinced that looking in a broken mirror brings bad luck. How horrified she'd be if she knew that last night I lost control and uncovered it. I was lying sleepless in bed and staring at it hanging on the wall, draped in a white scarf, when suddenly I couldn't take it anymore. I rose and tiptoed across the room, but when I pulled away the cloth, I discovered that the mirror was no longer broken. Or perhaps the cracks were invisible in the low candlelight. Looking at it, I felt the same shiver I'd felt that day in the pavilion—it was as if you were gazing at me through the glass. And when I touched it, I swear it trembled and gave way beneath my fingers like the surface of a lake."

Pearl applauded when she'd finished, but Esther stared at the document for a bit longer before shutting her laptop. She'd read the book a hundred times before but never felt the frisson of unease that had coursed through her body as she read the words aloud just now.

It was mirror magic.

"You've hooked me," Pearl said. "Who gave her the mirror? It has to be a lover."

"Yes," said Esther. "He calls her name in the night and she tries to go to him through the glass."

Pearl smiled. "So it's a romance."

"Not exactly," Esther said. "The mirror doesn't take her to him; it takes her to a different world where he can't follow."

"Ah," said Pearl, her expression dimming.

Esther wanted to explain that it was a good thing; that the narrator wasn't meant for her lover's world in the first place, that the novel was a story of liberation. But despite the hours she'd spent poring over the book to find all the right English words, none came to her now.

LATE THAT NIGHT, HOURS AFTER THE MIDNIGHT MEAL FOR THE THIRD shift had ended and the station finally settled into the rhythm of sleep, Esther untangled herself from Pearl's warmth and climbed carefully from the bed. Pearl woke, her eyes glistening in the darkness, but Esther made a comforting noise and a second later she was asleep again. Esther pushed her feet into her boots without lacing them, then felt along her desk in the dark until she found her pen and notebook. She held them in her hands, forcing herself to confront what she was planning to do. Too often she made choices without looking them in the eye, she let her choices make her, so later she could think, *Well, I didn't really have a choice, did I? It just happened. It wasn't my fault.* Unfortunately, knowing she had this tendency and recognizing it as it manifested were usually two different things. Now, though, she made herself face it.

I am doing this on purpose.

The bathroom down the hall was, like most of the bathrooms, communal, shared by the six other people who had rooms in this hallway, and Esther called out very quietly as she entered. She opened each of the three stalls to make certain no one was in there and then she locked the door and faced the mirror over the sink. It was a head-and-shoulders view of herself, a pallid cast to her light brown skin, eyes black with pupil despite the overhead light. Fear. She dampened a finger and touched it to the pattern of blood on the mirror's right side, one last attempt to wash the spell away, but it was as stubborn as dried varnish and didn't budge even when she scratched it with her fingernail. She wondered if others had noticed and how they'd explained it away to themselves. Nail polish; a flaw in the painted back; a coded message for the janitorial crew?

"Hello," Esther said into the mirror. She watched her mouth move. She touched the surface carefully. It felt like a mirror, cold and smooth. "If someone is there," she said, "I'd like to talk to you."

Long, heart-beaten minutes passed. Nothing. Not a glimmer, not a sound. The reflection remained accurate, Esther and the bathroom perfectly in reverse.

Esther took out the pen and her notebook. In large block letters, as neatly as her messy hand allowed, she wrote (both forward and backward, unsure of a magic mirror's logic of reflection):

WHO ARE YOU?
WHO ARE YOU?

She held the notebook up to the mirror, against her chest like a number in a mugshot and again she waited, feeling her pulse everywhere: throat, temples, wrists, belly. It was like being a child at a sleepover, chanting *Bloody Mary, Bloody Mary, Bloody Mary* and dreading the gruesome face that might appear, knowing on one level that Bloody Mary would not—could not—come, knowing on quite another that she absolutely might.

But the minutes circled by and . . . nothing.

Esther let out a whoosh of breath. She was relieved. She was disappointed. She was furious. If she was the punching type, right about now was when her knuckles would be bleeding from the shatter of silver shards. Instead, she slammed the notebook against the mirror loud enough that the bang echoed around the tiles but not hard enough to do any damage. She knocked against it like a bird who mistook the glass for sky.

WHO ARE YOU? WHO ARE YOU? WHO ARE YOU?

Nothing, nothing, nothing.

"Fine," Esther spat, and grabbed her notebook. She hadn't been expecting an answer, not really, but the impenetrability of it infuriated her.

She was turning to leave when she saw it.

A distortion. A shimmer like a pebble thrown into a pond, ripples moving outward, the reflection in the mirror still intact but wavering. Esther's breath caught. She turned back.

Surfacing through the glass was something flat and cream-colored. It was paper. Very nice paper, thick and toothy, expensive. It came through the mirror and dropped into the sink, where leftover droplets of water immediately began to curl its edges. Esther snatched it before the ink could smear, a few sentences in a gorgeous, old-fashioned cursive, though the letters were harried and dashed-off. At the bottom was what looked like a bloody fingerprint. She read it with shaking hands.

> *Esther: I am begging you to trust me. You and those you care for are*
> *in danger. Go home to your sister immediately. There is a cargo plane*

leaving in three days and you must be on it. Take these and do not communicate through the mirror again. I am not the only one watching.

Before these words had fully registered, something else was coming through the glass: a manila envelope, also bloodied in one corner. Esther opened it, her breath coming so fast she could hear it echo around the empty tiled room, and pulled out a small, navy blue bound booklet and several pieces of shiny, printed paper.

She turned the booklet over and blinked. It was a passport. A U.S. passport, and a stack of plane tickets. These, too, were stained minutely with the blood that had allowed them to pass through the mirror.

She flipped to the first page of the passport and found her own face staring back—her face as it had appeared just last night, inquisitive, staring into the mirror but superimposed on a gray background. Someone had taken a photograph of her in the mirror. Someone had made her a passport under the name *Emily Madison,* an eerie, WASPy facsimile of *Esther Kalotay.* The tickets were also for Emily Madison, and they were for three days from now. They traced a route out of Antarctica, through New Zealand, to Los Angeles, Boston, and, finally—to Burlington.

The little airport closest to her childhood home.

She sank to the floor, the tickets quaking in her hands, her mind spinning. She was so dizzy with confusion she almost missed the last thing that came through, but the clank of plastic on porcelain alerted her that something had fallen into the sink. She stood and found a plastic vial with milliliter measurements on the side, tightly shut. Inside was three milliliters of red liquid.

Blood.

There was a label on the vial, filled with cramped writing. That same graceful hand in miniature.

This is the path. It will provide the natural next step.

5

The water in Nicholas's wineglass was beginning to bubble.

Around him, the other guests—each clutching identical glasses—broke into excited murmurs, and Nicholas had a brief bird's-eye appreciation for the strangeness of the scene: a group of twenty people in dinner jackets and cocktail dresses standing among the sleek white leather sofas and black lacquer cocktail tables of this penthouse drawing room, the red damask walls boasting a Rothko, an Auerbach, and a splendid view of the glittering London night outside—yet everybody in attendance was staring with rapt attention not at the art or out the window or at one another, but into their wineglasses.

Everybody except Nicholas.

At the front of the room, posed dramatically in front of the black marble hearth, the host of the evening, Sir Edward Deacon, stood with a book in his hands, droning on and on in his florid, phlegmy voice. The guests' murmurs changed to gasps of delight and awe as the bubbles in their water turned from clear to turbid, taking on first a brownish, mineral cast and then deepening in hue as the host kept reading. People had begun lowering their noses to their glasses, inhaling the now-tannic bite and whispering foolish things like "Red! It's really turning red!" and "My god, it smells like wine!"

From just over Nicholas's shoulder came a long, inelegant snort, and he glanced around to see his bodyguard leaning to sniff his own glass, clearly imitating the other guests, and doing a poor job of it. For one thing, Collins was the only person in the room holding the wineglass by the bowl rather than the stem. For another, despite the decent suit Nicholas had picked out for him, he still looked like a last-minute extra in a film about the Boston Irish mafia, someone's daughter's pugilistic boyfriend maybe. Quite at odds with the smart milieu.

Sir Edward ended the reading, finally, letting the last word ring out in a sort of squawking triumph, and the guests quieted down, raising their eyes from the liquid in their glasses—now a dark, nearly violet burgundy—to their host. Sir Edward took his time shutting the book, clearly savoring the anticipation of his audience, then he held the volume aloft in one hand. His butler, who'd been standing to one side with a small, slightly bloodied dish of powdered herbs and a full wineglass on a tray, took a step forward. Sir Edward took the glass, replaced it with the book, and the butler stepped back again.

"My dear friends," said Sir Edward. "You hold in your hand the founding vintage of one of the finest winemakers in the world—a glass of wine that no one living can claim to have tasted." He paused, eyes sweeping the room. "No one, that is, except for us. It is my absolute pleasure to share with you tonight this 1869 Domaine de la Romanée-Conti." He paused again and everyone gingerly applauded, mindful of their glasses. "As many of you know, this project has been years in the making, ever since I first dreamed it up in the limestone vineyards of Burgundy—and it's a dream I never could have realized without the cooperation and collaboration of Richard Maxwell and Dr. Maram Ebla."

Richard was across the room from Nicholas but easy to see because of his height, and Nicholas felt his jaw clench as he watched his uncle incline his head, smiling, to accept the light applause. Maram was probably doing the same at his side, but she was obscured from Nicholas's view by a particularly broad man in a last-season Tom Ford jacket.

"And now, let us raise our glasses in a toast."

All around Nicholas, elegant arms were lifted, but he couldn't bring himself to move. *Cooperation and collaboration,* what bollocks. Sir Edward might've had the idea, just as Richard might've brokered the deal and Maram might've sent people to France to gather grape leaves and vineyard soil, but Nicholas was the one who'd spent nearly six months drafting the actual book; he was the one with the barely healed scar still pulling at the crook of his elbow; he was the one down nearly two pints of blood.

The toast had ended and now everyone was swirling their wine and raising their glasses to their lips, sipping, exclaiming, congratulating, patting Richard on the back, shaking Sir Edward's hand—and not a single one of them would be in this room if it weren't for Nicholas, and not a single one knew it.

He turned to Collins, who had a mouthful of wine and did not seem happy about it. "I'm getting air," he said. "Don't follow me."

Collins spat his wine back into his glass.

"That is disgusting," said Nicholas.

"Agreed," Collins said. "It tastes like socks."

The woman nearest him heard this and swiveled her long, pearl-draped neck to give him a look of absolute horror. He grimaced an apology and said to Nicholas, in a much quieter voice, "You know following you is pretty much my whole job description, right?"

Nicholas rolled his eyes and turned away, dodging a spiky metal sculpture and several wine-slurping guests, aiming for the sliding glass door that led to the balcony. He could hear Collins's heavy footsteps behind him as he pulled the door open and stepped out into the cold wet November air, but to the bodyguard's credit, he stayed inside. Through the glass, Nicholas could see him take up his awkward post in front of the door. He stuffed a big hand in one pocket, then took it out, then leaned with studied casualness against the wall and tried the wine again, mouth puckering.

Nicholas turned his back to the door, to Collins, to the party, and to all those glasses of shimmering garnet. Tiny misting droplets of rain touched his face and dampened his hair, and he was shivering a bit beneath his dark green dinner jacket, but the chilly air felt good after the warmth of the party. The balcony had two outdoor sofas and a small glass-topped table with a couple of chairs. Nicholas remained on his feet, leaning his arms against the metal balcony railing and looking out into the bright lights of the city night. He could see the lit-up dome and columns of St. Paul's Cathedral, and in the distance, the bright circle of the London Eye shone blue against the dull charcoal sky.

He had not yet sampled his own creation, and he raised the wineglass to his lips. Despite his irritation with Sir Edward and his uncle and—well, with everything, really—he had to admit this particular commission had been interesting. He'd enjoyed the research, which had necessitated writing a botanical historian at Cambridge to find out which herbs might have grown in a Côte de Nuits vineyard in 1869 and what weather events might have impacted the grapes (a particularly warm spring, as it turned out)—and the writing itself had been a rare challenge, a twisty manipulation of language to replicate not only the taste of the wine, but the color and its intoxicating effects. He was curious to see how it had all come together.

The flavor hit Nicholas's nose first, a dark and vivid burst of berry before a stony, silken slide on his tongue, an echo of dusty mineral and ripe red fruit and the languorous end to a long summer's day, like evening birdsong. A note of wood spice led to a long, gorgeously structured finish.

"Well, fuck me," he said aloud. He took another sip, then another. Deep down, he had expected it to taste like blood, but it did not. It tasted like wine; exquisite wine, sweet and earthy. (Not at all like socks, *Collins*.) He felt a flash of pride that managed, for the moment, to overcome his bitterness. There was no way to truly know if it was a perfect copy of the vintage Sir Edward had requested, but Nicholas felt confident in the closeness of the illusion.

That was all it was, though: an illusion.

Half the glass gone now, and Nicholas could feel the mellow burn of alcohol beginning to blunt the sharp edges of his bad mood, but that, too, was illusion of sorts. Once the spell wore off, as it would in roughly an hour, the wine in his body would turn to water once again.

When he was young and first starting lessons in history and current events, Nicholas had imagined writing books that could turn stones into bread and mud into apples, a heroic future in which he'd end world hunger forever. Maram had quickly dispelled him of these grandiose notions. Magicked stones and mud, no matter how much they tasted like bread or fruit, would turn back to stones and mud before they could be processed by the body. People may as well eat dirt.

He heard the slide of the glass door behind him and the swell of chatter from the party before the closing door muffled it once again, and Maram's voice came from somewhere to his left.

"Enjoying the results of your hard work?"

Nicholas did not like it when people came up on his blind side. He didn't turn to look at her, only stared out at the city.

"I'd rather drink terrible real wine than excellent fake wine," he said.

Maram moved deliberately into his field of vision and raised a single dark eyebrow. She was a small, sturdy woman with golden-brown skin and black hair now showing some gray, and often dressed in similar shades— tawny silk blouses, long camel coats, onyx earrings in silver bevels. Tonight she was in umber brocade and a black silk wrap. This color palette gave her the overall impression of a sepia-toned photograph, a person in perpetual pose, and her face was arranged now in a snapshot Nicholas knew well: the line etched above her oft-raised brow, the slight smile, the steady gaze.

"'Fake' is inaccurate," she said, always a stickler for semantics.

"Fleeting, then," said Nicholas.

"Everything in life is fleeting," she intoned, though Nicholas could hear the smile in her voice; she knew how he despised hackneyed philosophy.

"How's the scene inside?" he said. "Sir Edward still playing Jesus for his adoring masses? Have they started kissing his feet yet?"

"Why?" she said. "Would you rather they kiss yours?"

This stung a bit. He wanted credit, not genuflection. "And ruin my shoes with lipstick?" he said. "No."

"Richard's having a good time, at least," Maram said, and Nicholas followed her gaze through the glass doors. Past the vague distortion of city lights and his own reflection, he could see most of the party, and it was easy to spot his uncle's handsome, ageless face a head above most of those gathered, laughing. Nicholas's father, Richard's younger brother, had supposedly also been tall, and so as a child Nicholas had expected he would be, too, eventually, but he'd been cheated out of this particular family promise and sat pretty at a cool five foot nine.

"He's in his element," Maram said, which was true. The guest list was all wealthy people who fancied themselves patrons of the arts, and Richard was no exception. He was less patron and more collector—art was in fact the least of the valuable things he collected—but he loved any chance to rub shoulders with other enthusiasts.

Nicholas attempted a single eyebrow raise himself, though he could feel it was a disaster. Years of practicing Maram's brand of intrigue in the mirror and he only ever managed to look comically surprised.

"Wish he'd let me come along to that West End wrap party last week, instead," Nicholas said. "I like actors." His mother had been one, a Scottish stage actress whose programs Nicholas still kept in his bedside table.

"Naturally you like actors," said Maram, drawing her wrap tighter around her body. Her hair was glittering with mist. "Narcissus in the pond."

Nicholas ignored the jab. "All I'm saying is, this wasn't what I meant when I asked to come out, and you know it."

Another raised brow. "You wanted what, Nicholas—a club? Music so loud you wouldn't be able to yell for help if something happened? A dance floor so crowded Collins wouldn't be able to reach you in time?"

"I don't need a club," Nicholas said. "A pub would do. With, you know, people under thirty for once?"

"Collins is under thirty."

"People who aren't paid to be near me." As soon as he said it, he regretted it, because Maram's face—usually so arch and controlled—went suddenly soft with pity. He felt himself flush and turned away. He'd let himself forget that she was one of those paid attendants.

She'd worked for Richard and the Library since before he could remember, first as the secretary in charge of organizing his late father's notes, then as Nicholas's head tutor, and now as chief librarian and Richard's—well, girlfriend, Nicholas supposed, though that seemed a childish way to put it. Partner, then, in every sense of the word. Maram had always made it clear she had no interest in being his surrogate mother or even an aunt, yet she was still the closest Nicholas had ever really had to either; and now that he was more or less grown, he sometimes slipped up and considered her a friend.

But she was not. She was an employee of the Library, same as Collins, same as his doctor and his chef and the people who brought him breakfast and did his laundry. Same as everyone else in his life except for his uncle, because Richard *was* the Library. One could argue even Nicholas was technically his employee, as well as his nephew and the Library's heir.

"I know you've been lonely," Maram started. Nicholas twitched away from the hand she placed on his arm, the last of his fleeting wine sloshing in its glass.

"I'm *bored*," he said, "not lonely."

She'd succeeded in gripping his wrist, however, her red-painted nails digging into his skin even through the wool of his dinner jacket, and he realized her touch was not consolation, but warning. A man was opening the sliding door and stepping out to join them on the balcony—someone Nicholas did not know. He could see Collins emerge from the shadows by the door, his brow furrowed, clearly deciding if he should follow or not. Maram gave him a quick, subtle shake of her head and he melted back.

"Brrr," the man said, shutting the door. "Cold as a witch's tit out here." He was white, over middle age, with a strong American accent and a set of perfect teeth that were no doubt meant to make him seem younger but had the adverse effect, aging the rest of his face around their false youth.

"Mr. Welch!" Maram said, giving him the smile she reserved for people she didn't like, all cheeks and no eyes. "Been a while, hasn't it?"

"Five years," he said, shaking her hand. He held on a beat too long. "Shoulda known I'd see you here. Lord knows there's enough people in this crowd who could afford your—" he choked, coughed, cleared his throat, and found a way around whatever he'd been going to say. "Your product."

Maram gracefully extricated her hand. "And *I* supposed Americans considered it impolite to speak of finances at a party."

Mr. Welch laughed in a way that he probably imagined was "hearty." "Well, you can take the Texan out of Texas, but even after a few years here in merry ol' England, I like to keep things honest."

Nicholas was working to place him and must have appeared too interested, because Mr. Welch glanced his way.

"You're Richard's nephew, am I right? You a part of the—" another cough, this one harsh and painful-sounding. "A part of the—the—"

Even if Mr. Welch hadn't proclaimed himself a past client, Nicholas would have known from the forced pauses in the man's speech that he was under one of the Library's nondisclosure spells.

"The family business?" Nicholas finished for him. "Goodness, no. I haven't the head for it." He extended his own hand—quite wet now from the fine rain—and gripped Mr. Welch's, pumping it too vigorously. "I'm at Oxford, St. John's, reading theology."

He was, in fact, registered at the college—or at least, his name would appear on all the lists, if anyone followed up.

"Theology," Mr. Welch repeated.

"I'll admit I bullied Dr. Ebla into offering an independent advisory on my thesis—she got me access to the Laudian vestments, quite extraordinary needlework, have you had a chance to see them?"

"Can't say I have," Mr. Welch said, clearly bored by the lie, as Nicholas had hoped. His attention was back on Maram. "Oxford must be where you got that Doctor in front of your name."

"That's right," Maram said.

"But you're not English, originally," said Mr. Welch; a leading question that would have piqued Nicholas's own interest if he hadn't heard her evade it a thousand times before.

"I'm not," she said, still smiling, though the tenor of her smile changed subtly.

"Wouldn't have guessed from how you talk," said Mr. Welch. "You sound like the Queen herself."

"However *did* you guess, then?" Maram said pleasantly, then added, "I suppose you could liken my accent to . . . oh, to a good forgery, say."

Nicholas was interested to watch Mr. Welch's ruddy face grow pale. "Well," he said, backing away, "I'd better skedaddle before my wife comes looking. Nice to meet you, young man. Dr. Ebla, always a pleasure."

He let himself back into the party and Maram said, "We ought to go inside, too. You're shivering."

"No, I'm not," said Nicholas, then winced at how juvenile he sounded. "I am," he amended. "But I'd rather be out here shivering than in there making nice with—oh, for heaven's sake."

He'd caught sight of Richard passing Mr. Welch inside, both men nodded at one another as Richard made his way toward the balcony, and a second later, his uncle was sliding the door open. So much for coming out here to be alone.

"What did Mr. Welch want?" Richard said immediately, bending over Nicholas in concern. "Did he want to talk to you?"

"He was interested in Maram, not me," Nicholas said. "And, just a thought—perhaps chasing me out here isn't the cleverest way to deflect the attention you seem so worried about? At least Collins had the good sense to stay inside."

Richard looked startled and then sheepish and made a visible effort to relax. He glanced at Maram, who gave him a reassuring nod.

"It's fine, darling," she said.

"How are you feeling?" Richard said, settling a hand on Nicholas's shoulder and peering at his face. "It's frigid out here and you look a bit . . ."

"I look fantastic," Nicholas said. "Thank you for noticing. The tie's vintage."

Richard smiled but couldn't quite conceal his worry. Worried, worried, Nicholas thought—he was always so worried. It was exhausting to bear the constant brunt of all that kind concern. Richard himself never got sick and had never seemed to know precisely how to handle Nicholas's own health, or lack thereof.

"Perhaps it's best to get you out of here," Richard said.

Nicholas frowned. "Mr. Welch was a curious client; so what?"

"For one thing," said Maram, "he's the one who commissioned that forgery glamour you were so upset about, to sell a fake de Kooning—"

"Ugh, that commission was undignified."

"—and it's possible, even probable, that some of the magical forgeries he's profited from were sold to people at this very event."

Nicholas couldn't help but laugh. That put Maram's comment about her accent and the man's hasty retreat into perspective.

"For another thing," Maram went on, "you aren't having any fun. You said so yourself."

"More fun than I'd have locked up in the Library with Sir Kiwi!"

But she'd put a hand on his elbow and was steering him off the balcony, which he allowed only because he was, in truth, quite cold. They stepped back into the warm drawing room, which smelled like cologne and wine and the awful little canapés that had been served before the reading and were now being passed around by house staff dressed all in black. As they came in, Collins ate a mini-quiche like it was attacking him.

"Collins," said Maram. "The car."

Collins nodded and ducked away through the kitchen.

"This is ridiculous," Nicholas said. "If you sent me home every time someone asked me a question, I'd never leave the Library. Ah, hang on. I never *do* leave the Library."

"Bringing you here was a risk, anyway," said Richard. "I've already had several people asking about you."

"People are only interested in me because they're interested in you two, in the Library," said Nicholas.

"No," said Maram. "You attract your own attention."

Nicholas shrugged. Objectively, he was no different from any other standard-issue white man in his early twenties; perhaps a little better-looking and better-dressed, but even he, an alleged narcissist, could admit that was mostly money. Yet he was used to people—total strangers—glancing at him and then doing a double-take, squinting a bit as if they thought they should recognize him.

The only traits that might've made him stand out were his numerous neat scars, usually covered by clothes, and the prosthetic left eye that perfectly matched his sighted right one in appearance if not quite movement. But both these things were very hard to spot unless a person was looking for them, which few people ever were. Yet somehow, though Richard and Maram ought to have been more noticeable on the whole, it was always Nicholas that people focused on, as if they could somehow sense the power in his blood.

"That's not my fault," he said.

"No," Richard said. "It's *my* fault for allowing you to come tonight in the first place."

Nicholas took a long, slow breath, attempting to manage his simmering anger and failing. "You know, my father's choices make more sense to me every day."

The three of them were on the fringes of the gathering, facing the drawing room like actors playing to an audience, but at these words

Richard half turned, barely restraining himself. He looked more anguished than angry, and Nicholas felt a twinge of guilt.

"Your father's choices got him and your mother killed," said Richard, very quietly. "And I've spent my entire life making sure the same thing doesn't happen to you."

"You've spent *my* entire life, you mean."

"And I'll spend the rest of it the same way," said Richard.

For a moment, Nicholas couldn't speak. This was an old argument that had surfaced many times through the years, and until recently Nicholas's protests had been half-hearted, more to flex his independence muscle than to actually use it—but lately any thoughts of "the rest of his life" sent him tailspinning into a kind of grasping, frustrated hopelessness he couldn't articulate.

The problem was he knew exactly what the rest of his life looked like: a continuing monotony of marble hallways, needles, simmering cauldrons of blood, stinking herbs, crisp new paper, cramping fingers, doctor's visits, iron supplements, the same faces day in and day out. Once in a while, like tonight, he'd be trotted out on his short leash and allowed to sniff a few ankles before being tugged along home again.

The last time he'd felt this airless, this desperate for change, was ten years ago in San Francisco, when he was thirteen. Back then he'd been raging at Richard for weeks, alternately begging for and demanding more freedom, and what had happened? All Richard's fears had come true. Nicholas had lost an eye—and nearly his life, like his parents before him.

A tremor of remembered panic ran through him, and his anger defused suddenly, like a wire had been cut.

"I understand how you feel," Richard said, looking down at him with so much pitying affection that Nicholas couldn't return his gaze. "But being in danger is its own kind of lock and key. There's a freedom in safety, Nicholas. Remember that."

"Richard!" called Sir Edward from across the room, waving him over, "I want you to meet someone!"

A possible client, probably, which was no doubt why Richard had deigned to attend this farcical party, and why he would stay. To promote the product. The product being Nicholas, whom Richard dispatched with a sympathetic pat on the shoulder before stepping onto the carpet and disappearing back into the crowd.

"Come along," Maram said. "The car will be waiting."

A member of the staff fetched their coats, and the remains of Nicholas's anger vanished as he settled its weight onto his shoulders. He'd been constantly riding these waves lately, these little surges of rage followed by exhaustion, one feeding into the other in a feedback loop. He needed more sleep, probably. More exercise. (More iron, his doctor's voice droned in his head.)

Instead of any of that, he got a long, silent elevator ride down to a wet black London street and a lightly falling November rain, headlights shining off the pavement. Collins was waiting for them, arms crossed. One of the Library's cars, a sleekly anonymous black Lexus, rolled to a stop in front of Nicholas and Maram, and the valet climbed out and dropped the keys into Maram's outstretched hand, looking doubtful. No doubt he'd been expecting a professional driver, not a woman in a floor-length dress. But drivers were out of the question: only Richard and Maram's blood was on the Library's ancient wards, so only Richard and Maram could even find the place—and Nicholas, of course, because magic couldn't touch him as it touched other people, but he didn't know how to drive.

Nicholas climbed into the spotless leather back seat of the car and was joined by Collins, whose broad shoulders made the space suddenly seem smaller.

"Have fun tonight?" Collins said, smirking.

"Not as much fun as you had," said Nicholas. "Guarding the most precious treasure at the party."

"You mean babysitting," Collins said.

Collins had been hired six months ago and while he was probably not the first of Nicholas's bodyguards to disdain him, he was the first to show it—and for some reason Nicholas found this relaxing. His last bodyguard, Tretheway, also American, had been wide-eyed and deferential to Nicholas, but so casually cruel to other members of the staff that he'd asked Richard to let him go, unnerved by his double-facedness. Collins had only one face: a scowling one. It was evident that he resented being bossed around by a guy his own age, a guy he considered spoiled, soft. This only made Nicholas want to boss him around more.

"Put your safety belt on," he said.

Collins ignored him, busy loosening his tie and flicking open the top button of his shirt.

"Fortinbras," Nicholas tried.

This got a reaction. Collins's lips twitched and he shook his head. "Real close," he said. "Any day now."

"Pity. Fortinbras Collins has a nice ring to it."

The tires shick-shicked across the slushy pavement and Nicholas watched out the tinted back window as the building undifferentiated itself and became just one more light in a city made of them. He thought of Mr. Welch's distasteful commission; and then of how most of his commissions were distasteful, no artistry to them, only blunt demands. Even this last book, for all its interesting challenges, was ultimately nothing but fatuous nonsense, all hedonism and status.

Had it always been like this? Tiresome? Or was Nicholas just getting older? It was more difficult these days to bounce back after he'd written a book, his blood seemingly slower to replenish itself, leaving him weak and shaky and slow for days. And for what? Money? He didn't need more money. Nor did he need people to kiss his feet, obviously—but a "thank you" would be nice, or even a bare nod of acknowledgment from someone other than Maram or his uncle. For once, he wanted somebody to look at him and see what he could do. And to see, maybe, what it cost him.

Maram caught his eye in the rearview and gave him a small, sympathetic smile. "How's this," she said. "I'll take you to dinner tomorrow. We can come back into the city early, go to that boot shop you like, people-watch to your heart's content, and if you pick the restaurant, I'll make sure we get a reservation. Anything but bloody pasta."

Their chef was from Italy, and it showed, though Nicholas's meals tended to look rather different from everyone else's.

"Anything but bloody steak," he countered.

Maram rolled to a stop at a red light. "How about well-done?"

Nicholas opened his mouth to reply but suddenly, with absolutely no warning, the front-seat passenger door flew open, and a man launched himself into the car, slamming the door and turning in one fluid motion so he was kneeling on the seat beside Maram's, hand outstretched into the back. Nicholas had an impression of pale skin, a thick neck, broad shoulders, unfamiliar face, before he saw that the hand held a gun, and the gun was pointed directly at his head.

There was a beat of absolute silence.

Collins said, "Drop it."

"You shoot me, I shoot him," the man said. Collins had pulled his own gun, but he hadn't drawn it fast enough to aim; it hovered in his lap, his whole body rigid. Through the wet windshield, Nicholas saw the blur of green as the light turned. "Drive," the man told Maram.

"Oh my god," Maram whimpered, and she sounded so unlike herself that Nicholas's frozen mind finally roused itself to terror. "Oh my god—"

"I said drive."

Nicholas's vision had blackened and tunneled, and something roared in his ears: his own pounding pulse.

"Please," he croaked. It was the only thing he could think to say. He'd had to beg for his life once before and he'd said please then, too. *Please,* and later, *no.* "No," he tried.

Maram was driving now, darting terrified glances from the road to the stranger in the passenger seat to Nicholas in the back.

"What do you want?" she said.

"What do you think I want?" the man said. He was Welsh, with a low, growling voice that seemed tailor-made to intimidate. "I want you to drive me to the Library."

Maram, who was always so in-control, so calm, was shaking. "And then what?"

"Rest easy, it's not you I'm after. It's him." He hadn't taken his eyes off Nicholas. "We've been looking for you for a long time, boyo. What'll the Library do without their pet Scribe?"

Nicholas's blood went boiling hot, then freezing cold. This couldn't be happening. No one knew what he was, what he could do. He wanted to deny it, but it was San Francisco all over again, the terror, the disbelief, and his voice was locked somewhere deep in his throat.

"You need him alive," Collins said. "You won't hurt him."

"Try me," the man said.

Then everything exploded.

That was what it felt like, anyway: a deafening crack ripped through the car and pain burst in Nicholas's head. In the front seat someone screamed, and Nicholas was certain he'd been shot, certain he was already dead, but a second later he saw that Collins's gun was raised and the man in the front had pitched backward, slumped against the dashboard, his face obscured by the head rest.

Collins leaped out of the car, leaving his door wide open, the interior lights flashing on, and a second later he was up front, tugging the man's body out of the front seat and jumping in to take his place.

"Nicholas, close the door," Maram said. The fear was gone from her voice and in its place cold determination. She was already stepping on the gas and Nicholas, habituated to doing as she said, numbly leaned over to pull Collins's door closed. Before the lights went out again, he saw there was a gaping hole in the seat beside his head—a shot that had gone wide by less than an inch. His ears were ringing, and he was having trouble focusing his eyes. There seemed to be tiny shapes floating around the inside of the car and he blinked at them in dazed incomprehension.

"Bees?" he said.

"What?" Maram said sharply. "Were you hit? Collins, check if he's—"

"He's fine," said Collins.

"Fresh air," said Maram and rolled down her window. A few of the little shapes drifted out.

"Did you—did you shoot him?" Nicholas said. He could not piece together what had just occurred. There didn't seem to be any blood.

"Yeah," Collins said.

"Did you *kill* him?"

Usually, Collins spoke with barely concealed disdain, as if he were the only adult in a world of children. But for once Collins sounded like what he was: young. His voice cracked as he said, "I think so."

"Thank you," Nicholas said, because it seemed the appropriate response. Then he opened his own window, leaned over, and vomited into the wind, the illusory burning acid in his throat as it came back up. He could have sworn a honeybee, round and fuzzy, zipped past him and into the night.

When he was finished, Collins was on the phone, his voice now under control. "Roger that," he kept saying. "Roger that."

Nicholas could hear Richard's voice coming tinnily through the speakers.

"He wants to know if you recognized him," Collins said to Maram.

"I didn't," said Maram. "Give me the phone."

She and Richard continued on, a strained back and forth, but Nicholas couldn't focus on their words. He was still shaking, his hands trembling in his lap like trapped mice. Outside the tinted windows, London flashed by in a watercolored blur.

It had been ten years since he had woken in that hospital bed in San Francisco, face thickly covered in bandages. Ten years since his uncle had crouched at his bedside, tears streaming down his cheeks, gripping Nicholas's limp hand, and saying, "I promise I will never let anything happen to you ever again." Ten years since Nicholas had believed him.

Richard had been right. Safety was its own kind of freedom and Nicholas had been kept safe for so long he'd taken that freedom for granted. He leaned forward with his head between his legs and let himself be driven, as he was always driven, never behind the wheel, always buckled into the back seat of his own life.

"And here I thought nothing could be worse than the canapés at that fucking party," Nicholas said to his knees.

And Collins, probably because he, too, was in shock, seemed to forget his personal vow never to laugh at anything Nicholas said, and did.

6

It was no small decision, no small feat, to fly out from the South Pole—planes did not come or go at all in the winter, and leaving during the summer involved getting a seat on a tiny aircraft prescheduled for a supply drop, a plane whose weight was often calibrated down to the ounce; Esther would be lucky if they found room for 130 pounds of agitated electrician.

Not that she was going to leave.

Was she?

Another breakfast in the galley, another bowl of oatmeal she didn't taste. Pearl sat across from her, chatting to Trev the carpenter but casting Esther enough side glances that it was clear she could tell something was wrong. A bit of light research had told her the note that had come through the mirror was correct—a cargo plane was scheduled to come and depart with just enough time for her to make the flight listed on the tickets in her fake name. But using those tickets, that passport . . . it would be madness. Obviously, the whole thing was a trap.

Pearl was speaking to her, she realized, and she dragged her gaze up from her bowl. "Sorry, what?"

"I said, do you want to go for a ski tomorrow? It's supposed to be nice."

Tomorrow. A ski. Esther couldn't focus. "Maybe."

"Well, let me know and I'll reserve a couple pairs." Pearl peered at her. "You okay?"

"Might be coming down with something," Esther said, finally giving up on the idea of work that day. "I think I'm going to go lie down."

To her dismay, Pearl stood and followed her into the hallway, where she reached to grip her wrist. "You're not sick," she said, searching

Esther's face, though Esther made sure she would find nothing there except neutral interest. "Something's bothering you."

Esther shook herself gently free of Pearl's touch, tried not to notice the look of hurt that flashed in Pearl's eyes. "Right," she said, "my stomach."

Undeterred, Pearl crowded her against a wall, bracketed her body with her long arms so Esther was forced to look up at her. It was a power move, but when Pearl spoke, she sounded anything but powerful. "Did I do something?" she said.

"What? No, not at all."

"Your energy's been different since the party," Pearl said. "Weird. Distant. Like you're pulling away."

Even though they were technically in public, the hallway was empty and there were no nearby mirrors through which spying eyes might see them, so Esther let herself reach up and put a thumb on Pearl's lower lip, which was trembling slightly. "Whatever energy you're feeling from me, it's not about you," she said. "I promise."

"What is it about, then?"

Someone was walking down the hall and Esther dropped her hand. "Maybe I'm just coming to terms with the fact that we signed ourselves up for another six months without trees."

"You're not . . . you don't regret it, do you?"

"No," Esther said, infusing her voice and her face with a conviction she did not feel. But the worried line between Pearl's brows smoothed out at her tone. "And I really don't feel well," Esther added. "So it's that, too. Please don't worry."

Pearl looked at her, concern still clear in her lovely face, and for a wild second Esther imagined telling her everything, about books and magic and mirrors and her mother's murder and her father's rules—but a door slammed shut somewhere down the hall, and the fantasy burst. From the first sentence that explanation would be laughable. She felt a surge of anger flare through her unexpectedly: anger at her father for failing to find a way to protect her, anger at the person in the mirror who was yet another voice telling her to *run,* and even anger at her poor murdered mother, who'd died for the books instead of living for her daughter. With an effort, she smothered the flame of rage, cut off all its oxygen until she was calm again. Feelings wouldn't help her decide what she should do.

"Will you let me know if you need anything, at least?" Pearl said.

"Yes," Esther said. "I promise."

She sent notice to her supervisor that she was sick and then crawled back into bed to think. The mirror had told her not to speak to it again, but the mirror probably didn't have her best interests in mind.

Should she find another one of the marked mirrors, stand before it, and again demand answers?

I am not the only one watching.

If this was true, then there was more than one person behind the glass. And if she decided she *did* trust the mirror, it meant she was likely trusting one single person of several, or many. And there was at least one here at the base, too, with the book that activated the glass from this side. They were communicating, passing things back and forth.

So Esther's first step should be finding the person on this side—the person with the book.

She wished suddenly and fiercely that her sister was here, not only because Joanna was a book-bloodhound who'd have sniffed out the magic in ten minutes flat, but because Joanna was, if nothing else, an expert in these things. And Esther badly needed an expert.

There'd be physical evidence of the spell marking someone's body, but cuts and scrapes were hardly uncommon around here—Esther had a recently healed gash on her own ring finger from a slipped screwdriver, and most books needed nothing more than a pinprick and dollop of blood. Looking for injuries wouldn't help. She opened her laptop and waited for her work email to load, then pulled up the list of all the new employees that had been circulated a few weeks before. What she was looking for, though, she didn't know, and she closed it again in frustration.

The only action she seemed to be allowed was a decision.

To use these plane tickets, or not. To trust the person in the mirror, or not. They had quoted Gil, which in some way, shape, or form meant they *knew* her, beyond even her name. But you could be known by your enemy.

Or whoever was on the other side had simply seen her tattoos and used them against her.

It seemed so unfair that just when she'd decided to stay, someone else told her to leave. And she couldn't pretend any longer that the mirrors had nothing to do with her, which meant her father's paranoia had been well-founded all along.

She had known that, though. Deep down.

She'd tested it only once before, at twenty-two, after three years of painstakingly cobbling together an electrician's license from four different institutions. Her last school had been in Spokane, Washington, and she'd been dating a man she liked, though not as much as she liked Pearl: a journalism student named Reggie who'd moved to Spokane purely because that town loved basketball and so did he.

In late October she had broken her month-to-month lease and packed what few things she was taking with her, as she did every year, this time into a little Honda she was planning to drive across the border to Vancouver. Reggie had cried when she'd told him she was leaving and unexpectedly she had cried, too, and had let herself be convinced to come for one last dinner the day she was supposed to leave at eleven. She'd stay till ten thirty, she figured, and then start driving.

Instead, at ten o'clock, post-coital and exhausted, she had curled in the circle of his arms and fallen asleep. She hadn't exactly made the decision to test her father's warnings and stay; she simply hadn't left. It was a non-choice, an action that had been taken in the passive voice, so she didn't have to think about it or face what she was doing.

She had woken to the sound of someone screaming in her ear.

It took her a moment of panic to realize it wasn't a scream but rather the building's shrieking fire alarm system—and it took her another moment to see there was somebody standing beside the bed. Still bleary with shaken-off sleep, she glanced down, but Reggie was right next to her, blinking in gummy confusion. The person in their bedroom was a man, large, white, blond, holding a gun.

At that point she'd been moving around for nearly four years and had picked up some skills along the way. One of them was reading people, which she'd always been good at but had since honed to an art after realizing that if she didn't make friends fast, she'd never have them. And she could see on this man's face, scantly lit through the window by a distant streetlamp, that he was as startled by the alarm and her wakefulness as she was. The window was wide open, cold air coming in. It was right before dawn.

"What is this?" said Reggie. He was a big guy with a deep voice, and she saw the stranger tense. The fire alarm blared on and beside her, Reggie had gone very, very still. "You looking for money, man? What are you looking for?"

The man raised the gun. "Get out of the bed," he said, gesturing at Reggie. "I'm not looking for money, I'm looking for your girlfriend. If you get up and out of here, you won't get hurt."

"Do you know him?" Reggie asked Esther. She shook her head. Her voice was still in dreamland, inaccessible, but she was certain the man's face was completely unfamiliar. She would have remembered him, with his cleft chin and nearly invisible blond eyebrows. She thought she saw a square outline of something tucked into the front pocket of his thin black sweatshirt; the outline of what could be a book. But she was seeing things, she had to be seeing things.

"Get up," the blond man said once more, and then, when neither of them moved, he brought the gun down hard on Reggie's head. Esther screamed and Reggie fell back against the pillow, blood dripping down his face like a torn seam. He struggled to sit up and the man hit him again. This time Esther saw the whites of his eyes as they rolled back and he didn't stir, unconscious. She was shaking uncontrollably now and raised both her hands in the air.

"Good," the man said, and grabbed her by the wrist. His touch felt like a manacle. "Now come with me."

Suddenly, someone started banging hard on the apartment door. "Fire department!" A man's voice yelled, muffled but audible. "Open up! Anyone home?"

Esther met the stranger's gaze.

"Keep quiet," he said, squeezing her wrist tighter and leveraging the gun at Reggie's unconscious form, "or I shoot him."

"We're coming in!" bellowed the fireman outside. "Stand away from the door!"

A second later there was an enormous crunching sound and the stranger said, "Oh, for fuck's sake." He hesitated, but the thudding sound of footsteps was coming toward the bedroom door, and he cursed again, dropped Esther's arm, stuck his gun in the back of his pants, and went headfirst out the open window. A second later their bedroom filled with firemen, who had expected flames and found instead a man bleeding from a head wound and a woman screaming his name.

It turned out someone had called 911 and reported a fire in Reggie's apartment, maybe as a prank, maybe in error, but either way it likely saved their lives. The EMTs on the scene assured Esther that Reggie would be all right, but she would never forget the sight of his dazed, shocked face covered in blood as they loaded him into the ambulance.

Later she would half convince herself it was a coincidence, that the blond man had been there for money or, god forbid, assault, but not for her, specifically. But by the time she'd talked herself out of her own initial panic, it was many months later and she was living on an organic farm in Northern British Columbia, so off the grid she pooped in buckets of sawdust. Every few days she drove thirty-five miles into the nearest decently sized town to take a women's self-defense class, because never again did she want to feel so physically helpless in the face of danger.

The class ran for eight weeks and when it was finished, she enrolled in another, and when that one finished, she joined a boxing gym. When she moved from Vancouver to Mexico City, she'd switched to jiu jitsu; in Oaxaca, muay thai; in Los Angeles, MMA, which had agreed with her. It made her feel brutal, powerful, and in control, and she stuck with it for several years before she'd gone back to boxing. The sense-memory of Reggie's unconscious form in bed beside her and the grip of the man's hand on her wrist had faded over the years, but was still strong enough that, in all subsequent exercise routines, she preferred punching bags to yoga mats.

HERE AT THE STATION, IT FELT LIKE SPOKANE ALL OVER AGAIN, ONLY this time she had overstayed her time on purpose, mistaking purpose for deliberation and deliberation for logic. But her choice to stay had never been based on logic. It had been based on the swooping, giddy feeling that swept her body whenever Pearl touched her, the way her mere presence made Esther's pulse thrum between her legs. Lust, passion, weakness, whatever you wanted to call it. Any other incidental feelings . . . well, Esther's mind and heart had always been in thrall to her body.

How foolish of her to have thought that she could have this, something real. If she did not end it herself, it would end as it had with Reggie: in bloodshed. She couldn't put Pearl in danger.

Without thinking about it, she'd gotten out of bed and was lacing up her boots. Her body was making a decision as her mind was still catching up, and she followed as it took her down the warren-like hallways she knew so well, past the cafeteria, the gym, the medical clinic, to the suite of offices where she could count on someone to be sitting at the metal desk in front of the enormous computer, stamping proverbial paperwork and approving requests.

Today it was Harry, an older man with a kind, leathery face, who listened, dismayed, as Esther explained her position: her father had died and she'd been asked to go home to her family immediately, statements that were both true enough it was easy to deliver them with real emotion. The tears in her eyes, too, were not hard to conjure.

It was just a safety measure, Esther told herself, after she'd secured a spare seat on the next supply plane headed back to Auckland. She had two days to figure things out, to assess the actual level of danger and deal with it appropriately. Harry had sent paperwork to her inbox, a termination of contract, but until she signed it, she was not officially leaving. There was still time. She still might stay.

AFTERWARD, SIMPLY BECAUSE SHE DIDN'T KNOW WHAT ELSE TO DO, SHE went to sit in the greenhouse. She'd spent so many of her lunch breaks here, reading on the shabby, always-damp couch someone had dragged between pots of pepper plants and tomatoes. The greenhouse was small and square and always smelled soul-revivingly delicious, like healthy dirt and the promise of a self-regulating world, though the couch itself smelled like moldy basement. Mingled, the scents comforted her. If humans ever made it into space, bright boxes like this would keep them alive, as it had kept a part of her alive these past months. She popped a piece of tiny, jewel-like lettuce into her mouth and flopped down on the couch to stare up at the ceiling. The lights were a collection of approximate suns.

Esther herself had been responsible for maintaining these lamps, for keeping the station at least occasionally supplied with the taste of life. She remembered her first weeks here, pulling cable hundreds of freezing feet from the generator to the main building, stumbling over ice and loose rock, clumsy and uncomfortable in her insulated suit like a child in a too-snug jacket. Days spent in the oppressive beige of the underground interior hallways, the mess of wiring in the walls, some of it installed last week and some that hadn't been updated since 1968. Lying in her shoebox bedroom and watching the lights on her ceiling flicker, knowing she'd be the one to fix them. A sense of isolation so complete it was almost a sound, a grim buzz, the way she imagined magic sounded.

It amazed her, how once the unfamiliar became well-known you could never go back. What would it be like not to know the sucking, howling sound of a door opened into a Condition One snowstorm? The texture of frozen rubber, the unmistakable fishy cigarette reek of penguin shit? What would it be like not to viscerally understand the particular thrill of driving across roads of carved snow, knowing that if your radar sensor failed, you'd plummet into the ice? If she left—when she left—Antarctica would be a memory, then a memory of memory, and eventually it would be just a story. Pearl would be just a story, a swirl of remembered feelings, someone she'd talk about at bars to strangers who would become friends and then strangers again.

All these stories, what did they add up to?

A life?

She stayed in the greenhouse until past lunch, waiting.

Waiting for what? She didn't quite let herself articulate the answer, didn't quite let herself make a choice, because if she'd confronted it, she might have found it was a bad one. She was here for calm, she told herself. She was here because the greenhouse was quiet, removed. There was low foot traffic at this hour.

If someone wanted to talk to her, say, or to confront her . . . or even attack her . . . well, this was the perfect opportunity. An excellent chance for a threat to show its face and let her confront it, dispatch it, move on.

But nobody came.

Eventually she stood, stretched her tight muscles, and went back into the main station. She made her way through the halls, trailing a hand across the beige paneling. This place was such a neat, closed system of human necessity. Every job supported every other job, and every job supported the continued functioning of life. It was so much messier out there in the rest of the world.

But that was all right. Esther could handle mess.

Lost in thought, tense with unfulfilled adrenaline, she turned the corner of her hallway in time to see Pearl backing slowly out of her room. She almost called out a hello, but something stopped her. Pearl's face was turned away, glancing down the hall in a peculiar, almost furtive manner that raised Esther's hackles. No, Esther told herself, no, you're paranoid, you're on edge, Pearl has nothing to do with this.

Pearl turned and saw her then, face moving between surprise and relief. "There you are," she said.

"Hi," said Esther, smiling despite herself, despite everything. Usually, her face was like her trustworthy hands, completely under her control, but Pearl's presence seemed to be connected to the little muscles in her cheeks that pulled her mouth up at the corners.

"You weren't at lunch," Pearl explained, "so I brought you a bowl of soup. I forgot a spoon though, so you'll have to slurp it, sorry about that."

"That was thoughtful," Esther said. They were both standing in front of her closed door now. Pearl was in a pair of overalls and a bulky sweatshirt. Her hair was up so her neck was visible, long and slender and expressive like the rest of her body. Esther resisted the urge to touch it.

"You know me," said Pearl. "Always thinking. Where were you just now?"

"Bathroom," said Esther, and Pearl glanced in confusion toward the restroom, which was in the other direction. Esther said, "That one was full." She faked a yawn. "I'm gonna keep sleeping it off, but thanks for the soup."

Pearl reached out and slid two fingers into the neckline of Esther's sweater, tugging her closer. "D'you think you're contagious?"

Esther felt bitterness rise in her throat. That was one way to put it.

"Better to be on the safe side," she said, tangling her fingers with Pearl's to soften the gesture of moving her hand away from her throat. It didn't work. Pearl stepped away, nodding.

"Right," she said. "I'll leave you to it, then."

Esther's every instinct was shouting at her to say or do anything to relax the strained set of Pearl's mouth, a kind word, a kiss, but until she knew whether or not she was staying, those instincts had to be suppressed. If she was leaving it was better for Pearl that she start the process now.

"Thanks again for the soup," she said.

She didn't go back into her room until she'd watched Pearl disappear down the hallway. As promised, a bowl of soup sat steaming on her bedside table, and though she was quite hungry she sat on her bed staring at it, unable to eat. In the office she had forced herself to cry, and her eyes and chest seemed to want to reprise their earlier performance. They might have, too, if something hadn't prickled her senses.

Something about the configuration of her nightstand—with its clutter of books, lotion, hair ties—seemed different, as if things had been rearranged.

Or as if something were missing.

She knew what it was immediately and leaped up so quickly she jostled the bowl. Broth slopped over the edge and pooled on the white particleboard. She got down on her hands and knees to look under her bed, then began pawing through the discarded heap of clothes by her bureau, panic churning her stomach. Esther was messy but she was neither irresponsible nor forgetful, and definitely not with something as precious as Alejandra Gil's novel. The monetary value was only a fraction of what it meant to her.

But no matter where or how frantically she searched, the Gil, with its distinctively vivid green paperback cover, didn't appear. The blood was rushing to her face, and despite the chill of her room she was sweating, her hair escaping its ponytail and flying around her face as she searched. She tore apart her already torn-apart room. The tears she'd suppressed were now welling in her eyes. It was here, it was here, it had to be here.

It was not.

Finally, after what felt like hours, she stopped. She sat back on her haunches and gave in to a few seconds of pure unbridled despair, her face in her hands. Then she wiped her cheeks and took stock of things. The novel was gone. No—not gone. Taken. Someone had come in here and taken it.

There was only one person it could've been. Only one person who knew the novel was here, and knew its value, and only one person Esther was certain had been here while she was gone.

Pearl.

7

Nicholas woke gasping for air and kicking his legs against the tangled reeds of a nightmare. His hair was plastered to his head with sweat, his senses underwater, heart hurtling like a bullet train as he lay still, blinking to clear his sleep-blurred vision enough to concentrate on the bedroom around him. The light coming through a gap in the linen curtains was slurring and gray and the vines on his wallpaper wavered in and out of focus, but Sir Kiwi's yapping was loud and clear and grounding. He reached out and got a handful of her fur, felt her little tongue on his palm, and the vacuum of panic began to release him.

"All right," Nicholas said, cupping his dog's tiny, stubborn, barking head. "All right, all right, I'm awake."

Sir Kiwi calmed as he did, putting her paws on his shoulder and staring down into his face with her head cocked. He rolled to one side and groped on his bedside table for the novel he always kept there, a gilded 1978 edition of *The Three Musketeers,* opened it at random, and let his gaze fall to the middle of the page.

"In order to avenge herself she must be free. And to be free, a prisoner has to pierce a wall, detach bars, cut through a floor—all undertakings which a patient and strong man may accomplish, but before which the feverish irritations of a woman must give way."

He read a few paragraphs, steadying his breath to the rhythm of Milady's familiar rage, until the last remnants of his nightmare had faded.

He'd often had bad dreams as a child, and one of his earliest memories was of his governess's dour, impatient face looming over him in the dark, her froggy voice repeating, "Wake up, wake up, it isn't real." For years, the only nights he slept through were the ones when Richard read to him. They'd gone through all sorts of novels together, but Nicholas had loved *The Three Musketeers* by Alexandre Dumas the most. He'd been eight when Richard first read it to him and he'd probably read it a dozen times since. The book seemed to grow with him, new jokes and innuendos revealing themselves with each passing year, the world richer, the friendships deeper. How badly he'd wanted to live in that world! He'd even convinced his uncle to hire him a fencing tutor for a time, but the endless drills and lunges felt nothing like the duels of the novel. What was the point of fighting if there was nothing, no one, to fight *for*?

Recently the nightmares had become more frequent, and he'd taken to keeping the Dumas by his bed to read a few paragraphs whenever he woke up; a medicine to settle his nerves.

He dropped the novel back on the table and looked at the little brass clock beside it. Nine a.m., later than he usually slept. When he yawned, Sir Kiwi darted forward to try and lick the inside of his mouth, a truly revolting habit of hers that he barely fended off at the last second.

"Yes," he said, "I know what you want, give me a minute and then we'll go."

He pushed the dog aside and sat up to apply himself to the grossly satisfying task of unsticking the gunky lashes around his prosthetic. The eyelashes on his left side were sparser than on the right because of this morning routine, but he enjoyed the degunking process too much to outsource it to the warm face cloth that might've saved his lashline.

Soon enough he threw back the layers of blankets and stood, waiting through a wave of dizziness and shivering in his silk pajamas. Dizziness and constant cold: delightful side effects of regular blood loss. Quickly he dressed, then laced up a pair of solid-soled Brioni boots. His feet, at least, felt stable.

Because of the Library's specialized wards, this was the one place in the world where Nicholas was not required to have a bodyguard stationed outside while he slept, so he was surprised to see Collins standing to attention in the hallway. His big square body had been removed from its party suit and was now dressed in his standard not-a-uniform uniform of multipocketed black joggers, white T-shirt, ugly American high-top trainers, and the black felt-and-leather Gucci bomber jacket Nicholas had bought him last month because he couldn't bear to look at his rotating collection of cheap track jackets anymore.

"What're you doing here?" Nicholas said.

"Body guarding," Collins drawled, leaning hard on his Boston accent. He bent to extend a hand to Sir Kiwi. "What's up, bad dog? High five." Sir Kiwi patted her paw against his palm, and he dug into his pocket for a treat.

"But we're at home."

Collins straightened up as Sir Kiwi crunched the little biscuit. "Do you not remember what happened last night?" He clicked a penlight on his key ring and aimed it at Nicholas's right eye. "Let me see that pupil."

"No, I remember," Nicholas said, ducking away. "I just—does Richard think it's unsafe here?" He tried not to let his voice betray his nerves.

"Better safe than sorry," Collins said, and put a hand to his radio earpiece. "You want breakfast?"

"Coffee," said Nicholas.

"I'll get in trouble if I give you caffeine."

"You're the hero of the hour, you won't get in trouble. Besides, last I checked my diet wasn't under your jurisdiction."

Collins pointed at him. "Body." He pointed at himself. "Guard." But then he squinted and said, "All right, you look like you could use it."

Collins radioed through to the kitchen and ordered two coffees, then started down the hallway without another word.

Nicholas's suite of rooms was on the second floor of the manor house, in the West Wing, off a long corridor of floor-to-ceiling windows that were spaced with low velvet benches and waist-high decorative vases devoid of flowers. It had rained through the night and the glass was streaked with water, the sky a luminous mother-of-pearl that filled the corridor with a

strange, heavy-lidded light, bringing out the vivid reds in the carpet below Nicholas's feet but making all other color feel washed out.

The house had been constructed in the early seventeenth century for
one of Nicholas's ducal ancestors and renovated in the late eighteenth, so
the interior was all neoclassical doric columns and gilded pilasters, with
ornate stucco mantels and carved plaster ceilings. Outside, the walls were
plain stone, surrounded by rambling grounds that Richard referred to as
the "deer park" although it had been years since anyone had hunted there.
The furnishings were a testament to the succession of centuries the house
had seen: deep blue and red Savonnerie carpets from the Stuart period,
nineteenth-century Boulle desks inlaid with brass and tortoiseshell, silk
Chinese wallpaper, gilt rococo mirrors . . . a curated temporal layering of
luxury.

Nicholas made his way down the grand staircase, Sir Kiwi hopping
down in front of him. She was a Pomeranian whose russet fur matched
Nicholas's own hair nearly exactly, like they were from the same litter.
She was nine years old, shaped like a cotton puff, and weighed about
the same. She'd been a consolation prize from his uncle when he'd lost
his eye, a capitulation after years spent begging for a dog. He'd always
imagined himself with a sleek German shepherd or a big-headed pit bull,
something dangerous and loyal. Instead, he'd gotten Sir Kiwi. Perhaps
this had been Richard's idea of a joke, but the joke was on Richard, because Sir Kiwi was a creature par excellence. Not dangerous, perhaps, but
fierce and devoted and clever and an endless source of good cheer. She
was the best friend Nicholas had ever had. His only friend, really.

The grand staircase and lower reception hall were lined with oil por-
traits of dead people, all of them Nicholas's ancestors, some quite demonstrably so. There was the dowager cousin with his long nose; a great-uncle
with his sturdy chin; and his father, John, immortalized as a portrait of
a man with laughing brown eyes. Nicholas knew his own portrait would
be added someday.

Richard was not on the wall. He'd claimed modesty when Nicholas asked, but the one time Nicholas had been allowed into his private study, to celebrate the completion of his first book when he was eight, he'd seen that Richard kept in pride-of-place a portrait of his grandfather's great-grandfather—Nicholas's great-great-great-great-*great*-grandfather, founder of the Library—who looked so exactly like Richard that Nicholas had thought at first that they were the same person. It had scared him as a child because this founding ancestor, a surgeon best known for his speed with an amputation saw, had been painted in a bloody surgical apron holding a knife, and Nicholas had noticed that the ivory picture frame was only ivory on three sides: the bottom support was unmistakably made from the bone of a human leg. It was unnerving to see someone who looked like his gentle uncle so thoroughly doused in gore and surrounded by bone.

As a child, Nicholas had occasional heavily supervised playdates with the children of Library associates, but never here in his own home, and aside from lessons he'd usually spent his days alone. The house itself had become a kind of friend to him, and he had spent endless hours playing games with it: racing the pounding echo of his own footsteps across the black-and-white-checked marble floors of the empty Banqueting Hall; lying beneath the white Steinway piano in the never-used Green Drawing Room, staring up at the silent wooden ribs of its underbelly, hide-and-seeking with his own breath. Children in the novels Richard had brought him by the stack were always stumbling awed into mysterious old mansions seeking magic—and Nicholas had been lucky enough to have been born into it, surrounded by it, made of it. Once, this had been a source of wonder to him.

For most of the past decade, however, the endless hallways, fussy antique furnishings, and convoluted ornateness of the walls and ceilings had felt not wondrous but gloomy, oppressive. Yet sometimes he found it beautiful once again, as he did now. It was comforting to be within these familiar stone walls, snug behind the failsafe wards.

At the bottom of the stairs, Collins paused to listen to something on his earpiece. "Richard and Maram want you in the Winter Drawing Room."

"Sir Kiwi needs to go out first."

Collins rolled his eyes but relayed this information over the radio. "Richard says ten minutes max."

"Am I not allowed on the grounds without permission now?" Nicholas said.

"I'm just repeating what I've been told," said Collins, and then hesitated. "You should know—the rest of the staff have been confined to their stations today. I'm the only one allowed to walk around."

Nicholas turned quickly. "Why?"

"Safety precautions until your uncle can interview everyone with a truth spell. To make sure there aren't any . . . I don't know, inside informants, moles, whatever."

Nicholas groaned. "I suppose that's what I'll be doing the rest of the day, then. Writing truth spells." He'd barely recovered from the last book. "And you're the exception because of what you did last night?"

Collins frowned. "Guess so."

Collins looked as tired as Nicholas felt, his normally bright blue eyes dulled by exhaustion, and unbidden Nicholas recalled that unexpected crack in Collins's voice after the gun had gone off. Nicholas wanted to ask how he was feeling, if he was all right, but felt awkward doing so.

"Doug," he said instead, returning to his old standby of guessing Collins's first name.

Collins gave another expansive roll of his eyes and turned away, toward the main entrance. "Let's get your dog walked."

"Dougie, then? Douglas?"

Only Nicholas, Richard, and Maram could walk in the deer park; the Library grounds were included in the wards, and Collins would've been useless, too dazed from the addle of the protective magic to keep his feet once out the front door. Certainly no one else would be able to follow, so all told, the threat level was low. Nevertheless, Collins stood in the open doorway, arms folded, watching as Sir Kiwi dashed off across the wet grass with Nicholas following behind.

It had taken Nicholas a while to understand how other people perceived the house and its surrounding land. That is: they did not. Even those who knew the enormous house was there could not remember how to see it; they had to focus, and refocus, and argue against their own senses until those senses failed. It was why all the scant, carefully selected Library staff was live-in; if they left the premises, they'd never remember how to get back.

To Nicholas, however, who was immune to magic, and to Maram and Richard, whose blood was included as part of the warding spell they set each night, the house appeared as solid and obvious as anything, a gigantic stone manse settled complacently in the rolling green hills of West Berkshire. Brambles encircled the base of the house, though in summer those bare branches would be sagging with rose blossoms, yellow and pink and velvety red, and what looked now like black cracks in the stone walls would be green ivy crawling delicately upward.

The gardeners couldn't stand the mental strain of remembering the ground on which they worked and so the wildness of the lawn was kept barely in check by a small herd of cat-eyed goats, several of whom were milling about, chewing, paying no mind to Sir Kiwi, who was darting at them and then away with joyous barks.

Nicholas walked out to the man-made lake and sat on one of the damp stone benches, taking deep swallows of the cold wet air. He pretended to himself that he was simply appreciating the fresh healthy scent of it and not catching his breath after the pitiably short walk, but he couldn't ignore how his vision was swimming. He closed his eyes for a while, listened to the sound of the water moving in the wind. Writing a truth spell would probably put him in bed for days, but no need to focus on that now. He focused instead on how good it felt to be outside. He hadn't noticed how squeezed and claustrophobic he'd been feeling until that feeling had lifted somewhat.

When he opened his eyes again, they caught on the wet gravel drive that stretched out across the rolling land and distant, misty hills. The nearest road was about a half mile away and for a moment Nicholas's practiced imagination took over and he pictured it: walking down that drive, reaching the smooth black pavement, thumbing down a ride, disappearing.

But that fantasy held far less appeal than it had before someone had pointed a gun at his head. Anyway, he had nowhere else to go.

He stood and whistled for Sir Kiwi, then let her lead him back to the house and the stifling warmth of safety.

IN THE WINTER DRAWING ROOM, MARAM AND RICHARD WERE SITTING together on the cream and gold sofa, a sheaf of papers spread out on the low coffee table before them, along with an interesting-looking bundle wrapped tightly in waxed canvas. The bank of windows was sashed with heavy velvet drapes that had been pulled back enough for Nicholas to see the misty grounds he'd just left, and a fire flickered in the white stone hearth.

They were both dressed comfortably, Richard in a thick cardigan and Maram in a tan silk blouse. There was a silver pot with an arched spout sitting on a tray with an empty cup and a jug of cream. Nicholas went for it greedily.

"One cup," said Richard.

Nicholas sat on the other side of the low table in a pink armchair, its arms carved like lion's heads, and lowered his face toward his coffee. Richard leaned back on the sofa, ankle resting on his knee, but despite the casual posture his brow was creased with quiet worry.

"How'd you sleep?" asked Maram.

"Like the dead," Nicholas said. "Sorry, like the *nearly* dead."

"If you're managing to make jokes, then you don't understand the danger you were in last night," Richard said.

"I had a gun in my face," Nicholas said. "I'll venture to say I do understand."

"If Collins hadn't been there—"

"Yes, I'm fully aware, thank you," Nicholas said.

"How are you feeling?" Richard said.

In truth, Nicholas did not feel entirely himself; he kept seeing the metal barrel staring him down, hearing that sharp retort of gunfire, feeling the pounding of his heart, and then there were those honeybees he'd likely hallucinated (probably stuffing from the shot-up seat, he'd decided).

He sidestepped the question and asked his own. "Did this have anything to do with what happened in San Francisco?"

"We don't know," said Richard, his voice careful. "We're trying to find out. Regardless of who was involved, their intent was probably the same."

Grievous bodily harm, then. Fantastic. "Do you know what happened to that man after Collins shot him?"

Richard winced.

Maram said bluntly, "He died."

"And his body?"

"With some of our people in the Met," said Maram. "They're working to identify him, though no luck yet."

"It would have been nice," said Richard, "if Collins hadn't been quite so trigger-happy. If he'd thought about the fact that we might have some questions before taking that shot."

"There wasn't much time for thought," Maram said.

Richard rubbed his eyes with an elegant hand. "Still."

Nicholas found himself in the novel position of wanting to defend the man hired to defend him. "Collins saved my life."

"He certainly did," Richard said. "And he's getting a bonus for it."

"Great," Nicholas said. "What's the going bonus for someone's life these days?"

His uncle's jaw tightened. "*Your* life is priceless."

Nicholas would have been more moved by this if he wasn't keenly aware of its financial truth. Since his father had died when he was barely two, he was the last living Scribe. This knowledge came thanks to a spell Richard had inherited that scoured the earth for people like Nicholas— scoured, year after year, but never found. The Library's collection was the greatest in the world, its vast reserve of books loaned out to those in the know at high cost and in high secrecy, and culturally Richard maintained influence by partnering with universities and museums across Europe.

But financially, loaning out the old books did not pay nearly so well as offering customized new ones. So long as Nicholas remained alive, writing, and in the care of the Library, the Library remained rich; and so long as they remained rich, they remained powerful. Last night had come about because someone had traced the source of that power to Nicholas.

"Mystery creates intrigue, which creates desire, which creates commodity," said Nicholas. "Perhaps if you didn't keep me such a secret, I wouldn't have such a target on my back."

"I really don't have the energy for this argument today," said Richard, but he clearly couldn't help himself from adding, "Besides, that logic is absurd. A person won't try to steal the Crown Jewels unless they know the jewels exist."

"Please," said Maram, "let's stick to the subject at hand, shall we?"

"Are any of our books missing?" Nicholas asked. If the man was somehow a thief as well as a would-be murderer, they'd be able to find him easily enough. Every Library book had an "expiration date," a rechargeable spell dating back to the late twentieth century that had been affixed to each title in the collection and was added to every new book as soon as Nicholas had written it, in the form of a small, embossed symbol of a book on the back page. It was in fact a tracking spell that was automatically activated in the event a book had not been returned to the Library after the forty-eight-hour lending period was over; it alerted Richard to the book's precise location and had saved not only several books over the years, but once, Nicholas's life.

Maram, however, was shaking her head, galled at the mere suggestion that anyone could have squirreled a book out from under her loving care. "Nothing is missing," she said.

"Wouldn't that be easy?" said Richard. "No, at this juncture we haven't a single lead, so you'll be staying here in the house for the foreseeable future. At least until we can get a few answers—like how that man knew who you were. How he knew what you can do."

"And how long will that take?" Nicholas said, heart sinking.

"As long as it takes."

"What about you? Will you be locking yourselves up, as well?"

"Well, no, we can't," said Richard. "Too much to take care of."

"That reminds me," Maram said, "I'd scheduled that meeting with Conservation and Scientific Research for Friday at the British Museum, they have an eleventh-century emakimono they want me to look at, but—"

"Do you expect you'll keep me here for days? Weeks?" Nicholas said, voice as civil as he could manage. Even the threat of death couldn't stop the panic that rose in him at the thought of being trapped here indefinitely, stuck in this huge, echoing house in the English countryside in winter. "Months?"

Just then the parlor door swung open, and Collins appeared with another tray, this one laden with two steaming cups. "Tea," he said, setting the tray down in front of Richard and Maram with a rattle. He did not seem to like being pressed into maid duty.

Nicholas's coffee cup was nearly empty; he'd drained it without fully appreciating the rare taste, though he could feel the caffeine zinging through his blood.

"You won't even notice the time passing," Richard said, nodding a thanks at Collins as he reached for the tea. "We'll be interviewing every Library employee over the next few days and there's only one or two readings left on your last truth spell, so you'll need to write another as soon as possible. Tomorrow would be best."

"So you're saying I'll be too out of it from blood loss to be bored."

"Better out of it and safe than alert and in danger."

"Richard, he can't," Maram said, before Nicholas could reply. "The doctor said we ought to wait at least four months and he's only just finished Sir Edward's commission."

"A little anemia won't kill him," said Richard. "A traitor in our midst might."

"I'll be all right," Nicholas said to Maram, trying not to give in to irritation at the way she'd spoken for and over him. "I feel fine. Anyway, Richard's right. What do I need energy for if I'm stuck here?"

She stared at him, her big brown eyes unreadable. Then she looked back to Richard. "The interrogations can wait," she tried again. "Nicholas's health—"

"You can't possibly be suggesting I don't have his best interests in mind," Richard said.

It was an order and both Nicholas and Maram knew it. Nicholas had once admired the subtlety of his uncle's commands, though he'd never liked seeing them directed at Maram; in part because he didn't enjoy being reminded that her care for Nicholas was salaried, but also because his care for her was unpaid and unregulated and he was never certain how much of it he was allowed to feel. Especially when he was caught between the two of them; each, in their own way, his only family, paycheck or no.

"Of course I'm not," said Maram finally, and Richard turned back to Nicholas.

"Anyway," he said, "before you attend to the truth spells, I have a task you'll actually enjoy." He patted the canvas-wrapped bundle Nicholas had noticed earlier.

Nicholas perked up. "A vampire?"

"Got it in one!" Richard said. From inside his jacket pocket, he produced a leather-sheathed silver knife, and Nicholas couldn't help laughing. The knife was entirely unnecessary, but he appreciated the theatrics. "Vampire" was the Library term for a very specific subset of protection spell that dated back to fifteenth-century Romania, right around the rule of Vlad III—or, as he was more colloquially known, Vlad the Impaler, the original Dracula. The vampire spell was attached to books whose own spells had already been activated, as a sort of sadistic punishment for attempted tampering. Anyone who added their own blood to one of these activated books was drained absolutely dry—bled, effectively, to death. Quite nasty business. So nasty, in fact, that vampires were the only books the Library ever destroyed.

At least, Nicholas destroyed them. Only a Scribe could destroy a book whose spell was in progress, and Nicholas had always found such destruction intensely satisfying. He had spent so much of his life creating books that there was something wickedly luxurious about doing the exact opposite.

He unfolded the vampire from the tightly wrapped canvas and flipped through the pages, curious as always about the still-active spell that lay inside. Richard and Maram watched him read, equally curious.

"Somewhere," he announced after a few minutes, "there's a woolen blanket no moth can touch."

"A moth-repelling spell?" Richard said. "My god, what a lot of protection for a blanket."

"It must be a very nice blanket," said Maram, her hand drifting out to the book before she thought better, though she still looked at it longingly. It went against her nature to have a book right in front of her and not examine it.

Nicholas unsheathed the silver knife and poised it over the worn leather cover, feeling an odd twinge of regret. As soon as the spell was destroyed, the moths would descend. Wherever it was, the blanket someone had taken such pains to protect would succumb to the ruins of time like everything else. When Nicholas brought the knife down, it cut through the pages as easily as cutting dough, though after that first ceremonial stab he wrecked the rest of the book with his bare hands, tearing out the pages and rending the spine with a feral kind of pleasure. Richard watched, taking delight in Nicholas's delight. Maram seemed queasy and looked away after a time. She didn't like seeing violence done to a book, not even to vampires.

When the book had been thoroughly eviscerated, Nicholas stood and fed its remains to the fire, where they began their second life as ash and ember.

"Bravo," said Richard. "The vampire has been staked."

Nicholas sketched a bow, slowly, so he wouldn't get dizzy and add fuel to Maram's earlier concern.

"I suppose I'd best start writing, then," he said.

Collins could resent him all he wanted for enjoying luxury, but even he had never accused Nicholas of being lazy; not that it mattered what Collins, an employee, thought of him. But Nicholas reveled in luxury for the same reason he reveled in work and study. It was all he had.

"Good chap," said Richard, rising. "Collins, I'd love to give you the day off, lord knows you deserve it. But you understand that until we speak to everyone in the house, we need you to stay on the clock. You, at least, have more than proven your loyalty."

"Yes, sir," said Collins, but the bodyguard's eyes were not focused on Richard. They were focused on Nicholas. The expression on Collins's face was unfamiliar, the twist of his mouth softer than his usual scowl, his chin tilted downward, and when he caught Nicholas's gaze his own skittered away, as if he'd been caught out. It wasn't a look of irritation. It wasn't amusement. It wasn't even pity.

It was guilt.

But what could Collins possibly have to be guilty for?

"Maram, darling," said Richard. "My study."

Maram touched Nicholas's shoulder and followed Richard out, leaving Nicholas and Collins alone in the drawing room.

"What—" Nicholas started, but whatever expression he thought he'd seen on Collins's face was gone, and his eyes were fixed on the floor. He looked bored, tired, grumpy. Normal.

"What?" Collins echoed.

"Nothing," said Nicholas, and turned to leave.

8

Joanna liked dusting the books. It was satisfying to sweep the soft, luxurious paintbrush across their covers, along their spines. It reminded her of brushing Esther's hair, which Esther, a glutton for touch, had always begged her to do when they were young. Each of the volumes in the collection felt to Joanna like old friends, all their cracks and blemishes well known and forgiven, and save for the book Abe had died with, she knew the story behind each one. This one, sewn loosely with silk thread and bound in red cotton, had been found by her late paternal grandmother in a market in Montreal in the sixties; this one with a stiff leather cover had been tracked down by her father via a classified ad in the early nineties; this one, an Arabic scroll from Palestine, had been Esther's mother, Isabel's, from before she'd met Abe. Some of the spells within the collection were used up, but those books sounded the same as any with still-dark ink, as if whatever power that had once filled them still lay coiled inside.

She did not dust the book that had killed her father.

She'd asked her mother about it many times. Cecily had remained silent though, either refusing point-blank to answer any of Joanna's questions or lapsing into that infuriating cough she affected whenever she didn't want to talk about something. Maybe Joanna would try again today, at her mother's house for lunch. Probably it would end in an argument, but at least it would be a nice change of pace from the old standard they'd enacted the day before.

The note her father had left still lay beside it and she glanced at it quickly before moving on to the codex of wards, though the codex hardly needed tending; she used it too often for it to ever collect dust.

As she emerged from the basement into the kitchen she heard a long scratching sound in the foyer, and a pulse of hope beat in her throat. Hastily she emptied a can of tuna into a bowl and quieted her footsteps as she hurried across the kitchen, managing to open the front door so carefully it made no noise at all. There on the porch, like an expectant guest, sat the cat. He had one paw extended as if he'd been about to knock, but retracted it when he saw her and crept back a few steps.

Slowly, so slowly, she lowered herself into a crouch and set down the bowl of tuna. She put it halfway between herself and the cat and waited, breath held, as he craned his head forward ever so slightly and sniffed the air. He turned away toward the porch steps and her heart fell; he turned back, and it leapt. Then he was face-deep in the bowl making wet little gnashing sounds, and Joanna went to her knees to watch him eat. He was the color of autumn, all stripy silvers and swirling browns, and his eyes, slitted with pleasure as he ate, were apple-juice amber.

It was a cold morning. The temperature had dropped the previous night and Joanna had woken up shivering, the embers of the stove nearly banked under ash. Where had this little cat slept? His fur looked thick, but was it warm enough for the coming winter? She wanted to pet him very badly. He finished eating and sat back, licking his chops, eyeing her.

She held out a careful finger, pointing at his face. She had read once that cats liked this because the tip of a human finger looked like a cat's nose, and the cat put out his own nose to sniff, tail twitching. Then, as if he'd decided something, he stepped quickly forward and butted his head into her hand.

The delight she felt at this unexpected touch was so entire it was almost painful. She stroked his head, his cheeks, she scratched behind his ears. He was so warm and soft, so present, his eyes inquisitive, and she found herself beaming down at him as he came closer, his tail trailing along her kneeling legs. She felt a hum beneath her hand and for a moment she thought it was the books, that same many-timbred murmur, then she realized he was purring. For some reason this brought tears to her eyes.

She pet him for as long as he let her and when he wandered away she stood up with the half-eaten bowl of tuna. Holding it out, she backed into her house cajolingly.

"Here, kitty, kitty," she said. "Come inside where it's warm."

But he turned his head sharply at a sound she hadn't heard, leaped off the porch steps, and dashed across her muddy garden into the trees.

She watched him go, feeling a bizarre joyful pride that he'd let her touch him. It was rapidly overtaken with worry. Worry he'd be caught by a coyote, or hit by a car, or that it would snow overnight and bury him, frozen, before they'd even gotten a chance to get to know one another, before she had a chance to care for him.

There was a ragged comforter in Esther's old bedroom—perhaps if she put it out on the porch, he could make a kind of nest for himself, a place to get warm. He'd associate the porch with food and comfort, and by extension, Joanna, and soon enough he would deign to come inside.

She left the front door slightly ajar in case he changed his mind and hurried back into the house. In the living room she pushed aside the heavy wool army blanket she'd used to cover the stairwell and creaked her way up to the second floor, which was notably colder and darker. In Esther's room she found the overhead bulb was blown, but it didn't matter. It was still midmorning and the big window let in a milky light, so she could see her way to the closet just fine. Esther's bed was as it had been when she'd lived there, made up with the first and last quilt Cecily had ever made before deciding it wasn't a hobby for her, and a Nirvana poster curled on the wall. Otherwise, it looked like what it was now: a storage room.

Sometimes it was hard to remember a time when her whole family had lived under one roof, when her sister was in her life and her parents got along. In the months before Esther had left home without warning, Abe and Cecily had fought near daily, and for a while Joanna had blamed those fights for pushing Esther out. Abe and Cecily made an effort to keep their arguments from their daughters, sometimes even taking their fights into the forest so they could have it out away from any human ears, but the tension between them was so thick and sticky it was almost visible, like layers of cobweb.

From what Joanna and Esther could eavesdrop, the gist of their conflict had been this: Cecily was tired of living behind the wards. She was tired of living beholden to Abe's books. She wanted to drop the wards and sell the books and open their doors to the world. Abe thought this was patently insane.

Esther and Joanna had discussed their parents' fights but carefully avoided mentioning their own opinions, in part because it wasn't necessary—each knew whose side the other was on. Despite the fact that her own mother's murder could have been prevented by the wards, Esther had always made it clear that she did not plan to stay in Vermont forever.

When she left, she'd been making noises about applying to college—somewhere in Massachusetts or New York, she'd promised Joanna, somewhere close by. She'd buy a beater car and come visit, or pick up Joanna to take her away for long weekends.

"You can ignore your *calling* for a few days, I'm sure," Esther had said. "Long enough to go to a party or two."

But then, in early November, a few weeks after she'd turned eighteen, Esther came into Joanna's bedroom. It was late at night and Joanna remembered thinking it was strange that Esther was fully dressed in black jeans and combat boots, her hair pulled back. Joanna was already tucked beneath the covers, reading a novel about faraway misty islands and magic none of her father's books could ever summon.

"Excuse you, you didn't knock," Joanna said, so teenaged the memory still made her wince.

Esther came and sat on the side of the bed. Her face was eerily still. Joanna laid her novel facedown on her quilted lap. The air around her sister felt charged.

"Esther, what is it?"

"Nothing," Esther said. "Just wanted to say good night."

"Good night," Joanna said, half echo, half question.

Esther leaned forward and wrapped her in a hug, awkward because of the angle, her sharp chin digging into Joanna's shoulder. "I love you, Joanna."

"Love you, too," Joanna said, bemused, patting her back. "Are you okay?"

"Fine, fine, fine," Esther said.

The next morning, she was gone. So were all her favorite clothes and Abe's new station wagon. No note, no explanation. In her wake, the house turned into a battleground. Abe went around with his eyes rimmed red, his jaw clenched against tears, while Cecily followed him, keeping up a relentless argument that varied in volume and pitch but had one central theme: lowering the wards.

"This is no way to live," Cecily would say, her voice hoarse from shouting, begging, crying. "One child lost, wandering the world, no home, and the other locked up in this dungeon forever. It isn't life, Abe! Let them come, let them come and take what they want, anything is better than this hell!"

During this time, Joanna stopped going to school. It would have been her sophomore year, but she couldn't gather the energy to care, or leave the house. It felt like someone had reached into her chest and turned her heart to cold cement. There was a crushing weight in her lungs, and she couldn't catch her breath. She got winded just walking down the stairs, so she mostly stayed in her bedroom, staring at the ceiling, replaying that last conversation she'd had with her sister, trying in vain to find clues.

In the chaos Esther had left behind no one noticed Joanna's absences until it was too late for her to make up the classes she'd missed, and by then she'd decided not to return. Neither Cecily nor Abe could convince her otherwise, and later that year she got her father to sign the parental waiver so she could get her GED in Burlington . . . but in those long weeks after Esther left, school—and the future in general—had been the furthest thing from her mind.

Now, only half present, Joanna opened Esther's closet door. She jumped violently back when something moved inside, but a second later laughed, hand on her heart. It was her own reflection. She forgot she'd pushed Esther's old mirror in here, an enormous floor-length glass with a heavy wooden frame carved with grape vines. Cecily had loved this mirror, polishing the glass regularly and oiling the wood till it glimmered. Now it was dull with disuse. Joanna swept a hand over the dust and saw that her cat-induced smile still lingered on her face, her dimples coming out from hiding. They made her look young in a way she normally found off-putting, but today she didn't so much mind. She let them stay as she dug around for the comforter.

Arms full of down, she paused on the landing. Her own bedroom was at one end of that hall, her father's on the other. The only time she'd been in his bedroom since he died had been to search for his journals. She'd rarely gone in when he was alive, in fact, though she had paused at the door often enough to say good night, Abe nearly always awake no matter the hour, propped up in bed with his clunky laptop or a stack of documents or sometimes a novel—a book with a very different kind of power. Joanna would push the door open, lean in, and blow him a kiss.

"Get some sleep, Dad."

"Right back atcha, Jo."

If the cat came inside, her dad never would.

It was a nonsensical thought, but she felt herself having it all the same.

When she spread the comforter out on the porch, coiling it up so it looked inviting, it felt like she was making a choice. Making, perhaps, a change.

IT WAS JUST AFTER TWO BY THE TIME JOANNA PULLED UP IN FRONT OF her mother's place. When Cecily first moved out a decade ago, she'd lived in a bottom-floor duplex that was dark no matter the hour and smelled relentlessly of vinegar. Now she lived in a small, neat farmhouse on two acres of open land. Usually the land—and the house that sat on it—seemed staged by the Vermont bureau of tourism, so perfect was the image: the flat expanse of field stretching to the mountains, a sugar-white farmhouse with a pillared front porch and slate roof, a perfect little red barn.

Today, however, the uniform pewter of the sunken clouds overhead made the house look lonely and bare, the barn a smear of red adrift on an achromatic sea. One single alpaca stood in the pasture, head lowered to the brown grass. The rest of the herd must be in the barn.

The alpaca did not belong to Cecily—she rented out the barn and the fenced-in pasture to the animal husbandry department of the tiny college two towns over, and occasionally Joanna arrived to find students on the grounds, young people with bright eyes and loud, bossy voices who chattered about camelid vaccinations and toenail trims and other incomprehensible subjects. They treated both the alpaca and one another with competent, familiar affection, always laughing though Joanna could never figure out at what. Cecily kept inviting the students inside while Joanna was there, especially the shaggy-haired young men, but neither they nor the girls held any appeal; they all seemed somehow much younger than her, and much older at the same time, and looked at Joanna like they were taxonomizing her.

There were no cars parked here today.

Gretchen came running out to meet her, barking exuberantly, and Joanna tousled her brown ears, smiling at the dog's excitement. Cecily had wasted no time in getting a pet once she'd moved out, and though Gretchen was getting on in years, the border collie mutt still moved like a puppy, play-bowing and leaping in excitement. She pranced around Joanna's heels as they headed up the porch together, and Joanna let them both in after a quick rap on the door.

"In here!" Cecily said, and Joanna followed her voice to the kitchen, where Cecily was bent over the oven, peering inside. The whole room was warm and smelled deliciously like bread, a welcome change from the austere chill outside. "Almost done," Cecily said, straightening, and came over to kiss her, then wiped her own lip prints off Joanna's cheek. "Take off your coat, angel baby."

Joanna removed her coat and unwound the scarf from around her neck, hanging them over the back of a chair. Cecily's books hummed along the edge of her awareness, as they always did, though they seemed louder today. Maybe Cecily had moved them from their usual place in her upstairs bedroom.

"Coffee?" Cecily said, already pouring her a cup, then topping up her own mug. Joanna thought her mother might've had enough caffeine already—she seemed on edge, slamming the cream too hard on the table, rattling the cup in its saucer, glancing repeatedly over her shoulder as she moved around the kitchen. The dog seemed anxious, too, and paced a few times before she thwumped down at Joanna's feet, her body curled but her head still upright, alert.

The odd energy was contagious, and Joanna fought against a sudden feeling of disquiet. She took a sip of her coffee, told herself to relax.

Once it had astonished Joanna to see her mother here, astonished her to see any member of their family in such an ordinary, unhidden life, but now she could hardly remember what Cecily had looked like in the kitchen of Abe's house. Her memory of living with her mother was dimmed, or maybe her mother had been dimmed by that life. Now Cecily had a job, friends, a sweet dog, she'd been dating a horticulturist from the university. Oftentimes Joanna felt like a relic of her mother's old life, like a walking talking piece of the house Cecily had been so happy to leave.

"What've you been doing today?" Cecily asked, sitting across from Joanna. She was focused on Joanna's face, yet Joanna felt her attention elsewhere, one of her legs jiggling slightly.

Joanna thought back on her morning, which had been quite nice, really. So nice it made her tired to think of packaging it for her mother. One thing she knew would make Cecily happy, though, so she told her about the cat. Cecily was a great believer in animals for the soul.

"I don't think he was expecting how much he liked to be pet," Joanna said. "Tonight I'm going to see if he'll come inside."

Cecily smiled, but she seemed distracted, standing to check on the bread.

"What will you call him?"

"I don't know," said Joanna. "He's a tomcat, brown and sort of stripey, with really lovely amber eyes. Any ideas?"

"Well, I'd have to meet him," said Cecily. She said it lightly, but still Joanna's defenses began to creep up. Cecily ladled two bowls of carrot soup and refilled Joanna's coffee, and the two went quiet, eating.

"This is delicious," Joanna said eventually, an attempt to bring her mother out of whatever stressed-out funk she was in. "I made it at home, and it came out all watery."

"I add a mashed potato," said Cecily.

"I read online that chefs in Antarctica only get a shipment of fresh vegetables once a season," she said. "In the winter it's too cold for planes to fly—the jet fuel congeals. So if the summer season just started, Esther's probably eating fresh vegetables for the first time in months."

Cecily paused visibly, her spoon halfway to her mouth. "Yes," she said. That one syllable was so saturated with anxiety that Joanna, too, stopped eating.

"What is it?" she said, gentling her voice. She didn't like seeing her mother so agitated, especially when she didn't understand the cause. "You're always saying it makes you sad, that Esther moves so much, that she can't put down roots. I would have thought you'd be happy to see her staying put, for once."

Cecily laid her spoon beside her bowl. Her red lips were pressed so tightly together the skin around them had turned white, fine lines standing out in sharp relief. She shook her head roughly.

Joanna felt a prickle of alarm. "Please, tell me."

"I want to come to the house," Cecily said, which for once wasn't at all what Joanna had been expecting. "Just for the evening."

"What's that got to do with Esther?"

Cecily began to speak and coughed instead, that same harsh retch. Joanna started to her feet, but Cecily waved her down, shaking her head. "I'm fine," she said after a second. "Sorry. I just—" She paused and seemed to collect herself. "I haven't seen one of my girls in ten years and god knows when I'll ever see her again. And the other one . . . sometimes I feel like you're as far away as Esther."

"I'm right here."

"Your body is here in my kitchen," said Cecily. "Yes. You come, we talk, you visit in town, we take walks—and I'm happy to see you every time. Any time, any way I can get you. But you are my child, and I haven't stepped foot in your home since you were sixteen years old." Cecily's voice was shaking slightly. "I don't really know how you live. I don't know what your life looks like or how you really feel about it. And even when you are here, when I can see you, touch you, I know I don't have all of you. Part of you is down in that basement, with your books, locked up in that house—and you'll never let me in. Never."

Joanna sat, fingertips burning against her mug of coffee. This wasn't like Cecily's usual complaints. This was empty of reproach, of accusation, and full of real anguish. Her mother's eyes brimming with tears.

"Mom," she said. "You set fire to the wards."

"Yes, I did."

"Dad told me you'd do it again. And you would, wouldn't you? If you had the chance?"

Cecily was quiet. It was answer enough.

"I can't let that happen," Joanna said. "He made me promise."

"He's *dead,* Joanna," said Cecily. "He's gone and I'm still here."

Joanna thought of her father's dried-out tongue. She thought of the book he'd been clutching.

"When you tell me about the book he left behind," said Joanna. "Maybe that's when I'll let you in."

Cecily hurled her napkin to the ground like a child throwing a tantrum, but just like all the times Joanna had asked her before about the book, she said nothing. She was completely silent, her eyes blazing with frustration and rage.

Joanna closed her own eyes briefly and swallowed hard against the hot lump in her throat.

"I can't let you into the house if I can't trust you," she said. "You want the wards down, you've admitted it, and Dad died holding a book you refuse to talk about. I know you're keeping something from me. You have been for years. Maybe you have been all my life."

"So you keep things from me, in return?" said Cecily. "Is that it? You're punishing me?"

"I'm sorry if it feels like punishment."

"How did you get so cold?" Cecily said, and Joanna flinched. For a long, excruciating moment neither of them moved, Cecily staring fixedly at the table, Joanna's hands knotted together in her lap. Then, suddenly, Cecily let out a long, hard sigh. It was almost the beginning of a sob but when she looked up her eyes were dry, her face composed. "All right," she said. "You want to know about that book?"

Joanna sat up straight, her heart leaping. "Yes!"

"Go into the living room," Cecily said. Her tone was dull, lifeless. "Sit on the couch. Wait for me there. I'll join you soon."

Lunch, half-finished, was forgotten. Joanna stood, startling Gretchen, who'd been dozing on the warm tile. Then, despite her eagerness, despite the promise of finally getting the answers she'd sought for so long, Joanna hesitated. Her mother's shoulders were hunched, head bowed. Her expression was so bleak it was hardly an expression at all, merely a collection of features that made a face. For the first time, Joanna thought perhaps some things were better left unknown.

But it was too late for misgivings and her curiosity was too powerful, so she turned away to do as her mother had said. She went through the front hall to the cozy living room and sat on the scuffed leather couch, crossing her legs beneath her. From the kitchen she heard the faint sounds of her mother moving around, the scrape of a chair against the floor, the thump of a door. And on the edge of it all, the hum of Cecily's books, coating the edges of her awareness in sweet syrup.

Then she noticed the sound was growing louder.

The open places in her mind that were attuned to this specific sensation were slowly being filled, like honey dripping into the cells of a beehive, the buzz rising. She turned toward it, toward the wide doorway of the living room, and found her mother crouched there, one hand on the floor.

At first Joanna didn't understand what she was seeing.

Cecily was dragging her fingers along the lintel and when she stood, tears on her face, Joanna saw a streak of bright red on her hand, and red glinting wetly on the wood floor. A book was tucked under one arm and the hum had spiked, it was *active*, a hive of bees set loose in a field of flowers.

A spell in progress.

When Joanna and Esther had shared a room as children, Joanna had sometimes woken from nightmares terrified and wanting her parents but unable to make a sound. She'd had no air, no strength, nothing but a cracked sibilant hiss; yet somehow Esther had always known—had always woken up and screamed on her behalf, rousing their parents from their bed down the hall. She felt like that now, frozen. Her voice, always too quiet, arrested in her throat, but Esther wasn't here to help.

"My baby, please forgive me," Cecily whispered.

Joanna was already up from the couch and stumbling across the living room toward her, but at the drawn line of her mother's blood she hit hard against what felt like a wall, as unyielding as wood. She moved back the way she'd come, but slower, her hands out, already knowing what she would encounter: dried blood drawn across the windowsills, the doorways, invisible resistance on all sides, a circle of magic and blood that penned her in as surely as a fence kept a sheep from running.

She'd seen Cecily use this spell once before, many years ago, to trap a rabid coyote that had snarled its way onto the property, so Abe could shoot it.

"It's only for a few hours," Cecily said, tears dripping onto her collar. "I had no choice. You wouldn't—I have to—I can't make you understand."

The words thudded dully in Joanna's ears like a heartbeat, noise without sense. No choice. Understand. A few hours. Then she realized.

"The wards," she said. "You've trapped me here so I can't set the wards."

"I'm sorry," Cecily said again, and Joanna sank down onto the floor and screamed.

9

Nicholas's suite of rooms had originally been built for a private secretary, and as such were comprised of an anteroom that led to both his bedroom and to an attached study. This design was butterflied in Maram's quarters in the East Wing, though hers had been intended for a visiting lady, so what was now her own study had once been a dressing room. A few remnants of her study's past life remained in the forms of a walnut armoire and a full-length gilt Louis Philippe mirror, though the armoire was stuffed with papers, not clothes.

Nicholas waved Collins into his small anteroom and gestured to the low sage velvet sofa and matching armchairs.

"No need to stand in the hall," he said. "You can hang out in here. Play solitaire or whatever you do to keep yourself occupied."

Collins had a tray he'd been given by the kitchen, and waited while Nicholas unlocked his study door, eyes darting curiously past Nicholas's shoulder into the dark room until Nicholas took the tray and shut the door pointedly.

Nicholas had learned over the years that privacy was the rarest of his life's many luxuries, and following his uncle's example, he did not let other people into his study. Unlike Richard, however, who had an elaborate system of locks and spells to keep people out, Nicholas's door closed with a simple key, of which both Richard and Maram had copies. *Just in case*, they always said. He set the tray of food on his desk and locked the door behind him, Sir Kiwi at his heels, though at the moment she was more interested in Nicholas's lunch than in Nicholas himself.

Lunch was a pot of nettle tea, a spinach salad, and a plate of cold roast beef with a bowl of mustard. Iron-rich and not, overall, very appealing for his current mood, which would have preferred carbohydrates, sweet ones. He lit a fire in the marble fireplace to cut the damp chill of the air, then sat at his desk, moving his chair to one side so he could keep his seeing eye on the door.

When he was a small child, this room was where his governess had slept, but once Mrs. Dampett had gone and he'd started writing books in earnest, he'd taken it over. His bookcases were filled with perfectly useless novels, not a spell among them, and he'd positioned the leather-topped mahogany desk right between the three bay windows that looked out over the lake.

He could see it now, the water dark and rippling in the wind as Sir Kiwi curled into her favored position right on top of his feet. He smiled down at her and took a grudging bite of spinach salad, then opened his laptop and notebook and arranged them just-so before him. The laptop was, like everything he owned, top of the line, though he was sure many of its higher functions were wasted in a house with no internet connection. Mostly he used it for writing drafts of the words he'd later set to paper, or for watching the action movies he downloaded by the dozens whenever he was outside the wards and attached to a Wi-Fi connection.

He'd written many, many truth spells in his life and so the work mostly involved going through his past drafts and seeing if anything needed to be improved on or customized. A truth spell was, in fact, the first successful book he'd written on his own, an assignment Richard had set him when he was eight. His uncle had stored the finished copy behind glass and it stood on a plinth at the end of one of the Library's narrow aisles, complete with a plaque inscribed with its date of completion. According to Richard, his father's first book had been a truth spell, too. At the time, Nicholas had never felt so proud. Maybe never since, either.

He'd been a mere infant when his parents were murdered, and he had no memory of either of them. According to Richard, after Nicholas was born they had chosen to leave the safety of the Library wards in favor of "pretending at independence" in Edinburgh, and it was there they had been killed. Nicholas knew that Richard was still angry at his younger brother for leaving and it was an anger that Nicholas had inherited, to some degree. If his parents had simply done as he had done—as he was doing—and resigned themselves to life in the Library, they'd be alive today.

Though his father had been a Scribe, his mother had been like Richard and Maram—able to sense magic but not create it, like her own dead parents before her: one of the magical legacy families created when Nicholas's several-times-great-grandfather had founded the Library in the late 1700s and commissioned the spell that confined all magic to bloodlines.

It was hard for Nicholas to imagine what the book world had looked like before, with magical talent popping up in a person regardless of whether any family members were similarly skilled. He'd seen the book that held the bloodline spell only once, nearly fifteen years ago in Richard's study: a book so thick and complicated he'd immediately known it had taken the life of more than one Scribe to get it written. Three, his uncle told him later.

Almost harder to imagine than a world of randomized magic was a world in which there were so many Scribes that three of them could be bled to death for a fourth to write the spell.

Richard maintained that Nicholas's ancestor had commissioned the bloodline spell to ensure that magical knowledge was passed down instead of being lost among a scattered, disconnected populace, but Maram had once told Nicholas, privately, that his forefather had intended the spell to work somewhat differently. He'd intended it to confine all magical skills solely to his *own* bloodline, to his own children and their children on down the generations, but the spell had bucked that intention and become generalized instead.

Nicholas found the original goal of the spell absolutely brutal, if Maram was telling the truth—and he thought she was. Everything he knew about his ancestor made him seem distinctly unsavory. Though he had to admit, that bloodstained apron in the once-glimpsed portrait had not done his ancestor any favors in his overactive imagination.

Anyway, the man had got what he wanted, ultimately, hadn't he? There was only one Scribe left and it was his own great-great-great-great-great-grandson. Bully for grandad and a pity for Nicholas, who'd had to learn everything about writing from the reams and reams of notes the Library had spent the past centuries searching the world for, paying exorbitant prices to private dealers and institutions alike.

It was for the collation and preservation of these notes that Maram had first been hired, several years after graduating from Oxford with a doctorate in theology. She'd then designed Nicholas's entire education plan, employed all the necessary tutors, and generally made herself so indispensable she was now nearly as much a part of the Library as Richard himself. She likely knew more about the particularities of Scribes than anyone alive.

Going through his own notes and yawning, Nicholas wondered, not for the first time, who would organize his notes when he himself died. Perhaps his own child, though it was difficult to imagine how such a child might come about, considering how little time he spent in the company of people outside the house. It was a testament to his tragic social life that his only real crushes thus far had been fictional, namely the Musketeers and the women who loved them.

He yawned again. Despite the coffee he kept nearly nodding off over his laptop, and after a while forced himself to stand and shake off his afternoon torpor and stiffness. He was stretching when Sir Kiwi leaped up and began barking, and someone rapped on the door.

"Nicholas?" It was Maram.

He cracked the door. "Yes?"

She smiled, rattling a bottle at him. "Brought you some paracetamol," she said. "Can I come in?"

She knew how he felt about his privacy. She wouldn't ask to enter unless she had a reason. Warily, he stepped back. She bent to pat Sir Kiwi on the head and then went to stand by the printer, watching the pages slide out of its near-noiseless mouth. Nicholas, because he did in fact have a headache, shook a couple pills into his hand and swallowed them with the last of the nettle tea. He glanced up to meet Maram's eyes.

There was an odd intensity to the way she was looking at him, a stillness to her usually expressive face. The white light from the window lit up the furrows in her forehead, the lines at her mouth, and it made her look suddenly old and unhappy.

"What?" he said. "What's wrong?"

"Nothing's wrong," she said. "I just came to tell you that Richard and I will be in the Winter Drawing Room from about eight to midnight, sorting some things for the coming weeks. We're not to be disturbed."

"Noted."

She picked up a brass paperweight in the shape of a sparrow and examined it. "Until midnight," she repeated. "And you may want to plan on getting an early night. Richard will assist you with making ink tomorrow morning at seven."

"Seven," Nicholas groaned.

"He has a meeting in London at ten."

"I'm perfectly capable of making the ink on my own, especially if it means I might sleep past dawn."

"Richard wants you to wait for him." Maram scrutinized him with an expression that someone who didn't know her might take for irritation. Nicholas, however, recognized it as worry. "I tried again to talk him out of having you do it so soon, but both of you seem to think it will be fine."

"And it will," Nicholas said. "Pleasant, on the other hand . . ."

Maram let out a sharp, unhappy sigh and Nicholas looked at her more closely, taking in her pinched brows and the slackness of her tired skin. Last night had rattled her as much as it had Nicholas.

"I want you to get some rest," she said, stepping away. "You'll need your energy."

"For what?" Nicholas said. "Walking Sir Kiwi to the lake and back?

Lounging around reading spy novels? You need rest, too. Don't use up your energy worrying about me."

Maram shook her head. "In any event, Richard and I will be in the Winter Drawing Room from eight to twelve."

"So you said."

"It'll just be you and Collins on your own for those four hours, since Richard and I will be occupied. Quite occupied."

She was speaking slowly, a firmness to her words as if she were relaying something more important than mere logistics. It was unnerving.

"The adults need alone time," Nicholas said, raising his hands. "Understood."

She set the paperweight back on the desk with a loud clunk and gave him a quick, edgy smile.

Then she was gone.

"That was odd," Nicholas said to Sir Kiwi, bending to scratch her perked ears. "Wasn't that odd? Wasn't it? Yes. Almost as odd as you. Are you an odd little—" But before he could dissolve completely into baby talk, he saw something that made him straighten.

The sparrow paperweight was sitting on the bare wood of his desk. But now there was something stuck beneath it. A small piece of paper. Nicholas tugged it out and stared at it, even more confused than he'd been before.

The note was in Maram's neat script. A series of numbers and letters that didn't make sense, until he realized it was the Library's equivalent of a call number; its own specialized Dewey Decimal system.

PR1500tt.

It was the location of a book in the collection.

Nicholas read the number twice, then lifted his gaze to the window above his desk. He looked out at the mist that had settled into the folds of the hills without really seeing it, worrying the paper between a thumb and forefinger. Maram wanted him to go to the Library and find this book, and she wanted him to do so while she and Richard were otherwise occupied, that much was obvious. Maram often told him to revisit certain spells, quizzing him on them later. What he did not understand was why she hadn't simply told him outright. He couldn't see why such an assignment demanded secrecy.

He checked his watch. Just past five. He couldn't start writing the truth spell until he'd made the ink, anyhow, which apparently wouldn't be until the following morning, so if he started at eight, he'd have plenty of time to hunt this book down and try to puzzle out Maram's bizarre behavior. For now, he'd finish typing up this draft and maybe even squeeze in a nap.

He sat back at the desk and pushed Maram's note to one side, but found it difficult to refocus. Outside, the gray sky looked smooth as a shell, shimmering mother-of-pearl in places as the cloud cover thinned across the setting sun. A bird flashed by the window. It was as lovely as Nicholas had once thought magic could be.

How long had it been since he'd written a book purely for the sake of writing it, and not in service of the Library or some billionaire's dreams? When he was younger, before he'd started commissions, he'd done so fairly often; had been encouraged to do so, in fact, to come up with some outlandish idea and see if he could write it into being. It was considered part of his lessons. Like most children Nicholas had loved myths and fairy tales, but unlike most children he'd never seen himself in the plucky heroes and heroines who spat jewels from blessed mouths or spun wheat into gold or stumbled across magic beans, magic lamps, magic geese. His place was outside the stories, where someone, he imagined, was writing all the spells that made the magic possible. So he'd based many of his early, experimental books on the tales he enjoyed: an enchantment for a harp that made all who heard it weep; a spell to steal a person's voice and hide it in a seashell.

He couldn't read his own books and so was obligated to ask his guardians or tutors to read them for him, watching breathless with anticipation to see if his magic had worked. He'd had a few failures, which he supposed had been the point of allowing him the exercise—he'd learned for himself, for example, that magic could not directly transform a living body, no matter how often he tried to write a pair of wings or get an animal to speak—but his successes had been heady. For a while, it had felt as if he could do anything.

That feeling had faded over the years, along with the delight he'd once taken in his own abilities. Endless commissions had sapped any sense of play from writing, and as he grew older it became harder to convince his tutors to read the few spells he did write for pleasure. He got the feeling some were even a bit frightened of him, though the closest he'd come to accidentally hurting anyone was when he'd written an enchantment for a pair of shoes to make the wearer dance; a spell grudgingly read aloud by his then-classics tutor, a seventy-two-year-old woman in less than ideal shape for a half hour of frenzied waltzing.

There'd been a particularly depressing day when he was around ten, after he'd spent over a month obsessively drafting a book for a real-life magic carpet. He'd written it carefully to be the kind of magic that worked only on an object itself and not on the reader, so he would be able to experience his own book for once; he'd be able to climb onto the carpet and fly. Over the fields, over the pond, away from the Library.

If someone would just read it for him.

He knew full well that while perhaps Maram or Richard might deign to read the spell, neither were likely to let him climb aboard and try it out. But they were away for a few days on a collection trip in Chile and he hoped to circumvent their caution by convincing someone else, someone who might be less draconian about preventing what Richard called "high-risk behaviors," which included swimming, climbing, running too fast, sliding down banisters, riding in cars with anyone other than Richard or Maram behind the wheel, and spending time with other children, excepting the few pinch-faced, dull-eyed sons of Library associates who were sometimes allowed to visit.

His tutor at the time, Mr. Oxley, was recently retired from Eton, and had strongly intimated to Nicholas that he'd taken the Library position not for the joy of teaching but for the substantial remuneration. The man had laughed outright when Nicholas asked him to read the magic-carpet spell.

"What, so you can fly off and break your neck?" said Mr. Oxley. "A neck worth several times more than my own life, I might add—at least to some people, though my wife and children and grandchildren might argue otherwise, and so for their sake, thank you, I will decline."

Nicholas went next to the working kitchen, where the cook was chopping leeks and two of the domestic staff were drinking coffee at the table. They stood quickly when Nicholas came in, smoothing their aprons and smiling down at him. He'd used to like this, how everyone had to snap to attention when he entered a room, but lately he was noticing what happened to their faces as they did: how whatever natural expression they were wearing was wiped clean and replaced with this same bland accommodating smile. He'd started to wonder what it would be like to have someone smile at him because they wanted to.

"I need one of you to read a spell for me," he said. He did his best to imitate his uncle's deep voice, the natural command in it, but instead it came out whining, childish. He cleared his throat. "You don't need to know what it does. You just need to read it."

"Gladly," said the cook, "as soon as your uncle and Dr. Ebla get back and we can get their permission."

"*I'm* giving you permission!"

The cook was a slender, dark-skinned man with a head as bald as an avocado pit, and he'd been with the Library longer than either of the maids. He put down his knife and regarded Nicholas seriously. "Do you know what 'chain of command' means, Nicholas?"

"Yes," Nicholas said, then regretted admitting it. It was easy to see where this was going.

"Your uncle and Dr. Ebla are at the top of the chain here. So, much like you yourself, I can't do anything without their say-so."

"Where am I in the chain, then?" Nicholas said.

"Oh, that's complicated," said the cook, picking up his knife again. "There are a few things you can order me to do. For example, if you came in here demanding I give you one of the chocolate biscuits I just baked, those big ones cooling over there, well . . ."

Nicholas recognized a distraction when he heard one—but also, he wanted a chocolate biscuit. He demanded one, received it, and left to eat it at his desk upstairs. As he nibbled, he stared at the book he'd worked so hard on, filled with weeks of research and days of writing and several ounces of blood. He thought about how biscuits tasted very good while you were eating one, but as soon as you'd swallowed the last bite, the pleasure was over. Probably riding a magic carpet would be the same; wonderful while it was happening, but then it would end and the wonder would be gone. So, who cared, anyway? Magic was stupid and pointless. His talents were stupid and pointless. Probably he, Nicholas, was also stupid and pointless.

Now, much older, he sat at the very same desk, though sans biscuit. He looked from the draft of his truth spell, which hardly differed from the same wearisome spell he'd written many times over, to Maram's odd note. *PR1500tt.* An English-language book, transformational magic.

Curious indeed.

10

At eight o'clock, Nicholas dragged himself up from a nap and set off for the Library, Collins dogging his steps down the grand staircase and through the Great Hall.

The collection had once been contained only within the home's original library, which had been a modest space adjacent to the chapel and the formal dining room. In the late 1800s, however, Nick's great-grandfather had knocked down the walls and expanded the Library into the other two rooms, and it now took up fully half of the ground floor, temperature and moisture control minutely set to archival specifications. The entryway was a metal door that demanded both a retinal scan and a thumbprint, and only Richard, Maram, and Nicholas had access, though supervised staff came in regularly to clean.

Collins stood to one side, arms crossed, as Nicholas aligned his seeing eye with the scanner. "What are we doing down here?"

"I'm looking for something," said Nicholas. "You don't need to come in with me."

Collins nodded, and Nicholas hadn't been aware his bodyguard was tense until he saw his shoulders relax.

"Why do you hate books so much?" Nicholas said, curious. He'd always taken Collins's blatant dislike of magic as part and parcel of his nature, but wondered suddenly if there was more to it than simple surliness.

Collins cleared his throat. He seemed about to say something, lips moving soundlessly, then stopped, cleared his throat again, and swallowed hard. He let out a harsh, rasping cough and shook his head.

Nicholas looked at him, taken aback. He knew Collins was under an

NDA, of course, and he recognized the unmistakable hallmarks of trying to speak around the magical gag order. He did not understand, however, why the NDA should stop Collins from explaining an opinion. He wrote all the NDAs himself, though it was Richard and Maram who read them aloud, and they were a tricky bit of magic that allowed for the reader to fill in the exact terms of the enforced silence. For all he knew, employees might be prohibited from saying the word "whimsical," a word Nicholas knew for a fact Maram did not like.

Finally, Collins said, "All the books are written in blood."

Well, that was certainly true. Nicholas forgot sometimes that not everyone was as intimately familiar with blood in all its many forms as he was. "Fair enough," he said. A press of thumb to touchpad, and the metal door hummed open. He stepped through and thumbed the door closed again, then took a pair of white cotton gloves off the high round table standing right inside and pulled them on as the gears began to groan shut. At the last second, he glanced back at Collins and got a glimpse of his bodyguard's unhappy face before the thick metal separated them.

The lights in the Library were motion sensitive, and flickered to life as Nicholas moved into the room, illuminating the bookshelves one by one until he clapped loudly and the three enormous hanging crystal chandeliers blazed away the lingering darkness. The walls were many-angled, curved where the original library had been, straight through the old dining room, then swerving and peaked in the part that was once the chapel, and every inch of wall was lined with bookshelves.

Some had glass doors, and some did not, but all were richly carved dark English oak, the intricate wooden twists of blossoms and ivy shining beneath the brass lamps affixed to the top of each shelf. There were double-sided freestanding shelves as well, just as high and carved in the same fashion, some arranged in straight lines and some spiraling to match the curve of the walls, giving the place a tight, labyrinthine feel. Here and there were movable sets of spiral mahogany stairs tipped with brass finials, the underside of each step painted a glossy carmine that winked in and out of view as Nicholas walked the aisles, like a cardinal taking flight out of the corner of his eye.

The books themselves were organized according to a classification system devised by Nicholas's great-grandfather that separated them by age, place of origin, and function. There were over ten thousand, and not all of them were books in the strictest sense; some of the glass-doored shelves held scrolls, some folios, and the oldest "book" in the collection was actually fragments of a three-thousand-year-old papyrus written in Aramaic, the letters so faded by use that they were legible only with a specialized microscope. Once, it had been a spell to make a donkey double its strength for an entire day.

"What's the point of having it?" Nicholas had asked, peering at the flimsy, yellowed fragments, preserved behind glass. He was perhaps nine. "If it doesn't do anything anymore, you can't lend it out. Why do we keep books that don't do anything?"

"Everything we can learn about a book is valuable, not only what it can do," Maram had said. "The traces of ink. The methods of binding. The composition of paper. The Library is the sole carrier of a very ancient line of knowledge—how to make this special ink, make these special books. We have a great responsibility, both to preserve this knowledge and to keep it safe. In the wrong hands . . ."

"But I'm the only one who can make the ink," said Nicholas.

"Exactly," said Maram. She had turned her dark, lucent eyes on him. "So you mustn't fall into the wrong hands, either."

But he had.

It had been the last day of October when he was thirteen, in San Francisco, back when he'd been allowed outside the UK more often. He and Richard had been walking down the street, arguing. That year was the angriest Nicholas had ever been, a red haze of puberty in which he'd wanted any life other than the one being shaped for him, and on that particular day he'd been recovering from a challenging commission: a volume that had called a two-day hailstorm complete with lightning, which had been purchased by a billionaire in Sonoma County for the sole purposes of ruining his ex-wife's outdoor wedding.

Nicholas had wanted the argument they'd been having. He'd started it on purpose, by jamming the hailstorm book so roughly into his coat pocket that he knew Richard would not be able to stop himself from chastising him, and then Nicholas could start shouting, which he had. So heated was his fight with Richard that at first neither one of them had paid much attention to the van rolling down the street beside them, a garish vehicle advertising a local plumbing company.

Then Richard had said "They're keeping pace with us" in an odd tone Nicholas had never heard him use, and a second later he was grabbing Nicholas's arm and yanking him away from the street, but it was too late. The van door had already rolled open and several figures in black masks leaped out, metal glinting in their hands. Days later Nicholas had found bruises still livid on his arm in the shape of Richard's fingerprints where he'd clung to him, though by then those were the least of his injuries.

They'd knocked Richard out and grabbed Nicholas and driven him blindfolded and terrified for what felt like hours, then tied him to a chair and left him there—wherever "there" had been. Alone. He didn't know for how long. Long enough that he'd pissed himself several times. Then, finally, his kidnappers had returned. Multiple sets of footsteps. He had asked if they were the people who'd killed his parents and someone had laughed and told him yes.

From their rapid-fire questions, it was clear they were after the Library's closest-guarded secret: the secret of the Scribes themselves. They wanted to know how the books were being written and by whom, little realizing that the answer was tied to the chair in front of them. Nicholas told them nothing. Finally, after hours of interrogation and two broken fingers, a person who smelled like soapy lavender detergent had come and plunged a needle into his arm and that was where his memory ended.

When he woke he was in a hospital bed. He opened what turned out to be his one remaining eye to see Maram slumped in a chair at his side, exhausted in a way he'd never seen her before and would never see again. Behind her Richard was pacing.

After the doctors had told him the extent of his injuries, after Richard and Maram had explained how it had been the activated expiration date of the hailstorm book in Nicholas's pocket that had led them to him and saved his life, after he'd told them everything he'd learned from his captors, which was absolutely nothing, Richard had knelt at his bedside and taken Nicholas's hand.

"If we'd been fifteen minutes later—" he'd said, then stopped, voice shaking, unable to finish the sentence. When he spoke again his voice was steady, strong. "I will never let this happen again."

Nicholas had lowered his head, embarrassed by the emotion in Richard's words but thankful for it, too. Richard squeezed his hand and said, "No, Nicholas, I want you to look at me while I say this. I want you to believe me. Nothing like this will ever happen to you again. We're going to keep you safe, me and Maram and the Library. I promise you."

And he'd kept that promise. Nicholas had been safe—so, so safe—ever since. Grateful for the protection. Unquestioning of its necessity. Not dreaming, anymore, of any other life but this.

And because this was his life and he had more or less accepted that it was the only one he would ever have, he'd decided to take pride in what he could of it. He'd focused even harder on studying the books, his father's notes, on learning to write, and he'd long since memorized the layout of the library.

So he knew exactly where to find the book whose information Maram had copied into her note. It was on one of the curved shelves in the original library, very high up, and Nicholas had to push aside a large seventeenth-century globe and drag one of the spiral staircases over in order to reach it. It was bound rather crudely in undyed leather that felt rough to the touch. He took it down and read the informational card in its plastic cover.

Country of origin: England.

Estimated year written: 1702.

Collected: 1817.

Effect: Causes all admixture of chemical propellant, i.e., gunpowder,
to turn metal into Bombus terrestris *upon explosion.*

Ink sample: Blood type O negative, detected clover, balsam.

He remembered this book now; he'd studied it when he was learning transformational magic. He adjusted his gloves and began to page through it. He had no idea what Maram wanted him to look for and was prepared to flick through the pages and let his attention skim until it found traction, but he saw immediately that it wouldn't be necessary.

In the front of the book, tucked between the cover and the first page, there was a note.

This, too, was in Maram's handwriting and he read it over, a headache starting to throb behind his eyes.

It was another call number.

What was this, a scavenger hunt? He put the bullets-to-bees book back on its shelf and began weaving his way to the other side of the library entirely, where the old chapel had been. He was so focused on his path that he bounced his blind left side hard off the edge of a shelf and swore loudly in pain, though his voice was swallowed by the distant hum of the dehumidifier and the layers and layers of paper.

This next book was in one of the shelves beneath the stained-glass windows of what had once been the chapel, on a raised dais where the sermon would have been delivered. It was right behind one of two red leather Georgian wingback chairs that flanked a chest-high glass display case. The case held a fragment of a four-thousand-year-old limestone relief carving that depicted the Egyptian goddess of writing, Seshat, mistress of the house of books. Her name meant *She who is the scribe.*

This was not merely a relic, however. On the other side of the limestone slab were a series of meticulously etched hieroglyphics, taking up nearly the entire stone, and if one put a microscope to these etched characters, dark traces of blood were visible in the grooves. The long-dead Scribe who'd carved this spell had mixed their blood with herbs and clay and sealed it into the carving. It was what Maram called a "companion spell"—written to enhance the workings of other magic rather than stand on its own.

This particular companion spell could prolong the effects of any book for up to three hours, and the carving was priceless not only for its age, but because the magic was still intact—barely. There was enough blood present for one last reading, a near-miracle considering that etched or carved spells could generally support only two readings total. As long as Seshat was under Maram's protection, however, Nicholas knew those traces of blood would remain, and the four-thousand-year-old magic would endure, unread, forever.

According to Maram, Nicholas's grandfather had acquired this relic in 1964 at a curatorial meeting for a New York museum, via the use of a powerful persuasion spell that made the reader seem completely trust-worthy to anyone with whom they spoke, for thirty minutes. The spell had first been written, Maram told Nicholas, for the Dutch East India Company, to be used by slavers.

Nicholas had been thirteen, his empty socket still healing beneath an eyepatch, when Maram had told him this—she was sitting in one of the red chairs as he peered at the ancient carving, his fingertips just brushing the glass of the display case. That last part made him recoil.

"That's horrible," he said.

"Yes, it is," said Maram. "It was written in 1685."

The Library had been founded in 1685. Or anyway, that was the year Nicholas's founding ancestor had decided to turn his personal collection of books into the beginnings of an organization. That was the year he'd hired the first Library employees, and the year he'd appointed the first official Library Scribe—his sister.

Nicholas had a sinking feeling in his stomach. "Did a Library Scribe write that book?"

"That's right," said Maram. "In fact, it was the first commission, and the proceeds were used to renovate this chapel."

Nicholas looked down from the dais to the colored pattern of stained glass the sun painted across the carpet. "But," he said, knowing what he was about to say was childish and unable to stop himself, "I thought my great-whatever-grandad started the Library because he wanted to help people."

This was the story he'd been told: that the surgeon had seen so much suffering in his profession that in middle age he'd turned his purpose from medicine to magic, hoping to find a way to miraculously heal the human body. But books could not interfere with biology, at least not permanently, and over time the Library's auspices had expanded from mere study to include collection, preservation, and commission. Writing spells for slavers had not been included in this origin story as Nicholas had understood it.

"The Library holds power," said Maram. "And power is always a reflection of the world that has created it, regardless of intention."

"But magic could make the world better," Nicholas tried.

"No, it couldn't," said Maram, her voice sharp. "Your uncle understands this. You need to understand it, also. That is why we keep commissions small and personal, why you will never write for governments or corporations or leaders of political rebellions, no matter how intriguing their cause or how much money they offer. We are not here to change the world with these books, Nicholas. Part of the reason we collect them is to keep them *from* the world, because the world misuses power and the Library participated in that misuse for centuries. Do you see what I am saying?"

Nicholas had seen. But even now, he did not like looking at the carving, did not like looking at the serene lines of Seshat's ancient profile, and he avoided it as he climbed the steps of the dais.

On the outside, the books in this chapel section were as colorful as the books everywhere else, their spines bright leather or dull cloth or even hammered metal, but inside they were ghostly. This was where the Library kept the books whose ink had faded, whose magic had run dry. The book referenced in Maram's second note was a slim, elongated volume in a red leather cover with the customary placard in place.

> *Country of origin: Hungary.*
> *Estimated year written: 1842.*
> *Collected: 1939.*
> *Effect: Causes solid unliving objects to become translucent and breachable; allows bodies to pass through. Duration: Max six minutes per reading.*

There was nothing remarkable about it as far as Nicholas could tell on a first leaf-through. The book seemed to be no more than exactly what it was, a spell with scarcely forty pages to it, the ink faded nearly to the point of powerlessness . . .

But not quite.

Nicholas raised the book to his eye and squinted at the first page. The ink was faint, yes, but unlike every other book in this section, it was not entirely used up. There was magic in it yet. He began looking through it again and this time, when he reached the end, he saw something very interesting.

The last page had been written over. The ink, which had been faded and almost unusable, grew suddenly strong again. A different hand had changed the final words of the spell.

The last page had been rewritten by a different Scribe entirely, to make the book rechargeable.

Nicholas's heart picked up in his chest. Now this, this was something. A rechargeable book needed more blood than was usual; it needed all the blood a person could give.

Which meant someone, sometime, had died to rewrite this book.

He pressed one cotton-gloved fingertip to the faint brown stain where the page would take the reader's blood and read the notecard again.

Causes solid unliving objects to become translucent and breachable; allows bodies to pass through.

He looked up at the bookshelf, which was made of sturdy oak and metal nails, the shelves lined with books of leather and paper. Solid unliving objects. There was a visible section of wood where the book had been sitting, the back of the shelf sitting flush against the wall. Carved into the wood was a small symbol no bigger than the nail on Nicholas's smallest finger: a clear, deliberate X.

He stepped back to examine the rug beneath his feet. It was, like all the rugs in the library, woven wool and slightly worn down from the years. Was it Nicholas's imagination, or did the worn path look subtly different here? He knelt by the base of the bookshelf and took off his gloves so he could drag his fingers across the fibers, and it wasn't in his head: the rug was thinner not only in the center of the aisle but on the side, too—a barely perceptible swerve in the path that led to this book, to this bookshelf. The thinning pile went all the way to the foot of the bookshelf—as if the path led not to the shelf, but through it.

He rose to his feet. He stared at the rechargeable book in his hand and then again at the worn-down path of the rug.

Allows bodies to pass through.

There was something beyond this shelf. Something that could only be reached by using this book Maram had led him to, a book that anybody could read. Anybody at all could press their finger to the page and let the paper drink their blood, anybody could speak the words that would render this bookcase permeable, words that would dissolve the barrier of shelves and frame and allow the reader to move through it to whatever lay waiting beyond.

Anyone except someone who could neither touch nor be touched by magic.

Anyone except Nicholas.

By design, whatever lay beyond the shelf was inaccessible to him and him alone.

He put the book back with a shaking hand, obscuring that delicately carved X. He suddenly felt as if the bookshelves were looming over him, leering. If Maram wanted him to know about this, why not just tell him? Did she think him so bored he needed a child's game to occupy his time?

Collins was sitting on the floor in the hall outside, chin in his hand, though he got to his feet when Nicholas came back through the metal door. He took a step away when he saw that Nicholas wasn't closing the door behind him.

"You find what you were looking for?" he said.

Nicholas's mind was whirring. He himself couldn't work the magic, but that didn't mean someone else couldn't work it for him.

"You're not going to like this," Nicholas said. "But I need you to come in here and do me a favor."

Collins groaned. "I did you a favor last night by not letting you get murdered."

"I need you to read a spell."

"No," said Collins. "No way. I don't do that. Not in the job description."

"Please? I'll give you—" Nicholas paused, because he had no cash, only credit cards and a near-limitless bank account, which was useless for secret out-of-pocket expenses. "My watch," he finished. "It was eleven thousand pounds new. You could probably sell it for—"

"You paid eleven thousand dollars for a *watch*?" Collins said.

"Actually, it was a good deal, normally these go for—"

"My watch was thirty bucks and it works great," Collins said. "I don't need a new one."

"What, then?" Nicholas hissed, glancing up and down the empty hallway. "I have cuff links, tie clips, a couple rings, and Sir Kiwi's got that gold collar she never—"

"I don't want your money." Collins's eyes were narrowed in annoyance.

Nicholas thought of Collins's reaction when Nicholas had asked why he hated books. He lowered his voice further. "I'll write a spell to reverse your NDA."

Collins's expression changed so fast Nicholas nearly laughed. "I will," said Nicholas. "And in case you think I've turned suddenly selfless, I haven't. I'd prefer my bodyguard be able to answer my questions when I ask them—and it seems you can't do that under the NDA. So it'll be a win-win for both of us."

Collins clenched one hand and put it against the wall very gently.

"Who'll read it to me?" Collins said. "You can't."

"You'll read it yourself."

"What? It doesn't work like that."

Nicholas shook his head. "What do they teach you when you're hired? Yes, it works like that. People read their own spells all the time."

"How do I know you're not lying?"

Nicholas threw up his hands. "Because you saved my life and I already owe you?"

Collins looked away. Then he said, "Write me the spell first, then I'll help you."

"I can't," Nicholas said, frustrated. "You know that. I have to write the truth spells and I'll need to rest at least a few weeks afterward. I've lost too much blood recently as it is. But I need you to read that book for me now, tonight."

"So I have to just take your word for it."

Nicholas found that he wanted to be trusted. "Yes."

Collins frowned in thought while Nicholas waited, breath held. He wasn't used to it being this hard to get what he wanted, especially not from someone supposedly under his direction—or Richard's direction, anyway, which was the same thing.

"Fine," Collins said. "Ugh."

Nicholas debated fleetingly about whether or not he ought to go to the herbarium and find something to mix Collins's blood with—the spell was Hungarian, so paprika or meadowsweet were obvious choices—and the informational card had said *max six minutes* duration, which meant that without any herbal oomph they'd be lucky if the spell lasted three . . . but he was worried Collins would change his mind if the process took too long, and anyway, three minutes was plenty of time to see what lay beyond the bookcase. So he forewent the herbs and pulled Collins into the Library.

He waited until they were both inside to make certain the electronic door was firmly closed and locked behind them, and when he turned, he found Collins standing with one hand against the wall, the other pressed over his eyes as if overwhelmed by the light. Nicholas frowned. It was well-lit in here, yes, but not overwhelming—the brass lamps lining the shelves had a low, amber light, and the chandeliers overhead sent down a warm glow. But then Collins dropped his hand and stared out into the room, jaw falling open slightly.

"You've never been in here before," Nick remembered, seeing it through his eyes: the thousands of books in their tidy rows, the carved shelves on every winding wall, the glittering chandeliers, the changing ceilings, everything lush with color and texture and age and magic. No wonder he seemed overwhelmed. "What do you think?"

"Seen one library, seen them all," Collins said. "This one's nothing special." But his awed face suggested otherwise.

"Liar," Nicholas said, laughing. "Here, gloves."

Collins shoved his big hands absently into too-small white cotton, still looking around. "These are all . . . all these books are . . . ?"

"Spells, yes, for the most part." Nicholas started off down the aisles. "The majority are quite old, as you can see. All the ones written by Library Scribes are around that corner."

"There used to be a lot more of you, right? Scribes?"

"Supposedly," said Nicholas.

"I'm surprised they're not breeding you like a show pony."

"I'm not amenable to breeding—and besides, there's absolutely no guarantee any of my children would be Scribes. My father was the first Scribe born to our family since the Library's founding; my own birth appears to have been pure dumb luck." Nicholas glanced back. "Anyway, what do you know about show ponies?"

"I might know a lot. I might have grown up on a ranch."

Collins, growing up: it was a startlingly charming thought. Nicholas pictured a small square boy with bright blue eyes and a furious adult scowl. "*Did* you grow up on a ranch?"

Collins didn't answer, though, and the smile slipped off Nicholas's face. He should have known better than to expect Collins would answer; conversation wasn't part of the job description. Then he heard the rasp of a cough. He didn't turn around, unwilling to see on Collins's face the strain of fighting an NDA—unwilling to wonder why he'd be forbidden to disclose information that seemed so innocuous. Probably it was just a cough, perfectly natural. Besides, Nicholas had every intention of keeping his promise and reversing the spell—so maybe sooner, rather than later, Collins *would* be able to reply.

"Here we are," he said, leading Collins up the aisle beneath the stained-glass windows, to the dais. Collins watched with trepidation as Nicholas took the Hungarian book down from its shelf and held it out. "This is what I need you to read. Have a look through, it won't do if you stumble."

Collins looked at the description card. "It's in Hungarian."

"The language won't matter once the book feels your blood and knows your intention to read it. Once you start, you'll understand it as if it were English."

"I know that," Collins said.

"I don't have a needle or a knife or anything," Nicholas remembered. "Do you have something we can poke you with?"

Collins dug in his pockets and brought out a keychain with a small Swiss army knife. "You got a lighter? To sterilize it?"

"A *lighter*?" Nicholas said. "There's about a thousand kilos worth of irreplaceable paper in this room."

"So, no."

"You're not going to go septic from a prick on the finger, trust me."

Collins rolled his shoulders like a man gearing up for a fight and yanked off his gloves. "Fine. Let's do this."

Despite Nicholas's general exhaustion, his irritation with Maram, and his resentment at such a spell in the first place, he felt a little zing of excitement. The Library was full of secrets, but it had been quite some time since he'd encountered a new one. Collins held the knife to his finger and waited for the blood to well up before he pressed it firmly to the page and began to read. His voice was clumsy at first and then more natural, his accent lending the words a hypnotic kind of cadence.

It took about twenty-five minutes until, silently, the bookshelf began to blur. At first it seemed merely out-of-focus, but then its edges started to dissolve like a storm cloud fading into rain, and by the time the last word rang out, Nicholas's hand could pass through with no resistance at all. The bookshelf and the books on it were a vague dark haze and Nicholas could see through that haze to the wall.

Only it wasn't a wall.

"A door," said Collins.

It was. The bookshelf had faded to reveal the brass knob, the plain wood, the hinges fastened to the bare stone of the wall—a door like any other but hidden. And behind the door, when Nicholas reached forward through the intangible shelf and pulled it open, was a dark staircase heading up.

11

Are you sure I can't get you anything?" Cecily said. "A cup of coffee? Tea?"

Joanna didn't bother looking at her mother as she shook her head. She was lying on the couch with her gaze fixed out the window, tracking the slow fade of light as the sun sank downward, a bright coin tossed into a dark pool. With every dimming ray she moved further from the possibility of getting out and getting home in time to set the wards.

"You didn't finish your lunch," Cecily said. "I could reheat the soup?"

"You can't feed me into forgiving you," Joanna said. Her voice was hoarse from yelling.

"I know that," said Cecily, though her tone suggested she planned to keep trying. Joanna had been trapped behind her mother's spell for over an hour and wore herself out in the first fifteen minutes, screaming and weeping and begging for an explanation, and all Cecily had said, over and over, was "I can't tell you, I'm sorry, I can't tell you." She'd been crying, too, but neither of them was crying now. Joanna felt almost calm; perhaps she'd used up her yearly allotment of furious emotion. Cecily had positioned a chair in the doorway and was watching her daughter with sorry determination from outside the living room. Gretchen lay dozing at her feet.

"You want to steal the collection and sell it to the highest bidder," Joanna said. She'd been throwing out guesses, though her mother wouldn't tell her yes or no either way. "You're going to retire to Paris and eat croissants every morning."

"No," said Cecily. "Too many pigeons in Paris."

"You're going to burn the house down so I'll have nowhere to live and nothing to do and I'll be dependent on you for everything," said Joanna.

Cecily was quiet for a moment. Then she said, "I hope you can't truly imagine I'd do such a thing."

Joanna sat up against the arm of the couch. "I couldn't have imagined you'd trap me in your living room, either."

"It doesn't have to be like this," Cecily said. "I'll end the spell right now and we can get to the house in time for you to set the wards, if you'll only take me with you and let me in."

"If it's not the wards you want to get to," Joanna said, "then what?"

Cecily set her mouth and shook her head and Joanna lowered herself back down, eyes finding the afternoon sky again through the window. "That's what I thought," she said.

There was a part of her, buried so deep in fear she'd need a shovel to clear its face, that was curious to see what would happen when the wards went down. A part of her that felt a strange, soaring interest—almost elation. The wards were a tether as well as a safeguard. What would happen when her tether was cut? The house hadn't spent a night unwarded since Abe had first stepped foot in it nearly three decades earlier, infant daughter in his arms, the body of his murdered lover hundreds of miles away. What would happen when the protection he and Joanna had so painstakingly maintained, disappeared?

There were—or at least, had been—people out there who'd shown their willingness to kill for access to Abe's collection . . . but that had been almost thirty years ago. The dropping of the wards would mean only that the house would be like any other house; visible and accessible if you had the address, and no one, to Joanna's knowledge, had the address. So it was possible the cataclysmic event she'd always feared (swarms of armed men pouring through her windows? All her books carried off by malice and violence?) might not come to pass at all, or not anytime soon.

But what did Cecily want if not to expose the house *to* something, someone? In those weeks after Esther had left, Cecily had been like a person possessed, debating Abe constantly, trying to convince him to drop the wards, to leave the books, to give up his life's work. But why? For whom?

Cecily was the only person who could give her those answers, and Cecily refused.

Joanna gave it one last try. "I'll take you to the house," she said, and her mother straightened, "if you answer three questions under a truth spell."

Cecily's expression, which had been hopeful and alert, fell instantly. "I won't be able to."

"That's not possible," Joanna said, exasperated. Abe had put her under one, once, to show her what it felt like. She'd been twelve or so and he'd asked simple, silly questions he already knew the answers to: How do you make a fried egg? What's my favorite Allman Brothers song? Why did Esther get mad at you yesterday? He had told her to try to lie.

She couldn't. It had felt like the truth was a ribbon that unfurled on her tongue anytime she opened her mouth. No sense of striving or discomfort: she simply told the truth, over and over, her attempted lies transforming somewhere past her voice box.

"It isn't that I don't want to give you answers," Cecily said. "It's that I cannot. I know you don't understand and I'm sorry. If I could explain, believe me, I would."

Joanna felt a wave of helpless anger surging through her, and she shut her eyes tightly and held her breath against it until it passed. She'd tried anger, she'd tried tears, and neither had worked. Maybe part of her was curious, yes, but the rest of her was her father's daughter. She could not let the wards fall.

Cecily had refused the truth spell, but she'd seen her mother's posture change at the hope of a bargain, which meant Joanna could hope, too. For Joanna, a bargain was a chance to reach the wards in time; for Cecily it was a chance to restore some fragment of the relationship she'd broken when she'd drawn her blood across that door.

She stood from the sofa and crossed the room to stand in front of her mother and the invisible barrier, arms crossed. Cecily shifted in her chair as if she, too, might stand, but she didn't, just looked up at Joanna with wary eyes.

"You say you haven't done this in order to destroy the wards."

"I have not," Cecily said immediately. "I only need the wards down so I can get in. You can put them back up tomorrow, I swear it."

"But you won't tell me what it is you want to do."

"I *can't* tell you."

Joanna took a frustrated breath. Cecily kept repeating that word, *can't, can't, can't,* as if her silence were a matter not of will but of ability. Joanna decided to take this at face value. "Is it something I'd stop you from doing, if I could?"

Slowly, Cecily said, "No. I don't see why you'd stop me."

"Would you let me watch you do it? If I took you into the house?"

Cecily went very still, attentive like a dog in sight of a rabbit. Joanna could see her thinking, eyes darting back and forth as she considered this. "Yes," she said, finally.

Joanna felt a swell of triumph. She could set the wards and get some insight into her mother's motives at the same time.

"Here is my proposal, then," said Joanna. "We have about two hours before I need to set the wards. In those two hours, you will end this spell, let me blindfold you, and I'll take you to the house and let you in. You can do what you need to do and then I'll drive you back. If you try anything at all with the wards, or if you try to get into the basement, or if I tell you not to do something and you do it anyway, I'll never speak to you again."

Cecily started to respond and Joanna cut her off.

"I mean that, Mom." She weighed her voice with conviction. "And if you decline, if you leave me trapped in here while the wards drop and you break into my house, it will be the same. You will lose me as completely as you lost Esther, and you will never get me back."

The threat was sticky on her tongue, rotten. She said it knowing it was her mother's deepest and oldest fear. Cecily's eyes went shiny with tears and Joanna knew her own face likely reflected some of the grief she'd wielded like a weapon at her mother's underbelly. She'd never been able to hide her feelings, not like Esther could, but it didn't matter. She let her mother see.

"Okay, my love," Cecily said. "I will make that deal."

She licked her thumb, bent down, and wiped away the barrier of blood.

12

Esther did not know how to confront Pearl about what she suspected, or whether she should even try, but as it turned out, the decision was made for her.

She hadn't left her room after discovering the absence of her mother's book, nor had she slept. She'd locked her door and shoved her dresser in front of it then sat on her bed, so alert it felt almost like hypnosis. She'd been stolen from twice before: once in Buenos Aires by a group of eleven-year-olds who'd menaced her with broken bottles, and once in Cleveland by a guy who was disgusted to find that the only thing in her pocket was a cheap pay-by-the-month flip phone. "Man," he'd said, "you should be robbing *me,*" and they'd both surprised themselves by laughing. Both of those times she'd felt frightened and pissed off. She hadn't felt violated.

She did now.

Whether Pearl had taken the book to re-sell online or because she was somehow connected to the people who'd been after Esther all these years hardly seemed to matter. Either way it was a betrayal. Maybe, Esther thought, dull and staring at four a.m., she could avoid Pearl completely for two days, get on that plane, and leave without ever having to confront her, without having to face the fact that one of the only true relationships she'd had in her life had been a lie.

At eight a.m. after a sleepless night, she was still wide-awake, and so on edge that when someone banged on her door it felt like a forty-volt blast to the chest. She stayed motionless, clutching her knees, praying that whoever it was would go away, but the banging started again and to her horror it was Pearl's voice that spoke.

"Esther, I know you're in there! Open the damn door!"

Esther stood and took a deep breath, allowed herself to close her eyes, to feel her breath coursing through her body, to feel her feet on the ground. Then she opened the door.

Instead of letting Pearl inside, she edged out into the hallway. She didn't want to be close together in a small room with this person she thought she'd known. Pearl's face was twisted in an unfamiliar expression that Esther belatedly identified as rage; she'd never seen good-natured Pearl truly angry before.

"Can we go in your room?" Pearl demanded.

"No," said Esther.

Pearl's nostrils flared and something moved in her chin. Esther, taken aback, realized she was about to cry.

"You weren't at breakfast," Pearl said.

"I'm not hungry."

Pearl's chin puckered again, and she said, "Were you ever planning on telling me?"

"Telling you—?"

"Don't, Esther. Don't. I saw Harry from the office today and he asked me how I felt about you leaving. I laughed and told him you weren't leaving, I said we'd decided to stay on another season together, and he looked at me like I was a sad little idiot. I *feel* like a sad little idiot."

This was not at all how Esther had pictured their confrontation going. "I—I'm not leaving, I—"

"No?" Pearl said. Her lashes were wet. "Why would Harry lie to me? I mean, either he's lying or you are, which is it?"

Esther re-centered herself, tuning in to her breath, moving in and out. It wouldn't help to get emotional. "Is this why you took my book?" she said. She wanted Pearl to know, unequivocally, that *she* knew.

"What are you talking about?"

"You know what I'm talking about. *La Ruta,* the novel I'm translating. The one whose price you were so interested in."

Pearl's face lost some of its anger and began to look frightened. She dropped her eyes from Esther's and then seemed to force them back up. "I didn't take your book."

"Did they tell you it would stop me from leaving?" Esther said, so calm, so quiet. "Is that why you took it, to stop me?"

"No, Esther, what?" Pearl's voice was rising in pitch, and a couple curious people had paused at the end of the hall, drawn by the drama. "I'm not trying to stop you, but I don't understand what's happening. We agreed to stay here, we agreed to stay *together*, and now you're leaving? Without even talking to me about it? I don't understand your reasoning or this . . . this reaction you're having!"

"Who are you working for?" Esther said, still very quietly.

Pearl's eyes went wide. "You're not making sense."

Esther wasn't going to get anywhere, she could already tell. This interaction had spun so far beyond her control she didn't know how she'd ever rein it back in line. It was a brilliant tactic on Pearl's part, to throw Esther so off-guard she'd be on the defensive instead of the attack, but she wasn't going to play into it. Defensiveness made a person say things they'd regret.

"We're done here," she said.

Pearl was crying now, tears streaming down her cheeks, and it was harder than Esther had expected to keep the sight from affecting her. *You don't want to make Pearl cry!* bleated her stupid, soft heart. *Apologize!*

"Fine," Pearl said. "I'm going skiing with Trev, so you have a few hours to decide if you want to talk to me like a human being. If you do, I'll give you one more chance to explain yourself, because I love you. But only one chance. I don't deserve this."

Because I love you.

Esther hated her for saying that. Slowly but firmly she stepped back into her room and closed the door in Pearl's tearstained face.

"Fuck you!" Pearl said, and there was a thud as if she'd kicked the wall, but Esther stood still, her entire body at alert, inches from the door she'd just closed. After a long minute she heard Pearl walk away, footsteps fading down the empty hall. She didn't move for a long while afterward, and when she finally did turn away, it was to sit on her bed and resume staring at the door.

Pearl had specifically told her she was going skiing with eager, flirty Trev, a fact that seemed unnecessary to share unless she thought Esther would be jealous, but that would be the hurt pettiness of a spurned lover, which wasn't really who Pearl was. She would know that the first thing Esther would want to do would be to search her room looking for the Gil, and this declaration of her intent to be absent all day had to be nothing less than an invitation.

Which meant, probably, that the book was *not* in Pearl's room at all—but something else was. A trap.

Pearl had a mirror above her sink, same as Esther did. This must be a trick to get Esther to go into Pearl's room where she could be observed, where whoever was on the other side could verify that she was on to them.

She gripped her head, which felt like it might split in two. This paranoia, these cyclical thoughts, this was how her father must have felt most days of his life. She was still so angry at him, but for the first time she understood viscerally the fear he had lived with and understood, too, that it was a fear she had always trusted, deep down—until she had decided to stop trusting it and called this chaos down upon herself.

I'm sorry, she told her father, tears welling in her eyes despite herself. She would've given anything to be able to call him, to hear his voice, deep and attentive. He used to go into town and use the public library computers to Skype her, and she'd talked to Joanna like that sometimes, too. Cecily, who'd gotten a cell phone the week she'd moved out of Abe's house, had often called and texted her, and twice flown across the country to see her for the weekend, against Abe's nervous wishes. She'd been in contact with her family until she'd decided that contact was too difficult. Until it had become easier to cut ties on purpose instead of struggling to maintain thinning threads that would someday break and her heart along with them.

Esther stood up, frustrated with herself for sinking into maudlin tears at precisely the time they were least helpful. She might be paranoid, like her father, and for good reason, like her father—but she was *not* Abe. She couldn't operate on supposition and inklings. She had to *know*.

She waited, pacing, for another thirty minutes, enough time for Pearl and Trev to bundle up and be on their way, and then she went by the equipment room to see if Pearl had checked out skis and walkie talkies yet. She had, which meant they were out of the station.

Esther had been in Pearl's room countless times and had no trouble imagining the layout. She would be able to open the door, crouch low, and enter without any fear of being reflected in the mirror on the dresser, and if she positioned herself at the correct angle, she thought she'd be able to see the mirror's surface well enough to know if there were any telltale blood marks on it. She'd see the marks, but the mirror wouldn't see her.

Esther crawled through the door as quietly as she could and closed it behind her with a barely audible click. She was kneeling on the floor in the darkness of Pearl's bedroom, the overhead off, no window. She could just make out the looming form of Pearl's dresser and the glint of the mirror atop it, but it wasn't bright enough to see what might be on the glass. She reached up and opened the door again, only an inch, letting more light spill in. It wasn't enough.

So she stood up, dusted off her knees, closed the door, and turned on the light. Let them see her. It wouldn't make a difference. Whatever they were planning to do to her, they planned to do it regardless.

And, despite the evidence, despite all her suspicion and paranoia, she realized there was still a part of her that trusted Pearl; a part of her that trusted, when she turned to face the mirror, that she would find nothing except clean, absolving glass. She'd crossed her fingers without realizing she was doing it and her breath caught high in her chest, unmoving as she scanned the glass. Empty, empty, empty. A sweet, melting relief began to spread through her limbs—and then she saw it.

The rusty smear of blood, at all four corners.

Her breath came out in an explosive curse and she staggered backward onto Pearl's bed, a place she'd been many times before, a place she'd so recently been happy. She had not truly believed in Pearl's betrayal until she'd seen the blood. She hadn't wanted to believe it. But the evidence was there, clear as anything.

Well, if those assholes were watching, whoever they were, let them watch. Esther began tearing Pearl's room apart with no regard for order or stealth, looking not only for her own book but for the book Pearl must have used to activate the mirror spell. She searched the bed, the pillowcase, beneath the mattress, upturned all of Pearl's drawers. She pulled the meager furniture away from the walls, looked behind the mirror, went from corner to corner in that little white box, searching . . . and found nothing.

Afterward, she sat on the floor in the middle of a heap of sweaters and underwear, flushed and nearly shaking with frustration. Of course Pearl wouldn't leave the books here, *of course,* or she wouldn't have given Esther an express hint to look in her room while she was out. Esther had known this was a trap and had stepped directly into it, telling herself all the time that it was her decision, that she was in control.

She rose from the detritus of her frantic search, delivered a vicious kick to the dresser, then picked up one of Pearl's discarded boots and smashed it into the mirror. The crack and crash of broken glass was only briefly satisfying, and the silvery shards clung to the frame like teeth in a mangled jaw. She slammed the door on her way out.

She'd barely eaten anything in the last twenty-four hours, so she went to the kitchen, still shaking, and begged a plate of breakfast leftovers from a disgruntled cook. Alone at a table in the empty mess hall, she barely tasted the food, her eyes fixed on nothing. She felt as if the station walls were dissolving around her and the ice creeping in.

As she chewed the last bite, the double doors banged open, and Trev burst through them. He had a wool hat balled in one hand and snow goggles hanging around his neck, his bunny suit unzipped and hanging around his waist with his legs still encased in insulated fabric. His expression was anxious, though it relaxed somewhat when he saw Esther, and she found herself rising even as he hurried over to her.

"What is it?" she said.

"The medic says she'll be okay," Trev said first, which raised her alarm instead of calming it as he'd probably intended, "but Pearl fell while we were skiing and really messed up her arm. Broke her wrist and hit her head pretty hard, too."

"Oh god," Esther said, forgetting for a moment that she shouldn't care—should even, perhaps, be relieved. "But she—you said she'll be all right?"

Trev ran a hand through his hair, face pale. "Yeah, I mean, she definitely blacked out for a minute, which was like, pretty scary, honestly, but she knew the date and her name and everything. I was too freaked out to try and move her myself, so I radioed for help and a group of people came and took her back to the infirmary. That's where she's at now."

"Well," said Esther, still torn between conflicting emotions, "it's lucky you were with her."

"I know, right? Anyway, she keeps asking for you. And she's like . . . pretty agitated about it? Kinda freaky. So I told the medic I'd come find you, bring you back to calm her down."

Esther hesitated. This had to be another one of Pearl's tricks, but if so, she couldn't parse it. "Did you *see* her fall?"

"No, she was behind me. I definitely *heard* it, though."

Maybe she was faking, Esther thought, but why? "What about her wrist? Did the medic say it was broken, or did Pearl—"

"They already set it and everything," Trev said. He half turned, moving toward the doorway, clearly expecting her to follow, and Esther did not know how to refuse without looking like a grade-A asshole. And her nerves had calmed as soon as she'd gotten something in her stomach, which meant her curiosity was once again more powerful than her self-preservation. So, shaking her head at herself, she went after him.

Esther had been to the infirmary a couple times for work-related injuries and had always found it bright and bustling. Today, though, it was dimmer and quieter than normal—the overhead lights had been shut off and the desk lamps were reflected in the full-length mirror fixed to the opposite wall. There was no one at those lit desks and Pearl seemed to be the only patient, curled up on one of the cots with her mop of blond hair spread out over a pillow, the sound of her heavy breathing suggesting sleep. The other four beds were empty.

Esther moved toward Pearl's still form. Her eyes were closed, her face slack. Asleep, or pretending. Her still face made Esther's traitorous heart thump painfully.

"She seems to have calmed down all right without me," she said, but Trev didn't answer. She turned to find his back to her, his head bowed over the doorknob. He was locking it. From the inside. "What—" she said, and he turned. His anxious expression had fallen away, and he was grinning at her, completely at ease.

"Let's get this over with," he said, jingling the ring of keys in his left hand.

In his right hand, he held a gun.

13

Why does everything around here have to be so fucking creepy?" Collins asked, his voice echoing oddly in the dark stairway. He'd gone first up the steps, maybe out of force of protective habit, though both he and Nicholas had experienced a spike of panicked doubt when the bookshelf began to solidify again behind them. In order to come back through that same door Collins would need to read the spell aloud again. There was a small shelf set into the wall of the staircase that fit the book perfectly, so they left it behind and started up the wooden stairs, guided by the beam of Collins's keychain penlight.

Despite the light it was very dark, and Nicholas did not like the dark. He'd been in the dark for days when he'd been kidnapped and in the half dark ever since, always aware that he was one eye infection away from darkness of a more permanent nature. This, coupled with the steep climb and the general intrigue, meant his heart was beating rabbit-fast by the time they reached what seemed to be a long, dark landing that took them to the left. The stairs had zigzagged three times, leading them up the house's stories.

"Are we in the attic or something?" Collins said, gazing down the black hall.

"Thereabouts," Nicholas said, trying not to let Collins hear how out of breath he was. He reached out to touch the wood on either side of him, gauging the width of the passage, which was narrow. "To be specific," he said, "I think we're in the attic walls."

Collins made a noise of displeasure. "Is Richard hiding a crazy wife up here, or what?"

"Why, Collins, I didn't have you down as a Brontë fan."

"I had a thing for Jane. Hot little weirdo. So, what's up here?"

"Nothing, as far as I know," Nicholas said. "Bare boards, mouse turds."

Collins started walking. Behind him, Nicholas was mapping out their steps—they'd climbed through the south wall and turned left, which meant they were headed east, walking in stacked parallel to the corridor that led to Richard's rooms on the third floor and Maram's on the second. After a few minutes Collins stopped abruptly, and Nicholas saw that the passageway had ended. There was no doorway at this end, nor any opening, and Nicholas assumed it was a dead end. But then Collins said "Oh," and crouched to shine his light downward. Beneath his feet, the metal handle of a trapdoor flashed into view, and when he pulled it up with a grunt, there was another steep staircase going down.

"Curiouser and curiouser," said Nicholas.

"Creepier and creepier," corrected Collins, and Nicholas couldn't argue. He was less prone than Collins to being spooked, but the darkness and inexplicability of the staircases and passages were eerie even to him. Collins had already started down the steps, however, despite his own clear hesitance, and Nicholas followed. This staircase wasn't quite as dark as the hall above it—there was a faint line of light beneath the door at the bottom, which seemed promising.

"Where do you think we are in the building?" Collins asked over his shoulder, footsteps dull in the close wooden space.

"West Wing," Nicholas said.

"That's where your uncle lives."

"Yes."

"Shit," said Collins, "maybe he really does have a secret wife. Or maybe he and Maram use these passages for a late-night rendezvous and—"

He stopped talking because he'd pulled open the door, found a light switch, and was now squinting in the sudden brightness. He stood still, peering out at whatever lay beyond the door, and right as Nicholas was about to push him forward, he went of his own accord. He said, as Nicholas joined him, "Mirrors."

This was accurate. They were standing in a room full of mirrors.

Or, not full, exactly: the small room itself was empty save for two heavy wooden chairs pulled up to a round table. It was the walls that were filled, lined with full-length mirrors, ten of them in total and identical. They were wider than normal, wide enough for two people to stand side-by-side, framed simply in dark wood and hung with no embellishment on the white walls. In each one of their forty corners was a dried, reddish-brown smear of blood.

Each mirror also had a handwritten label tacked atop it, in what Nicholas recognized as Richard's handwriting. He began reading the labels automatically—*Kitchen, Gym, Bathroom North, Bathroom West, Clinic*—but then he glanced again at the glass itself and all his attention focused laser-sharp.

"There's another door over here," Collins said, but Nicholas wasn't listening.

The mirrors did not reflect the room he and Collins were in. They did not even reflect Nicholas himself. Or not exactly. It was like looking into a clear pond: Nicholas could see the suggestion of his own reflection on the surface, the refraction of light, but he could see through, as well, to different rooms entirely. Many of them appeared to be bathrooms, but the mirror labeled *Kitchen* showed, yes, a kitchen, a large one from the looks of it, with stainless-steel tubs and gigantic ten-gallon pots and a man with his hair held back in a tie-dyed bandana bent over an enormous frying pan. The *Gym* mirror showed several weight benches, and, in the background, what looked like a row of treadmills. There was someone here, too, a bearded man doing squats, sweat rolling down his forehead.

Nicholas had written the spell that linked these mirrors. Could this be the reason Maram had sent him here? So he could see the results of his hard work?

"Check this out, it's a whole other room," Collins said, and Nicholas looked up to find him leaning out of a door, beckoning.

Nicholas glanced back at the mirrors and then reluctantly dragged himself toward Collins. His reluctance turned to wonder, however, when he stepped through the door and found himself, unmistakably, in Richard's study.

He'd only been in this room once, right after he'd successfully written his very first book, but he'd been aware the visit would be a rare one and so his memory of it was sharpened with particular attention. From what he could see now, not much had changed. Like most of the rooms in the house it had expansive windows and high ceilings, not so different from Nicholas's own study though larger and more opulent, the marble fireplace ornate in a way that was impressive as well as functional. Shelves crowded most of the wall space, towers of gleaming wood that held not books but objects, artifacts that had hypnotized Nicholas when he'd sat here as a child: a fist-sized dog of red clay, a meticulously painted Cypriot amphora, a stuffed capuchin monkey with glassy obsidian eyes, an enormous sterling bell. It was like the back room of a museum. He knew most of these objects must be attached to a spell somewhere or had been once.

"Don't touch anything," he told Collins.

"Wasn't planning on it," Collins said.

"I cannot stress how very much we shouldn't be here," Nicholas said.

"You want to leave?"

Nicholas certainly did not. He understood now why Maram had been so uncharacteristically secretive—she'd be in even more trouble than Nicholas if Richard learned she'd told him how to get in, yet she had told him. She knew how curious he had always been about this place, the one room in the house that was stubbornly closed to him, so perhaps this was a gift to soften an otherwise dreadful week. He couldn't remember the last time she'd so directly gone against Richard's wishes and the gesture warmed him even as he worried they'd be caught.

Collins had stopped in front of Richard's vast walnut desk and was staring at the painting of Nicholas's great-great-great-great-great-grandfather on the wall behind it. The ivory-framed portrait gazed down at them, the surgeon austere in his blood-crusted apron, the oil paint shining thick and darkly red. There was even blood beneath the nails of the man's hands, a delicate detail that Nicholas noticed with some measure of respect.

"Is that a leg bone?" Collins said, pointing to the bottom section of the frame.

"It is," Nicholas said.

"Is that some British shit? Putting human bones on picture frames?"

"He was a surgeon," said Nicholas. "Famous for his speedy amputations, which I imagine must have included plenty of legs."

"And what, he kept them after he'd sawed them off? To make furniture, like a serial killer?"

"He kept one, at least," Nicholas said, not wishing to give Collins the satisfaction of his own discomfiture, but in truth he did find it off-putting to imagine someone strapped to a table in an old surgical theater, screaming as his ancestor hacked through bone and tendon while curious medical students scribbled notes.

Nicholas turned away, shaking his head, to examine the rest of the room. There were a few other frames on the wall but instead of art they held more objects: a mummified bat who'd been pinned behind glass, a Victorian brooch of knotted human hair, a woolen blanket embroidered with gray moths.

On Richard's desk were two things that appeared interesting. One was a leather binder full of old yellowing pages, each individually laminated to delay the aging process. A quick perusal of the first few pages suggested they were the drafted text of a book Nicholas had neither seen nor written, and the drama of the opening lines alone convinced him it deserved a closer look. *Flesh of my flesh,* it began. *Bone of my bone. Only mine own blood can end me.*

The other thing that drew his attention was a cloth-bound book nearly as thick as a novel, and he found himself drawn to it despite the twinge of fear and disgust the depth suggested. A book of this thickness would take at least an hour to read aloud, which meant, for the second time that day, he was looking at a book a Scribe had given their life for—somebody like

Nicholas had given all their blood to supply the ink to write this book. He turned the front cover and looked down at the neat, cramped handwriting, then flipped to the back.

The spell was rechargeable, though not endlessly so like the wards or the spell that had faded the bookcase for those few minutes. It could only be recharged once a year on the anniversary of its first reading, and as he noticed this, he realized at what spell he must be looking. He read the first few pages to get a sense of the text and confirm his suspicions that yes, it was the spell that located Scribes. The same spell Richard performed every year only to tell Nicholas, every year, that he was still the only one.

It was a complicated piece of writing, and despite the unease Nicholas felt with the amount of blood necessary, he found himself reading it with interest. It was the kind of spell his father referred to as "crystal ball" magic in his notes and what Maram called "intuitive divination"—an object-connected spell that delivered a specific piece of information directly into the reader's mind. The Library's expiration date was the only other such spell Nicholas had ever encountered, connected over and over again to the books and to Richard's mind.

Nicholas had written object-connected spells before, such as the one that linked the mirrors in the other room, but he'd never written this kind of "crystal ball" spell. Nor would he ever. Intuitive divination demanded more blood than a single body could provide.

Still, it was fascinating to see the choices this anonymous Scribe had made, particularly the clocklike structure of the paragraphs and the way they used rhyme to double down on the cognitive connection. He could learn a lot from a spell this powerfully specific and wondered why Richard had never shown him before. Curious about the nature of the linked object, he carefully turned the pages, searching to see what the spell had been fastened to.

He found it in the middle of the spell: a directive to connect the reader's cognition to "the view from the body that gives life to power."

What on earth did that mean?

He knew it would be repeated somewhere in different terms at least three more times, and he bent closer to the pages to look. He found "The sight of the heart that pulses the force," which didn't make things much clearer, so he scanned onward. He was so focused that he jumped when Collins spoke to him.

"I think you need to see this," Collins said. He was across the room, standing in front of one of the shelves.

"In a minute," said Nicholas, rereading to find his place again.

"Nicholas," Collins said, and something in his tone made Nicholas glance up. "You need to see this."

Oh-so-carefully, Nicholas set the book down on the desk and came to join Collins where he stood, apparently transfixed, in front of a large glass jar with something suspended in the middle.

"Look close," Collins said. "Maybe I'm crazy, but . . ."

Humoring him, Nicholas looked at the jar. It was at the height of his head and about the same size, with a few bloody marks that were probably part of a spell to keep glass from breaking. The lid, too, seemed to have been spelled.

Nicholas turned his attention to the contents of the jar, though he wasn't certain what he was looking at: some kind of small orb floated in some kind of liquid, which wasn't water, he could tell that much. It was thicker, a kind of translucent viscous goo, and the orb was not so much floating as suspended.

It was an eye.

Or an eyeball, to be precise, removed from the skull with surgical precision. It was facing them. Nicholas could see the red cloud of veins and ligaments that trailed it like a comet. He was no expert, but the iris so closely resembled the painted version of his own prosthetic that he figured it must have come from a human. Beside him, he felt Collins shift his weight, clearly disturbed by the sight. Nicholas did not feel much better. His own left socket tingled in sympathetic response and his stomach churned. It was uncanny to be stared at, literally eye-to-eye, by something so ghastly yet so recognizable. So familiar.

Too familiar.

"Collins," Nicholas said, and the word came out hoarse. He turned to face his bodyguard. Collins stared back, jaw clenched, and a shiver ran through him. He said, "It looks like mine."

Collins swallowed but didn't speak. He nodded.

Nicholas turned back to the jar. He'd spent more time than most people looking at his own eyes, especially as a teenager, comparing the two in the mirror to see if the false one was noticeable, and unlike most people he'd often held an exact replica of his own eye in his hand while cleaning it; he'd turned it this way and that, examining the craftsmanship and admiring the variations in color that made it so realistic, the flecks of greenish gold among the brown, the ring of lighter amber around the iris, the blood vessels made up of tiny red fibers.

He knew his own eye when he saw it and he was seeing it now.

"Hey," Collins said, "stop, get up."

Nicholas, perpetually light-headed, had become suddenly much more so, and was now sitting on the ground. It was as if his body had decided he'd be able to use his brain better if he cut all other sources of energy. Collins prodded him with a sneakered toe, not quite a kick.

Nicholas said, "What is my eye doing in a jar on a shelf in my uncle's study?"

"I didn't put it there," said Collins.

"Richard must have gotten it from—from those people, the ones who kidnapped me," Nicholas said. "Right? But why would he keep it? And why wouldn't he say anything about it to me? It looks perfect, I mean, they could've stuck it back in or something, I don't know how eyes work but you can sew fingers and hands back on if the cut's clean enough, why didn't they . . ." He rubbed his face roughly, working to focus, to understand.

"Nicholas," Collins said. "Whoever took your eye, I think, I mean, I think it's probably the same person who stuck it in that jar."

Nicholas's mind skimmed these words, not ready yet to settle on them. He pushed himself to his feet and stumbled back to the desk, squinting through the haze of a headrush as he flicked through the pages of the spell book he'd just been examining. He didn't have to look to know what he would find.

The view from the body that gives life to power.

The sight of the heart that pulses the force.

The eye of a Scribe.

Nicholas thought of that room in San Francisco all those years ago, the sound of his piss dripping from his chair, the feeling of zip ties cutting into his wrists, the endless darkness. He couldn't ignore the implications of what Collins was saying.

It had been the Library itself that had taken him. The Library itself who'd so carefully removed his eye and preserved it in a glass jar for this spell.

And the Library was Richard. Richard and Maram.

They had staged a kidnapping and taken his eye and then staged a rescue, proving all their own warnings and justifying the close watch they'd kept on him ever after, cementing his reliance on them. His *trust* in them. Richard's face when he'd woken in the hospital, the tears in his eyes. Maram's pacing. Had it all been theater?

Nicholas did not want to believe anything that was running through his mind. He wanted to think he was panicked, foolish, paranoid. But he was standing in a secret room that had been perfectly designed to keep him out. To keep him ignorant.

All this time, he had been told he should be frightened of whatever lay beyond the protective wards of these familiar walls. All this time, he'd believed the danger was external.

But perhaps the greatest threat had always been inside.

Without meaning to, he found his fingers tightening on the pages of the spell to which he'd unwittingly sacrificed his eye. It was object-linked, which meant it was technically still active, and only a Scribe could destroy an active spell. If Nicholas followed his instincts and tore this book to shreds, Richard would know without a doubt it had been him. But he was so furious he didn't care. He grabbed the page he was holding and pulled as hard as he could, expecting to feel the satisfying rip as it tore from the binding.

Nothing happened.

The page did not even wrinkle beneath his fingers. He tried again with another page, and another, and another. None of them showed the barest sign of being touched, much less torn. He scratched at the cover and clawed at the thread of the binding, desperate and furious, and might even have started using his teeth if Collins hadn't reached out to grab him.

"Hey, hey, hey," Collins said, "it's not working, it's not gonna work, breathe for a second, c'mon." He'd taken ahold of Nicholas's shoulders and spun him around to face him, his big palms warm and weighted. "Breathe," he said again. "You're freaking me out."

Nicholas breathed, or tried to. He knew later he'd be embarrassed that Collins had seen this loss of control, but right now he was too appreciative of his steady presence to care. After a few long moments, Nicholas had himself more or less together and was thinking clearly.

It made sense that he couldn't destroy the book, he realized. Two Scribes had written it; two Scribes would be needed to ruin it.

"We need to get out of here," Nicholas said.

"Agreed," said Collins. He dropped his hands from Nicholas's shoulders and Nicholas moved away to look back at the book that lay crouched, unscathed, on the desk. Next to it, the leather binder looked businesslike and innocent.

Did Nicholas even want to know what other secrets Richard was keeping? Nothing could be worse than being stared at by his own eye.

His hands were shaky, but sick curiosity was creeping in on the tail end of his frenzy and he opened the cover of the binder again to look at the yellowed linen paper within.

He read the first ten or so pages, then started at the beginning again, unable or unwilling to make sense of the spell being suggested.

"What is that?" Collins said.

"That's what I'm trying to work out," said Nicholas.

"We really should leave."

"I know," but Nicholas kept reading.

As he'd subconsciously known it would, this drafted book, too, demanded two Scribes. But it was not only blood it seemed to be looking for. *Bind with the body. Sew with the sinew. Bond with the bones.* The entire book was to be made of the unlucky Scribe who gave their blood—as well as their skin. Their tendons. Their hair. Everything.

"This isn't possible," Nicholas said.

Collins, who'd been pacing back and forth from desk to door as Nicholas read, paced back to the desk. For someone who claimed to hate books and magic, he looked very interested. "What isn't?"

Nicholas read another few sentences to be sure. "These are notes on another spell that uses part of a Scribe's body as an object-anchor . . . but the object connects to a *life.* So you could connect your life to, I don't know, a Scribe's tooth, for example—and so long as the tooth exists, so do you."

Collins furrowed his brow and Nicholas readied himself to try to explain, but Collins said, "Immortality. That's what you're saying."

"In essence, yes."

"But it's not a book. Not written, I mean."

"No," Nicholas said, staring down at the first page. *Flesh of my flesh . . .* "It's only a draft."

"And it would take two of you," said Collins.

"Yes," said Nicholas.

Collins's voice was hard. "Is this why your uncle's looking for another Scribe?"

Another Scribe. So Richard could melt their bones for glue, shear their hair for thread, skin them to make leather. Carve a pen from their fingers. Drain them of their blood. Then force Nicholas to use the gory remains to write a spell that would keep someone alive forever.

14

For weeks after it was written, Nicholas's flying carpet spell had languished in the lowest drawer of his desk. He'd covered it with a mess of papers and even an old T-shirt, not wanting to think about it, but as the weeks passed, he felt strangely like he'd shut a part of himself away in that drawer, too, muffled beneath a layer of paper and cloth. It felt like the volume and color of the world had been turned down, everything quiet and beige, dull and exhausting. He couldn't even muster enthusiasm when Maram proposed an outing to London to pick up the pair of new Adidas trainers he'd been begging for, prompting her to frown at him and press a hand to his forehead.

As always, he couldn't help leaning into the unexpected touch. She quickly took her hand away and said to Richard, "He doesn't have a fever, at any rate."

They were in the dining room eating a very pink rack of lamb rubbed in rosemary, and the bloody, herbal smell was nauseating. It reminded Nicholas too much of making ink to tempt his appetite.

"You've been out of sorts for weeks," said Richard, "and Mr. Oxley tells me you barely got an eighty percent on your last test, which isn't at all like the hardworking student I know you to be. Is anything wrong?"

"No," Nicholas said, pushing a pile of sautéed spinach around his enormous porcelain plate. "Everything's boring."

"We could go to the cinema tomorrow," Richard suggested. "Or see a play."

"No."

"A record store, then."

"No."

"Madame Tussauds?"

At this, Nicholas looked up, interested despite himself. He'd wanted to go to the wax museum for ages. Richard smiled and said, "I can ring them tomorrow morning and rent it for an afternoon next week. We'll have the whole place to ourselves."

Nicholas deflated. He didn't want to wander around an empty museum while Richard watched him look at unmoving figurines of people. "No," he said.

Maram, clearly impatient with the whole thing, said, "Oh, leave him. You can't bribe someone out of a sulk."

Stung, Nicholas shoved his plate away. "May I be excused?"

"Go ahead," Richard said, forehead creasing, and Nicholas could feel his uncle's concerned eyes on him as he escaped from the dining room. He was already regretting turning down a trip to Madame Tussauds, but dignity demanded he give it a few days before announcing that he'd changed his mind.

The very next morning, however, Richard knocked on his bedroom door and said, "Get dressed—something comfortable. I've got a little surprise for you."

He had a duffel bag slung over one shoulder and was wearing jeans, which was enough of a sartorial novelty that Nicholas's interest was piqued. After Richard had shut the door again, he climbed out of bed, pulled on his clothes, and found his uncle waiting for him in the antechamber, sitting on the low sofa with an ankle resting on one knee, foot bouncing up and down with restrained energy. Nicholas managed to hold back his questions until he'd followed Richard down the staircase, through the corridors, and into the main entrance hall of the house.

Richard flung the doors open onto what was an altogether lovely morning in late spring. The sky was a peerless blue and the deer park covered in lush, emerald grass studded with daisies and clover and the brilliant sunshine yellow of buttercups. Insects and bumblebees hummed, birds chirped, and everything smelled sweet and fresh. The gardener goats munched great mouthfuls of tender grass, their coats looking soft as rain, their ears pricking curiously as Nicholas and Richard tromped past.

"What are we doing?" Nicholas asked, finally.

"Tell me," said Richard, "where are the boundaries of our wards?"

This was hardly the first time Nicholas had been grilled on this, and hardly the first time Richard had answered a question with a question, so he quickly rattled off the answer. "The road to the north. White fence to the east. Copse of trees in the south. The barn in the west."

"Very good," Richard said. They were at the lake now, and he stopped, heaving the duffel bag onto the stone bench to unzip it. Nicholas looked down, confused, as his uncle began to pull out what seemed like yards of rough bright fabric. His breath caught in his throat when he realized what he was looking at: a flat, woven rug. Richard shook it out and lay it on the grass beside the water, then took out the other item in the duffel.

Nicholas's flying carpet book.

"Rumor has it you went behind my back with this," Richard said, holding it in his hands and thumbing idly through the pages. "You were asking others to read it for you. You knew I'd disapprove, clearly."

Nicholas was quiet, trying to gauge his uncle's mood, to decide if he should defend himself or protest or apologize. Finally he said, "I worked really hard on it."

"Yes," Richard said, and closed it. "I can tell. It's absolutely beautiful work, Nicholas. I'm really impressed."

These words were like sun flooding an unlit room. Nicholas attempted to force his expression into one of nonchalance, but it was too difficult; he felt himself beaming. "Okay," he said, fighting the embarrassment caused by his own transparent happiness. "Good."

"Here's what we'll do," Richard said. "I'll read the spell and try out the rug first, and then, if it seems safe, I'll let you on it with me."

"Really?" Nicholas blurted. "You promise?"

"So long as it seems safe," Richard repeated. "And so long as we don't go past the wards."

"It will be safe," Nicholas said, breathless with sudden, ferocious excitement. "I put it in the book, you'll stick, it won't let you fall."

"*You* won't stick."

"But I'll hold on so tight! I promise!"

"Well, let's see," Richard said, and took a knife from his pocket, along with a small bag of what Nicholas guessed was a powdered mixture of black henbane, esphand, and the dried petals of cyclamen persicum. "Sit," he ordered, and Nicholas sat on the edge of the stone bench, practically vibrating with impatience, watching his uncle prick his finger and press the bloodied mixture of herbs to the page.

Because of the spell's difficulty it was rather a long book, the product of two separate sessions of bloodletting more than a month apart, and Richard did not hurry his way through it. Just as when he read to Nicholas at night, his voice was resonant and engaging, and as Nicholas listened to his own meticulous words read aloud so expertly, pride began to radiate through him. He had done beautiful work. His uncle was really impressed. And now they were going to fly.

By the time Richard had finished reading, the sun was high in the sky and the carpet had risen about a yard off the grass and was floating there, its corner tassels moving in the light breeze. Richard leaned to test his weight with his hands before sitting gingerly and lifting his feet from the ground. The carpet did not give beneath his weight. He sat cross-legged and gripped the two front tassels and pulled them up—instantly the carpet rose another yard. He pulled the left tassel—the carpet floated left.

"Marvelous," Richard said. "And it'll last how long?"

"A half hour, I think," Nicholas said excitedly, "and it won't just drop, it'll start sinking slowly and then land on the ground so you can climb off."

With no warning, Richard yanked on the tassels so hard the rug banked straight upward, shooting into the air like a kite as Richard, absolutely fearless, stayed improbably seated, fastened by magic to the rug's wooly back. Nicholas nearly got a crick in his neck following Richard as he shot up, up, up, then veered to the left and did a quick, tight circle above the lake, maybe twenty yards in the air, his face and body obscured by the bottom of the carpet. It looked very small from Nicholas's vantage point, and then grew bigger as Richard shot back down to the ground, so fast that Nicholas feared he'd crash, but he pulled level just in time.

His thick hair, peppered with gray that had never crept any further than his temples, was tousled by the wind, and he was grinning like a schoolboy.

"Bloody fantastic," he said. "All right, Nicholas, climb on. Safest thing is if you sit behind me, I think. Promise you'll hold tight?"

Nicholas was already scrambling to get aboard, kneeling behind his uncle and, after a beat of hesitation, looping his arms around his waist as if riding behind him on a motorbike. Richard was not much given to hugs and Nicholas hadn't initiated one since he was a very small child, and this was the closest they'd been in quite some time. Nicholas leaned against his uncle's back and looked out over his shoulder as Richard pulled the carpet upward, much more slowly than he'd done for himself a moment before.

As the carpet rose, so did Nicholas's heart, until he felt it would burst from happiness. When Richard paused some five yards above the pond he said, "Higher!"

So they went higher. They went high enough that Nicholas was giddy with it, clutching his uncle so tightly he could feel his ribs creak, but Richard didn't object. From above, the lake looked like a brilliant blue puddle and the goats small as mice, while the great stone walls of the house—so chilly and impenetrable when Nicholas was on the ground looking up—appeared flimsy and quaint, a doll's house in perfect detail. They hovered there for a while without moving, pointing things out to one another: the toylike car puttering down the road, the roses like splashes of color from a shaken paintbrush, the flock of trilling birds that rose from one tree and alighted in another. Then Richard guided the carpet down to somewhat less-dizzying heights and urged it forward.

They swooped over the field and wove through the tops of trees, and when he begged Richard to pick up speed his uncle obliged, dipping so low the carpet left a swathe of rustling grasses in its wake as it hurtled across the grounds. They looped around the house, climbing ever higher until they were level with the topmost spires of the copper-shingled turrets, and Nicholas laughed aloud from sheer joy, from the danger and thrill of the flight.

"You did this, Nicholas," Richard called to him. "Your blood, your words. How does it feel? Do you feel powerful?"

"Yes!" Nicholas shouted, because he did. But even more than powerful, what he felt was purely, sublimely happy.

Eventually the carpet began to sink, as he'd written it to; down, down, down, until it lay itself on the grass like a tired child and came to rest. Nicholas rolled off, still feeling the swoop and climb in his belly, the wind in his hair.

Richard smiled at him. "Still in a bad mood, then?"

Nicholas couldn't deny he felt better than he had in weeks. "No," he said honestly. "That was amazing."

"If you'd asked me about your book right from the start, instead of keeping it from me, we could've read it together days ago," Richard said. His tone was mild, not reproachful. "I hope next time you'll trust me. Secrets are bad news, Nicholas. In the end, they'll only make you feel worse."

At the time, it had not occurred to Nicholas to wonder how his uncle had found the book in the first place; how he must have gone through Nicholas's study and maybe even his bedroom to find where Nicholas had hidden it. At the time, he was too dazed with satisfaction and gratitude. But that night, long after he'd thanked Richard and promised not to keep anything from him again, he lay in bed going over the events of the day and felt a twinge of resentment. Even at ten he'd known that Richard's view of secrets went only one way: secrets kept from Richard were bad, but secrets Richard kept, himself? Well.

Now, many years later in Richard's study, he thought of his uncle's long-ago words with fury.

Secrets are bad news, Nicholas. In the end, they'll only make you feel worse.

He was still standing at his uncle's desk staring down at the draft of that abhorrent spell. Collins had stomped into the next room and suddenly popped his head round the door.

"Get over here," he said. "Now."

"Excuse me?"

Collins's head disappeared.

Nicholas took a second to rearrange the desk, so it looked as it had when they'd come in, then took one last look around the study, forcing himself not to skim over the enormous jar and its grotesque inhabitant. He needed to remember.

In the other room, Collins was staring intently at one of the mirrors, arms crossed. Nicholas came to stand at his side. They were in front of the one labeled *Clinic,* which framed a room that looked like a nurse's office in an American high school movie, with a large desk and several beds separated by curtains—though none of the curtains were closed and there was no one at the desk.

There was someone in one of the beds, however; someone with a lot of blond hair and a pale, sleeping face. And standing at the foot of the bed, her own face in profile, another woman, this one dark-haired and light-brown-skinned and wearing a sweater Nicholas couldn't help noticing was very ugly. Just as he started to turn away, however, Collins said, "Wait," and someone else came into the frame from the side, then turned to stare right at the mirror.

"Tell me," Collins said, pointing. "Is that Tretheway?"

Nicholas realized with astonishment that Collins was right. It was Tretheway, his former bodyguard.

"I thought that asshole was fired," Collins said.

"I thought so, too," said Nicholas.

"Can he see us through the mirror?"

"Not if it's the spell I wrote last May, which it must be," said Nicholas. "You can pass things back and forth but it's one-way vision only. Come on, I don't give a damn what Tretheway's up to."

"Hang on," Collins said. "The girl."

The dark-haired woman had turned, and she, too, was staring directly into the mirror. Nicholas nearly took a step back, so purposeful and intense was her gaze, her eyes bright beneath thick, expressive eyebrows. She stared searchingly, then turned away again. Tretheway had disappeared from the frame. She was facing his direction and saying something.

"Do you know her?" said Nicholas. There was something familiar about her, maybe. "Is she one of ours?"

Collins didn't answer. He was staring at the glass as if transfixed and Nicholas reached out to pull him away, but the woman looked back at the mirror and Nicholas paused. Tretheway came into the frame again, his back to the glass, mostly hiding the black-haired woman, one of his hands rigid at his side. He was holding a gun.

"Oh shit," said Collins.

The woman was speaking again, her hands were up like she was calming a dog. Tretheway cocked his elbow almost casually, pointing the gun at her, and for a second both were so still it looked like the image had frozen on the screen. Then, so suddenly that Nicholas found himself gripping Collins's sleeve in alarm, she leaped into action, throwing herself forward in a tackle that sent both her and Tretheway flying to the ground and Collins let out a shout like he was watching a football match. The two were half out of sight of the mirror now, only their lower bodies visible, boots and knees tangling in a desperate scuffle.

"Whose side are we on?" Nicholas said urgently. "Do they both work for the Library?"

"I don't give a shit about the Library," Collins spat. "I hope she throttles him."

Nicholas didn't think she would. Tretheway was strong and well-trained. But just as he thought this, the woman reared into view: she'd gotten the upper position with Tretheway beneath her, though her lip was dripping blood and one of Tretheway's hands appeared to yank her forward, and then they both vanished again.

"Oh fuck," said Collins.

Through the mirror someone swung back into view. It was Tretheway this time, bruised and bloodied but grinning. It was clear from the set of his shoulders and the position of his arms that he was strangling the woman beneath him.

"Get up," Collins begged her. "Get up, get him."

Only then did Nicholas notice that the blond person in the bed had risen. She was in a cloth gown with one arm strapped to her chest in a sling, looking unsteady on her feet. In the other hand she held a flower vase with what appeared to be a single plastic flower glued inside it. She was creeping up to Tretheway's side, her face terrified but determined. She raised the vase in a trembling hand. It was clearly the only weapon she'd been able to find and it looked useless and pathetic.

Her swing, however, was neither of those things. With surprising power, she brought the vase down on Tretheway's head, and he lurched to one side, half vanishing again. The blond woman leaned quickly down and when she stood, she was holding the gun.

She looked at it.

She looked at Tretheway, who was rising, his broad back obscuring their view again, blotting her out until all they could see was his pale sweater.

The scene that came next was all the more horrifying for being completely silent. Tretheway jerked once, the wool of his sweater going red below one shoulder blade, and then he keeled over. Gone from the frame. All they could see was the blond woman, gun out, mouth open, visibly shaking.

Nicholas's hand was still clamped on Collins's arm, all thoughts of leaving vanished from his head. The woman in the sling appeared to be screaming the same word over and over, maybe her friend's name, sinking to her knees. It was too late, Nicholas thought numbly. Tretheway had been shot, yes—but not before he'd strangled the dark-haired woman to death while Nicholas and Collins watched.

But then she surged into view, her face red, cheeks hollowing as she gasped for air, and Nicholas released his own breath. At his side, he heard Collins do the same. The woman with the gun dropped it and grabbed onto the dark-haired woman with her good hand, both of their mouths moving frantically at one another. Nicholas could not even begin to guess what they were saying, but the blond woman had stopped screaming and was now weeping, her shoulders shaking. She looked back toward where Tretheway was lying, invisible.

"Is he dead do you think?" Nicholas said.

Collins looked ill. "I don't know," he said.

Suddenly the two woman both turned toward the mirror in tandem. The blonde in the sling was still crying but she was nodding now, too, and they moved closer to the frame, crouching down to where Tretheway must be lying. The black-haired woman was apparently rifling through his pockets and came up with a slim book that Nicholas recognized. It was one of many simple memory-wipes he'd written over the years, and he felt a jolt of total otherworldliness, watching this stranger handle an object he'd bled and sweated over.

An object designed to suck in whatever reader was unlucky enough to lay eyes on its first page.

"Don't," he said aloud to her, "don't look, don't say the words," but it was too late—she was already skimming the first page of the memory wipe spell. She flipped through to the next page, then the next, yet had no visible reaction to the spell written in Nicholas's own blood.

The magic did not touch her.

"That's impossible," Nicholas breathed.

A second later she'd shoved the book into the back waistband of her jeans and dragged Tretheway into view by his armpits, his head lolling on his neck, and the blond woman gripped the leg of his coveralls with her good hand. They dragged him closer until they were right on the other side of the glass, the black-haired woman so near that Nicholas could see splatters of Tretheway's blood on her face. She grabbed Tretheway's limp hand. On Nicholas and Collins's side, the glass rippled. Like a worm through wet soil, Tretheway's fingertip came through to the last knuckle, the nail black, the bones twisted from its journey through the mirror. The finger disappeared and the two women began to struggle with the body.

No sooner had Nicholas wondered what they were doing than he understood.

"They're pushing him through," he said.

The finger had been a test. Now Tretheway's hair prickled through like spikes of growing grass, and then came his bruised forehead, and his face, which was now horribly misshapen—his nose smashed to one side, his jaw misaligned, his eyes sucked back in their sockets as if by an invisible vacuum.

His shoulders stuck and then suddenly began to come through—and wrapped around one shoulder was a small, brown hand with bitten nails. Nicholas gaped at it. The second it had come through the black-haired woman yanked it back, holding it up to her chest in a panic, examining it, clearly expecting it to be warped like Trev's body was warped, but it seemed to be all right. A second later she resumed her struggle and the rest of Tretheway's shoulders came through. At that point the magic did its work and gulped the rest of his body into the room with Nicholas and Collins, spitting it out to lie crumpled at their feet. The gun came tumbling with it.

Neither of them could do anything other than stare. If Tretheway hadn't been dead before, he certainly was now, and the contortions of his mangled flesh were sickening. His skin had held together but everything within had not. He was twisted and bulging beneath that thin unbroken surface. When Nicholas looked back at the glass, the mirror—and every other mirror in that room—had gone blank. They were only mirrors again, disconnected from the life that had charged them on the other side. The life that had just ended.

15

The only positive thing about this whole godawful situation was that Esther now knew that Pearl hadn't betrayed her.

Trev's body had gone through the mirror like it was passing through mercury, not even a trace of blood left behind on the cold, hard glass. As soon as he'd vanished, Pearl let out a low moan and sank onto the infirmary floor.

Esther, her whole body aching from the fight and buzzing from the adrenaline of what had felt like near-death, spat frantically onto a clean patch of her sweater sleeve and began to rub the blood marks on the mirror that had opened it in the first place. She was terrified that if she left them up, someone would step out from the frame and kill her and Pearl where they stood. Living things could not pass through mirrors, she knew this—or thought she'd known it, but despite the test she'd made of Trev's finger, despite how it had come back bruised and twisted and wrong, there had been that terrifying instant where her own had slipped through the surface, and she had felt nothing at all. Perhaps it was the passage from one place to another that ruined a body, and not the entry.

Trev had not been fully dead when they'd pushed him through, but if there had been any doubt as to whether the journey through the mirror had finished what Pearl's shot had started, it was laid to rest now, as the rusty stains of his magic came away easily beneath Esther's scrubbing. His living blood had activated the spell from this side; his still-living blood had allowed his own body to pass through; and now that he was dead, the spell from this end was broken.

She wiped away the last of the blood from the glass and crouched in front of Pearl.

"Thank you," she said. There was a lot more she wanted to say, starting with *I'm sorry*.

"Please tell me I'm hallucinating," Pearl said. "Please tell me I'm on drugs, tell me this is a bad dream."

"It's a bad dream," Esther said. She was scanning Pearl, looking for traces of Trev's blood. There was a little on her fingers and wrists. "You need to wash your hands."

"I need to wash my *brain*," Pearl said. At any other time, this would have made Esther laugh. But it was clearly not a joke and the fact that Esther planned to do more or less exactly that made it even less funny.

She went over to the sink in the corner and soaked a wad of paper towels, then came back to Pearl and carefully wiped down her hands, cradling them in her own palms. There was a streak of blood on her face, too, though whose Esther didn't know, and she cleaned that as well. Then she looked down at herself. Her sweater was only lightly stained but there were a few smears on the floor, and the thigh of her jeans was soaked red. Pearl's infirmary gown was wet and red at the hem.

She would take care of that in a moment. If they had a moment. If no one tried the door of the clinic, found it locked, and raised the alarm. She had no idea what Trev had told the medic to make her leave or how long she'd be gone.

"Do you know where they keep those gowns?" Esther asked Pearl, and to her great relief, Pearl nodded. "Okay, change yours and put the dirty one here, then get into your bed. I'm going to clean the floor."

Pearl did as she was told, her movements jerky and dissociated, and when she'd gotten into a new gown—struggling a bit with her sling—and climbed onto her bed, Esther went to the supply closet and filled a bucket with soapy water.

"He attacked me," Pearl said. "Trev. When we were skiing. One second we were talking, and the next he just—his face changed, and he came at me and—" She stopped, her breath coming short. After she'd caught it, she said, "Who *was* he? What just happened? How did you know you

could put him through the—the—put him through the—" She seemed
unable to complete the sentence. Another shaky breath. "What the hell is
going on, Esther?"

"He was after me, not you," said Esther.

"Yes, thank you, I got that bit. *Why?*"

Esther was mopping as quickly as she could, emptying and refilling
the bucket until all traces of blood were gone, which did not take nearly as
long as she might have feared. None of this would stand up to a forensics
team, but by the time anyone noticed he was missing and began to worry,
Esther would be long gone.

She hoped.

Besides, there would be no trace of his body, no murder weapon, and
there were no cameras in the clinic—why should anyone suspect foul
play? And there were no witnesses, either. Or there would be no witnesses
by the time Esther was done.

"Where did the nurse put the clothes you wore skiing?" Esther asked
Pearl.

"I don't know. Esther, please, just look at me for a second and *explain.*"

Esther squeezed her eyes shut, then opened them and turned. The
book she'd taken off Trev's body would completely erase Pearl's memory
of the past twenty-four hours—it would reset her back before the shot,
the ski, the argument—but this Pearl, the one trembling on the bed and
staring at Esther with desperation, still remembered. This Pearl deserved
something, didn't she? And why not the truth? It was a thought too se-
ductive to turn down. Just for a moment, she and Pearl could live in the
same world together.

"It will sound crazy," she said. "But try to believe me. Remember
that you just saw Trev go through a mirror."

"I don't know what I saw."

"Yes, you do. If you can't accept that, you won't accept anything I'm
about to tell you."

Pearl bit her lip, quiet. Then she said, "Okay. Yes. I saw it."

Esther turned back to search for Pearl's clothes as she spoke. "Magic exists," she said, "and it's channeled through certain books. My family can sense those books, they can hear them, though I can't. My father spent his whole life collecting them, and he has—or had, they're my sister's now—hundreds. Incredibly valuable."

She'd found the clothes folded in the metal medicine cabinet in a plastic bag, and she shucked her own bloodied garments and jammed them into the bag in place of Pearl's.

"When I was a baby," she said, "a group of people broke into our apartment in Mexico City to take the collection. They didn't get the books, but they killed my mother. I don't know the details. All I know is that afterward, my father took me and went underground. Or to Vermont, anyway." She was shivering at the sink in her underwear, washing her hands and face as best she could, afraid to turn around and find disbelief on Pearl's face. "It's not only that I can't hear magic, I'm also immune to it. We don't know why. But when I was eighteen my father realized that the wards he used to block our house from being found didn't block me, so all anyone had to do to find my father and stepmother, and my sister, and the whole collection, was find me."

She paused to hitch Pearl's clean jeans up around her waist. Pearl was taller and slimmer, but she could roll the hems and the oversized sweater was plenty long enough to cover the fact that the pants barely buttoned, and in the mirror—only a mirror again—Esther appeared clean and unbloodied, if a bit bruised around the face.

"My dad gave me a choice," she said, turning back to Pearl. "I could stay home and put my family in danger, or I could leave and never come back. Obviously, I chose the latter."

Pearl was staring at her. She seemed to have calmed down a bit while Esther was talking, or at least she wasn't visibly shaking anymore, though she was nearly as pale as the walls.

"Get under the covers," Esther urged.

"Please come here," said Pearl.

"We don't have time—"

"*Please.*"

Esther swallowed hard and went to sit by Pearl on the bed, stiff and awkward until Pearl flung her good arm around Esther's shoulders and buried her face in Esther's neck. Then Esther did the only thing she could: she shifted position until she was holding Pearl very close, careful of her broken arm, her lips against Pearl's soft hair. She could feel her own face, normally so biddable, acting of its own accord, her mouth screwing up tightly, her eyes watering.

"I will believe you," Pearl said, voice muffled against Esther's skin, "until another explanation presents itself."

"There are no other explanations," Esther said. "I gave you the truth."

"Is that why you were going to leave?" Pearl said, pulling back a little to look at Esther. "Because Trev was . . . after you?"

"Yes," said Esther.

The hope on Pearl's face was so painful. "So does this mean you'll stay?"

It always came down to this. With Joanna, with Reggie, with Pearl. Esther was a danger to those she loved simply by being herself.

"I can't," Esther said. "They know where I am. You already got hurt because of me, and both of us almost got killed."

"But you said Trev was going to use you to get to your family, to your father's books. He wasn't going to kill you," Pearl said. "Right? He only wanted to question you, or—"

Esther shook her head. "What I've told you is the extent of what I know." She touched her throat, which would be purple with bruises soon enough and ached from where his hands had squeezed. "It *felt* like he was going to kill me."

"Instead," said Pearl, "*I* killed *him.*"

"You didn't, technically," said Esther. "He was alive when we put him through the mirror."

"Oh, god," Pearl said, and wiped her wet cheek on her good shoulder.

The room was as cleaned as it was going to get. Esther had a bag of bloodied clothes tied up in one hand but anyone who entered would see nothing out of the ordinary at all. It was absurd, how normal everything looked. Pearl was still shaking in tiny tremors.

"You don't have to remember it," Esther said.

Pearl's tears were pooling in the corners of her eyes and sliding down her pale cheeks. "What do you mean?"

Esther showed her the book she'd lifted from Trev's pocket. It was new, she noticed—bound like a modern hardcover, by machine. She had never seen a book this new.

"Is that a—I feel ridiculous saying it out loud," Pearl said.

"A spell book," Esther said. "Yes. It'll take away your memory of the past day, so you won't remember holding the gun or pulling the trigger, you won't remember being attacked. None of it."

Pearl didn't look relieved, she looked horrified. She recoiled from Esther's touch, her nostrils flaring. "And I won't remember any of what you just told me."

"Well, no."

"And when I think about Trev," she said, "I'll think about him as a fun new friend and I'll wonder where he is, I'll worry about him. Without knowing that I was the one who killed him."

"You didn't kill him," Esther repeated.

"I shot him and now he's dead," Pearl said. "Anything else is semantics."

"I like semantics."

"I don't want to forget what you told me," Pearl said. "A whole season together and this is the first time you've really been truthful." Through all this she had been crying steadily, one slow tear at a time, and Esther touched one of those wet tracks on her cheek with as much tenderness as she could manage without breaking down herself. "And it seems dangerous to forget what I did. I feel it *here*." She pressed her palm to her chest. "My body's going to remember even if my mind doesn't. Won't it?"

"I don't know," Esther said.

The slow tears came a little faster, Pearl's mouth trembling uncontrollably, and she sucked in a shuddering breath, getting herself under control. "But . . . but if people notice Trev's gone missing and ask me what happened, I don't know if—I don't think I could—I'm not a good liar, Esther, you know that. I don't know how to handle this. I don't know what to do."

Esther said nothing. She didn't even nod. This choice had to be Pearl's alone.

Suddenly Pearl gripped her hand, hard, her fingers pressing into Esther's palm. "Promise me something," she said.

"I'll promise you anything I can without lying to you again."

Pearl nodded. "If magic really does exist, and you really can erase my memory, and I let you do it—you have to promise to come find me again once you're safe. You have to promise to tell me everything that happened, and tell me again about your parents, and the books. Fill in all the blanks. I don't want to forget forever. I want to *know*." She took a shuddering breath. "But I don't think I can handle knowing right now. Alone."

Esther wanted this to be a promise she could keep. "Yes," she said. "I promise."

"Swear to me," said Pearl, extending her little finger, but instead Esther uncurled her other fingers and pressed a kiss to her palm.

"I swear it."

"Okay," Pearl said. "Do it before I can think too hard about it."

"I can't do magic," Esther said.

"So then—?"

"You have to do it yourself."

"How is that possible?"

"You have to read this book out loud. Wherever it says 'you,' say 'I,' and where there's a place for a name, you say your own. When the spell starts catching, it'll take you through to the end, I think. It won't interrupt itself with its own effects. Or they usually don't."

Pearl was staring at her. "The way you're talking about this . . . the way you handled Trev, I feel like I never really knew you."

The wave of feeling came so fast Esther didn't have time to pull up her defenses. "You did," she said. "And you will again, because I'm coming back, remember? You'll get to know me. If you still want to."

Pearl reached out and Esther thought she was reaching for the book, but then her good hand was cupped around the back of Esther's neck and Esther leaned on instinct, her mouth meeting Pearl's and feeling the give of those soft lips as they parted beneath hers, the scrape of those sharp teeth. She closed her eyes and let herself have this one second of luxury: being kissed by someone who knew her, all of her. Then she pulled away and set the book on Pearl's lap.

If Esther could have been touched by magic, she might have used the spell on herself, afterward, to wipe the memory of its unfolding from her mind. It took Pearl twenty minutes to read it, twenty minutes that Esther spent panicking someone would try to come through the door, but no one did, and she watched the magic take Pearl over word by word. She watched Pearl's eyes go dull, her mouth moving not by her own will but by the will of something else, a force that powered the voice it was in service to, the magic carrying itself forward as Pearl's eyes grew more and more fixed on the page, her tone more and more monotonous, until finally she spoke the last word and her hand dropped from the page and she slumped forward like a doll abandoned mid-play.

"Pearl," Esther said, immediately terrified that the spell had gone wrong somehow, and Pearl would be like this forever, a hollow shell of magic, but at the sound of her name Pearl picked her head back up, her expression confused but alert.

"Esther?" She sat up straight. "Ow, what the hell. My arm, what the, where am, is this the clinic?"

Her voice was so natural, so wiped of the fear that had shaken it minutes before, that Esther felt a chill roll down her spine. She took the book from Pearl's lap and tucked it under one arm. "You had an accident," she said. "You'll be okay, but—what do you remember?"

"Remember?" Pearl repeated, like it was a foreign concept.

"You went skiing this morning and fell," Esther said. "You broke your wrist and hit your head, it's a concussion but not a bad one. The medic said it's normal to experience some memory loss."

"I thought amnesia was only in movies," Pearl said, gingerly touching her head. She looked a little scared again, but that was appropriate for the situation. "Where is the medic?"

"She stepped out for a second," Esther said, through a lump in her throat so painful she could barely pronounce the words. "Let me go and find her."

She stood, preparing to leave, then paused.

"There's one thing I don't want you to forget," she said to Pearl. "Even with your concussion. I don't want you to forget that I really care about you. More than I've cared about anyone in a long, long time. Whatever happens next . . . that isn't going to change."

Pearl looked frightened. "What do you mean, whatever happens next? How bad is this head injury, exactly?"

"I'm not worried about your head," Esther said, smiling in the most reassuring way she knew how. "I just want you to remember how I feel about you."

"Okay," Pearl said, half smirking. "Got it. You"—she employed air quotes—"*really care about me.*"

Esther knew Pearl wanted more, wanted something else, a different configuration of words, but now wasn't the time for truth. Maybe that would come later when Esther fulfilled her promise.

"Yes," she said. "Now rest."

THE MEDIC, IT TURNED OUT, WAS IN HER BEDROOM SLEEPING. THIS WAS discovered after Esther hadn't been able to find her and, worried about what Trev might have done to her, she'd alerted the office. They'd paged her on the intercom, and she showed up ten minutes later, cheek creased from the pillow, completely confused. She was under the impression it was the beginning of the day, not the end of it, and didn't seem to remember Pearl being brought to the clinic, though she didn't seem terribly concerned about her lapse in memory.

"Long hours will do that to you," she said to Esther confidingly.

No, thought Esther, magic will do that to you, but she only nodded and smiled.

The first dinner shift had started, and the halls were full of people returning from work, some of them talking and laughing, some of them yawning and quiet. Esther felt caught out by every hello that came her way, waiting for someone to say, "Hey, have you seen Trev?" Or "Hey, how come you look like you spent the afternoon disposing of a body?" But why should they wonder such things? Only Esther's world had been warped.

With as much subtlety as possible, she crept around the station wiping away every blood mark on every mirror: the gym, all the common bathrooms, the kitchen. Each time she approached a mirror her heart seized up, thinking something or someone would break through, but nothing, no one, did. By the time she'd finished, it was seven o'clock. Her plane was in twelve hours. In twelve hours, she'd be gone.

Finally, she went to what had been Trev's room and stood in front of his door, steeling herself, though for what she didn't know. Inside, the small space was tidy and uncluttered save for a sweatshirt dropped at the foot of the bed. Esther wiped away the blood marks on the mirror above his personal sink.

Then she started moving through a perfunctory search, looking for her stolen novel and for answers to questions she didn't know to ask. She opened drawers, rooted through folded sweaters, even opened the contact lens case on Trev's nightstand and looked down at the tiny empty puddles of saline solution.

She found dried yarrow and several other herbs she didn't recognize, and, wrapped in a towel and tucked beneath the mattress, she discovered the book he must have used on the mirrors. Like the memory wipe this book was also inexplicably new, bound in the same neat, mechanical fashion. Somewhere, she knew, there was a mirror book that had to be nearly identical, in the hands of people who wanted to kill her.

And someone, maybe, who wanted to save her. Someone who was helping her get out.

The Gil novel was, to her grief, nowhere to be found, and aside from the book and herbs there was no other evidence that Trev was anything other than the Colorado carpenter he'd been playing. She rewrapped the mirror book in Trev's towel and carried it with her to her own room, where she methodically shredded every page of both it and the memory wipe, until her trash can was full of confetti and the spines of the books flapped hollow and useless.

Then she began packing.

16

Only as Joanna was leading her mother up the porch stairs and to the front door did she realize that she'd never actually seen anyone move against the wards and into her house.

Cecily was blindfolded and clinging to Joanna's arm. She couldn't keep her balance and seemed to have no awareness of anything but Joanna, who had to lean down and physically tap each one of her mother's feet to get her to lift them to the next step. It was frightening to see Cecily so slack-jawed and helpless, like a flashback and premonition at once, reliant in the circular way of both infants and the very old.

Joanna guided Cecily through the door, and she stumbled into the foyer with a gasp, then bent forward with her hands on her knees. Joanna took off her boots and went to the kitchen to get her mother a glass of water and when she returned Cecily had untied the scarf from her eyes and was staring at Abe's old brown leather jacket, still hanging on the coatrack.

"Here," Joanna said.

Cecily gulped the water and handed the glass back, her red kiss on its rim. "That was horrible," she said.

Joanna resisted the urge to say *good*. "Take off your shoes."

Cecily obeyed. How strange to have another person in her home. How strange that it had once been Cecily's, too.

"What did the wards feel like?" she asked, curious.

Cecily was peering into the hall mirror and running her hands through her hair, surveying herself as Joanna had seen her do a thousand times before, but at Joanna's question she dropped her hands as if startled to catch herself in the instinctive act.

"Like being in a dream where you can't see or hear anything," Cecily said, "but you know you're on a boat and the boat is sinking."

Joanna could not fully imagine this description, but she accepted it. She hung their coats by Abe's on the old coatrack and watched as Cecily traced one carved wooden hook with her finger.

"The same," she said.

"Most of the house is," said Joanna, though as soon as she'd spoken, she wondered if that were true. Cecily hadn't taken much with her when she'd moved out and neither Abe nor Joanna had added much new, but still, she knew the house felt different than it had when her mother—and sister—had lived in it. It had felt smaller back then, cozier.

Cecily was trailing past her into the kitchen, where the late-afternoon sun was shining through the window above the sink, sparking off the copper kettle and the peeling yellow walls. Joanna felt grateful for this warm, flattering light, grateful that the kitchen was presenting its best face for judgment, and then angry with herself for this gratitude. It didn't matter what her mother thought. Her mother had tricked her and trapped her.

"He never retiled the floors," Cecily said, scuffing a foot along a buckling wave of linoleum. But even Joanna, who felt raw and sensitive under Cecily's gaze, could tell it wasn't a criticism; her mother's voice was low with complicated emotion.

"No," said Joanna. "Though we did get a new toaster."

Cecily smiled and too late, Joanna remembered her anger.

"You have thirty minutes," she said. "Do what you came here to do."

"I need a needle or a knife," Cecily said.

Joanna plucked her little silver knife from the drying rack. "I'll carry it. You tell me what to do with it."

She could see on her mother's face just how much Cecily disliked the intimation that she posed a threat. "You can't think—"

"My house," said Joanna. "My rules."

Cecily looked as if she might argue but then visibly gave up. She turned and left the kitchen to walk through the dining room, and too late

Joanna remembered the spread of materials she'd left out on the table: the strips of leather, skeins of thread, the jar of glue, stacks of different kinds of paper. She saw her mother's eyes take it all in and hoped that Cecily would not put the clutter together into a conclusion, but Cecily sucked in a sharp breath and turned to her with an expression of fear that seemed outsized to the situation.

"Jo," she said. "You haven't been . . . you can't . . . write the books?"

It had started out a statement but ended as a question.

"Only experimenting," Joanna said, and Cecily's features shifted from afraid to relieved. Joanna could imagine what she'd been thinking— that if Joanna learned to make the books herself, she'd be too deep to ever emerge, she'd be gone. Maybe she was even right. Joanna wouldn't ever know.

Cecily paused in the living room, taking in the blankets, pillows, folded piles of clothing on the corner armchair.

"You sleep down here?"

Joanna did not owe her mother any explanations but her defensive urge kicked in again and she said, "It's warmer. And it saves on heating bills."

"You mean it saves on the glamour spell you use to fill the propane tank."

"Heating bills," Joanna repeated.

Cecily parted the tacked-up blankets that separated the living room from the staircase leading to the second floor and Joanna followed. The temperature dropped as they climbed, and Joanna shivered, wishing she hadn't removed her coat. She trailed her fingers along the banister, the wood still polished bright from years of her family's hands.

Despite her fury, her hurt, despite what Cecily had done to bring about this situation, part of Joanna did not feel angry at all to be follow-ing her mother up these stairs that she'd been climbing for so many years alone. It was the same childish part of herself that thrilled at the soft press of the cat's head in her hand.

Cecily stopped at the second-floor landing and looked around. She took a step toward the end of the hall and the largest bedroom, the one she'd once shared with Abe, then put her back to it and surveyed the other two doors. She could feel her heart thudding in her throat as she waited to see what her mother would do. She did not have a single guess.

It was Esther's old room that Cecily moved toward. She cracked the door tentatively, as if someone might be sleeping inside, then she pushed it open more fully and stepped in with Joanna on her heels. It was even colder in the room than it had been on the landing, and the chill made everything seem dreary in a way that might have been cozy in warmth. Kurt Cobain stared down at them from over boxes of ordinary books, Abe's old clothes, broken furniture Joanna meant to someday repair.

Cecily skimmed the room with her eyes, one hand light on her collarbone as if she wanted to press a hand to her heart but was holding back.

"There used to be something else in that corner," said Cecily.

Joanna looked at the corner by the closet, now taken up by a small set of drawers filled with crafting and sewing supplies. "Can you give me a little more to go on?"

"No."

Joanna racked her memory, visualizing the room as it had been when it was Esther's. "The mirror?"

Cecily said, "Where is it?"

In answer, Joanna crossed the room and opened the door to the closet. Inside, the huge mirror shone a faceful of winter light back out at them and Cecily let out a sound of relief that was almost a groan. When she spoke again her voice was agitated, as if the sight had spurred her into new urgency.

"I need a piece of paper and a pen," she said.

There was notebook paper in the set of drawers and Joanna found an ancient blue gel pen that somehow still worked. She passed both to her mother, her movements jerky with a tension Cecily mirrored as she took them.

Cecily leaned the paper on the top of a taller dresser. Her eyes were narrowed in concentration and once or twice she stopped to reread before continuing, and Joanna held herself still rather than crowding her mother's space to see what she was writing. When Cecily finished, however, Joanna held out her hand.

She could see her mother's hesitation, her reluctance, but she handed over the piece of paper.

The words were nonsensical, two bullet-pointed paragraphs; Joanna read them twice without understanding.

• I don't know if you're still there, or if this comes too late. You can see why I am reaching out. Please find a way to tell me you have this under control or tell me what I can do.

• It is time to break my side of our agreement. As soon as you get this message—if you get this message—please end it.

—C.

"What is this?" Joanna asked.

Cecily, predictably, said nothing. She reached into the pocket of her cardigan and removed a stiff piece of paper. Joanna registered pink sky, square font. Esther's Antarctic postcard.

"I need your knife now," said Cecily.

Joanna considered refusing until she received a clear answer, except she was by this point fairly certain her refusal would bring not more answers, but fewer. Time was running out and she wanted to see what Cecily planned to do next. She handed her mother the knife, handle first, and with a quick jab, Cecily reopened the cut she'd used earlier to draw blood barriers to keep Joanna in her living room. She smeared bright red onto the corner of the postcard and onto the note she'd written and folded the postcard into the piece of notebook paper like a loose envelope.

Then she closed her eyes and took a long, slow breath. "I don't even know if this will work anymore," she said. "It's been ten years since I last used it."

Joanna said nothing. Cecily was speaking to herself, her gaze inward and focused. As Joanna watched she reached forward and pressed her bloody thumb to the mirror: a print at the top, on both sides, at the bottom.

Joanna was watching closely as Cecily did this, but it was not her eyes that registered any change. It was her other sense, the ear-within-an-ear, that felt the shift. Everything was quiet and then it wasn't, not quite. A hum, low and slow, building in Joanna's head. The sound of a spell surging into place—and with no book in sight. It was a spell that was somehow already ongoing, a spell in progress that needed blood not to activate but to reactivate.

Quickly Cecily reached out and held the note-folded postcard against the mirror. Only it was not *against* the mirror, because the mirror offered no resistance. The glass shivered and parted like water for a stone, and like a stone, the note and postcard sank in and were swallowed.

Joanna's hand clamped around her mother's wrist as soon as she registered what was happening, but she was too slow, and it was too late. Cecily's hand was already empty. Frantically, Joanna reached out to wipe away her mother's blood from the glass, even though she knew full well that the stains, though still wet, would budge for no one except Cecily.

"Stop it, sweetpea," Cecily said. Her face was calm, all the urgency drained from her posture; she'd done what she had come to do.

"What did you do?" Joanna said. Her voice came out tremulous. "Who's on the other side of that mirror?"

For clearly there was somebody, there had to be: a nameless figure who'd been crouched behind glass in this closet for god knew how long, waiting to be activated. Goosebumps spread across her arms.

Cecily took Joanna's face in her hands and after a reflexive twitch away, Joanna stilled and let her mother stare her in the eye. Even now, the touch of her mother's cool hands on Joanna's hot, agitated cheeks comforted her.

"Nothing can come back through the mirror," Cecily said. "Your wards will prevent it. I can only pass things through."

"To where? To whom?"

"I know I am asking you for something difficult," Cecily said. "I am asking you to trust me, with no explanations. Someday I hope I will tell you everything and you'll understand completely, but for now, I need you to believe that what we want is not so different. I'm not acting against your interests, and I would never do anything to harm you. Tell me you know that."

Joanna did know it; or at least, her body knew it, her heart and her gut. But her mind insisted that such knowledge was incompatible with what Joanna had witnessed over the years. She'd seen Cecily try to burn the wards and then leave Abe when her plan wasn't successful. She'd listened when her father told her not to let Cecily back in, listened when they'd kept arguing well after Cecily had moved out. She'd fielded hundreds of unveiled requests from Cecily to reenter the house and hundreds of veiled criticisms she couldn't help but believe had been formulated in part to make Joanna give up on the wards of her own accord. Cecily had made no secret of wanting Joanna to leave this house, leave the books, leave the only protection she had. Wasn't wishing someone unprotected the same as wishing them harm?

The only counterargument was the fact that she knew Cecily loved her.

"Trust me," Cecily said again. "For three days. Then I'll come back and suspend the spell."

"You'll *end* it," Joanna said.

"I can't do that," said Cecily and let go of Joanna's face. "The book is on the other side, I put it through as soon as I cast it, many years ago."

When Joanna looked in the mirror, she saw only herself, her own huge, thinly lashed hazel eyes staring back at her. She saw Cecily at her side, saw the room behind her, the piles of junk, the purple edge of Esther's old quilt. Touching the glass felt like touching any glass, cold, hard, fragile. Where was that other room, that other mirror? Who was behind it?

In the end it was not Joanna's trust in her mother that won out. It was her curiosity.

"Three days," she said. "Then you suspend the spell, you wipe away your blood completely."

"Yes," Cecily said immediately. Relief was written all over her face and Joanna wanted, desperately, to know why. But Cecily wouldn't tell her anything. Perhaps the mirror would.

17

Ever since he first began writing books, Nicholas had made all his ink in one of the two basement kitchens. This was where he'd had his practical lessons as a child. Unlike the newer kitchen, which was the domain of the domestic staff, this kitchen hadn't been updated since the late nineteenth century, and its wooden walls, pitted flagstone floors, and iron stove were stained with decades of oily smoke. With smoke—and with blood. Nicholas was fairly certain a forensics investigation would light the whole place up like a rave.

As it stood now, the kitchen was lit only by the early-morning sun, and Richard was silhouetted against the window with his back to the door as Nicholas came in.

Nicholas could make the ink by himself, but it was easier, quicker, and less painful with someone to help him, and usually he would have been pleased to have not only Richard's company but the rare warmth of his full attention. This morning, however, the sight of his uncle provoked only a sick surge of fear deep in his belly.

He'd barely slept the night before, tossing and turning until his sheets were a ropy tangle and Sir Kiwi had left the bed in protest to sleep on the floor. He kept picturing that jar, the eye, those carefully severed veins, the fierce, protective look Richard had worn when he'd promised to keep Nicholas safe, and Tretheway's mangled body lying in that mirrored room.

Last night he and Collins had left the study immediately, hurrying back through the passageway so Collins could read the spell and get them through the bookshelf. Nicholas had half expected Richard or Maram to be waiting for them on the other side, accusatory, furious. But no one was there. They'd gone back to Nicholas's chambers without encountering a single soul, and despite the dead body lying in the room right next to Richard's study, no one had come to speak with them.

"We had nothing to do with Tretheway," Collins had insisted. "We just happened to be there when it happened. He'd be dead even if we'd never found that passage."

This was true, yet all night Nicholas had been certain that at any moment Richard was going to burst through the door of his bedroom and accuse him of murder. And what would Nicholas accuse Richard of? The possible charges were too awful for him to articulate.

Now he couldn't help but tense as Richard turned from the kitchen window toward him, backlit so it was hard to see his expression.

"Good morning," he said.

"Morning," Nicholas said, trying to keep his voice even. Surely Richard had found the body by now, hadn't he? Surely he knew Tretheway was dead. Did he know Nicholas had been there when it happened?

But when Richard stepped out from the glare of sunlight, Nicholas saw he was smiling—a natural, welcoming smile, unstrained and completely normal.

"All right?" he said. His voice, too, was normal. "I know it's a bit early for you."

Nicholas forced himself to smile back. "I'll manage. Thanks for getting everything set up."

Among the instruments—the needles, the basin, the tubing, the gum arabic, the candles—sat an enormous glass of orange juice, and Richard pointed to it.

"Drink," he said. Nicholas picked up the glass and took a sip, though it felt like battery acid in his dry mouth. He watched Richard frown into a box of twenty-one-gauge butterfly needles.

"Those'll take forever," Nicholas said. His own voice, too, sounded perfectly casual, not a hint of a quiver that might betray his nerves. "Are we out of the straights?"

"No," Richard said, "but you're out of good veins."

"I only blew one last time," Nicholas said. "And that was almost two months ago."

"Those veins are a precious commodity," Richard said. "We want to be careful with them."

Nicholas took another long swallow of orange juice, waiting. But Richard said nothing else, simply began setting up the kitchen floor for a circle, as he always did. Slowly, Nicholas's pulse began to come down. If Richard had seen the body, he did not seem to have connected it in any way with Nicholas. Collins had been right. All Nicholas had to do was act like his normal self, not give anything away.

He set his glass down and began rolling up his sleeves, examining his scarred forearms for a likely spot, though he was having trouble focusing his vision. The momentary calm had dissipated and in its wake his heart rate climbed again, because regardless of Tretheway, regardless of whether Richard knew or not what Nicholas had seen, he *had* seen his own eye floating in goo.

How many times had Richard helped him with bloodletting? How many times had his uncle's caring, capable fingers wrapped the pressure cuff around Nicholas's upper arm and taken the plastic covering off a new needle? How many times had Nicholas sat there and let Richard tap his veins like a miner picking for ore? Those same hands had taken his eye from his head and blamed it on strangers.

His own hands were trembling.

Act normal, he told himself desperately, *act normal.* But how could he? How could he let Richard stick a needle in his skin after seeing that jar?

"You know," he said, lowering his shirt cuff, "I'm actually not feeling that well."

"Oh dear," Richard said, and came at him with an open palm. Nicholas tried not to flinch away as his uncle felt his forehead. "You don't have a temperature."

"I'm just not feeling very well."

"It's natural, after what happened the other night," Richard said.

"But we've got our top people on the case, and you know nothing can hurt you in here."

A lie. Richard could hurt him. Nicholas knew that now.

"Can't the ink wait?"

"Not if we want to get to the bottom of this," Richard said. "Someone told your attacker what you can do, which means somebody close to us, close to the Library, has betrayed our trust. We need truth spells if we're going to get answers, and the longer we wait, the less likely it is we'll ever learn what happened."

"Maybe I don't care what happened," Nicholas said.

"Ah," Richard said, drawing the syllable out slowly. He set down the box of needles. "Being attacked the other night made you feel powerless and so you're asserting power where you can—I quite understand. A natural reaction." He held out his hands in resignation. "Well, I can't argue with a trauma response, can I?"

Richard was baiting him, not even hiding it, and Nicholas knew this, but somehow knowing didn't help. Richard's stupid mind games worked anyway. Even as Nicholas told himself to turn away and leave it, he said, "I don't feel *powerless,* I feel *ill.*"

"This must be Maram's influence," Richard said. "Don't let her baby you—you know your own limits better than anyone."

"These are my limits!"

Richard's air of tolerant good humor faded, and he peered at Nicholas more closely. His voice was tinged with real worry when he said, "What's this about, Nicholas? If you're ill, you're ill, but I don't think that's what's troubling you. Sit, talk to me."

Richard sat at the table and gestured to the chair across from him, and Nicholas, despite himself, sat.

"Good," said Richard. "Now. Tell me what's going on."

Nicholas folded his trembling hands into fists in his lap. Richard's face hadn't noticeably changed since Nicholas was a child. He knew every fold and quirk of every one of Richard's expressions, had even seen some of them on his own face in the mirror, the family resemblance surfacing at surprising times. It was a face that had infuriated him countless times—and comforted him even more. He had trusted his uncle all his life. Was his own trust so easy to break?

"Excuse me," said Collins from the doorway. Both Nicholas and Richard jumped, their shoulders jerking in surprise at the sound of his voice.

"Good lord, Collins," Richard said. "How long have you been lurking there?"

"Sorry," said Collins. "I just wanted to ask if you've seen Sir Kiwi's squeaky pig? The one in the tux. She's going bananas looking for it."

Now Richard and Collins were both staring at Nicholas expectantly. He worked to get his thoughts in order. "The squeaky . . . it's—should be in my room, probably under the bed."

"Thanks," said Collins. "Apologies for the interruption."

Richard had already turned away from him, but Nicholas glanced again at the open door, where Collins stood unmoving. Over Richard's shoulder he shook his head—once, twice, his eyes boring into Nicholas's. Then, the words clear and exaggerated, he mouthed: *Don't tell him.*

A second later he'd closed the kitchen door behind him and was gone.

"So what is it?" Richard prompted.

His head was pounding. He dropped it into his hands and when he picked it back up, he had pasted a rueful smile onto his face.

"Honestly, you're right," he said to Richard. "I'm sorry. I'm just being stubborn for the sake of it. God, am I that easy to read?"

Richard hesitated, then grinned back, clapping him on the shoulder. "Only to one who knows you as well as I do. Not ill after all, then?"

"Only ill-tempered. You know I'm useless this early in the morning. Let's get this over with so I can go back to bed."

He could see that Richard was glad to take him at his word, glad to spring back into action and begin the ritual they'd done so often together. Nicholas told himself it wouldn't be so bad, a truth spell needed about twenty thousand words, and they could get that with under a pint.

Probably he'd barely feel it, if they went slowly enough and he didn't try to stand too quickly afterward. Richard had done this for him hundreds of times—there was nothing to suggest today would be any different.

The only difference was that Nicholas did not trust him anymore.

He drank some more juice to ready himself for what was coming. It was the mental effects he dreaded most, the way too much blood loss blunted the corners of his mind, slowed him down, made him want to sleep and nothing else. And making the ink was the least time-consuming part—he'd still have hours left of work, of careful, breath-held writing. How was he supposed to collect his thoughts if he'd barely have time to think?

He wondered if the spell itself would suffer from how badly he didn't want to write it.

Richard was arranging the collection bag. Nicholas finished his juice and then forced himself to survey the contents of the table in earnest. A bowl of still-damp soil, stones, water, and feathers.

"We're going elemental this morning, I see," he said, picking up a red candle.

"If there's no objection."

"None here."

Ink needed ceremony, but as with the addition of herbs, there were no set rules for what that ceremony should be, though the ink came out noticeably darker if a Scribe had some connection—emotional, geographical, familial, or all of the above—to the ritual that helped create it. Nicholas's magical imagination had been heavily shaped by the fantasy novels he'd loved as a child, and many of those fantasy novels had themselves been influenced by earth-based spiritual traditions from the British Isles; so because of this, he made his best ink within a strong framework of natural symbolism. The ink he made under such ceremonial conditions was darker than any other, which meant there were more uses to a single book and the spells lasted longer, their effects stronger.

He had set up a circle so many times in this kitchen that it was nearly second nature—the bowl of soil at the north with a heap of stones and a small lamb skull; fresh flowers and incense to the east; to the south, a dish of desert sand and a burning candle; to the west, water and blue silk. In the center, an amethyst geode Richard had given him when he was a child.

"Ready?" Richard said when he was done. He was holding the pressure cuff and Nicholas sat again to let him fix it around his arm, the familiar, constricting sensation almost comforting despite his rattling pulse. Richard fastened the Velcro and paused, his hand still on Nicholas's arm, his gaze distant.

"What?" said Nicholas.

Richard blinked as if rousing from a dream, though his eyes were still unfocused. "Oh," he said. "Nothing. Just . . . I remember doing this with your father when we were young." He smiled to himself, an insubstantial, melancholy smile that solidified when he raised his head to Nicholas. "He was stubborn, like you—and like you, he could admit it. Sometimes, Nicholas, you remind me so much of him I can hardly . . ." He trailed off, then cleared his throat and began busying himself again with the instruments. Then he said, "I feel very lucky to have you, that's all."

Nicholas swallowed. He had to fight hard to push away the swell of complicated feeling that moved in him at Richard's words.

He watched as Richard rose to light the white candles clockwise, and then he began to grudgingly murmur the invocations for each cardinal direction as the candles flared to life, his voice hoarse in his own ears.

"No singing today?" Richard said, as he returned to Nicholas's side to push the needle into his arm.

The magic was always stronger when Nicholas sang, especially in the context of making ink for a truth spell, as he was doing now. Usually when he wrote truth spells, he sang "The Bonnie Banks o' Loch Lomond," a Scottish folk song he could swear he remembered his mother singing to him. Yet the memory was a pure lie. He had been scarcely two months old when his mother died, far too young for that kind of specific recollection. Emotionally, however, the memory *felt* true—and the tension between truth and figment made for fantastically powerful ink.

Today, however, the thought of raising his voice in some silly tune while his uncle watched was insupportable. He shook his head once and Richard did not push him, only sat back in the chair across from him to wait. The familiar honeyed blur of magic hummed to life in Nicholas's ears, in his bones, and even in the face of so much uncertainty he relaxed into it, into the rightness of it, the certainty of his purpose. And despite everything, he felt gratitude swell along with the churn of slow wings. How many people in this world could claim to know exactly what they'd been made for?

He sighed, watching the jewel-toned blood slide through the clear tubing and into the plastic hospital-issue bag that Richard held so lovingly in his elegant hands. It pooled at the bottom like a dark mirror. Nicholas tilted his head back and closed his eyes.

Whatever horrors he'd imagined did not come. The ink-making went off without a hitch, as it always did, though Nicholas felt a bit woozy as he stood over the cauldron and watched the powdered herbs dissolve into the thick darkness of his blood. He had claimed nausea earlier and now, as if he'd cursed himself, it had come to pass, and the brain fog he'd been fearing was actually something of a relief. His thoughts felt slipperier, less urgent, though his anxiety had not decreased.

"I have a meeting in London today," Richard said, "but I'll be back well before supper. Maram and I interviewed a few employees yesterday with our last truth spell, and I'm pleased to say the chef is fully reliable and back on duty, so do let him know if there's anything in particular you'd like."

The thought of food was stomach-turning. Nicholas nodded anyway. Richard scrutinized him and said, "Back to bed with you. Though if you do manage to get some of the writing done today, I'd much appreciate it. The sooner we're back to our full complement of staff, the better. I don't think Collins much likes being bodyguard, butler, and scullery maid all at once."

"I can't say I like it, either," said Nicholas. "He makes a terrible maid."

"Well," Richard said, "he'll have to endure it for a bit longer—this kitchen needs tidying and I haven't the time." Richard checked his watch and clapped Nicholas on the shoulder: a dismissal Nicholas was only too glad to take.

THE JAR OF INK WAS WARM IN HIS COLD HANDS AND NICHOLAS FOUND himself holding it close against his chest as he trudged up several flights of stairs, then through the portrait gallery and to his room. Collins was in the anteroom listlessly throwing a miniature tennis ball for Sir Kiwi, who left off her chase as soon as she saw Nicholas. It was always gratifying to be greeted so enthusiastically, and Nicholas bent to greet her in return. When he straightened the blood roared in his ears and he staggered once before regaining his balance. Collins looked away.

"I didn't forget what I promised you," Nicholas said. "I need a few days' rest but then I'll write the reversal to your NDA."

"So you can interrogate me," Collins said.

"Yes," said Nicholas, and to his surprise, they both laughed. It wasn't that anything was funny—it's that nothing was. Nicholas's vision was blurring, and he dug a fist into his seeing eye, feeling the weariness setting in. "I'm going to sleep for a bit," he said. "I'm taking Sir Kiwi. If we're in there longer than an hour, bang on my door, will you?"

Collins started to answer then stopped, his posture changing into something straighter, squarer, his eyes fixed over Nicholas's shoulder. Nicholas turned to see what he was looking at and found Maram standing at the entrance of the anteroom. She was in one of her fawn silk blouses with a luxurious bow at the neck, a bag slung across her shoulder and her camel coat draped over one arm. Her black boots were heeled. She was going out.

"You're both here," she said. "Good. Nicholas, can we go into your study? Collins, too. I need a word with both of you."

"You certainly do," said Nicholas. "I followed that note you left me."

"In your study," Maram said, "quickly, quickly. Richard's coming up to check on you in a few minutes."

She was herding them across the anteroom and Nicholas fumbled for his key with one hand, the jar of ink still clutched in the other. Maram pushed past him with uncharacteristic impatience, her own key already out and in the lock, and a second later they were in Nicholas's study, and she'd locked the door behind them.

The curtains were drawn and the study was dark, but Maram yanked the brass pull of a nearby standing lamp and light flooded the room. Nicholas set the ink on the desk and sat down in the chair, resisting the urge to put his swimming head between his knees. Sir Kiwi leaped onto his lap and he clung to her soft fur.

"Were you there last night, when it happened?" Maram asked, her voice low and urgent. "With Tretheway. Did you see?"

Nicholas was too surprised to answer but Collins said, "Yeah, we were there. We saw the whole thing."

"Who was it? Who pushed him through?"

"Two girls—women. One of them blond, one with dark hair."

Nicholas looked at his bodyguard. He had not hesitated to answer Maram, who let out a long breath of either relief or agitation, Nicholas couldn't tell.

"All right," Maram said. "All right." She whirled suddenly on Nicholas, all rippling silk. "And you. Did you see, in Richard's study? Did you see what I wanted you to see?"

"I—I saw, I don't know what I saw, it looked like, but it wasn't, was it?"

"What wasn't? Say it."

"My eye," Nicholas said, "it looked like my eye."

"Yes," Maram said. She began to say more but choked, one manicured hand flying to her throat, her eyes squeezing shut against a sudden coughing fit, and it was as if Nicholas's entire body was submerged in ice as her rasping went on, and on. Every Library employee was under a silencing spell, Nicholas knew that. It had never occurred to him though, not once in the past twenty-odd years, that Maram might be as well. She was an employee, yes, but she was also Richard's partner. She was more Library than Nicholas himself. Yet she had let Richard read her the NDA, had bound her silence like any servant or bodyguard.

No wonder she had not told him about his eye. What else had she been unable to tell him, all these years?

Maram had recovered herself before Nicholas had and was now rummaging around in her handbag. She pulled out a thick manila envelope and pressed it into Collins's hands. He opened the flap quickly, glanced inside, and said, "What, right now? Today?"

"As soon as Richard and I leave," Maram said. "Remember what to do when you get where you're going? You drop them. As soon as you can."

Nicholas should not have been surprised to find that Maram and his bodyguard had been keeping secrets from him, had, apparently, an entire preexisting relationship that allowed them to speak in such shorthand. Everyone had secrets from him. One more shouldn't have been a shock. But his mouth was hanging open anyway.

"What is this?" he said. "Maram?"

"You have to trust me," she said. "I know it's going to be hard and I'm sorry I can't explain. This would all be so much easier if I could."

Sir Kiwi suddenly leaped from his arms, darting to the study door. She let out an excited, high-pitched yap.

"That'll be Richard," Maram said, crossing the room quickly and opening the door, then crossing back to sit in the armchair by the fire, arranging herself in a relaxed, casual posture. Quickly she said, "Collins, hide that."

Collins leaned over Nicholas to open the desk drawer and shove the manila envelope inside, and had just taken up his customary post by the door when Richard poked his head in. He, too, was dressed to go out, already in his black wool coat.

"Ready?" he said to Maram. To Nicholas, "I'm taking her with me for the day. You'll be all right here? You don't need anything?"

Channeling his actress mother, Nicholas said, very calmly, "I do, actually. If you've time, will you check and see if my order's in at the bookstore?"

"I'll call once we're out of the wards," Richard promised. "And you're feeling all right?" He winked. "Not ill?"

Nicholas rolled his eyes good-naturedly. "I feel fine."

"Good." Richard clapped his gloved hands together. "Then maybe you'll have that book written by evening."

"We'll be back in a few hours," said Maram, and rose, readjusting her coat over her arm. She paused by Nicholas's desk chair, hesitating, and he saw that her hand was gripped so tightly around the thin leather strap of her bag that her knuckles were white. When she bent toward him, he stiffened, genuinely confused about what was happening, because Maram had never kissed him before. But she did so now, a quick brush of her lips against his cheek. She said, "Good-bye."

"Open or closed?" Richard said, swinging the study door exaggeratedly.

"Open's fine," Nicholas said, and they disappeared. He listened as their footsteps thudded across the carpet of the anteroom, then began clicking down the marble corridor, fainter and fainter until he couldn't hear anything at all. He said quietly to Collins, "What's in that envelope?"

"Shh," said Collins, striding to the window and twitching open the curtain. Nicholas pushed himself to his feet and joined Collins at the window. The early sun had faded back into mist and the green fields were glimmering, the long black driveway shining like a snake in the grass, coiling toward the distant road. Silently he and Collins stood shoulder to shoulder, watching until the Library car rolled into view and began making its way down the drive, away from the Library, toward London.

Only when it had vanished from sight completely did Collins turn from the window toward the desk.

He opened the manila envelope and unceremoniously dumped the contents onto Nicholas's desk.

"We gotta go," he said.

"Go?" Nicholas echoed, picking up the first thing he saw and examining it in bewilderment. It was a slim green paperback novel with a Spanish title, rather old, and Nicholas opened it to find a note in Maram's handwriting between the covers. He began to read it—*Show this to the woman in the*—but then stopped, distracted by the other objects that had been shaken from the envelope.

A fat stack of Euros in a rubber band, and two blue passports.

Collins quickly flipped each passport open in turn to skim the first page and handed one to Nicholas. "This is you."

Nicholas looked inside. It was him. And it wasn't. The photo was him, but the name said *Nathaniel Brigham* and the citizenship was Canadian. Folded inside the passport was a series of plane tickets and another note, also in Maram's hand:

Trust me.

"Pack your shit," said Collins. "We're leaving."

Nicholas found his voice. "What on earth are you talking about? Did you and Maram plan this?"

"Kinda," said Collins, sweeping the book into the envelope again. He started shuffling through the stack of tickets in his own passport, nodding.

"What do you mean, *kinda*?"

"I mean pack your shit," Collins said, and jammed the tickets and passport into his back pocket. "Our first plane leaves from Paris tomorrow, which means we have to get to London, catch the last Eurostar, and cross the channel tonight, and it's already late, so move."

"Are you out of your mind?" Nicholas said. "No. These tickets are in *coach,* I'm not going to—"

"Nick," said Collins, and the nickname was enough of an odd surprise to shut Nicholas up. "You saw what was in that jar. You know what it means."

"It means, well, it means—"

"It means you're not safe here," said Collins. "And you never were."

"You do remember that someone recently tried to kill me? I'm not safe out there, either."

Collins scrubbed a hand through his dark hair and stared at Nicholas with an expression that was equal parts frustration and pity, and Nicholas suddenly remembered his odd, guilty look in the Winter Drawing Room the day before. A wave of exhaustion crashed over his shoulders, and he slumped against the desk, putting his head down on his arms.

"No one tried to kill me, did they," he said, voice muffled against the desk. "It was Richard again. He wanted to frighten me."

Collins didn't answer. Probably he couldn't. Nicholas kept his head down, concentrating on his breath. The bees. Of course. He could see the placard of the book Maram had sent him to just the other day: *Causes all admixture of chemical propellant, i.e., gunpowder to turn metal into Bombus terrestris upon explosion.* She'd charmed Collins's gun so that when he shot it, bees would come out instead of bullets. Collins had playacted the rescue, just as Richard and Maram had playacted their concern. Only Nicholas, with his real fear, had not been acting.

He needed one second of darkness and quiet, one second to gather his thoughts, but Collins punched him hard on the shoulder.

"No," he said, like Nicholas was a bad dog. "You can have your breakdown when we're in the car."

"What car?"

"Whatever car we steal once you drag me across the wards to the road."

Nicholas stared at him, unmoving, and Collins threw his hands into the air like he might wrap them around Nicholas's neck. His blue eyes were nearly all pupil, Nicholas saw, and his normally laconic voice was more animated than Nicholas had ever heard it.

"We have one chance," Collins said. "One chance to get out of here. If we don't leave now, Richard and Maram will come back, and nothing will—I won't be able to—we'll never—" he choked, hacking on the words, then cursed. "Don't you trust Maram? You have to trust her."

Nicholas looked at him. "And you."

"Yeah," Collins said. "You have to trust me, too."

Again, Nicholas pictured that jar on its shelf in Richard's study. He remembered rope cutting into his wrists and the bright haze of the hospital room. It had taken him a while to adjust to being half-blind. At first, he'd been a mess, dropping glasses off the edges of tables, bumping into things, his head always pounding with the strain. Now, though, he was used to it. His left shin was still bruised more often than not, and he was never going to win any prizes at catch, but those things didn't actively bother him. After ten years, being monocular felt as much a part of him as being right-handed or getting freckled in the sun.

So you see, said a voice in his mind, *it's not so bad, what was done to you. Lots of people have it worse, but look at you, you live a life of luxury in a beautiful home, you want for nothing. You don't really mean to give that up out of spite for something that happened so long ago, do you?*

The voice was reasonable, affectionate.

The voice was Richard's.

Nicholas looked at his study, at the lovely rug, the lovely furniture, the lovely view of the water and rolling green beyond. Comfortable and unchanging, like everything in his life. But his life *had* changed. It had changed the moment he'd seen his lost eye: the moment he'd seen the truth of what Richard had done to him.

Not only that. He'd seen the truth of what Richard still might do. Nicholas had another eye, after all. He had a whole body full of blood for the taking, and Maram, who knew all of Richard's plans, was telling him to run.

Collins was staring down at Nicholas and vibrating with the effort of restraining his impatience, his jaw tight and his lips pressed together. He was frightened, Nicholas realized. Truly frightened.

Richard was Nicholas's only family, his sole guardian, and still he had done what he'd done to his nephew.

What might he do to Collins, who was not family, or even a friend, but a mere employee?

Nicholas had argued with his uncle so many times over the years, fighting to loosen his restrictions only to feel them growing ever tighter, chains made from links of hard, rattling fear. Fear that Richard had instilled in him, first with stories of his murdered parents and then with false threats and real injuries. And Nicholas was still afraid: desperately so.

But the only thing more terrifying than the thought of leaving the Library was the thought of staying.

"We're bringing Sir Kiwi," Nicholas said.

Collins took a deep breath through his nose and closed his eyes. When he opened them again, he did something unexpected, and smiled.

"Duh," he said.

PART TWO

THE SCRIBE

18

The cargo plane sat on the runway, looking like a toy against the vast expanse of snow. Above, the sky was still the rich dark blue of night, but the horizon line glowed pink with incipient sun. Dawn was breaking over Esther's last day on the Antarctic continent.

She made pointless small talk with the people on duty as she waited for the plane to load, every word and movement made with a heightened sense of surreality, as if she could reach out a hand and alter the fabric of the world. That's what killing was, wasn't it? To remove someone from existence was to rip a hole in what was real. She had not shot Trev herself, yet she felt as if she had and she knew, if the gun had been in her hand, she would have. Killing had been added, suddenly, to the list of what she was capable of. It had gone from unthinkable to possible. Was this how people tipped over into darkness?

In a daze she finished filling out her paperwork. In a daze she said good-bye. The lack of food and sleep compounded her sense of unreality and she worried, as faces blurred together and her movements became more and more mechanical, that she might pass out, but she did not.

Pearl would wake this morning alone in her bed in the clinic and Esther would be gone. She wouldn't know why. She'd be in pain. Her body would be telling her that something horrendous had happened and her mind wouldn't know what it was. She wouldn't remember the promise Esther had made, the promise to come back for her and tell her everything, but Esther would remember. Would Pearl even speak to her again, after what Esther was doing now, leaving without a word? There was no way to know.

Somehow, she climbed aboard the small plane. She strapped herself into the little, blue-padded seat, watching the back of the pilot's head as he made adjustments she didn't understand, and she thought suddenly, yearningly, of sitting in her father's old red truck with her sister, how safe she'd felt behind the wheel, how in-control. Her senses filled with the loud rumble of the plane's engine as it zoomed down the runway. Outside her window it was daylight, as it would be here for the next few months. The ground was endless, white, receding. The station dollhouse-sized and then teacup-sized and then ant-sized and then gone.

She leaned her forehead against the cold window, fighting back tears. She had done this so many times: watched a twelve-month life recede below her as she flew away from it. A year felt so long unless it was all you had.

Before now—before Pearl—the most difficult departure had been flying away from Mexico City, because she'd so clearly remembered flying into it. Remembered looking down at the endless carpet of lights and thinking one, at least, might illuminate an answer.

Isabel, like Abe, came from a family that could hear magic, and like Abe's family they had been collectors. Abe had never told Esther her mother's maiden name and all Esther really knew about her grandparents was that they'd owned a bookstore stocked with ordinary books both new and used . . . unless you knew the right combination of phrases to gain admittance to the back, where the stock was decidedly different. This was how Abe had met Isabel, he was visiting from New York, she was home after graduate school to take over the family business.

The first words he'd spoken to Isabel had been in Spanish, and she'd corrected his pronunciation even as she'd taken a golden needle from a chain around her neck, pricked her finger, and pressed the bloody tip to a wall that suddenly became a door. His standard line, when Esther asked him what Isabel had been like, was always: "She never missed a beat."

Abe claimed to remember neither the name nor the location of the family's store, though Esther did not believe him in the slightest. Her first week in Mexico City she landed a job doing under-the-table electrical work for an expat interior designer and bought a by-the-month smart-phone, and every afternoon after work let the maps app lead her from bookstore to bookstore in a city crammed full of them. In and out of the dusty, cluttered stores on Donceles; in and out of the hip, upscale ones in La Condesa and outside Coyoacán; she even looked in the chains, in the Gandhis and Sanborns.

At first each bookstore felt magical. Not the kind of magic Esther had grown up with but the kind she'd read about in novels, the kind that was all possibility, the chance that with one right turn in the forest or one fate-ful conversation with an old woman a person's life might change forever. She would enter a store and take in the march of spines lined up on the shelves, the dust motes glittering in the sun, the mouthwatering smell of paper and cardboard and glue and words, and think, *this is it*. Every time.

It never was.

To each clerk and bookstore employee she repeated the same phrase, the first words her father had ever spoken to her mother, the phrase that had granted him entry into the bookstore's secret room: "Sé verlas al revés." A palindrome. *I know how to see them backward.* But all Esther ever received as a response were cocked heads, puzzled smiles. "I haven't heard of that one," they'd say. "Is it poetry? An art book?"

Esther was not a creature easily cast down. She had learned this about herself early on, when she'd become aware that much of life was either an opportunity to be discouraged or to press on, and she'd always chosen to press on. That fall she visited over two hundred bookstores and found not a single sign of either magic or evidence that her mother had ever been involved in them.

She'd Skyped with her father at the end of October, she locked in the bathroom away from her roommates, Abe backlit by the overhead lights of the local library. The row of computers behind him was all occupied by teenagers playing a jerky first-person shooter game, and ev-ery so often she could hear one of their triumphant cries through Abe's headphones.

"Can't you give me anything else to go on?" she had begged. "A neighborhood, a landmark, their last name, anything."

This time he hadn't claimed not to remember. Instead, he'd pressed his fingers into the back of his neck like he did when he had a headache and said, "Honey, please. It's better to drop it."

"What happens if I leave next week, stay away for a year, and then come back?" she said.

She'd been gone five years by that point and already Abe looked older, his face ossifying in folds at the stress points. "That's a risk I'm gonna beg you not to take."

She smacked her head back against the bathroom wall in frustration. "It would be a lot easier to follow these rules if I understood them."

"You do understand them. You just don't like them."

"Why once a year? Why November? Why—"

"Asking *why* isn't going to change anything. I could explain it all to you, every specific little detail of the wording of the codex, but I know you, Esther—it'd only make you think you could outsmart it, find a loophole. But if there was one, don't you think I would've figured it out years ago? Don't you think I want you to be able to stay in one place, to have a normal, steady life—to come home?"

Abe was like Joanna, his emotions always writ large across his face and waiting to come out his eyes, which were tearing up now, their rims reddening. It made him look even older.

Esther suddenly realized she would never see her father in person again.

The thought cracked her open so completely that she had to hang up before she wept in front of him. She closed her laptop and sat there in the corner of the tiny bathroom, the tile cool against her bare feet, and cried until one of her roommates banged on the door.

Then she did something she tried never to do. She gave up. She wasn't going to press on. She could feel it in her entire body, the absolute discouragement: leaden limbs, chest of stone, throat of petrified wood. A few days later she was on a plane. It was a midnight flight and she looked down at that ocean of lights and remembered descending a year before, when the city had seemed incandescent with possibility. Leaving, the plane rose, and the lights were obscured by clouds.

Now Esther stared at the tiny dot of the research station as it vanished from sight, and her body again registered the same heavy, unfamiliar feeling she had felt on the floor of the bathroom in Mexico City. She did not want to use the word "despair."

Pearl was safe, which was what mattered. Esther, too, for the time being. She had delayed disaster once more. She just didn't know if she would have the energy to ever delay it again.

"I made it," she said aloud, trying to convince herself it was true. Her voice was lost in the roar of the plane.

19

The house felt echoey the day after Cecily had been there, as if the floor-boards and rafters were clinging to the sounds of voices. The weather had left off its flirtation with winter and was dallying once again with fall, warm enough that Joanna let the stove's simmering coals fade to soft white ash for the first time in days. She checked Cecily's mirror, but nothing had come through and the glass was solid beneath her fingers. The streaks of her mother's blood were still stark and un-smudgeable.

When she went out on the porch to drink her coffee and deliver more canned tuna, the cat was curled up in the comforter she had left him. He startled awake at her arrival, then yawned, his mouth pink and cavern-ously complicated.

"Good morning!" she said, thrilled to see him in the blanket, and put the tuna down. He yawned again and then stirred himself to investigate his breakfast, and she slid down against the side of the house to sit with him as he ate. When he was finished, he began to busily clean himself. His actions were comforting in their pure explicability.

Joanna had always known that there was quite a lot she didn't under-stand: about the world, about the books, about her parents and their his-tory. But when the physical and emotional boundaries of one's life were small, when one had walked every inch of one's allotted space many times over, it was easy to forget ignorance and feel a sort of mastery, instead. This house, that path, those books, that mountain; Joanna was used to being the expert and used to the safety that came with expertise.

But the events of the previous day had revealed—or recalled—exactly how inexpert Joanna really was. All along, in her own house, there had been a magicked mirror crouched dormant and waiting. All along, Cecily's secrets had gone far beyond her desire to drop the wards, though it wasn't her desire that had ever been a secret, but her reasons. All along, gears had been turning, and Joanna hadn't even known there was a machine.

Worst of all, perhaps, was the realization that she was not even an expert in herself.

She kept returning to that moment in her mother's living room, trapped behind the spell and believing the wards would come down, that moment of sudden, ecstatic relief. She hadn't even known she'd had those feelings in her and suddenly there they were, like someone had shouted their names. For the first time, she'd fully understood that if the boundaries of the wards were dropped, the boundaries of her life would drop along with them.

Was that what she wanted?

Cecily had been asking her this question in various forms for years and Joanna had never truly listened; in part because it always came not in the form of a question but of advice, unsolicited and full of "shoulds." A question left room for Joanna, while advice only had space for Cecily. Joanna needed space.

The cat finished his spit-bath and came over to investigate Joanna's coffee cup. When she put her hand on his back, it was slightly damp from his ministrations, but the pleasure of being allowed to pet him was too great to deter her. Soon he was purring, a hoarse rumble.

"If you came inside," she told him, "we could do this all the time. You'd have a million soft things to curl up in. There's a woodstove and an ugly armchair you could scratch to pieces. I'd take care of you."

But when she stood after a while and opened the door, again he refused. He twined around her legs, hopefully nosed the empty tuna bowl, then darted off toward whatever adventures awaited a small cat in a large forest. She tracked his streaking figure until she lost him amid the trunks and dead leaves and pine needles.

Joanna understood his reluctance to enter the house. For him, the forest was the known world. Its dangers and pleasures could be anticipated. And maybe he sensed with his wordless cat brain that coming inside would forever change his experience of outside. Cold was easier to bear when you'd never been warm.

20

Esther made it through Christchurch and onto her connecting flight to Auckland without a hitch, but the pitch of her nerves didn't dip as she stepped off the runway into the bustling Auckland airport. She kept expecting her falsified documents to trip an alarm that would send people springing from the woodwork to arrest her, or tail her, or kill her, and "Emily Madison" had passed through the Christchurch check-in and security with a pulse so high she'd been worried the scanners would detect it somehow. But they hadn't.

Now safely in Auckland and standing in line for flight 209 to Los Angeles, Esther shifted her bag on her shoulder and breathed deeply. To calm herself in the hours before boarding, she'd gone to a bar and parked herself at the counter and had two very strong beers, counting on the booze and the chatter and the muted rugby match to work their soothing magic on her, but the alcohol had the opposite effect. She felt twitchier than ever and kept overcompensating for beer-slowed reflexes by whipping her head over her shoulder at every movement, to catch the eyes she felt sure were on her.

"Step to the side, please, ma'am."

Esther realized the gate agent was speaking to her, and she paused, one empty hand still held out for the passport that wasn't coming. "Sorry?"

"I'm told you've been selected for additional security checks," the gate agent said, handing Esther's passport to the uniformed guard who'd appeared at her shoulder. "This gentleman will escort you."

Esther gaped, too confused to be frightened yet. She had been anticipating this since she'd stepped into the airport with a forged passport, but it had come at the very second she'd stopped expecting it and now she was disoriented, unprepared.

"What is this about?" she said, pitching her voice to sound calm and authoritative but only making it halfway.

"Additional security checks," the uniformed guard said, repeating the gate agent's words, but instead of the comforting lilt of her Kiwi accent, his voice was all flat American. He had a bland white face with dark cowlicked hair and a defensive mustache, under which his mouth barely seemed to move as he spoke. "Come along, miss." His hand hovered at her arm, a threat of physicality.

"But my flight," she said, one last useless grab at control. "I'll miss it."

"This won't take long," the guard said. Esther didn't move, her mind whirring for an out, imagining breaking into a run and dashing back through the airport, past security, out into the parking lot, running. Or maybe she could slip away from the guard somehow and sneak out without making a scene, maybe she could beg for the bathroom and maybe the bathroom would have a window and—and—

His fingers closed around her arm.

"Let go of me," she said. "I'm coming."

But his grip tightened instead of loosening, and he led her away, past the line she'd so recently been a part of. Curious faces swiveled to watch as they passed. A young Asian woman with enormous red plastic glasses took a few steps after them, and the expression of sympathetic concern on her face jump-started Esther's own fear, as if it had needed a mirror to see itself. She felt breathless and dizzy as the guard brought her down the hall to a door set near-invisibly in a white wall, and before she could understand that she was losing her one chance to break away and run, he ushered her inside.

There she found a room of harried-looking people getting their shoes swabbed by security officers, along with a table spread with partially un-packed suitcases and a few big, beeping x-ray machines. Aside from her guard she was one of the lighter-skinned people in the room and she almost relaxed, thinking maybe it really was just a random security check after all (and this was certainly the first time she'd ever found herself *hoping* for some commonplace racism), but the guard steered her past the security equipment and through another door, down a narrow hallway, and into a tiny room that held a desk, a computer, and a pink-lipsticked woman staring at the screen. She glanced up when they came in and nodded.

"Room four," she said.

Room four was at the end of yet another hallway, and the guard pushed Esther in before him, then locked the door behind them with a click that echoed horribly through Esther's nerves.

The gray room was bare but not empty: in one corner was a large cloth-covered object.

In the other corner was a person.

A grown man, sitting slumped against the wall with his head hanging onto his bare chest. He was in only boxers and socks and Esther felt a thrill of pure panic run up her spine. Would she, too, have to submit to being undressed and searched? The man in the corner raised his head and looked blearily up at her, and something about his face was so uncanny that at first she didn't realize what exactly she was seeing—but when she did understand, she let out a small, involuntary noise.

Aside from a streak of drying blood on his forehead, he looked exactly like the guard. Exactly. Same bland features, dark hair, defensive mustache. Same face.

"Don't mind him," the guard said in that flat American voice. The man said nothing, eyes unfocused, head sagging back down.

"What is this?" Esther said, dropping her duffel bag and turning to the guard. She kept her voice firm to maintain some shred of dignity and control, but the guard merely smiled at her.

"He's had a few sedatives," the guard said. "He'll be all right, don't worry."

Esther was not worried about the man on the floor. She was worried about herself.

The guard leaned down to the unclothed man and took a fistful of his hair in one hand, jerking back his head with its identical face. Almost tenderly, like a mother wiping away dirt, the guard licked his thumb and rubbed off the blood that was smeared across the man's forehead.

"Let's give it a moment," the guard said, "and see if you remember me."

Esther had no idea who the guard was and was about to say so, when suddenly she saw that he did, in fact, look vaguely familiar. Something to do with the set of his mouth, maybe, or the tilt of his eyebrows, which were so light they seemed to disappear against his browbone.

She blinked. The mustache hiding his upper lip faded away as she stared at him, and his brown hair was lightening rapidly to a cornsilk blond that matched his eyebrows. His soft chin was now hard, with a decisive cleft in the center. In the space of seconds, he had a completely different face—and suddenly she did remember him. Reggie's apartment in Spokane and this man's pale face hovering above their bed, the glint of his gun in the dark. The way Reggie's head had snapped back when the man hit him.

Esther said nothing, because if she spoke he would know without a doubt that she was absolutely terrified, and she wouldn't give him the satisfaction.

"Where'd you get this passport?" the blond man said, taking it from his pocket and flipping through it. "It's good work."

"Isn't that how you found me?" she said. "Weren't you tracking it?" If she tackled him right now, she could catch him off-guard, she could angle it so his head would slam against the wall and—

With a gesture so casual Esther could tell he was enjoying himself, he pulled his jacket aside and rested his hand on the hilt of his gun. The tense line of his arm said he knew exactly what she was thinking, and he wouldn't give her the chance.

"Tracking your fake passport?" he said, and threw it at her feet, laughing. "Come on. There was only one flight off your research base scheduled for weeks—it wasn't tough to figure out you'd be on it. I've been following you since you got to Auckland."

"Are you going to try to kill me again?" she said.

In answer, he backed toward the cloth-covered object in the corner opposite the drugged man and tugged the cloth away with a flick of his hand to reveal a large mirror. It was leaning against the wall, its silver surface dotted in blood.

Esther's heart, already in her throat, surged further upward. Magic had been all over this airport since she'd walked in, it had been stalking her, and she'd gone to a bar and had a drink like a senseless lamb lapping at a trough before a slaughter. Her sister would have known. Joanna would have sensed the magic the second the blond man approached with his face-stealing glamour, but Esther was ignorant and insensible to it. Useless.

She was so angry she almost forgot to be frightened.

"I'm not going to kill you," the man said. "Not outright, anyway. I'm going to push you through this mirror. Do you know what going through a mirror does to a person?"

Esther didn't answer.

"You do know," the man said. "Because you did it to Tretheway. He was a good friend of mine, by the way."

Trev. He must be talking about Trev. "You saw me do that?" she said, skin crawling at the thought that it had been him behind the mirror the whole time, watching her.

"We saw the aftermath," the man said. "That was enough. He looked like he'd gone through a meat grinder."

We again. Esther swallowed. "Are you going to shoot me first, like I shot Tretheway?"

She was stalling and he knew it, but he let her, as she had suspected he might—because if this was revenge, he'd want it to go slow.

"Maybe," he said. "You shot him right here," he tapped his shoulder, "but I think I'd aim a bit lower. A gut shot sounds nice, doesn't it?"

Amid her panic, a tiny ray of relief shone. So he thought she had shot Trev, which meant he—or *they,* whoever *they* were—hadn't seen Pearl. They wouldn't know she was involved; they wouldn't go after her. Pearl, at least, was probably safe.

Was he bluffing about shooting Esther right here in the airport? Surely someone would come running at the sound of a gunshot. Unless everyone in the vicinity was somehow working with him . . . but then, why go through the trouble of taking the guard's face? She thought of the pink-lipsticked woman at the desk, the way she'd nodded at the blond man; she, at least, was likely in on it.

"I can tell what you're thinking," the man said, smirking. "You're thinking you'll fight me, you'll get my gun, you'll turn the tables, blah blah blah."

It wasn't at all what Esther had been thinking—but it was true that the scenario he'd described was pretty much her only option, and her best weapon, surprise, was no longer possible. Her mind flashed desperately on all the chances she'd missed to escape: she should've turned and run when the gate agent had confiscated her passport, she should've run while he was marching her down the hall, she should've run before he'd locked her in this room, but she didn't, she hadn't, she'd frozen, and now she was utterly and entirely shit out of luck.

Unless . . .

Unless Pearl had been right, back on base, that Trev had never wanted to kill Esther in the first place. If Trev had been seeking information about her family instead, if what he really wanted was access to her sister and her sister's books, then this blond man probably did not want her to die, either. The gun was just a threat, and the mirror wasn't there to kill her: it was there so whoever this man answered to could watch him interrogate her.

"I won't fight you," she said, spreading her arms out, testing her theory. Taking a chance. "Go right ahead and give me that gut shot."

He shook his head at her, as if he was disappointed. "You wanna make it easy for me?" he said. "Fine." And he flicked off the gun's safety.

Esther's limbs went numb. She'd been wrong. He wasn't asking her a single question; he really *was* here to kill her. He aimed the gun at her legs, finger finding the trigger, and said, "Let's start with the knees."

Every muscle in her body tightened as she stared at his trigger finger, preparing to throw herself out of the way, preparing herself for the crack of a shot—but the next sound that echoed through the room wasn't a crack, but a click.

The door was opening.

"What the—" the blond man said. His eyes darted from Esther to the opening door and back to Esther, gun still level in his hand. Nothing happened, no one entered. Holding the gun in both hands now, like he thought he was in a spy movie, the man backed toward the open door, glancing out into the hall, and because this was the only chance she had, Esther took it.

She lunged to one side and then the other in case he shot and threw herself toward the door—right as it slammed shut again under its own power.

"Jesus," the blond man yelped, and Esther hurled herself against him, getting so close he wouldn't have an angle to shoot, but she didn't have much leverage and her body hit his with a soft, weak thud. It shouldn't even have been enough force to make him stagger—yet he did stagger, badly, and a second later he collapsed at Esther's feet, cracking forehead-first against the ground. He went absolutely still.

Esther stared down at him. After a few seconds had passed and he didn't move, she did, because there would be time to unpack this new mystery later, if she survived. Even if his collapse was another trap, it was also the only hope she'd felt since this man had closed his fingers around her arm at the gate, and she wasn't going to waste any time. She pulled her duffel bag back onto her shoulder, scooped her fake passport up from where it had fallen on the ground, and glanced back at the drugged, half-naked mustached man in the corner, whom she'd nearly forgotten. She did not know what she could do for him at this point except wrestle the gun from the guard's limp fingers, empty the bullets into her palm, and smash the butt of it against the mirror as she left the room.

Her body screamed at her to run, but she didn't, because running invited chasing. Instead, she walked quickly down the hall, slowing only slightly when she saw that the pink-lipsticked woman was slumped back in her ergonomic chair, mouth wide open, unconscious behind her computer. There were no signs of a struggle. Goosebumps rose on Esther's arms. She didn't stop moving though, only dropped her handful of bullets into the wastepaper basket beside the desk as she passed. Back in the main room, harried-looking travelers were still submitting to searches and questions. A few of the security personnel glanced at her without much interest as she passed toward the door. She focused on projecting an air of absolute confidence and ease despite the fact that her hands were trembling and she was cold-sweating uncontrollably. She even managed to smile at a uniformed woman, and a second later, she was back in the main airport.

Everything felt unreal, staged: the overhead lights, the speckled tile of the floor, the hum of a passing cart loaded with luggage, all the people calling for their kids and queuing at gates and frowning at their phones. She didn't look behind her to see if anyone was following but she did pick up her pace a little, glancing up at the signs to find the direction of the exit.

Suddenly, someone grabbed her wrist.

She yanked away on instinct and whirled around, but no one was there—in fact, the closest person was nearly ten feet away, a man in a business suit standing at a vending machine. Her breath was coming fast, almost in pants, her whole body alight with nerves; had she imagined the feeling of cool fingers grabbing her?

"I'm right next to you," said a voice in her ear, and this time when Esther whipped around, she felt the unmistakable brush of fabric against her hand. "Don't say anything," said the voice, which was light and female and had a New Zealand accent. "And don't leave this airport. They have people waiting at the exit for you in case you try. Go into the nearest washroom and wait for me."

"Wait for—who are you? *Where* are you?"

"We'll talk in a sec," said the voice. "All you need to know right now is that I'm the one who saved you back there, and I promise I'm on your side."

Esther started walking toward the exit again, even faster this time. She had never heard of any circumstance under which listening to a disembodied voice had been the right course of action.

"Esther," the voice said, those cool fingers touching her wrist again— and then, in faltering, unimpressive Spanish, "La ruta nos aportó otro paso natural. Did I say that right? Please believe me when I tell you not to leave this airport."

Esther didn't know if it was the sound of her own name or the sound of that familiar phrase that slowed her steps, but she did stop. She stood there, duffel bag digging into her shoulder, T-shirt damp with anxious sweat beneath her jacket, teeth gritted against a scream of frustration. She just wanted to take one step that belonged to her, make one move that she had independently decided to make, but at every turn it felt as if her strings were being pulled by unseen hands.

"The last time I trusted that particular sentence," she said quietly, "it led me here, straight into a trap."

"That trap wasn't laid by the person who sent me," the voice said. "I swear it." Then, with a gusty sigh that ruffled Esther's hair, "Please, come into the washroom and hear me out? Being invisible is actually so uncomfortable, it's like bees are crawling inside my skin. I'm really over it."

If this little glimpse of humanity was a trick, well . . . Esther was tired and friendless and let herself fall for it. Silently, her jaw still clenched in fury, she turned on her heel and stalked into the nearest restroom, then stood there, arms crossed, as a tiny redhead finished putting on a layer of mascara in the mirror and hurried out, casting Esther a nervous glance. Once the redhead had gone, one of the taps turned on by itself, and a paper towel unrolled itself from a dispenser, tore itself from the roll, and floated over to dampen itself beneath the water. It began scrubbing away at something unseen, and then a young woman stood over the sink, holding a book and a paper towel with traces of blood from where she'd wiped it off the page.

"Ugh!" she said, shaking herself like she was casting off spiderwebs. "That was really unpleasant. You all right?"

Esther stared. It was the girl she'd seen in line what felt like hours earlier: the Asian girl with the huge red glasses who'd watched her being dragged off by the blond man. She seemed to be a few years younger than Esther and was wearing a black blazer, a black messenger bag, and very clean white sneakers. She looked like the kind of Young Professional that Esther had seen on TV but never met in real life.

"You're okay," the girl said, answering her own question. "Just a bit shaken, I imagine."

A woman and two children entered and both Esther and the stranger went quiet, waiting for them to do their business, which seemed to take forever and involved a lot of arguing over whether or not the little girl actually had to pee. (It turned out she did; Esther had to listen to her do it.)

When the family left, Esther said, "What did you do to those people back there? The guard and the woman at the desk?"

"I injected them with a tranquilizer," the girl said earnestly, pushing the red glasses up her nose.

"Who told you to do that?"

"I do wish I could answer you," the girl said, "but, you know." She mimed zipping her lips and tossing away the key. "Now listen, you've missed your flight, which really threw a wrench in things, but I got it sorted. That's why it took me some time to break you out of there, by the way, my apologies for the delay, though he wouldn't have actually hurt you. I'm told they want you alive."

With this last horrible pronouncement, she stuffed the book in her messenger bag and passed Esther a sheaf of boarding passes, all in Emily Madison's name.

"Your new flight to L.A. leaves in about thirty minutes, which is good, because the tranquilizer only lasts an hour or so and we want you gone by the time those people wake up and start yelling."

Esther clutched the boarding passes in her hands. This stranger's cheerful, no-nonsense attitude reminded her of Pearl, if Pearl was the kind of person who could ever keep a pair of sneakers clean, and though she wanted to resist, being told what to do by a pretty, authoritative girl was like balm to her frazzled soul.

"You won't tell me who you work for?"

"I can't tell you who sent me here," the girl said. "I *can* tell you my day job's with the Ministry for Culture and Heritage? But that isn't exactly relevant."

"If I take this flight," Esther said, "what will happen to me?"

"Hopefully nothing bad."

Not exactly the words of reassurance Esther wanted. "And if I don't take it?"

The girl looked at her in sympathy. "Nothing good."

21

Half an hour later, as Esther moved cautiously down the aisle of the plane toward her seat near the back, nothing on the flight seemed out of the ordinary. All the people around her were preoccupied with the business of stowing luggage and wrangling infants and loudly asking the flight attendants if they sold compression socks aboard and if not, why not. But any one of these people could be cloaked in magic and Esther wouldn't know it. They could all have books in their carry-ons. They could all be working under mysterious orders, for people they wouldn't name, for reasons no one would explain to her. They could all be threats.

Yet here she was. Closing herself voluntarily into a flying metal tube instead of making a getaway into the outback of New Zealand (did New Zealand have an outback?). Trusting a stranger, again, simply because she happened to know a sentence in Spanish, a sentence that meant a lot to Esther, a sentence that moved her. Literally, lately.

She'd been assigned a window seat. Neither the middle nor aisle seat were occupied yet, and she put her duffel in the overhead compartment and settled herself in, gazing out at the tarmac. If someone *was* going to kill her on the plane, fine. She'd rather die in the blue sky than in that gray detention room.

When she turned her gaze back to the aisle, someone was blocking it, staring down at her. Two someones, actually, both of them young white men around her own age. One was tawny-haired with reddish stubble, handsome and well-dressed, while the other man, towering behind him, was very tall and broad-shouldered, with bright blue eyes and a mouth that looked like it was about to curse.

Nothing about their appearance could quite explain Esther's sudden inexplicable conviction that she did not want to be seated next to them.

It was only that the way they were looking at her pinged a warning bell inside her, and the wide, practiced smile the shorter one offered did nothing to quiet it. Her heart kicked into high gear as he double-checked their seat numbers.

Not here, she thought, *please, not here,* but a second later the man was hoisting his bag into the overhead and then sliding into the seat beside Esther, another bag perched on his lap. His big friend folded himself into the aisle seat, scowling at the way his knees pressed up against the seat-back in front of him.

The smaller man's carry-on gave a small shake and a muffled whine, and Esther understood, with a flicker of reluctant delight, that it held a dog. The guy twisted in his seat, angling his whole body toward her, and running his palms down the thighs of his trousers as if he were nervous, though he still had that easy smile on his face. He looked expensive.

"Hello," he said. "God, I'm glad to be sitting. Airport was an absolute madhouse, wasn't it?"

His accent was the kind of English that made Esther think of horse races and corgis. She nodded infinitesimally but made no other reply. He was undeterred.

"We couldn't get on our last flight, there was this sudden problem with our tickets when we were about to board, so we had to scramble to get rebooked on this one," he said. "Torment! Where are you headed?"

She gave him the most unimpressed look she could manage. "Same place you are," she said.

"Right, naturally," he said, and seemed finally to take her hint. He bent over to slide the carrying case under the seat in front of him, then unzipped one of the mesh windows so he could put his hand inside. Esther caught a glimpse of wet black nose and fluffy fur and clenched her fingers into fists. It had been nearly ten months since she'd seen a dog and the urge to pet this one was overwhelming. She hoped once the plane was in the air the guy might put the carrying case on his lap again, maybe even let the little dog stick its head out and say hello. He zipped up the window and sat back in his seat, picking a hair off his dark trousers.

"What kind of dog is that?" she asked, unable to help herself.

"Pomeranian," the man said, nudging the carrying case fondly with his booted toe. His boots were high-quality leather, waxed laces.

"Don't worry," he added. "She's good on planes, she won't yap the whole way."

Up close Esther was realizing that the dog's owner was younger than she'd first thought, but surface-aged by a visible pall of exhaustion. His skin was sallow, lips chapped, and there were purple half-moons beneath his eyes, one of which was very bloodshot. The nice clothes and posh accent had distracted her.

The broad, blue-eyed man had leaned over his friend's lap and was staring at Esther with the fixed intensity of a cat looking at a squirrel, until the posh one dug an elbow into his ribs in a gesture he clearly thought was subtle. They didn't speak to one another, but at least they didn't try to speak to Esther either, and little by little she began to relax. Her nerves were shot right now, after all; she was reading danger into nothing.

The overhead intercom crackled to life, the flight attendant cheerfully thanking active military members and members of the Gold Wings Plus program, and soon enough the plane was barreling down the tarmac. Esther's stomach lifted as the wings caught air and the ground began to shrink beneath them, gem-green and patchworked with roads and buildings, then replaced by the sparkling blue of the bay as they set off across the open water.

She turned from the window and opened the mystery novel she'd bought at the airport hours before. It was performance more than anything else. She was far too keyed-up to make sense of the words. The man next to her took out his own book though he didn't open it, and yes, she was all nerves, but still she would've sworn that something about his energy was off. He kept jiggling his leg and she wondered if he was afraid of flying. He'd said his dog was good on planes but mentioned nothing about himself.

"What're you reading?" he asked suddenly, swiveling toward her again, moving his whole head like an owl.

She showed him the cover rather than speaking, hoping he'd finally read the signs that she didn't want to engage in conversation.

"You like books?" he said, his voice quiet beneath the roar of the engine, and was she imagining it, or was there a subtle emphasis on the word "books"? She glanced at his friend, who was leaning past him slightly, back to staring at her.

"Yep," she said.

"Have you ever read this one?"

Perfunctorily she glanced down at the book in his lap, and the physical recognition hit her before the mental one did. Her heart skipped a beat and then resumed at ten times its original speed, her face tingling in shock. It was *La Ruta Nos Aportó Otro Paso Natural* by Alejandra Gil. Not only that, it was her own copy, unmistakably. She'd know it anywhere, that crease in the corner, the tiny rip at the spine.

"Where did you get that?" she whispered. She didn't choose to whisper but her vocal cords weren't working, her throat too tight, her breath barely pushing through her lungs.

Once again, the jaws of the trap were closing around her.

"Maram gave it to me," he said, as if the name should mean something to her.

"I don't—" She struggled for air. "I don't know who that is."

"She knows who you are," said the blue-eyed man, in a surprisingly strong Boston accent.

"But *we* don't," said the English one. "Who are you?"

How was she even supposed to answer that question? "I'm the person you stole that book from."

"We didn't steal anything," the Englishman said, looking affronted, which seemed a very unfair thing for him to feel given the fact that he had the book and she did not.

"Then give it back," she said.

The man looked at his friend, who shrugged and nodded, and to Esther's complete astonishment, the book was suddenly in her hands. She hugged it tightly to her chest, not caring if she looked like a kid with a stuffed bear.

"If you don't know Maram, why'd she send us to you?" the guy said. He seemed to be talking not only to her but to his friend, too. "Because she did send us, didn't she? Had to've. She said to show this book to the woman in the mirror, and our tickets—Paris to Zürich to Singapore to Auckland. If I'm honest, I nearly pissed myself when we recognized you in the queue."

"When *I* recognized you," the man at his side corrected.

"Right, when Collins did."

"Sean."

The Englishman looked briefly confused, then nodded. "Yes. Sean. This is Sean. And you are?"

"I'm not telling you my name," Esther said, incredulous. "I'm not telling you anything until you explain why you have my book, why you sat next to me, and who the hell you are."

"Look, we're just as confused as you are," said the Englishman.

The big blue-eyed one—whose name was very obviously *not* Sean—leaned forward so he could look at her over his friend's lap. "We saw you," he said, his voice barely audible over the rumble of the plane. "We saw you fighting Tretheway through a mirror."

Esther nearly lost her grip on the Gil. "It was you?" she said. "On the other side? All that time? You're the one who gave me the tickets?"

"What? No," said the Englishman.

"Shhh," said the other, although they were all talking quietly, and she realized that the three of them had leaned forward, heads together.

She sat back abruptly and put her hand to her seat belt, even though the gesture was absolutely pointless, because where would she go?

The big one saw the movement and said, "We aren't gonna hurt you."

He looked extremely capable of hurting her.

"No," agreed the Englishman, and he at least didn't look like he could do much damage. Already she was sorting them into bad-guy types: the brawn and the brains, though she was yet to see real evidence of the latter. "We only want answers," he said. "Like why was Tretheway after you? And what's your connection to the Library? And where were you when you had that fight? And is that blond girl all right? And why didn't that book have any effect on you? And—"

"Stop," Esther said, "slow down, I don't understand half of what you're saying. What Library are you talking about? And wasn't Trev—Tretheway—wasn't he the one who spelled the mirrors in the first place? So aren't you all on the same side?"

"We're not on Tretheway's side," the big one said loudly, then, in a lower but no less furious voice, "Tretheway's a fucking dick."

Esther was far too frightened and far too tired to trust her instincts right now . . . but she couldn't help thinking that neither of these people seemed like they wanted to kill her, which was encouraging. But famous last words: I don't *feel* like I'm about to be murdered.

The Englishman held up a finger. "Okay, first things first. Magic books. Why don't they work on you?"

Esther was suddenly dizzy. She had never heard anyone outside her immediate family so much as acknowledge the existence of magic, much less put it so plainly, *magic books*; a term that seemed almost ludicrously charming compared to her lifelong experience. It was the novelty of this more than anything that made her suddenly honest.

"I don't know," she said. "They just never have."

His eyes—one bloodshot, one oddly white in comparison—were locked on her face, searching, as if she were an instruction manual in a language he didn't understand. "You can't read spells?"

She couldn't see any reason to lie. "No."

"And they have no effect on you?"

"None."

His eyes widened even further and he shook his head slowly, then more vehemently. Then, out of nowhere, he started to laugh.

It was the laugh of someone so tired that their exhaustion had turned to energy, wired, crackling, half-hysterical.

"Oh Jesus," he said, putting his head in his hands, still laughing. "Oh no."

"What?" she said. "What?"

He shook his head again, shoulders shaking.

"*What?*" the big one said, and Esther felt briefly consoled that she was not the only confused party.

"I figured it out," said the Englishman. "I figured out why Maram sent us to you." He looked back up at her, his mouth still twisted in a manic grin. "You're like me," he said, and started laughing again. "You're a fucking Scribe."

22

In Boston it was snowing.

"We should've got off in L.A.," Nicholas said, shivering on the pavement in front of the decrepit duplex Collins had led them to. Collins had climbed the cement steps and was waiting for an answer to his resounding knock while Sir Kiwi strained the end of her leash, searching for a place to pee on the small patch of dead grass Nicholas supposed passed for a lawn.

"What was that, Nicholas?" Esther said. He and Collins had dropped their false names somewhere over the South Pacific. "You're not loving this gorgeous New England weather?" She'd been pacing the curb with far more energy than Nicholas would expect from someone who hadn't slept since they'd left New Zealand.

"Bit too much like Old England for my tastes."

Nearly thirty hours ago, right as Nicholas and Collins set out across the Library grounds, it had started sleeting, and Nicholas hadn't been fully warm since. Thank god for Collins's reminder that he needed a proper coat or he'd have fled in just his sweater. He had packed his backpack and Sir Kiwi's carry case in the kind of dreamlike haze that made time go all syrupy, moving around his bedroom picking things up and putting them down again. He needed his toothbrush, obviously, but did he need his Church loafers? Did he need his linen dressing gown? What about cuff links?

"No, no, no," Collins had said, pulling everything out of his backpack and shoving Nicholas onto the bed. "Sit. I'll do it."

Nicholas had been too tired and too woozy to argue. The only things he'd insisted on were his old copy of *The Three Musketeers*, a rolled-up blood collection bag, and several clean needles because he'd never traveled without them, plus a falsified prescription for insulin so TSA wouldn't confiscate the syringes. He'd felt a stab of humiliation at how quick and efficient Collins was compared to him, but that humiliation had vanished when he'd had to practically carry Collins across half an acre of warded Library grounds.

He'd seen people go through the wards before, naturally he had, but they'd always been in cars, so the effects were both shorter-lived and less noticeable. But Collins had barely been able to keep his footing, his eyes rolling around in his head like a horse having a fit, muttering nonsense as Nicholas had dragged him through the tall wet grass toward the road, both of them stumbling under Collins's not-inconsiderable weight. As soon as they'd passed the perimeter of the wards, Collins had fallen to his knees and retched, cursing, the knees of his trousers soaking in the sleet-wet grass. Then he'd got up, squared his shoulders like nothing had happened, and set off down the black pavement to find a car to steal.

Which gave Nicholas yet another reason to lift Collins's NDA as soon as possible: he wanted to know where on earth he'd learned to hot-wire cars. Though that wasn't what they were planning to do now, here in Boston. Now, they were getting a car the legal way, by borrowing one. Apparently.

It had been Esther's idea not to take the final leg of their flight to Burlington, and instead remain in Boston and find their way to Vermont on their own.

"But the tickets—" Nicholas had said, on a plane somewhere above the American Midwest.

"Exactly," said Esther. "You may trust this Maram person, but I for one have never even met her. I don't like the thought of her knowing our every move, knowing our moves because she *planned* them. This is our one chance to shake the trail a bit. We'll end up where she wants us to, but we'll do it our own way."

"How?" Nicholas had demanded. "You need ID and passports and all that to rent a car, so it'd be as trackable as taking a plane would be. Same with buses, I imagine."

Esther had been quiet, which meant she was conceding his point—and Nicholas had found himself quietly pleased that he already knew her well enough to recognize this. Twenty-four hours of air travel and concentrated conversation had rather speeded them past the initial stages of mere acquaintanceship, and a quarter of the way through his life, Nicholas thought he might be in the process of making his very first unpaid friend.

"I can get us a car," Collins said. He'd been quiet for most of the conversation so far because it had been preceded by the snack cart, from which he'd procured a single-serving bag of Cheez-its that had taken most of his attention. He tipped the last scatterings of orange dust into his mouth and wiped his hands.

"How?" said Nicholas.

"I'm from Boston," said Collins. "I have people."

"Family?" Nicholas said, interested by the prospect of seeing which giants must have copulated to produce Collins, but Collins shook his head jerkily.

"People," he'd repeated. "Who can get us a car."

"He's got people who can get us a car," Esther said to Nicholas.

"Yes, thank you, I'm right here."

"So it's settled," she'd said. "We won't get on the plane to Burlington."

And they had not. Instead, as soon as they'd landed in the Logan terminal they found a payphone, something Nicholas had only ever seen in movies. Collins had tucked himself into it and had a short but intense-looking phone conversation that had resulted in a squalid, thunderous subway ride to this hideous house on a nondescript corner of a gray city street.

From his vantage point Nicholas could see a laundromat, an Irish pub, a Salvation Army store, another Irish pub, a pizzeria, and a store whose sign was a hamburger circled by planetary rings, like Saturn. An older woman with a cigarette clenched between her teeth paused nearby to let her squat, beetle-like mutt lift a leg against someone's car tire and release a waterfall of steaming piss.

"That's a lotta pee pee for a little boy!" she exclaimed.

If this was how the other half lived, Nicholas thought, perhaps he should've stayed and taken his chances in the Library.

Esther stopped pacing so abruptly Nicholas looked up and followed her gaze to the door, which had swung open. Collins's broad back obscured whoever stood inside but he ducked his head, listened, then turned and trotted down the stoop to where Nicholas and Esther were waiting.

"She wants us to come in before she gives us the car," he said, running a hand through his hair. "Don't say anything, all right? Except please and thank you or whatever."

"Who is *she*?" Esther said.

"Lisa," said Collins, already heading back up the steps. Esther was after him like a shot—where did she get that energy?—but Nicholas hesitated, feeling a flicker of nerves. Despite his curiosity to get a glimpse of Collins's life before the Library, part of him worried that when he and Esther left today, Collins would not be with them. He would opt to stay here, in his own city, with his own people, free from Maram and the Library's machinations. Not a choice Nicholas could hold against him; after all, they were both, in their own ways, hoping for freedom . . . though what Nicholas's own freedom might look like was unclear.

He hoped it would not look like Boston.

He followed Esther inside.

The woman who'd opened the door—Lisa, presumably—was waiting for them in the dark-wooded foyer, which was cluttered with coats, boots, and hats. Nicholas had been expecting someone shady and brutish, someone more like Collins, but Lisa was neither of those things. She was a dark-skinned Black woman of perhaps forty, with a broad, animated face, purple lipstick, and a faded pink Cape Cod baseball cap.

She was peering at Nicholas and Esther with interest. "Coworkers of yours?" she asked.

"No," said Collins. "I quit."

Her expression, which had been light and somewhat mocking, changed. "What do you mean, quit? No one quits."

"It's complicated."

Lisa had a small gold cross around her neck. She toyed with it as she studied him. "We can give you a car," she said. "We can't give you protection. You know that, right?"

"Did I ask for protection?"

Esther turned to Nicholas with a raised eyebrow. *What the fuck,* she mouthed. Nicholas shook his head at her.

Lisa stared at Collins until he looked away, then she sighed. "I probably shouldn't even bother asking questions. Could you tell me anything even if you wanted to?"

Nicholas felt his eyes widen.

Collins said, "No."

"Figures." She glanced down and seemed to notice Sir Kiwi for the first time. "*Okay!*" she said. "Okay, now that is *cute,* my gosh. How is it with cats?"

"She's never met a cat, actually," said Nicholas.

"He's British," Lisa said to Collins. It sounded accusatory.

"So was Bowie."

Lisa put a hand to her heart. "Touché."

"I'm not British," Esther said brightly. "Thanks for lending us a car."

"Don't thank me till you see it," Lisa said. "All right, drop your bags here for now and come on in. Tansy's bringing the car over, but she'll be another ten minutes or so." She kept talking over her shoulder as she pushed through a heavy door into the downstairs unit. "I made an orange cake last night, if you're hungry."

"The boozy one?" Collins said.

"If you consider two meager tablespoons of rum boozy."

Nicholas didn't care about cake. He'd stopped, fascinated, in the entry to Lisa's living room. He'd never actually been in a normal home before. He'd been in innumerable penthouses, and hotels, and even a few upmarket bed and breakfasts, but never a space that existed purely for the purpose of someone's common daily life.

"Have a seat," Lisa said, and pointed to Collins. "You—come into the kitchen with me."

They left through a doorless arch at the end of the room and Esther threw herself immediately onto a couch, which was covered in a fuchsia sheet that sent up a visible cloud of pale cat fur as she sat. Nicholas looked down at his dark clothing and despite being quite tired, decided against sitting for the time being, and crouched to let Sir Kiwi off her leash so she could explore. While she darted into every corner and made a thorough inventory of all the various smells, Nicholas stared.

"Is it normal for a house to be so . . . small?"

Esther looked around, incredulous. "This room is huge."

"Hmm," said Nicholas.

Esther laughed, lounging on the cat-fur-covered couch as if it were velvet. Even in their brief acquaintance he'd noticed that she always managed to look comfortable, somehow. "Not used to visiting the homes of commoners, are we, Prince Nicholas?"

"I'm not a prince," said Nicholas. "Technically, I'm a very minor baron."

"Excuse me, your majesty."

"The correct honorific is *my lord*."

"No," said Esther. "Not even as a joke."

Nicholas went back to cataloging the mismatch of the furniture around him. The fuchsia sofa was almost subdued compared to one of the armchairs, which was upholstered in a striped fabric of orange and yellow, and the other armchair, though a sensible neutral tan, had been piled with rainbow-hued cushions. There was only one rug atop the worn floorboards, a mint green Moroccan Boujad that might've been nice once but was now threadbare.

Nicholas had read the word "threadbare" in books but hadn't ever actually *seen* it.

The walls were covered in art, some of which was quite lovely—a gold-framed oil portrait of a black-and-white cat with a little nub of a tail asleep in a garden—and some of which was frankly disturbing. He stepped closer to examine a drawing of a naked woman with a very full bush pulling a three-headed snake out of her vagina. She looked delighted about the whole thing. Nicholas stepped away again.

Well, at least the place was warm. Deliciously so, in fact, the kind of warmth that went straight to the chilled core of him, running through his bones like molten gold. It was a warmth that could only come from flame, which meant there had to be a fireplace somewhere, though he didn't smell smoke.

Just as this thought crossed his mind, Esther said, "Nicholas."

He turned. She'd risen from the couch and was crouched in the corner of the room, looking at something. He joined her and found that what had caught her attention was nothing more than a large rock, sitting unadorned on the wood floor. Aside from the fact that to the best of Nicholas's knowledge rocks did not generally belong in houses, this one was utterly unremarkable.

"Yes, she's got rather odd taste, hasn't she?" he said.

"Get down here," Esther said.

Reluctantly, Nicholas knelt on the floor beside her. Sir Kiwi, excited to see humans closer to her level, trotted over to join them. Nicholas gave it his attention, examining the rock's gray contours, the flecks of mica. It was even warmer down here, somehow, and he rolled up his sweater sleeves.

"On closer inspection, I see that, yes, it is indeed a rock," Nicholas said.

"Put your hand over it," said Esther. "But don't touch."

Humoring her, Nicholas obeyed, but a second later snatched his hand back with a grunt. "It's hot!"

"Yeah," said Esther. "In fact, I'm pretty sure it's heating this whole room."

He looked closer at the rock and saw, barely perceptible if you weren't looking for it, dark brown smudges that had to be blood. "But that's . . ."

Esther nodded. "Magic."

"You wouldn't believe what that spell saves on heating bills," said Lisa, coming out from the kitchen with Collins in her wake. He was holding a platter of sliced cake.

Esther said, "Propane or electric?"

Lisa looked amused. "Electric. Why?"

"Professional curiosity." Esther stood.

"You have a book," Nicholas said to Lisa, because he couldn't think of the right way to frame this as a question.

"We have lots of books," said Lisa, and glanced sideways at Collins. "No thanks to your employer."

"His employer?" Nicholas started to say, but Collins shot him a sharp, silencing look.

"The cake's really good," Collins said, putting the platter down on a mirrored coffee table. "Have some."

Sir Kiwi let out a yap so excited it was nearly a howl, and Nicholas saw a small white cat sashay into the room, tail high and swaying. It batted its green eyes at Nicholas and then let out a warning hiss as Sir Kiwi approached, flashing needle-sharp teeth. Sir Kiwi rolled immediately over onto her back.

Esther said, mouth full of cake, "How long does that heating spell work? I mean, how many uses can you get out of it?"

"That's what makes it so great," said Lisa. "Once it's activated to the rock, it'll stay hot until you end the spell. So we just keep it in the basement in an unplugged mini fridge during the summer and never deactivate."

"Now that's a spell I'd love to look at," Nicholas said, and refrained himself from repeating Esther's words: *professional curiosity.*

Lisa cut her eyes at Collins. "I'm sorry," she said. "I promised not to take you upstairs. To quote Tansy, we don't give tours to sellouts."

Collins's face crumpled a little, his expression folding on itself.

"Who's we?" said Esther. "You and Tansy?"

Lisa was looking steadily at Collins. "I guess you're still making a habit of keeping things from your friends." To Esther she said, "There's a lot more of us than just me and Tansy. Membership's up to twenty-eight since our last meeting."

"Membership?" said Nicholas.

Lisa nodded but didn't elaborate.

"Hey, I know you're already doing us a favor," Esther said, "but you wouldn't happen to have a computer I could use, do you? I need to send an email." Lisa hesitated and Esther added, "I promise it's nothing to do with . . . all this. It's personal. You can watch me write it if it makes you feel better."

With a shrug, Lisa went to retrieve a battered laptop covered in political stickers and opened it, typing her password onto its worn keys. The screen needed a good cleaning, Nicholas noticed. She opened a web browser and pushed the laptop across the coffee table to Esther, who leaned over it and signed onto her email, eyes scanning eagerly. Something on the screen made her let out a breath like she'd been punched, and Nicholas decided cat hair was a fair trade-off for curiosity and sat next to her on the couch.

The email Esther was reading was all in caps.

ESTHER ARE YOU KIDDING ME WITH THIS SHIT? YOU DISAPPEAR IN THE MIDDLE OF THE NIGHT AND LEAVE ME THIS COMPLETELY INADEQUATE LETTER PROMISING "EXPLANATIONS"? "SOMEDAY"? I DON'T WANT EXPLANATIONS SOMEDAY, I WANT YOU BACK HERE, IN PERSON, YESTERDAY. WHERE THE FUCK DID YOU GO? I DON'T

EVEN KNOW WHERE TO BEGIN WITH HOW ANGRY OR HURT OR
HOW WORRIED I AM ABOUT YOU. I HAVE A BROKEN ARM FOR
CHRISSAKE HAVE YOU NO PITY. THAT NEW GUY TREV IS MISSING
AND EVERYONE THINKS HE WALKED OUT ONTO THE ICE AND DIED
IN A HOLE SOMEWHERE. PLEASE TELL ME YOU'RE NOT OUT THERE
ON THE ICE IN A HOLE. I AM SO MAD AT YOU!!!!!!!!!!

Esther glanced up, her cheeks pink. Lisa and Nicholas were both
peering unabashedly over her shoulders, rapt.

"What?" Collins demanded. "Read it out loud."

"Absolutely not," Esther said.

"It's from the girl she ditched in Antarctica," Nicholas told him.

"Jewel?" said Collins.

"Pearl," Esther said, and hunched further over the laptop to hide the
screen as she typed her reply, but Nicholas and Lisa leaned over with her.
"Guys," Esther begged.

"You said I could watch," Lisa pointed out.

Nicholas didn't bother making an excuse, just read aloud for Collins's
sake as Esther wrote:

Dear Pearl, I am so glad to read your voice, even if you're e-shouting
at me. I am not on the ice in a hole, I'm all right, except for how shitty
I feel about leaving you. I can't be there yesterday, but I promise I
will be in touch soon and I WILL explain. Until then, please try to
trust me when I say I absolutely had to leave. I'm thinking about you
all the time and I miss you in lots of ways I can't write down because
I'm on a public computer.

"Go ahead, write them down," Collins said.

"Yes, we don't mind," said Nicholas.

"Okay," Lisa said, leaning back, "let's give the girl a little privacy."

Nicholas gave her a betrayed look but turned away so Esther could finish her email in peace. He'd never felt so passionately all-caps about another person as Pearl seemed to feel about Esther, and certainly no one had ever felt that way about him. He expected to be sad about this realization, and instead found that he was mostly curious. Maybe if he really did manage to get free of the Library once and for all, if he began to lead a life on his own terms, all-caps was a feeling he himself might someday find.

Esther closed the laptop as a muffled bang sounded from the direction of the entryway.

"That'll be Tans with the car," Lisa said, standing. "Did you all get enough cake?"

They trooped back out through the dark entryway, and Nicholas cast one last curious glance at that bright living room, warmed by magic. He'd never seen a book employed like this, to do something so utterly practical rather than luxurious, and it sparked something in his chest, a long-dormant ember. For the first time in a long while, he had the urge to write uncommissioned, purely out of interest in magic itself. To think about what it could do; how it might be useful. How he might be useful.

Outside, leaning on the hood of a scratched-up red car, was a tall, bulky white woman, her hair in two long silver braids as thick as snakes. She was probably over sixty and wearing a pair of plaid wool overalls that looked so warm Nicholas couldn't even begrudge her their ugliness. This was Tansy, he supposed. Tansy regarded Collins coolly, jingling the keys in her hand. She had faded tattoos on her bare fingers, Nicholas saw, and he recognized the four suits of the tarot: a cup, a wand, a sword, and a pentacle.

"The prodigal son returns," Tansy said, her voice scratchy but resonant. She moved her attention squarely to Esther. "Hi there. Can you drive stick?"

Esther stepped forward immediately, all shining eyes and dimples. "I sure can," she said.

"Hell no!" said Collins.

Tansy swung her head to stare at him, braids swinging. "Last time I saw you work a clutch, you stalled out on a highway."

"That was like ten years ago!"

"It was two."

"I'm the only one who knows where we're going, anyway," Esther said, letting Tansy drop the keys into her outstretched palm. *"Thank you."*

"Remind me why we're lending him a car?" Tansy said to Lisa, then before Lisa could answer, "I'd think you could afford a hundred cars by now."

"Yeah, you'd think," said Collins.

"Are you planning to call your sister?"

Nicholas leaned forward, interested.

"I can't right now," Collins said. "Don't tell her I came through, all right? It's not safe."

Lisa, who'd come to stand by Tansy's side, frowned. "Should we be worried?"

"That's your choice," said Collins.

"Oh," said Tansy. "You want to talk about choices?"

"I just want the car, you guys. C'mon."

"All right, all right," said Tansy. "Take it, it's yours. We don't need it back anytime soon, for obvious reasons." She narrowed her eyes at Collins. "Like you, it's on its way to being trash."

"Tansy!" said Lisa.

"Ouch," said Collins, but he smiled at Tansy, and she reached out and squeezed his arm. Whatever ire lay between them, there was affection, too, and Nicholas had the sudden thought that Tansy must be, in some way, Collins's family.

"Get in," Collins told Nicholas, and he wound Sir Kiwi's leash around his hand to bring her closer.

"Is that fluffy little pom-pom going with you?" Tansy said.

Collins clapped Nicholas on the shoulder as he passed. "He sure is."

"Ha, ha," said Nicholas, focused on opening the trunk. The handle felt rusted shut. Finally it creaked upward and he began to load in their few bags, wrinkling his nose at the dirty fabric interior.

The car itself was older than any vehicle Nicholas had ever been inside: the seats were a beige vinyl that had split at some seams, revealing ragged, infested-looking stuffing, and the metal parts that encircled the wheels were bitten through with rust. Nicholas took the back seat out of habit, buckling Sir Kiwi's carrier in beside him before dropping a treat into it and cajoling her inside.

Esther and Collins had piled into the front. Lisa was leaning through the driver's side window to talk Esther through what seemed to be a complicated headlight situation. Collins was folded up in the passenger seat, arms crossed, clearly displeased with his position, and Nicholas was glad to be in the back seat where nothing was required of him.

He waved through the window at the two women and tilted his head back, his eyelids almost immediately sinking down as if weighted. The car started beneath him with a growl, and he felt them pull away from the curb, but he couldn't bring himself to open his eyes.

"Who were those people?" Esther asked.

"Lisa and Tansy," Collins said.

"I liked them."

"Of course you did." His voice sounded very far away.

Then, what felt like mere seconds later, Nicholas snapped to attention. The car was moving fast. There was a blur of trees out the window instead of buildings, and Collins was kneeling backward in the passenger seat and leaning over the center console to unzip Sir Kiwi's carrier. He froze when Nicholas cracked open his seeing eye.

"I fell asleep," said Nicholas.

"Yeah," said Collins. "Sir Kiwi was getting whiny stuck in her dog box."

Nicholas waved for him to sit down and attended to Sir Kiwi himself, letting her out to explore the back seat. He felt groggy and unrested. "How long was I out?"

Collins looked to Esther.

"Thirty minutes, maybe," said Esther. "Not long. Go back to sleep, if you want."

He did want to, and instead dug around the pocket of his jacket and found his eye drops. His prosthetic eye felt like it had been rolled in sand. "Who were your friends?" he asked Collins.

"Lisa and Tansy," said Collins, just as he'd said to Esther.

"Oh, sod off. What did Lisa mean when she said she couldn't give you protection? How do they know about books? What's this membership thing she was on about? Why's Tansy so angry with you? Do they know about your NDA? Why—"

"Look, you can ask questions until your throat hurts, but I can't talk about it," Collins said. "Literally. Can't. You want answers, you keep up your end of the bargain."

Breaking his NDA. Nicholas squeezed another drop into his eye, resisting the urge to rub. "Does this vehicle have heat? I'm freezing."

"It's cranked," said Collins, putting a hand over the front vent. Nicholas pulled his cold-stiffened hands into his sleeves and got Sir Kiwi to sit on him, but even the tiniest blankets were more effective when they didn't wriggle.

"Feels warm to me," Esther said.

"Nicholas is sickly," Collins informed her.

"Oh, come on," said Nicholas.

"Are you?" Esther asked, glancing at him in the rearview.

"He's anemic," said Collins. "For obvious reasons."

Esther didn't understand right away. Then she said "The books," and her eyebrows flattened along with her mouth. "The more you tell me about this Library," she said, "the more confused I am about how you ever thought the people who own it were, I don't know, the good guys?"

"I never said I thought they were good," Nicholas said. "I just didn't think about it either way. When you're growing up, you don't ask whether your family's *good,* do you? Especially if you don't know anything else. They're just your family."

"And I suppose being, like, insanely rich helped grease things along."

Nicholas felt a bolt of irritation, and Esther, whose eyes were on the road, must've felt his reaction somehow, because she added quickly, "I'm not making fun of you for being rich. That's clearly Collins's territory, I wouldn't dare infringe."

"Thank you," said Collins.

"I only mean," said Esther, "that when things are very beautiful and comfortable on the surface, it can be harder to see the ugliness underneath."

"It wasn't all ugliness," Nicholas said, though he didn't know why he felt the need to protest. He was too tired for this conversation by half. "My uncle inherited the entirety of the Library, inherited our family's legacy. It's a lot of responsibility. I should know, being next in line."

"It's manufactured responsibility," said Esther. "Your family took that responsibility on purpose, just like my family did. You say 'responsibility,' I hear 'power.'"

"Well, aren't they the same thing?"

"No! And anyway, I don't know how you can defend the man you tell me staged a kidnapping and committed real violence against you to keep you loyal to him."

Nicholas's fingers tightened in Sir Kiwi's fur. "I'm not defending him," he said.

"Leave him alone," said Collins. "He learned about the eye thing what, seventy-two hours ago? It'll take a second."

"What will take a second?" Nicholas demanded. "I left, didn't I? Don't I get some fucking credit for leaving?"

"Yes," said Collins.

The car was silent for a while after that, only the loud wheeze of the engine and the swish of the wheels on pavement. Nicholas slouched down and stared out at the green blur of passing trees and the steady lines of traffic they passed queuing at the exits.

Then he said to Esther, "What about your family?"

"What about them?"

"Do they know we're coming?"

"No," said Esther. "Joanna doesn't have a phone. And I want to leave Cecily, my mom—well, stepmom—out of it for now."

"So you're just gonna show up after however many years, boom, no warning?" said Collins.

"The fewer people know our plans, the better," said Esther. "I'm still not convinced your friend, Maram, isn't trying to get us all in one place to murder us. Especially if you're right and I'm—whatever you think I am."

"You are," Nicholas said, for the five hundredth time. Her doubt frustrated him. They had two axes of undeniable proof: her utter invulnerability to magic and the fact that her father's orders to move every year coincided exactly with the activation of Richard's annual Scribe-seeking spell.

And then there was the fact that Richard had told Nicholas over and over, all his life, that he was the last and only one of his kind.

Just a few days ago, Richard's insistence might have seemed proof in the opposite direction, but whatever Esther said about his loyalties, Nicholas was coming to accept that nearly everything he'd known about himself had been a lie, so it stood to reason that this lie, upon which his entire identity was formed, should also be false.

"We'll test it as soon as we get to your house," he said. "Do you think you'll be able to get hold of any blackthorn?"

"I have no idea," Esther said, "because I have no idea what that is."

"It's a tree," Nicholas said. "Berries, branches, or seeds will do, but it can be tricky to find, we might have to call a specialty store to get some seeds, or—" he stopped, because Esther was grinning at him in the mirror.

"Nicholas," she said. "If you're asking about herbs, I did a bad job explaining my sister to you. She's a specialty store unto herself."

"What's blackthorn do?" Collins said, swiveling in his seat to look at Nicholas, an expression of guarded hope on his face.

"Many things," said Nicholas, "but in this particular circumstance, it's going to help break your NDA spell. A spell Esther here is going to write."

"Oh, great," said Collins. "Give me to an amateur." But his eyes were crinkling at the corners.

Esther, on the other hand, was silent, as she had been on this topic since Nicholas had made the connection on the plane over New Zealand. He could feel the disbelief rolling off her in waves, and underneath it, something else. Something tense and bitter that didn't make sense to him. Shouldn't she be pleased, to be told that what she'd always thought was a weakness was in fact the deepest form of power?

If anyone should be unhappy, Nicholas thought, it was him. And there was a small, childish part of himself that did not like to believe he wasn't, after all, special. Unique. The one and only.

But when you were the one and only, it meant you were alone.

Nicholas had been alone all his life. The past few blurred days had been dreadful: a complete upheaval of his entire life, horrific revelations he hadn't even begun to process, and he wasn't *sickly,* Collins, but he couldn't deny he felt like absolute wrung-out shit. Yet for all that, he was also more exhilarated than he'd been in years. Almost giddy. Granted, he'd lost a lot of blood, suffered a multitude of shocks, and barely slept, so his emotions mightn't be entirely rational—but still.

In helping him escape Maram had proved once and for all that she cared about him; he and Collins were maybe, possibly, becoming friends; he and Esther could maybe, possibly, become friends; Sir Kiwi was safe; and he wasn't alone.

"Hey, Nicholas?" Collins said in the mirror.

"Hey, Collins?"

"It's fucking creepy when you smile to yourself like that."

Nicholas smiled wider. Esther took an exit too fast. Collins braced himself against the window.

23

Joanna was standing at the kitchen counter trying to open a well-sealed jar of tomatoes when she heard an engine. She froze, jar in hand, a butter knife poised to pry off the flat metal of the underlid, and listened. There it was: a rattle that sounded closer than the occasional whoosh of the passing trucks she could hear in winter when the deciduous trees dropped their muffling leaves and the sounds from the county road made it down her long driveway.

She put down the tomatoes.

Surely it was a trick of the wind, a noise somehow carried from the far-off street. Her senses strained at their leashes, verifying what a dog could've sensed without twitching an ear, but instead of passing, fading, disappearing, the sound was growing closer. It was an engine—a car—a loud one—and it was on her driveway.

But that wasn't possible. She took a step and stopped, took a step, and stopped. Her heart was suddenly beating so fast she felt breathless. She did not know what to do. It was past seven and she'd just come up from setting the wards, she'd felt the tingle and swish as they reasserted themselves, so this sound, this car, this coming-closer, *was not possible.*

Her palms had grown damp in the space of seconds. She wiped them on her jeans. There was a hunting rifle in the back hall closet, and she moved swiftly to retrieve it, though even as she shook out bullets from the age-softened box and fed them into the barrel, she recoiled at the idea of actually shooting anyone. How much time did she have to get used to the idea? A minute? Less?

The vehicle was growling closer.

Joanna went to the door and turned off the hall light. From this angle she could see the dark driveway through the small, four-paned window but couldn't herself be seen. The rifle felt slippery in her sweating hands, and she could hear herself panting in quick gasps. Panic wouldn't help. She forced herself to assume a posture of calm, relaxing her shoulders, unclenching her jaw, willing her body to trick her mind, but as she did so, the headlights of a car flashed through the thin branches and another surge of adrenaline knotted any muscle she'd managed to relax. The car rounded the bend in the drive and came fully into view.

Joanna leaned forward, desperate to catch a glimpse of the passengers through the car's front windshield, but the sun had set, and it was too dark to see anything until the car rolled to a stop by her truck and the porch light illuminated two figures in the front seat.

One of them was big and square, and the other was small with lots of dark hair. That was all Joanna could make out at first. The big one drew her gaze, but even as her attention snagged fearfully on wide shoulders, another part of her was sluggishly attempting to make sense of the other passenger. Their silhouette struck her deep in the pit of her stomach, and she lurched with sudden vertigo. Her body had recognized the driver before her brain had caught up.

Then her brain caught up.

The driver turned toward the light and Joanna saw, clearly and unbelievably, that it was her sister.

Esther's face registered in every single part of Joanna's consciousness at once. It was like a flash bomb had gone off inside her head, her ears ringing, her heart slamming. Esther. Esther was *here,* in the driveway. She squeezed her eyes shut and opened them again. Esther had not disappeared. Esther turned off the car's engine.

Joanna couldn't move, could barely breathe, and she jumped an inch off the ground when the rifle slipped from her fingers and hit the floorboards with a thud. She picked it back up, shaking. She watched as her sister—her sister, here, home—ran her hands through her hair and said something to the person beside her. Then she climbed out of the front seat and the slam of the car door was so loud, so tangible, it ricocheted through Joanna's body like a shot.

She rocked back from the door, her free hand pressed to her chest, the other still clutching the gun. How many times had she dreamed of this? Of her sister, come home? Yet the only thing she could do was peer through the window like it was a television screen, like whatever was on the other side couldn't possibly come through onto this side, into her life.

Esther was out of the car now and standing by the hood. She gazed at the house, her face still and unreadable in the shadows—and older, grown-up. Behind her, a third person Joanna hadn't noticed spilled out of the back seat, along with a small puff of fur, but Joanna couldn't tear her eyes from her sister.

Esther took a breath so deep that it was visible in the rise and fall of her chest, then turned and went around to the passenger side of the car. She opened the door and leaned in to tug the other person upright. Both the other people appeared to be men, and although the big one was much, much taller than Esther, and much, much broader, he clung to her shoulder like he would fall over without it, which probably, thanks to the wards, he would.

The back seat passenger, however, seemed impossibly unaffected. He was pacing the dark front yard, his face tilted toward the sky rather than the house, and he didn't seem dizzy or confused at all.

They were perhaps three truck-lengths from the house and she could hear their voices though she couldn't make out what they were saying. The man pacing the yard had made it to the tree line, and Esther called loudly to him, waving him back. Even without understanding the words, her sister's voice hit Joanna like a hammer against glass. It was unchanged, that voice. It sounded like Joanna's childhood, sunlit and safe and gone.

Both Esther and the other man were standing on either side of the big one now, supporting his weight. They were coming toward the porch and its yellow glow. They were at the porch steps. If either of them looked up now they would see Joanna's pale face staring through the glass, but both were intent on their companion, getting him to bend his legs to climb the stairs. They managed to haul him up the first one. Then the second. Two steps left.

There wasn't nearly enough time for Joanna to regather all the little pieces that had shattered at the sound of her sister's voice.

So she straightened up, pulled her shoulders back, and assumed a posture of control. This was her house. She turned on the hall light again. She opened the door.

Esther was right there.

They stared at one another. Joanna could feel how wide her eyes were but couldn't control it and Esther's mouth curled into a smile, reflexive, so familiar. For a moment she looked exactly like herself, like Joanna's memory of her, good-humored and lovely in a way made vivid with energy, but then Joanna's eye began cataloging the changes. Her face was still round but it was thinner, her chin pointier, those Kalotay dimples deeper, and there were faint lines in her forehead that deepened as she raised her eyebrows; an expression so recognizable Joanna could almost feel it on her own face.

"Hi, Jo," said Esther. She jazzed the hand that wasn't holding up her companion. "Surprise."

Joanna had wanted Esther to come home since the minute she'd left. She'd imagined this exact scene so many times over the years, imagined wrapping her arms around her older sister, imagined crying into her hair, both of them talking at once, volleying questions and answers, imagined accusations and apologies and reconciliations. But now Esther was here, and Joanna couldn't do any of those things.

She was so happy to see her.

And she was so angry.

She hadn't realized before how angry she was—furious, really. Furious that Esther had left without looking back, had apparently given up every modicum of love between them, had not even returned for Abe's funeral, had left Joanna here alone to rot and die in this rotting, dying house. She was so angry she couldn't speak.

The silence was broken by the big man, who let out an inarticulate groan.

"Can we come in?" Esther said. Her eyes darted to the rifle still in Joanna's hands. "They're on our side, I promise."

Joanna cleared her throat. "What side is that?"

"I have a lot of stuff I need to tell you," said Esther.

"Ten years' worth of stuff?"

"Yes, but—no—specifically, like, seventy-two hours' worth of stuff."

"Look at poor Collins," said the back seat passenger, and Joanna was startled to hear that he was English. The big one—Collins?—was rolling his head around on his shoulders, his jaw slack, moaning piteously. It was a pathetic sight, but Joanna was distracted by the feeling of two very small paws on her shin, and she looked down to find a dog jumping up at her, bright-eyed and wet-nosed. It was so blatantly adorable it looked like it had been cut-and-pasted.

"Down, Sir Kiwi," said the English man. "Or the nice lady might shoot you."

"Who are these people?" she asked her sister. She'd meant it to come out firm. Instead the words were plaintive. "Why do the wards work on his friend but not on him?"

"I'm Nicholas," said the self-declared Nicholas, and held out a hand with such confidence that Joanna found herself shaking it without having quite made the choice. He had cold fingers, a strong grip, and a very convincing smile in a nice-looking, slightly puckish face. "Your other question has a longer answer."

Joanna took back her hand. She turned away from him to her sister, waiting, but Collins's knees buckled, and he started gagging, and there was a flurry of action to lower him to his hands and knees on the porch.

Nicholas looked at Joanna, his face full of impatience. She noticed that he looked very tired, dark circles under his eyes, his mouth drawn, cheeks sallow beneath light reddish stubble.

"I can't read magic and I can't do spells," said Nicholas. His concern for Collins seemed to make him more inclined than Esther to answer Joanna succinctly. "Nor do they work on me. That includes your wards. Collins here isn't so lucky, obviously."

His explanation floored her. She'd thought Esther was unique in her untouchability.

"He's like you?" she asked her sister. Esther shrugged and looked away. It was Nicholas who answered.

"More than you know," he said. "Which we will explain presently, but Collins doesn't have that many brain cells to spare, so please, could you let him in before he loses one too many?"

There seemed to be no point in continuing to assert any silly semblance of power, so Joanna began to step back, then paused. She did have a chip she wanted to bargain for, after all.

"He can come in on one condition," she said, turning to her sister and willing her voice not to shake. "You have to look at the book that killed Dad."

Esther swallowed. "I will," she said. "Or Nicholas will, he's the expert."

"You didn't say anything about a killer book," said Nicholas, sounding alarmed. But then he added, "I'll look at anything you like, just let us in."

Joanna stepped back and watched as Esther and Nicholas hauled their friend up and forward—watched as strangers entered her house for the first time in her entire life.

"Sir Kiwi!" Nicholas called over his shoulder, and the little dog darted between Joanna's legs to follow them inside. She closed the door behind them and turned around.

Collins was leaning heavily against the wall, appearing slightly sick, though lucid. With his eyes properly focused and his head held up, Joanna saw what she'd missed at first, but what she could not miss now, even in her heightened state: he was, to her mingled alarm and interest, very good-looking.

"Christ," he said. "That was as bad as the wards at the Library."

"Least this time we didn't have far to go," said Nicholas.

Even this snippet of conversation raised a thousand questions in Joanna's head. "Wards," Collins had said, as casually as he might have said "truck" or "sandwich." She could feel Esther staring at her but it was too much to meet her sister's eyes again so she addressed the men instead, leaning on the only script she'd been given for this kind of situation: Cecily's hostessing script.

"Are you hungry?"

"Starving," said Collins, so loudly that he drowned out Nicholas and Esther's replies.

"I was about to make chili," she said. "I'll trade you dinner for an explanation."

"That depends," said Esther. "Will you be adding peanut butter to this chili?"

This time Joanna did look at her. She'd made peanut butter chili once, when she was twelve years old, a culinary experiment she and Abe had quite enjoyed, and Esther and Cecily had decried as blasphemous. Esther's eyes were bright and intent. She was saying, *I still know you.*

"I love chili," said Collins.

"Come into the kitchen," said Joanna.

Even with her back turned, she could feel Esther's presence, could feel her taking in the house. She wondered what was going through her head after so long away. As she had with Cecily, she couldn't help reframing her own view of the house, seeing it through her sister's eyes: the dinge and fade of everything seemed even dingier and more faded than usual. The once-bright carpet in the hallway was threadbare and dulled, the lines of the molding were soft with dust, and the kitchen was slumped around its warped linoleum center.

"I love the retro vibe," said Nicholas. "Look at this avocado fridge."

Joanna glanced at him to see if she was being made fun of, but he looked genuinely enthused, dinging a fingernail off one of her hanging copper pans with an approving nod. The dog, Sir Kiwi apparently, had made it her business to sniff in every corner, her tiny nails click-clacking as she applied herself to the task.

"It looks exactly the same," said Esther. "Like stepping into a memory." She opened the breadbox, which held not bread but Abe's collection of vinegary hot sauces, as it had since they were kids, some of them browned with age. She stood there staring at the red bottles, one hand at her throat. Joanna had to turn away before her own grief rose up and took her over.

The two men made themselves comfortable at the kitchen table and it had an odd, transformative effect on the room, to have strangers in a space only family had ever been. The kitchen felt smaller and livelier at once.

"Water?" Joanna said. "Beer?"

"Coffee, I think," said Esther. "It's been a long couple of days."

Collins said, "But don't give him any." To Nicholas, "You had some earlier."

"I think we left that rule at the Library, don't you?"

"It's not a Library rule, it's a medical rule," Collins said.

"Well, seeing as I didn't pack any nettle tea—"

"I have nettle," said Joanna.

"Told you," Esther said to the others.

The three of them seemed to be following threads of conversations that did not include Joanna. She turned to her coffee maker as they chattered away, dumping out the soured remains of her morning. She was feeling so many things it was almost like feeling nothing at all. One repeated word, however, had stood out to her.

She said, "What is the Library?"

The small group at the table went silent. She started to face them and then thought better of it, her nerves too frayed for three pairs of eyes, and busied herself with her abandoned tomato jar, applying herself again to the lid.

"That's as good a place to start as any," said Esther.

"The Library," Nicholas said, "is an organization dedicated to the collection and preservation of rare and powerful manuscripts from around the world." He sounded like a BBC announcer. "We enjoy partnerships with venerable institutions such as the British Museum, the Biblioteca Ambrosiana, Oxford, Cambridge, and the American Ivies, as well as providing lending and creative services to private individuals."

Collins let out a hearty snort. In Joanna's hands the jar lid finally came free with a pop and the lush, acid scent of tomatoes wafted into the air, a breeze from another season.

"By rare manuscripts," Joanna said, "do you mean . . ."

She had never spoken of books with anyone outside her immediate family and found she couldn't finish the sentence.

"Yes," said Nicholas. "It's a family organization and I grew up there. Rather like you grew up here, I understand."

"How many books does the Library have?" she said.

"Oh," said Nicholas, "ten thousand or so?"

She whirled to face him. "Ten *thousand*?"

"We've been around for hundreds of years," he said. "My great-great-however-many-greats-grandfather started collecting on an amateur level in the early 1600s, and more recently my great-great-grandfather started lending them out, building connections, capital—he's the one who started offering commissions."

Joanna felt her mouth hanging open and slowly shut it. Collecting on an *amateur level*—was that what she and Abe had been doing? When she thought about it at all she'd assumed her own collection was one of the larger ones, if not the largest. Why else would anyone have targeted them and killed Isabel?

"So you really are an expert," she said, swallowing her pride. "Good. I said I'd let you in if you looked at my father's book. Will you?"

"He'll look tomorrow," said Esther. "There's more we have to tell you right now."

Joanna was shocked all over again at the sight of her sister sitting there at the kitchen table, lovely and adult and still so far away. "But we made a deal," she said.

"Jo," Esther said. "Nicholas doesn't just collect books."

"Technically *I* don't collect them at all," he said. "Maram's got her little army of workers out in the field for that."

"He writes them," said Esther.

Joanna was holding half an onion in her left hand, which was still bandaged. Under the gauze her cut was healing well, while in the refrigerator her useless, unmagical ink still sat in its ramekin, dark with blood and ash.

She said, "What do you mean?"

"Sir Kiwi," said Nicholas, snapping at his dog, who was engaged in an experimental scrabble at a peeling corner of tile. "Leave it." He turned back to Joanna and said, "Right, Esther mentioned that's been a question for you. How the books get written. Well . . ." He spread his arms, mouth twisting in a bitter, self-deprecatory way. "This is how. I've always known us to be called Scribes, capital *S*, but probably that's a dramatic Library thing, I don't know."

The coffee maker burbled a warning that it had finished brewing and Joanna reached for it numbly. She was attempting to put together Nicholas's words in a way that made sense. This strange, posh young man with the designer dog did not match her image of the people who'd created the books she'd spent her life studying and protecting. Always, in all her reveries and musings, she had imagined women. Old ones, wise ones, witches. Their kind, wrinkled faces had lingered in her subconscious for so long that she didn't even know they were there until she was asked to replace them with this face: young, male, untried.

"How do you do it?" she said. A question that was also a test. She wasn't at all convinced he was telling the truth.

"With my blood," he said. "And herbs, and ritual, and occasionally, the phases of the moon."

All of this, Joanna had attempted.

"But it's the blood that's most important," said Nicholas. "My blood, specifically. I could write a book without herbs, ceremony, or moon, and it would still have an effect, though a weak one. Whereas someone like you could bleed yourself dry and burn ten thousand candles beneath a total eclipse and end up with only a stack of paper."

Nicholas couldn't have meant this to sting, but it did. The cut on her hand felt suddenly silly, a mockery of all her efforts over the past few years.

"And you?" she said to Collins, whose eyes—very blue—were fixed on her. "Are you one of these . . . Scribes, too?"

Collins darted a glance at Esther and shook his head. "No," he said. "I'm like you."

She turned back to Nicholas. "What makes your blood different?"

"I don't know," Nicholas said. "How come you can hear magic and other people can't?"

Joanna's stomach lurched. She looked at Esther, who must have seen the betrayal in her face, because she looked away. Her sister had told these men a secret Joanna had spent her entire life keeping.

"I can't hear anything," Nicholas went on. "Or feel anything or do anything. That's why wards don't affect us." He gestured to Esther, whose expression was suddenly very calm. "No magic does. Scribes can't work it—we can only write it."

Us, Nicholas had said. Joanna stared at her sister.

"Nicholas has this theory," Esther said, flicking her fingers as if to wave it away.

"A theory we'll test soon enough," said Nicholas. "You're going to break Collins's NDA."

"Tell Jo about the NDAs," said Esther, as if she wanted to change the subject as soon as possible.

"What is he saying?" Joanna said to Esther, then answered her own question. "He's saying you can write magic."

"Maybe," said Esther.

But Joanna knew instantly it was true. She knew it like she knew the moon would rise, night after night, whether or not anyone could see it. Joanna might be able to hear books, but Esther was the truly magical one; she always had been.

How wrong Joanna had always been, about everything.

24

Here," said Joanna, putting a folded blanket in Esther's arms. She added a pillow. "Let me know if you need more."

"Thank you," Esther said, feeling uncomfortable and oddly formal. She and her sister were standing in the living room, where Nicholas was passed out on the couch and Collins was crammed into the reclining leather armchair, eyes crossing as he tried and failed to stay awake. It had been past two in the morning when Nicholas had nodded off at the table and broken his coffee mug, and Esther had to admit she wasn't far off from doing the same. She was at the point of tiredness where nothing seemed real, as if she'd already started dreaming. Or maybe it was being back in this house that felt so dizzying and unreal. Maybe it was looking at her little sister and seeing a grown woman.

Joanna had prepared dinner while her three guests had finally managed a full, beginning-to-end explanation of what had brought them there, and then she'd filled them in on her own account of the past few days. Esther had gone cold when she'd heard that Cecily had used mirror magic; it was too close to what she herself had just been through. She'd experienced a bright zing of hope that perhaps it had been her mother behind the glass the whole time, her mother who'd orchestrated everything to bring her child home to safety, but Joanna said she'd seen what Cecily had put through the mirror and it wasn't a passport. It was Esther's own postcard and a note as inexplicable as Joanna herself.

Esther remembered her little sister as a quiet, complicated, marvelously strange teenager, and though she'd grown into a quiet, complicated, marvelously strange young woman, it wasn't quite a linear growth. As a kid she had been incapable of hiding her feelings or pretending to feel differently than she did, but what had been charming in her childhood, a vulnerable kind of warmth, was disconcerting in an adult. Disconcerting, but not off-putting. The opposite, in fact. Her sister's face was mobile and legible in the way of someone unused to imagining themselves seen by others, and as a result it was oddly hard to look away. Joanna's sweet awkwardness had turned to a compelling kind of charisma. She wasn't certain Joanna herself was aware of the shift; though, Collins, at least, seemed to have noticed. Esther had caught him sneaking interested looks at Joanna since they'd arrived.

On her sister's readable face, Esther read two things very clearly in relation to her sudden reappearance: Joanna was absolutely thrilled, and Joanna was absolutely furious.

Esther had not yet fully examined her own feelings, because they were so big she was worried they'd eat her if she let them open their mouths.

Now Joanna was politely leading her up the stairs of her own child-hood home as if she were a guest in a B&B. Esther thought she might scream with the weirdness of it. It was, she reflected, a testament to how bizarre her life had recently become that she found her younger sister's politeness even weirder than the fact that tomorrow morning she was supposedly going to bleed into a cauldron and embarrass herself by at-tempting to write a spell.

Dustballs had gathered in the corners of the steps, the runner was wearing thin, and the upstairs hallway felt so echoing and empty her throat began to close. She remembered running through this hallway, up and down those stairs, in and out of all the rooms, remembered shrieking and laughing, hiding in her parents' closet to jump out and let them pre-tend terror; and later, she remembered tiptoeing past these closed doors to sneak out and meet—what was his name, the boy she'd met at the county fair? Harry something. She remembered banging on the bathroom door and shouting for Joanna to hurry up. She remembered living here.

"You can't sleep in your old room," Joanna said. "Not with the mirror in there."

"It's not dangerous, though, right? You said the wards wouldn't let anyone put anything through, or see through to this side."

"They won't," Joanna said. "But still. Too creepy. You can take my bed. I'm going to set up a futon in the dining room and sleep down there, to keep an eye on things."

"An eye on Nicholas and Collins, you mean."

"Yes."

"Could I . . . do you mind if I just look inside?"

"No, go ahead. The overhead light's out," she added, as Esther pushed her way through the door.

"Lucky you've got an electrician in the house," Esther said, but Joanna had retreated back down the stairs. Esther turned on the standing lamp.

The room was full of old furniture but still recognizably hers. Her Kurt Cobain poster, her purple quilt, her glow-in-the-dark ceiling stars, her white bureau, her cold lava lamp in the corner. This was the room in which she and Joanna had constructed elaborate Playmobil villages, the room she'd snuck out of countless times, where her parents had come in to kiss her good night. All this, too, she remembered. She remembered Cecily rubbing her back and singing an off-key German lullaby as Esther fell asleep, remembered her dad lying on her bed with Esther on one side and Joanna on the other, his arm warm beneath her cheek, his voice pitching high and then low as he did all the voices for the story he was reading aloud.

She was glad not to be sleeping in here, after all. And when she crept in, she was relieved to find that Joanna's room, at least, had changed somewhat—she'd gotten a new desk, a new bureau, and had repainted the walls from her high school lavender to a cool, adult gray. It looked nice. She sat on the bed for a while, preparing herself, then went back out into the hallway.

In front of her parents' closed door she paused. This was where Cecily and Abe had slept all through her childhood and where Abe must have slept alone after Cecily had gone. Esther was bone-tired and shaken up and she didn't have time to succumb to emotion, but she needed to look inside this room with an urge so strong it felt like instinct. She needed to see evidence both that Abe had been here and that he was now gone. Even years later it felt inconceivable.

She had been living in Oregon when he'd died and after she'd heard, had driven out to the gray, surging coastline to sit on the rocks and mourn him alone. Joanna's voice was still ringing in her ears along with the waves: *Come home, I need you, I can't do this without you.* It hadn't seemed like the right time to explain that staying away was a last fulfillment of their father's wishes. She didn't want to warp Joanna's memory of him. Let her sister have one family member who'd never disappointed her, she'd thought. At the time it had felt like a gift but now she wasn't so sure.

The bedroom was almost exactly as she remembered it, though all traces of Cecily were gone. The light green walls were the same, and the green bedspread, and the nightstand piled high with books, and the dresser cluttered with tchotchkes, with the remnants of Abe's life: a watch, a comb, a framed photograph of his daughters, and a photograph of Isabel holding an infant Esther. The only photo of Isabel Esther had ever seen.

Esther swiped her thumb over her mother's image, clearing her of dust. In the photograph Isabel was supporting Esther on one knee like a tiny ventriloquist's dummy, a posture Esther had always found oddly distant in comparison to the pictures of her and Cecily. Cecily always had her face squished up next to Esther's, beaming. In this one the upper half of Isabel's face had been cut off and only her mouth was visible, curled in a secret smile, a smile that was for herself and not for Esther or for the person behind the camera. Esther loved that smile. It made her mother look like a person, not a ghost.

She put down the photo and went to sit on the edge of her father's bed, looking to his nightstand to see what he'd been reading. A couple detective novels and a copy of *Cook's Illustrated*. She picked up the magazine and leafed through it until she found a recipe he'd circled and dated, as he'd always done. He'd wanted to cook a cassoulet. She wondered if he had.

His reading glasses were sitting on one of the novels, so familiar she had to turn away. Then she picked them up, feeling their spindly metal weight in her hands. She unfolded them and put them on, the room around her swelling and softening through the glass. The nose pads pinched, and she remembered the marks they'd left on Abe's face, red divots standing out on the skin of his nose, and for some reason it was this detail that opened the gates she'd been keeping so tightly latched.

Someone knocked lightly on the half-opened door and somehow Esther wasn't surprised to see Joanna standing there. She looked up at her sister, whose face was blurred by tears and by Abe's lenses.

"Hi," said Esther.

"Hi," said Joanna.

For a moment, neither spoke. Then Esther said, working hard to steady her voice, "You haven't even hugged me."

Joanna took one step further into the room. "You didn't hug me, either."

That was true. Esther touched the bed next to her and Joanna hesitated before coming slowly over to sit, pulling her long braid over one shoulder and holding on to it like it was a lifeline. Esther moved closer, reached up to wrap her arms around her sister's narrow shoulders, and for a moment it felt terrible: Joanna was stiff and unfamiliar, a stranger. Then, infinitesimally, she relaxed into the touch, her back curling slightly because Esther was shorter and had been since they were kids, and suddenly, like they'd both remembered how, they were hugging one another for real, Joanna's head on Esther's shoulder, Esther's face pressed into her sister's hair. They hugged the same way they had always hugged, Joanna tucked into Esther's arms as if she were the smaller one, and Esther squeezing her so tightly she could feel Joanna's bones creak under her grip. Her eyes had closed of their own accord but still tears were somehow pushing their way onto her cheeks.

When Joanna spoke, Esther could hear from her voice that she was crying. "Why didn't you come home?"

Esther gave it some time, because she hadn't hugged her little sister in ten years, and she wasn't quite ready to stop yet. Then she drew back, took off Abe's reading glasses, wiped her eyes, and told Joanna the truth.

The truth that Abe had told her, when she was eighteen, that her immunity to the wards was endangering everybody in the house. That Abe had given her a choice. She could stay and put herself and her family at risk—or she could leave and spend the rest of her life running. It hadn't really been a choice because they had both known what she would do.

Joanna was silent as she listened though her feelings played out on her face like it was a stage. Shock, comprehension, dismay, fury, and finally, as Esther finished speaking, a sadness so deep it felt like leaning too far over the edge of a quarry. Esther had to look away before she lost her balance.

"Dad knew," said Joanna. "He always knew you were a—what did Nicholas call you? A Scribe."

"If I am."

"You are," said Joanna. "And he knew."

"Yeah," said Esther. "Probably."

"He used me," said Joanna. "He knew you'd never protect yourself the way you'd protect me, so he told you to run for my sake, not your own. But he didn't give *me* a choice."

Esther shook her head. "What kind of choice could he have given you?"

"The same one," said Joanna. "To protect *you*. I would have. I'd have gone with you or you'd have stayed here and we could've figured something out together. It wasn't fair that he put it all on you. You were a *child*."

"So were you."

"I hate him," said Joanna, though her face told an entirely different story.

"I don't," said Esther. She felt the heat of tears in her eyes again. "I miss him."

Joanna covered her face with one hand, her back rising and falling, but her other hand reached out and found Esther's. Despite her grief for her father, despite her exhaustion, despite everything, Esther felt a profound sense of . . . what was it? Something expansive and dizzying, like lying on her back under a night sky so filled with ancient stars that she felt the tininess of her own life like a flickering candle beneath them. Awe. That after ten years, Joanna was still her sister.

"But I don't understand what this means," Joanna said eventually. "Why that person—what was her name?"

"Maram."

"Why Maram sent all of you here. Do you trust her?"

"I don't know her," said Esther. "So no. But . . ." She struggled to articulate her thoughts. "At least something's happening. Something different. I couldn't go on the way I have been."

Joanna's fingers tightened on hers, a silent press that felt like understanding. In the room around them, the small, ordinary relics of their father's life lay quietly where he had left them: a watch waiting to be fastened, a handful of quarters waiting to be spent, a novel waiting to be read. For a while Esther and Joanna sat there together on the bed, both knowing they would soon need to break the stillness, stand, and move onward, but not quite yet. For just this moment, the world—like the watch, the quarters, the novel—could wait.

25

This is a vampire," Nicholas said.

A patently ridiculous sentence, but still, Esther looked down at the book Joanna had brought up from the basement and shivered. It sat spread open on the coffee table, limned in soft light, and looking far more innocuous than it had any right to. She and Nicholas and Collins had all slept late, so it was already midmorning, a day as gray and chilly as the one before. The living room was warm with wood fire and stuffy from the sleep of three people, but Esther could feel the cold coming off the window glass. The closeness she'd felt with Joanna last night had ebbed; this morning her sister felt distant, perched on the piano bench with her long hair loose around her shoulders, her gaze fixed on the book in front of Nicholas, beautiful like a portrait and as remote. In the light of day, she saw that while Joanna was still unmistakably Abe's daughter, with the same dimples and thin-bridged nose Esther had also inherited, she looked more like Cecily now that she was an adult. This, too, made Joanna feel far away.

Probably Esther shouldn't have been surprised to learn she could still feel that same old jealous ache she'd felt as a child, searching her face in the mirror for signs of her own birth mother, her own family, but there it was, like a trick knee in the rain. Another ache was the thought of how physically close she was to Cecily, mere miles away, yet still so far. If her stepmother hugged her right now, she thought, she might start crying and never, ever stop.

"A vampire?" Joanna repeated.

Collins, who was standing in a corner slurping coffee, said, "Oh, shit."

"Have you been touching this with your bare hands?" Nicholas demanded.

"My dad said to keep it away from blood, not skin," Joanna said, sounding a touch defensive. "What do you mean, vampire?"

"A vampire is a fifteenth-century spell that protects activated books," said Nicholas. "It kicks in as soon as anyone attempts to add their blood to the spell in progress, which your father must have done. I'm very sorry," he added, and he did look sorry.

"You're telling me he died because of some . . . some magical booby trap?"

"I'm sorry," Nicholas said again.

Joanna put her head in her hands and Esther, feeling uncertain, went to sit beside her. Joanna turned toward her with a wretched expression, mouth twisted the way it had when she was a kid trying not to cry.

"He should have known better," Joanna said, and Esther understood why this information was hitting her sister so hard. For Joanna, their father had always been the pinnacle of knowledge, yet he'd been killed by nothing more than a stupid mistake. A mistake that had taken Nicholas less than a minute to spot.

"Had you ever seen anything like this before?" Esther said. "A—what'd you call it, a booby-trapped book?" She already knew the answer and miserably, Joanna shook her head. "So dad couldn't have known," Esther said.

Joanna shook her head again, eyes wet, and Esther's own throat tightened in response. She didn't know what to say to comfort her. Her sister had been the one to find their father, after all. She had seen firsthand the brutal cost of Abe's mistake.

"Joanna," Nicholas said suddenly. Something in his voice had changed. "Where did your father get this book?"

Joanna looked up, eyes still damp. "I don't know," she said. "He never talked to me about it. I didn't even know he had it until he died."

Nicholas held the book out, his grip odd, like he was holding something rotten he'd wrestled from his dog's mouth. "This is a Library book. Was a Library book."

Esther's pulse quickened immediately.

"How do you know that?" Joanna said.

"Did you notice this symbol?" he asked, opening to the back cover to show them a small, embossed gold book, and when Joanna nodded, "It's not decorative, it's functional. It's the mark of a spell we call the expiration date—we put them on every book that comes through our collection."

Esther pulled her feet up onto the bench and linked her arms around her knees, the urge of a frightened animal to make itself compact, reduce the target area. "What does it do?" she said. "The expiration date."

"It's an object-connected intuitive divination spell," Nicholas said, and Esther saw that Joanna, despite everything, smiled at this, clearly pleased with the jargon. Nerd. Esther felt differently.

"Say that again in dumb-dumb, please."

"The spell adheres to an object," Nicholas said, "and conveys information directly into someone's mind. In this case locational information, to Richard's mind."

"A tracking spell," Joanna said.

"Exactly," he said, pointing at her. "No, don't look so alarmed, the Library can't find us unless you take the book outside the boundaries of your wards. You haven't, have you?"

"No," Joanna said. "At least, I haven't in the past two years. I don't know about before. But what does the book itself do?"

"Well, I haven't seen this exact book," Nicholas said, "but I think— no, I'm certain—that I *have* seen a draft of it."

Collins, who'd been standing, sat down heavily on the closest surface, which was the record player. Cassettes rattled and a cardboard record cover fell to the floor and Joanna half rose, concerned—though for Collins or her record player, Esther wasn't sure.

Nicholas was holding the spine very close to his right eye, squinting at the binding. "If this is the book I think it is . . . I'm relatively certain it's human."

A hot, sour feeling rose in the back of Esther's throat. "What do you mean, human?"

"I mean the thread looks like it could be a combination of hair and sinew. The glue is likely rendered collagen." He pinched the cover between thumb and forefinger. "The leather's probably human skin."

"Okay," Collins said, "great, well, if you need me, I'll be outside screaming."

"I don't know how your father got his hands on it," said Nicholas, "or who it's attached to, but—"

"*Who* it's attached to?" Esther interrupted. "Don't you mean *what*? If it's another object-permanence spell or whatever?"

"Object-connected," said Nicholas, "and yes, that, too." He paused for breath. "Sorry, I forget I'm literally the only person alive who's been forced to learn this. Look, any book written by two Scribes has two points of magical action. This one has an object-connection and a body-connection."

"So it's connected to both an object and a person," said Joanna.

"Yes," Nicholas said. "Until today, I didn't even know this kind of thing was possible."

"But what does it do?" said Esther.

Nicholas was rubbing his temples again. "It connects a person's life-force to an object," he said. "As long as the object is intact, so is the life."

Esther looked at Joanna, waiting for a recap, but even Joanna didn't immediately understand what he was saying. When she did, her eyes went huge.

"It's an immortality spell."

Nicholas nodded. "As much as anything can be, yes."

"You said it's in progress," Collins said. "So it's attached to someone?"

"Yes," said Nicholas, and glanced at Joanna. "It obviously wasn't your father, because, well . . ."

"If it was, he'd be alive."

He rubbed his face roughly. "I don't know what to think about this. Sir Kiwi!"

Esther turned to see that the dog had gotten hold of someone's boot and was lying on the hearth, gnawing on it enthusiastically. At Nicholas's voice she froze, made eye contact, then resumed her gnawing.

"I should take her out," said Nicholas. "We'll look at the book again later. After we prove my theory." He looked pointedly at Esther, who kept her expression neutral.

Today, she was going to write a book.

"How long will that take?" Joanna said.

"Well, seeing as it's her first one, and all the writing has to be done by hand, we're probably looking at an eight-hour process, all together," Nicholas said. "You'll make ink and write this morning; the pages will dry by late afternoon; and we'll bind it in the evening. Then Joanna can read it to Collins."

"Yay," said Collins.

"If getting rid of Collins's NDA is really so important," Esther said, "if we're in such a hurry for answers, maybe now isn't the time to test a wild theory. Maybe you should write the spell yourself."

"No," said Nicholas, plucking a few dog hairs from his expensive-looking sweater. "The sooner we can test you, the sooner we have at least one answer—and speaking for myself, a definitive answer about *anything* sounds lovely right now."

"Also," Collins put in, "if we take any more blood out of Nicholas, he'll probably die."

Nicholas made a grudging noise of affirmation.

"So you want to take it out of me, instead?" said Esther, but it was a show of protest. She wanted to know. She did. She just wasn't certain which answer she was more frightened of.

"Yes," Nicholas said, and stood from the couch. He staggered once, then caught both his balance and her concerned eye on him. "Don't worry," he said, "you'll only be bleeding enough for a single book, you won't even feel it. By the way, Joanna, do you have any candles? And if so, how many?"

THE QUESTION OF CANDLES WAS A SIMPLE ONE, WITH A SIMPLE ANSWER: many. Nicholas's next question, however, was far more complicated. He wanted to know if there were any symbolic traditions Esther had a strong connection to—specifically with regards to sharing secrets, or breaking silence.

"Traditions," Esther repeated. "Like . . . religion?"

Nicholas shook his head. "Overtly religious traditions rarely work. I'm talking about creating a ceremonial context that feels powerful to you personally. And we're making this ink to break a silencing spell, so think perhaps about . . . volume? A tradition of being loud, or a tradition of being quiet. Telling secrets. Sharing truth. Does that make sense?"

It didn't, quite. Esther put her mind to it anyway. She had never been given to spirituality, though she had gone through a short, exploratory religious phase as a preteen. Cecily and Abe, while both technically Jewish, were hardly practicing. However, Esther had done enough research into her biological maternal roots to know that most Mexicans were Catholic, so at twelve she'd convinced her parents to take her to Mass the next town over. The church was lovely, mossy stone with dramatic stained-glass windows, and behind the pulpit, Jesus stared down from an enormous crucifix. Esther had gazed up at his mournfully heroic face, his chest and thighs muscled and bare, his ankles slender, and believed she felt the faith of her people coursing through her veins, holy and tingling.

But the mass itself had been so boring that even her fantasies of rescuing Jesus and giving him a tender, thorough sponge bath couldn't keep her awake. By the end of her twelfth year Esther had lost her zeal for religion and was channeling it into a zeal for Kurt Cobain's delicate, tragic eyes, instead.

Esther relayed all this to Nicholas and was met with a sigh of poorly hidden frustration.

"You're still hung up on theology," he said. "That isn't what I—"

"The truck," said Joanna.

The three of them—Esther, Nicholas, Joanna—were sitting around the kitchen table, Sir Kiwi at Nicholas's feet. Collins was nowhere to be seen (according to Nicholas, he always made himself scarce for this part) and until now, Joanna had been mostly quiet. Esther turned to her.

"Dad's truck?" said Esther. She'd seen it in the drive when they pulled up, worn and red and as familiar as the house itself.

"Yes," said Joanna. "Nicholas said to think about volume, didn't he? About secrets."

"Is the truck very loud?" Nicholas said, furrowing his brow. He was clearly not following Joanna's logic . . . but Esther was. She could almost feel the soft leather of the steering wheel beneath her hands, the rattle and shake of the pounding speakers as she cranked her music as loud as it would go and screamed the lyrics out the open windows, turning now and then to grin at Joanna's pained expression in the passenger seat beside her. They'd had their best conversations in that truck. The truck was where Esther had first admitted aloud, both to Joanna and to herself, that she had a crush on a girl; and the truck was the only place Joanna would ever let herself complain about the books, the only place she'd admit to feeling resentful of the pressure.

"Genius," said Esther. Obviously, Joanna was a natural at this. She turned to Nicholas. "Can we do the ceremony outside, in the truck?"

Nicholas pressed his lips together, considering. "Yes," he said, though the word was drawn out, doubtful. Then, with more confidence, "Yes. I can work with that."

The setup took the better part of an hour, Nicholas consulting with Joanna now and then on the availability of certain tools and conscripting Esther to carry armloads of supplies out to the truck. Nicholas clearly had an aesthetic vision, and though Esther was initially skeptical, she had to admit that by the time he'd finished, the cab of the truck no longer looked quite so much like a truck; or anyway, it did, but a truck in which someone might make magic. Layers of gauzy red fabric darkened all the windows against the winter light and filled the cab with an eerie glow, while colorful cushions and blankets hid the lines of the seats, and a multitude of tea candles flickered on the dashboard. Still, despite the changes, the truck felt as familiar to Esther as her own heartbeat. She gripped the steering wheel with one hand and put the other on the gear shift, feeling herself settle into the space, all the old ease and comfort coming back to her body. She felt, for the first time in days, safe—a feeling that was in and of itself magical, and which no candles or gauzy fabric could approximate. Nicholas sat next to her in the front seat and Joanna squeezed into the back, all of them bundled to their ears against the chilly air, though Esther could feel the warmth of the many candles caressing her cheeks.

"Are you ready?" said Nicholas.

Esther did not know how to answer that, exactly. Was she ready to let him stick her with a needle and fill a bag with her blood? Sure. Was she ready to possibly reassess everything she'd thought she'd known about herself and her relationship to power and to her family and to the world in general?

Was anyone, ever?

"Ready," she said.

"All right," he said. "Sing."

Esther said, "Now?"

"Now."

She didn't know any meaningful prayers or chants but Nicholas had promised this didn't matter. Religion was beside the point, he'd said; it was *connection* that mattered. So Esther cleared her throat, put both hands on the wheel, and channeled her devotion as best she could.

Very quickly it became clear that "Smells Like Teen Spirit" was not made to be sung a capella.

She saw Nicholas wince before he schooled his face into an encouraging smile. He and Joanna nodded along as she sang the first verse, though their nods became more infrequent as she moved into the section that was entirely comprised of the word "hello" over and over. She tried to remember how it had felt to drive the back roads as a teenager, blasting her music and scream-singing at the top of her lungs, not worrying about how she sounded because it was the volume that mattered, the power of her own voice . . . but she couldn't quite get there.

She completed the chorus and the second verse, added some guitar-riff noises, then paused. "Should I . . . like . . . feel anything? If this is working?"

"I don't know what you'll feel," said Nicholas. "For me it's . . . it's as if there's a length of ribbon coiled in my chest and someone's unspooling it. Plus bees."

"Bees?"

"Or honey. Same thing."

Esther couldn't let that one go: "With due respect, no they're not."

"Joanna?" Nicholas said.

"Yes," said Joanna, from the shadows of the back seat. "Bees or honey. They're the same."

Esther fell silent, unnerved by this nonsensical solidarity.

She tuned into herself, feeling for bees or honey, but there was only the everyday tide of her pulse. "I don't feel anything," she said. "Nothing unexpected, anyway."

For the first time she could see Nicholas's total certainty begin to waver around the edges, and she felt a sudden childish choke of disappointment. Of course she wasn't magic. It was ludicrous she had ever allowed herself to believe otherwise. She was an ordinary person with ordinary blood and ordinary skills, like reading blueprints or calibrating flowmeters.

He said, "Is there another song that you have a stronger connection to? One with less . . . yelling, perhaps, and more . . . sharing?"

Esther began to run through the jukebox in her mind, then hesitated. An idea had come to her, though she was embarrassed to say it aloud. "Do I have to know it by heart?" she said. "Could I read it, instead?"

"I don't see why not."

"It's religious."

Nicholas sighed. "Do you have a connection to it?"

"Yes. Sort of."

"We may as well try."

Esther swallowed and glanced at Joanna. "What happened to that book of prayers Dad used to pull out sometimes?" she said. "With the Mourner's Kaddish? Do we still have it?"

Joanna's face went taut with understanding, and she nodded before pushing open the back door and vanishing in a gust of cold air and bright sun. Esther settled back in the driver's seat, hoping this would work and irritated to realize how badly she'd let herself want this. Even after all these years, even after Abe was gone and it was too late, she was still striving to find a place for herself in her family, grasping for anything that might finally tell her, *Yes, you belong.*

Joanna reappeared quickly with the old prayer book, its pages yellowed by age, its spine cracked. She'd already flipped to the right page and when she opened the driver's door to hand it in, Esther grabbed her by the wrist.

"Will you sit up here with me?" she said. "Like you used to?"

Joanna glanced to Nicholas to see if he'd mind, but he was already out the door and clambering into the backseat, re-situating himself and his supplies. "It's a good idea," he said. "We can work around the odd angle."

Joanna took his place beside Esther in the passenger seat, relaxing back almost automatically, one booted foot coming up to settle on the dash, and Esther smiled. This, too, was familiar.

"You're supposed to say this standing up," Esther said to Nicholas. "Is it okay if I kneel on the seat?"

"It doesn't matter what you're *supposed* to do. Do whatever feels right."

Awkwardly, Esther raised herself to her knees, bending her head a bit against the roof. She had forgotten, until now, that she'd had a fleeting resurgence of that old desire for religion in the months following her father's death, and had gone to several Portland churches and synagogues attempting to mourn. Her grief had felt so heavy and she had wanted to find somewhere to put it, a container big enough and strong enough and old enough to hold it.

She'd wanted to *share* it.

These were the feelings she focused on as she squinted down at the page and began to recite the Mourner's Kaddish; her deep grief for her father, and the endless, yawning chasm inside her that had always sought to be a part of something bigger. Of a family, of a tradition, of the whole unknowable world.

She thought of Abe as she'd known him in childhood, loving and good-humored and eccentric and impractical, a great dancer and a meticulous cook who'd made her a five-course meal every year on her birthday. She thought of how safe she'd felt when he hugged her, how she'd always been able to make him laugh until he cried. She imagined all the people who'd been reciting this same prayer for their lost fathers for thousands of years, in thousands of homes beneath thousands of skies, while ancestors from her other line drank wine together in church each Sunday, holding it on their tongue as blood. She felt Joanna reading over her shoulder to recite the Kaddish along with her, very quietly, this mystifying person who had never understood Esther's ache for belonging, because Joanna had always loved Esther so completely that to her it must have felt like a completion. There were thousands of years of wine and blood shared between them, a lineage of ritual and belief and longing and connection, of magical thinking and of real magic.

And suddenly Esther began to feel it.

Crystals of old honey on her body's tongue, long hardened, were loosening in the warmth of her spilling blood, turning from grain to syrup, a slow sweet hum of wings unfurling from deep within her and looping outward, solid and multitudinous, the comb in her chest and the workers in her veins and the hive all around her.

Nicholas said, "Esther?" just as Joanna said, "I hear it."

Esther was trembling. This was what Joanna and Abe had been hearing all those years. This was what they'd devoted their lives to listening for—and meanwhile Esther had believed she was on the outside when really, she'd been inside all along. She *was* the inside. The warm, humming center. It came from her.

"It's working!" Nicholas said.

Esther laughed, exhilarated. "What, now you're surprised?"

"It's one thing to suspect," he said. "Or even believe. It's another to know. Quick, roll up your sleeve."

Esther wriggled one of her arms out of her coat and rolled up her sweater sleeve. The equipment Nicholas had brought looked sterile and medical, out of place in the red, glowing candlelight, and Nicholas leaned over the center console to tie an elastic around her forearm with the practiced air of a doctor. Then he took her wrist in his cold fingers and aimed a syringe, pausing to look up at her, questioning. She nodded.

There was a slight sting as the needle pierced the soft skin. "Excellent," he said. "You've got lovely veins, mine are squirrely. Now keep going."

Esther started the prayer again, sinking into the warm, buzzing glow as blood began flowing from her arm. She felt a tugging pressure from somewhere inside her chest, a wide wash of sweetness that encompassed her whole body then focused down into her arm and came out vivid red through the tube and pooled in the bottom of the plastic bag. The last time she'd seen this much blood was when she and Pearl killed Trev and pushed him through a mirror. Had that really been only a few days ago? She'd confessed to that secret; both Joanna and Nicholas knew, and telling them had removed some of the weight.

She thought of Collins, then, of how long he'd been silent and alone. She was doing this for him, after all; pouring out a piece of her heart so that he, too, could share of himself.

She finished the prayer and no one spoke for a while, all three of them attuned to that inner sound, the endless, honeyed hum. This was the first time Esther was hearing it, yet she felt, somehow, that she'd been listening to it forever. That perhaps it was the first sound she'd ever heard, and perhaps would be the last, when her time came.

"How old were you?" Esther asked Nicholas eventually. "When you first bled like this?"

"Eight," said Nicholas. "I was a late bloomer."

It was meant as a joke, and Esther smiled dutifully, though she did not find it funny. Nicholas should not have been forced to do this at eight; just as Esther should have been given the option. She found that she desperately wanted to begin writing, to see how the feeling might change as the ritual changed, if the power would ebb and flow or stay the same, this steady pour of syrup.

"This ought to be enough," Nicholas said, leaning into the front seat again. "Here we go—" He did something deft and slightly uncomfortable to the needle in Esther's arm and suddenly it was out, though the feeling, that beautiful thrum, lingered in its wake. Nicholas said, "You all right?"

He was pressing a wad of paper towel to the bright bubble of blood that sprang up in the needle's wake, his cold fingers gentle. The memory of that all-encompassing feeling still pulsed inside her. She wanted more.

Nicholas tilted the bag to the candlelight. "You're very well-oxygenated, look how red this is."

"This is more clinical than I thought it would be," Joanna said.

"It isn't always," said Nicholas. "Sometimes the work demands a more specific method of getting the blood out." He weighed the bag casually in one palm like he was measuring flour for a cake. "Anything to do with heat or fire, for example, you've got to burn yourself open. Which is difficult, since burned flesh tends to want to meld, not part." He glanced at Esther's face and laughed. "Man up, Esther. No one's coming at you with a lit match. Yet."

Esther's annoyance over this *man up* did a pretty good job of distracting her from the thoughts that had been twisting her expression. She hadn't been thinking of herself. She'd been thinking of Nicholas again, of what had been done to him.

Nicholas, oblivious, was handing the bag of blood up to Esther. "Let's go inside and char some herbs."

They blew out the candles and left the truck with its cab still draped in fabric. In the kitchen, Nicholas turned out all the lights and lit more candles, and the three of them clustered around the stove. They blackened a pot of herbs and Nicholas stirred them with a wooden spoon while Esther poured the blood in slowly. It was so similar to the picture she'd always had in her head of evil witches that she almost laughed—and then she started feeling things again. The stirring of translucent wings. Everything was dim and flickering and the surface of the ink was so dark it reflected the candlelight back at her, a pool of red-tinged night shimmering with stars.

"That should do it," Nicholas said eventually. Esther took a long, slow breath and stopped stirring, letting the feeling fade as the liquid calmed and stilled. "Now comes the harder bit. Actually writing."

26

Joanna supposed it made sense that Esther did not in fact write the book—she copied it. It was Nicholas who did the actual writing, typing away on the desktop in the dining room until he finished a document full of the kind of looping, recursive sentences Joanna would recognize anywhere, nonsensical on their own but accruing meaning with each repetition: *. . . and from the closed mouth is a closed chain, and the closed chain opens like a mouth. Every link is a mouth that opens like the closed mouth will open.*

"This reminds me of your emo poetry phase," Esther said, skimming the first few pages as they were spit from Joanna's dusty printer.

"Bad enough you stole my diaries," Joanna said, and plucked the pages from Esther's hands to look at them herself. "Worse that you remember what was in them."

"It isn't poetry," said Nicholas, leaning back in his chair and looking miffed. "And let the record show that if I did write poetry, it would be excellent. This is magic. I might be able to teach you the basics of ink-making in a morning, but the words themselves took me years to master, so show some respect, please."

"It'll work, though?" Esther said. She set the stack of paper on the dining room table beside the well of blood-ink. In the light of the 1970s faux chandelier, the ink was as dark as her eyes. "Even though the words didn't come from me?"

"Yes," said Nicholas. "In fact, I wonder if it'll be strengthened by the collaboration. Or maybe that only works if one of us gives our life to the writing of it. There's a lot I don't know about working with another Scribe."

"There's a lot I don't know about this house," Collins said, and Joanna jumped. He'd come up behind her without warning and was standing at her back, nearly a head taller and twice as broad as she was, though he slouched a bit as she turned, as if to make himself less intimidating. "Sorry," he said. "I didn't mean to scare you."

"You don't," Joanna said, and it was true. Despite his size and a certain sense of pent-up energy about him, there was something oddly calming about his presence. Nicholas was all sardonic drama, Esther all activity and energy, and Joanna herself had already burst into tears twice today— Collins was easily the least reactive person in the house.

"I was just wondering if maybe you'd give us a tour of the place," Collins said. "While Esther's writing."

"You've seen most of it," Joanna said.

"I mean your collection," Collins said. "Your books."

Nicholas had been folding and numbering the pages that Esther was preparing to write on, but at this he looked up.

"Yes," he said. "I heartily second that request."

Joanna glanced at Esther. "You don't need us?"

"I just fill the pen and go at it, right?" Esther said to Nicholas.

"If by 'go at it' you mean give the process your full concentration and utmost care, yes. Remember, the writing needs to be as legible as possible. If you mess up you can't cross anything out, you'll have to start the whole page over."

"Then no, I don't need you. In fact, probably better for me if you're all out of the room instead of breathing down my neck."

Joanna hesitated. Hiding the collection, protecting it, had been the singular purpose of her life for so long that it seemed impossible to reassign herself so easily. Abe would be appalled she was even considering it . . . but then again, Abe had no room to criticize. Trusting one another over all others was a central tenet of his rules, and he'd lied to her all her life, which meant his rules were at best hypocritical and at worst, moot. If only she could get her feelings to catch up with her logic. Every time she experimented with anything other than grief for her father, like anger, or bitterness, she thought of how he'd looked the last time she'd seen him, sprawled out on the cold, damp ground, drained by that mysterious book.

A book that, thanks to Nicholas, was no longer such a mystery.

"All right," she said.

Nicholas got to his feet then swayed, gripping the back of a chair, face pale. Collins's expression moved from neutral to threatening in one impressive twist of his features, but Joanna was starting to read him well enough to think he might be worried, not homicidal.

"Head rush," said Nicholas. "Lead on."

WHEN JOANNA HAD IMAGINED SHOWING OFF THE COLLECTION, IT WAS always to a faceless fantasy of a person who'd be impressed. She'd imagined somebody following her down the basement stairs and through the trapdoor to the secret underground room, where they'd exclaim at the mystique of the passageway and the locked door, admire the pristinely labeled cabinet of herbs, marvel at the hundreds of antique volumes lining the orderly shelves. "Good god!" the stranger would exclaim. "This is remarkable!" Or something along those lines.

What she hadn't imagined was opening the door for someone who not only had twenty times more books than she did but an entire English mansion to put them in, plus magical blood pulsing through his veins and centuries of lineage to back him up. Flicking on the overhead lights and waiting out the roar of magic, she was almost embarrassed at how small and paltry her collection appeared.

But Nicholas seemed genuinely enthused.

"The Library buys entire private collections fairly often," he said, peering through a glass cabinet, "so I've seen the books themselves, but never visited them in someone's residence. May I?"

"Go ahead," she said, and felt a little thrill of fear and pride as he opened one of the cabinets and slid out a book. Collins was examining the shelves of jarred dried herbs, his face impassive.

"I'm out of vervain," she said, then felt instantly silly when he glanced at her, brow furrowed. Right. Why on earth would he care about the state of her stock?

But he said, "Running low on blackthorn, too. Is there enough for a reading?"

"Enough for three," she said. Behind them, Nicholas was murmuring to himself about dust jackets.

"It's amazing down here," said Collins, and Joanna flushed, unaccountably pleased at his approval, though it shouldn't matter to her what these strangers thought.

"Are they organized?" Nicholas called to her. "What's your system?"

"Right now they're grouped by how many estimated uses they have left," Joanna said, glancing away from Collins. "I reorganize them a lot, though, just for fun."

She was aware, too late, how extremely un-fun this made her sound, but Collins saw her face and said, "Don't worry, Nicholas is no fun, either."

"Well, I haven't been given much of a chance, have I?" Nicholas said, carefully putting the book back in place. "For all we know, I might be absolutely amazing at karaoke."

"Karaoke's for people who suck at dancing." Collins had been squinting at a jar of powdered calendula but he looked up again at Joanna and said, "So where do you keep your wards?"

"Since when are you so curious?" Nicholas said before Joanna could answer. "Usually you're halfway across the room at the mere mention of books."

Collins shrugged. "What can I say. Shit got interesting."

"The wards are here," she said, "up front," and Collins came over to the desk to look, Nicholas following more slowly. The codex of wards sat in pride of place on the stand Abe had built for them, barely larger than her spread hands but the most precious thing she owned. When Nicholas reached out she said, much louder than she meant to, "Don't!"

He jerked away so quickly he stumbled backward into Collins, who'd been leaning over his shoulder to look.

"Sorry," she said. "Only—please, don't touch."

Nicholas raised both hands. "I won't," he said, "I promise. Will you open them for me, maybe? I'd like to see inside."

Joanna found she was trembling slightly, taken aback by her own forceful reaction. It was catching up to her, having so many people in her space, and she felt like her heart rate hadn't settled since they'd arrived. But she took a deep breath and moved to the sink to wash her hands, letting the sound of running water and the hot rasp of the air dryer fill the uncomfortable silence her outburst had left in its wake. When her fingers were perfectly dry, she opened the wards to their first page, calming a little at the familiar feel of the age-softened pages and the tight scrawl of the writing inside.

Nicholas stayed a step back, bending at the waist with his hands in his pockets to look as she showed him each of the fifteen pages one by one.

"Amazing," he said. "It's identical to the ones the Library uses, except my father edited ours so communication spells could pass through. Mirror-spells and the like—they wouldn't work here."

"But I told you my mother put something through a mirror the other day."

"Nothing can come back through, though. In the Library something could. Where did your father get these again?"

"They were Esther's mother's. Her family had them."

"Curious," said Nicholas.

"Joanna, would you add my blood to the wards while we're down here?" Collins said. "So I can go outside without falling over?"

Joanna answered without checking herself for courtesy. "No."

"Come on," Collins said. "Someone's gotta walk the dog."

"Hello," said Nicholas, raising his hand.

"Okay, but someone's gotta walk *me,*" Collins said. "I can't stay cooped up in the house all day, I need a little exercise or I'll go nuts. Please? I'm begging you. I'm the only one who's bound by the wards here. Plus, you can take me off them anytime."

Joanna examined him. He did seem too large to be confined, and he'd been pacing the house all morning—stomping up and down the stairs, rattling around in the kitchen, wrestling way below his weight class with Sir Kiwi. Too, there was something about him she implicitly trusted, and it wasn't (she swore to herself) because he was good-looking. Good-looking, blue-eyed men were usually the least trustworthy of anyone—how many times had she read of a villain with "icy blue eyes"? But Collins's eyes weren't icy at all. They were homey, soft, an old-denim blue like a pair of perfectly worn-in jeans, and they were focused on her now, full of hope. She found she didn't want to say no to him. But . . .

"No," she said again.

Collins gave Nicholas a beseeching look and Joanna recalled the way she and Esther used to ask their mother for something and then move on to Abe when Cecily said no, hoping for a more satisfactory response. She could tell that in this situation, she was Cecily.

"I agree it doesn't seem entirely fair that he's the only one confined to the house," said Nicholas, and then both of them were looking at her, two sets of pleading eyes. Only her family had ever been on these wards—but then, until recently, only her family had ever been in the house at all. Changes were happening whether she was ready for them or not, and after years of resistance, it was easier now to give in.

"Fine," she said, picking up the silver knife from the desk. "Give me your hand."

Collins came forward very quickly, as if afraid she'd change her mind, and rolled up his sleeve unnecessarily. His hand, she saw, was like the rest of his body, large and strong and well-formed. It was lightly calloused, with taut veins that ran along the backside and up his muscular forearm, and his fingers were long and blunt-tipped, his nails well-kept in their broad beds. Joanna stared down, feeling the warm weight of his palm in hers, until Nicholas cleared his throat and she jerked back to attention.

She swallowed hard and pressed the knife into Collins's pointer finger, then watched as he pressed it to the back of the codex right next to her own bloody fingerprint. Right where Abe and Cecily's blood had once stained the page. She thought she felt the wards shiver as they shifted to accommodate him and he stepped back, staring down at his still-bleeding finger as if he couldn't meet her gaze.

"I'm sorry," Collins said, voice quiet. "I know how hard all this is for you."

Joanna flexed the hand that had been holding his. "It's all right," she said.

She closed the wards and set them back behind their glass door on the desk, above the vampire book, which on Nicholas's insistence was tightly wrapped in an old jacket. She could still hear it, though, a deep, discordant gong cutting through the peaceful hum of the other books, a wrong note played over and over.

Nicholas's attention, too, was on the book.

"Do you mind," he said, "if I take this back upstairs with me? I'd like to have another look at it."

"Be my guest," said Joanna.

UPSTAIRS, ESTHER WAS BOWED OVER HER WORK, THE FINISHED PAGES accumulating across the dining room table to dry. Nicholas gave them a professional once-over, looking down his nose like the judge of a pony show, saying, "Very nice, very nice, oh, *very* nice," until Esther reached out to shove him away.

"You're making it extremely hard to concentrate," she said. "What if I copy a word wrong and accidentally turn Collins into a chicken?"

"I did notice you're out of eggs," Nicholas said to Joanna.

Collins himself had vanished with Sir Kiwi as soon as they'd come back upstairs, slamming the door behind him like he couldn't wait to get out. As she watched him leave, Joanna had felt a flicker of dejection that she decided was jealousy. She would have liked to take a walk, herself, but was nervous at the thought of leaving Esther and Nicholas alone in the house, writing their magic. It was partially her paranoia—she didn't want to leave them without supervision—and partially her desire to be included even though she was powerless to help.

After a while she contented herself with going out onto the cold porch, where she was somewhat disappointed to find that Collins was nowhere to be seen—he must have taken Sir Kiwi into the woods. But she smiled in delight when she saw that the cat was waiting for her, twining around the railing with his tail raised. She'd been worried the unfamiliar smells of dog and people would scare him off.

"It's a party in there," she said, reaching down to stroke his head. As always, she was amazed by how warm he was, how present. "Are you sure you won't come in?"

He pushed his face against her fingers and wove himself through her legs, and she wondered if he'd let her pick him up. She wanted badly to hold him in her arms. But when she reached down with her other hand and touched his side, he leaped away.

"All right," she said as he retreated, his cidery eyes admonishing. "I'm sorry. I didn't mean to rush you."

She couldn't help wishing someone with a kind voice would say this very thing to her.

Collins was coming back; she could see his figure between the branches and hear the crackle of twigs and dead leaves beneath his heavy feet as he moved up the path. He emerged from the thicket behind the overgrown swing set, Sir Kiwi's leash wound around one hand, his eyes focused on the ground in front of him, his mouth grim. When he glanced up and saw Joanna standing on the porch, he froze.

"What're you doing?" said Collins.

"Saying hi to the cat," she said.

Collins frowned, then seemed to notice the way Sir Kiwi was wheezing at the end of her tether. "The cat," he repeated, as the animal in question bounded off the porch and streaked toward the woods. Sir Kiwi let out an agonized yap and Collins stared off into the dark trees as the cat vanished.

"Are you all right?" Joanna said.

"It's nice out here," he said. "You clear that path yourself?"

"My dad and I did," she said. "And Esther. Years ago, when we were kids."

"But you've kept it clear. That must be a lot of work." Sir Kiwi had trotted up the porch steps and was straining her leash to try and jump on Joanna's legs. Collins stayed a few paces away on the grass, looking up at her. "How far does it go?"

"It circles the property," she said. "Tracing the outline of the wards. It's about three miles altogether. Did you get to the stream?"

Collins nodded. He seemed to be relaxing from whatever bad mood had gripped him. "Yeah," he said. "It's beautiful out there."

Again, as she had in the basement, Joanna felt a flush of pleasure; and again, she told herself it did not matter what Collins thought. But he was right, she had worked hard on that path, and in so many ways it was a part of her just as the books were, or this porch, or her own blood. It was her blood, after all, that kept this house safe within the circle of forest.

Collins started up the stairs, boards creaking, and she stepped back to give him room. He paused right in front of her, his eyes locked somewhere over her shoulder, his lips set in a thin, unhappy line. It was a face full of bad news, and she was suddenly certain that whatever he was about to say next, she didn't want to hear it. She braced herself, pulse climbing, as his gaze lifted briefly to hers.

He said, "Everything here is beautiful."

Then he brushed past her and into the house, Sir Kiwi leading the way. Joanna stood, astonished, and confused, listening to the slam of the door behind him. His expression had been as dire as she'd yet seen it, tension radiating from every line of his body despite his words.

All of them were under a lot of stress, she reminded herself, and Collins no less than any of the others. He must be anxious about the spell Esther was writing, preoccupied by the thought that it might not work, or even by the thought that it would, that soon whatever silence he'd been under would be broken. Constraints could be comforting. Joanna knew this better than anyone.

When she opened the door to go back inside, the sound of the vampire book hit her all over again. Collins was in the foyer wiping Sir Kiwi's muddy little paws with an old towel, but he released the last hind leg as Joanna came in, and when Sir Kiwi skittered away, he went after her. Joanna followed him back into the living room, where they found Nicholas sitting on the couch with the book to one side, massaging his temples. Joanna thought, slightly impressed, that she had never met any human or object who managed to look so deluxe and so depleted at the same time.

"What's wrong?" Collins demanded, hovering over him.

"Stand down," Nicholas said, "good lord. You're not actually my bodyguard anymore, remember? Nothing's wrong, only a headache. And this book is foul."

The sound was stuck in Joanna's head, a bitter film on the back of her tongue that she tasted every time she swallowed. Knowing what the book was made of hadn't changed the sound itself, but it was harder now to hear the wrongness of it and not think of skin, bone, sinew, suffering.

"Are you done looking?" Joanna said.

"For now," Nicholas said, frowning. "I keep thinking there's something more, something I'm not understanding, but . . . I don't know."

Esther wandered in from the dining room, stretching, and leaned against the doorjamb.

"Can I put it back in the basement?" Joanna said. "It's really unpleasant to listen to."

"Yes," Nicholas said, and Collins, who'd been about to sit on the sofa beside Nicholas, stood again. Then he started to sit. Then he changed his mind and stood. Nicholas frowned up at him and Joanna was glad she wasn't the only one who'd noticed his weird behavior. "Collins," said Nicholas, "are you all right?"

"You're finished writing?" Collins asked Esther.

"Yes, a second ago," said Esther.

Collins turned to Nicholas. "What next?"

"Now we wait for the pages to dry so Esther can bind them."

"How long will that take?"

"Not long, thirty minutes? Forty?"

"Don't put the book back downstairs yet," Collins said, eyes locking with Joanna's. His voice sounded strained, like he was fighting to keep it level. "Please. Not until the spell's ready."

"Why on earth not?" Nicholas said.

"I can't tell you."

Joanna exchanged a baffled glance with Esther, the book droning on the coffee table like a distant chainsaw. "Can I put it in another room, at least?"

"Anywhere except the basement," said Collins.

Wanting to allay whatever inexplicable anxiety had hold of him, Joanna went to stash the book in the pantry, where its low, unpleasant buzz would be muffled by several doors, but she could still hear it faintly as she moved around the house. It was quieter, however; bearable.

Esther's ink dried quickly, and Joanna watched in interest as Nicholas walked her through the process of binding. He ended up doing most of it himself, a quick coptic binding sewn with ordinary black cotton thread, the leather cover cut from an old jacket and stitched on instead of glued to save time. The binding itself did not matter much, Nicholas explained, so long as the book was bound. Ancient forms of magic, like scrolls or prelinguistic carvings, had once had to be similarly "finished" before the spell would take effect—the blood-mixed clay had to be fired, the kollesis perfectly aligned.

She watched Nicholas stitch the binding with a practiced hand and marveled at how many of her lifelong questions could be answered by the simple fact of his presence.

Nicholas put the final stitch in place and tied off the thread, then snapped it between his teeth and grinned up at Esther. "Congratulations," he said. "You've written your first book."

"Don't congratulate me until we know it works," Esther said, but Joanna could hear quite clearly that it would. The finished product looked very little like the other books in Joanna's collection: its pages were comprised of cheap white printer paper and its binding was neat but very simple, its cover a stiff and unadorned leather. It wasn't the appearance that Joanna cared about. She cared about the sound. And this homemade volume, written in a single day by her own sister's hand with blood from her own sister's body, hummed like a beehive in the heat of July.

"All right, let's do this," Collins said, his entire body practically twitching with anticipation. "Read it to me."

Beneath the comforting sound of Esther's spell in her hands, Joanna could still hear the ugly murmur of the book in the pantry, a tug on her mind's ear. She set the new book back on the dining room table and turned toward the kitchen. "The vampire is distracting. Let me just put it down—"

"Leave it," Collins snapped, and she whirled on him, stung by the harshness in his voice. He cleared his throat, making a clear effort to modulate his tone. "Come on, Joanna, please. Read me the spell first, then do whatever you have to do in the basement."

A jitter of nerves surged through Joanna's body. "Why don't you want me to go in the basement?"

Collins blanched. "It's not—I didn't say that."

"You didn't have to." Joanna was already moving away from him, away from Nicholas and Esther's disconcerted faces and into the kitchen, ignoring Collins calling her name, his voice a full panicked pitch higher than she'd ever heard it. She didn't stop to grab the book from the pantry; a sudden, certain instinct had shoved her concerns firmly elsewhere.

As she pushed open the wooden door in the basement, she heard immediately that something felt different—or sounded different. It was like listening to a song she knew by heart and realizing one of the instruments was missing from the background. Her pulse was racing even before she went to the desk and registered the off-kilter space of it.

The shelf that held the wards, a shelf that had never in her entire life been empty, was.

She fell to her knees, searching behind the desk, under it, around it, as if she'd carelessly knocked the wards off somehow, but she knew she wouldn't have done that, she knew that wasn't what had happened, and she ran back through the basement and up the stairs without even locking the door behind her. She burst back into the dining room and went straight to Collins, rocking to a stop in front of him, so breathless with rage that she could barely get the words out.

"What have you done?" she said.

Collins looked down at her, his face white, his pupils huge in his blue eyes. He swallowed hard but said nothing.

"What?" Nicholas said. "What are you talking about?"

She kept her eyes on Collins's, refusing to look away. Her whole body was shaking with adrenaline and fear and hurt. "He took my book of wards," she said.

Still Collins was silent. Nicholas said, "That's ridiculous. He didn't touch your wards."

Collins cleared his throat. He shook his head. When he opened his mouth, his voice was rough.

"Yes," he said. "I did. I took them. And I won't give them back."

27

For a moment after Collins spoke, no one else did. But to Nicholas it did not feel like silence. There was a roaring in his ears as the blood rushed to his head and his mind brayed a denial despite Collins's own confession. Collins stepped back until he hit the dining room wall, and looked from Joanna to Nicholas, his expression bleak. Nicholas knew his shock and hurt had to be written plainly on his face, but he couldn't control his expression even to salvage his broken pride.

"Collins," Joanna said. Her voice was uneven, and she put both hands on the dining room table as if she couldn't keep her balance. Nicholas was glad he was already sitting down. "It is five o'clock. We need to set the wards in two hours or the house won't be protected anymore, it won't be hidden, anyone could find us if they know where to look."

She was giving him the benefit of the doubt, which Nicholas thought was ludicrous. Collins obviously knew exactly what hiding the wards would do. Esther stepped around the side of the table, fists balled at her sides like she was preparing to fight him, and Collins crossed his arms over his chest—not in his usual tough-guy way, but like he was protecting himself, like he was scared.

"Where did you put them?" Joanna said, and when Collins didn't answer, she turned to Nicholas and Esther and said, "We have to search the house."

"They're not in the house," Collins said. "Joanna. I'm so sorry. But you're not gonna find them."

Joanna slammed her hand down on the table, the gesture so unexpected that Nicholas jumped. It was the loudest sound he'd heard Joanna make since they arrived. "Tell me where they are."

"I need you to read me the spell," Collins said.

"Not until you give me back my wards."

Already Nicholas was rewriting his understanding of the past few days, polishing the lens on every interaction he'd had with Collins and recasting it all in a sick, sallow film of shame. He thought with lurching disgust of the version of himself he'd been only minutes before: a pitiable person who'd believed he and Collins might actually be becoming friends.

"Maram told me to do it," Collins said, his eyes darting up and down between Joanna and Nicholas. "She told me the place we were headed had wards and I had to get them down as soon as possible. She said to tell you when I'd done it."

Maram, too, then, had been pretending. She'd never really given a shit about Nicholas; he was merely a pawn in the Library's inexplicable game, like he'd always been a pawn. He couldn't look at Collins. He gripped the wooden arms of his chair and stared at the table instead, at Esther's first book. Only moments ago he'd been thrilled at her success and thrilled at the prospect of breaking Collins's NDA, of finally learning his name. He was so, so stupid.

"Why?" Esther demanded. "Why would she tell you to do that?"

"I don't know!"

"You didn't think to *ask*?"

"Obviously I asked!" Collins and Esther were bellowing at one another now. "She couldn't tell me, because she's probably under the same—" he broke off, hacking into his arm, unable even to name the spell that kept him silent.

"Oh, convenient," Esther said. "You can't explain yourself because you'll choke to death if you try. Perfect."

"Wait," said Joanna. "That cough." She looked suddenly more intent than furious, peering at Collins's face, which was flushed from lack of oxygen. "Collins, is that what happens when you try to talk about something you've been spelled not to?"

Collins didn't answer, because the NDA prohibited answering questions about itself, but Esther said, "If he's even really under a spell in the first place."

"Hold on," Joanna said, stepping backward so quickly she hit the dining room wall. A watercolor painting of a mountain trembled in its frame. "Hold on."

Collins had recovered his breath. He said, "Maram gave me a message. She said we have to find the thing Richard will use to find us."

"What the hell does that mean?" Esther demanded.

"I don't know," Collins said, and took a step toward Nicholas, who drew back in his chair on instinct. Collins stopped moving. "Say something," he said, "please."

"Hold on," Joanna repeated, but she seemed to be talking to herself and Nicholas's head was spinning too fast to worry about her right now. His focus was all on Collins, on Maram, on the stolen wards and the unbroken NDA, but none of it made sense.

"Even if he's telling the truth," Esther said, "and he thinks he's somehow, I don't know, *helping* by hiding the wards—"

"*He* doesn't think he's helping," Collins said, "he knows!"

"—even if," Esther repeated, louder, "he thinks he's helping, why the hell does he trust Maram, and why the hell should we?"

"Read me that book, Joanna," Collins said, and reached out like he might touch her, then curled his hand shut as she, like Nicholas, shied away from him. "Please. I'm begging you."

Nicholas saw that Joanna had taken the newly written book in her arms, was holding it protectively away from Collins, backing up from the dining room table and toward the door leading to the kitchen. "Your cough," Joanna said to Collins, "I've heard it before, the same exact one."

"What?" Esther said. "Where?"

"Mom." She clutched the book more tightly and looked at Nicholas. "I think our mother is under the same spell. Silence. An NDA."

Her words brought a moment of quiet.

"That particular technology," Nicholas said, "was developed by the Library. By my father. I've seen his notes."

"So what does that mean?" Joanna said, her face pale.

Nicholas thought of Abe's awful book. "It means that at some point, both your parents must've had a connection to the Library."

Joanna lifted her chin and drew herself up to her full height, which Nicholas only belatedly realized was tall, maybe taller than he. The long hair, the big eyes, the quiet voice, it all made her seem small, but she wasn't.

"I want to use this on my mother," Joanna said. "Not on Collins."

"Joanna," Collins said, his voice low and imploring, and she looked like she was about to start spitting fire.

"I don't owe you a goddamn thing," she said.

"But I stole your wards," he tried. "Don't you want to know *why*?"

"It won't work, anyway," Nicholas said. "I wrote Collins's NDA, I know the language of the original, so I know the language needed to undo it. There's no possible chance I wrote your mother's, I imagine she's under an older version, from my father's tenure as Scribe."

Joanna looked crushed. "But—"

"Stop, all of you," Esther said, clapping her hands to her ears. "One thing at a time! Look, Nicholas asked Collins why he trusts Maram, and that's something we need to know above all else. She's our puppet master, she brought us here, we need to figure out *why*."

"Yes," Collins said, pointing at her.

"I wrote that book," Esther told Joanna. "So I think I should decide what we do with it. And I want to break Collins's NDA."

"Thank you!" Collins said.

"Nicholas?" Esther said.

Nicholas was very used to being ordered around. He wanted to protest, to assert himself, but the truth was he didn't know what to assert himself *toward,* and there was a not-insignificant part of him that showed its neck at the commanding tone in Esther's voice. "Your call," he said.

"Jo," Esther said, her voice noticeably softer when she addressed her sister. "Is this all right? Will you read the spell?"

Joanna looked down at the book in her hands, thumbs moving back and forth over the leather cover. She nodded at last, resigned. "I'll get the herbs and the knife," she said.

"Meet us in the living room," Nicholas said. "Collins should be sitting down for this."

Collins sat on the couch and Joanna started to sit next to him, then seemed to think better of it, and sat on the coffee table before him instead, the book in her lap. Nicholas stood a pace or two away, arms folded, while Esther perched in the leather recliner, one foot pulled up on the cushion like she might spring away. Joanna glanced between the two of them nervously.

"Nicholas, could you maybe not loom so much?"

"I'm not looming, I'm—"

"Standing over me, glaring," said Joanna. "It's making me nervous."

Grudgingly, Nicholas stepped back. "Better?"

Joanna nodded. In a voice that started soft and then went hard, like she was remembering to be angry, she said, "Collins, are you ready?"

"I'm ready," he said.

She opened the book on her lap and took a deep, slow breath. Then, without so much as a flinch, she stabbed the point of the knife into her ring finger and dipped the bloody tip into the bowl of herbs. Collins watched her every movement, his posture tense and anticipatory, his breathing fast. Joanna pressed her finger to the page and began.

Nicholas had expected her to be a tentative reader, small-voiced and uncertain, but he kept forgetting she had been doing this her entire life. Her voice was confident and continuous and beautifully modulated, rising and falling as if she were in conversation with the words. Once she began reading, she did not lose focus: not when Sir Kiwi leaped onto the back of the couch to yap out the window at a squirrel, not when Nicholas had a wave of dizziness and sat heavily on the piano bench, not when

Collins's hands began to tremble in his lap and he started swallowing convulsively.

Nicholas and Esther were both leaning forward, Nicholas watching so intently his eyes were getting dry, and a few times Collins looked back up at him, jaw set, to give him a little nod that Nicholas couldn't interpret. Nicholas didn't feel the magic as it began to work but he knew Joanna would be hearing it, and he could see its effects in the lines of Collins's body, his shoulders stiffening, the tendons standing out on his neck, his shaking hands balling into fists as he breathed through the discomfort of the lifting spell.

Joanna let the final word ring out and Collins gasped, a sound like water sluicing through a grate. He slumped forward, one hand on the couch to support himself, the other flying to his throat, wheezing.

Joanna closed the book and set it on the low coffee table, and Nicholas demanded, "Well?"

"Give me a fucking second, Jesus," Collins rasped.

"But it worked," Esther said. She had gotten to her feet and her mouth was twitching like it wanted to break into a smile, but she wouldn't let it. "I wrote a spell," she said, "and the spell worked!"

"We don't know that yet," Nicholas said. "Something happened, but—"

"My name," Collins said experimentally, "is Nicholas."

"What?"

Collins had an expression Nicholas had never seen before, a grin that transformed his whole face, lit up his eyes, erased the scowl lines around his mouth. "That's my first name," he said. "Nicholas."

"What?" said Nicholas. "No."

"Nicholas Collins," said Collins, and held out a hand toward him. Before he quite knew what he was doing, Nicholas was leaning over the coffee table to take it, Collins's palm very warm against his own perpetually freezing fingers. They shook.

"All this time I've been guessing," Nicholas said, "and you're telling me we have the same name?"

"Well, I've always gone by Nick," said Nick Collins. "Holy shit, it feels good to say that out loud!" He glanced at Joanna and, somewhat more tentatively, offered her his hand, too. "Nick Collins?" he said.

Nicholas watched the uncertainty play out on Joanna's face—one beat, two, and she didn't move, Collins's own hopeful face beginning to fall as the seconds ticked by. Then, right as Collins began to pull his hand away, she reached out with an abrupt, decisive gesture, and Nicholas couldn't help but feel secondhand relief as Collins beamed at her, cradling her hand in both of his. He turned toward Esther next, but then seemed to think better of it—she was literally sitting on her hands.

"Wait," said Nicholas. "What am I supposed to call you now?"

"Collins," said Collins decisively. "And I can hear them, by the way. Books. Magic. Whatever. Every bodyguard you've ever had can hear them, that's why we get recruited."

"But you hate books," Nicholas said, dazed.

"I didn't used to," said Collins. "I used to love them. I worked security for a collective in Boston who pooled their books—their homebase is Lisa's house, she and Tansy are members, like I used to be. My little sister Angie, too. That's how the Library found me, when they wanted to buy our collection and ended up buying me instead. My friends, including Lisa and Tansy, and probably Angie . . . they all think I sold out for the paycheck, but it wasn't like that." His face shuttered. "Turns out I'm a hot commodity, a trained bodyguard who can hear magic. When I turned down their job offer the first time, Richard sweetened the deal with a little blackmail. The Library offered money for our collection, sure, but Richard's got enough of his own magic that he doesn't need to pay to take ours. Buying the books was just the easier way. He said so long as I came to work for the Library, if I submitted to the NDA and stayed in line, the collective would be safe. And he didn't just mean the books. He was threatening my friends, too." He glanced at Esther, seeming to seek some sort of sympathy. "And my sister."

"But you're not in line now," Joanna said.

"No," Collins said grimly, "I'm not. But Maram told me if I got Nicholas safely out of the Library, she'd make sure no one in the collective would be hurt."

Esther snorted. "And you believed her, just like that?"

"Give me some credit," Collins said. "She let me read her a truth spell. She wouldn't have been able to promise if she didn't really mean it."

So that was why Richard had found Nicholas's last truth spell so faded. He started to get to his feet, felt a flood of nausea and leaned hard on the piano keys without meaning to. A discordant clang made Joanna jump like a startled rabbit. "Sorry," he said.

"Sit down," Collins said, and Nicholas sat. He wasn't sure if the waves of vertigo were from Collins's words or from an underproduction of red blood cells, but either way, he was feeling distinctly unwell. He snapped his fingers for Sir Kiwi, who trotted over, black eyes bright, having a grand old time. She sat obligingly on his foot.

Esther had settled back in her chair, but she kept changing position, restless. "So, Maram gave you a bunch of marching orders and told you if you did what she said, she wouldn't sic Richard on your friends. Fine. That still doesn't exactly sound like a reason to trust someone. In fact, it sounds a whole lot like more blackmail."

"That's not why I trust her," said Collins. "I trust her because she's protecting someone on the outside, too, only Richard doesn't know about it."

Nicholas felt a jolt of agitation he couldn't explain, a sensation of falling, and Collins cleared his throat.

"The night of the gala," he said to Nicholas, and hesitated. "I think you already figured out they staged that attacker, right?"

Nicholas nodded. "The bees," he said.

"What attacker?" Esther said. "What *bees*?"

"I had to fake-kill a guy to scare Nicholas into thinking people were after him," said Collins. "Maram put a spell on my gun, it turns bullets into bees."

"It's a beautifully written spell," Nicholas murmured.

"Real, living bees?" Joanna said with interest.

"I don't know, they definitely buzzed," Collins said, and waved his hand; the bees were beside the point. Sir Kiwi took this wave as an invitation and got off Nicholas's foot to leap onto the couch next to Collins, circling once before settling next to his leg. Nicholas felt a stab of annoyance at her disloyalty. "Maram did it in her study, the spell, with Richard watching." Collins cut his eyes over to Nicholas and then looked down, hand settling on Sir Kiwi's head. "I didn't like it, obviously, but I didn't have a choice. And I couldn't tell you. I'm sorry. I would have. I wanted to."

Nicholas was having too many feelings to add forgiveness to the list. "What were the exact terms of your NDA?" he said.

"I couldn't say anything about my personal life," Collins said, ticking it off on his fingers, "I couldn't say anything about the Library itself, and I couldn't repeat a damn thing Richard or Maram said to me. Not in writing or aloud. That's a pretty standard contract, by the way. Maram's probably under a similar one. Anyway, she did the spell, gave me back my gun, Richard left the room, then she asked me . . ." He swallowed. "Asked me how I felt about watching you bleed to death."

Nicholas wasn't expecting this and it hit him somewhere between his throat and heart. "I—what? I'm not, I wasn't—"

"Yeah, you were," Collins said. "Slowly, maybe. But even in the few months I was with the Library I could see it was getting worse, Richard wasn't giving you any time to recover. I know how much blood a person can lose before it becomes a problem. I knew it was becoming a problem." Collins cleared his throat. "I told her I didn't like it much."

"Virtuous," said Esther.

"That's when Maram told me she had a plan," he said, glaring at Esther. "A plan to end it—not only what was happening to you, but the Library itself. My contract, everyone's contract, the whole hellhole of a place, collapsed."

"Oh, fun," said Esther. "There's nothing I love more than being an unwitting participant in someone else's big dramatic scheme."

"No," Nicholas said, shaking his head, "That's not possible. Maram loves the Library. She always has. She sought the Library out, not the other way around, she convinced Richard to hire her as soon as she was out of Oxford." He said it again because it bore repeating. "She loves the Library. And she loves Richard. What possible reason could she have for wanting to destroy it?"

Collins ran his fingers through Sir Kiwi's fur, looking suddenly nervous. "I asked the same thing. And she looked at me for a long time, like she was deciding something. Then she went into her bedroom and came out with a photograph—an old one, like from a disposable camera, with that little orange date in the corner. The image was murky, kind of green, it looked like a rainy landscape . . . but there was a little bit of dried blood in the corner. When she rubbed it off, the image changed."

He wasn't looking at any of them anymore, seemingly focused on stroking Sir Kiwi, whose tongue was out with pleasure from the attention.

"It was a lady in a hospital bed," he said. "Holding a new baby. It took me a second to realize the lady was Maram. She was a lot younger, but she looked pretty much the same."

Esther raised a skeptical eyebrow. "What does a baby have to do with anything?"

Nicholas stared at her—at that dark, arched brow. He had seen that expression before. Seen it nearly every day of his life. He had even practiced it in the mirror. And he knew, all at once, why Esther had looked familiar when he'd first seen her through the spelled glass.

It was there, in the sweep of her jaw, the decisive bow of her upper lip, the heart-shaped hairline. Those faint lines in her forehead that would grow deeper as her eyebrows kept up their constant dance. It wasn't a direct resemblance, less photo-image and more impressionist. But as soon as he noticed, he could not unsee it.

She looked like Maram.

Maram, who'd gathered all of them here together in this room in the middle of rural Vermont, who had appeared in Nicholas's life at the same time Esther's mother had vanished from hers.

"What?" Esther said, because Nicholas was staring at her—and so were Collins and Joanna. Esther's face was arranged in a sort of helpless confusion, which was how Nicholas knew she wasn't confused at all.

She, like Nicholas and Joanna, was starting to understand what Collins was about to tell them.

"The NDA didn't let her explain anything straight out, so at the time, the only thing I understood about the photo was that Maram had a kid," Collins said. "Big secret, sure, but not enough to make me trust her—and I told her so. She said to wait, she said soon I'd figure it out. I think that's why she told Nicholas how to break into Richard's office, not only so he'd recognize his eye, but so I'd see the Scribe-seeking spell and look through those mirrors to Antarctica. And I did figure it out. I realized Richard's spell had finally found another Scribe: someone else to bleed, someone else to kill. And the person he'd found was Maram's daughter."

PART THREE

BLOODLINE

28

Nicholas had no memory of his own parents and few photographs. The only pictures he had of his mother were from her theater days, playbills and old cast photos in which she was nearly always in costume, her smiling lips painted, her skin unnaturally smooth and matte, her dark hair curled. He'd read the text of all the plays she'd acted in and knew she'd often been typecast as an ingenue or a naïf, a lovely girl whose narrative tensions existed not for the sake of furthering her character but for dramatic or comedic effect—and this was the role she seemed to play offstage, too. A young woman unlucky enough to fall in love with the Library's prized Scribe, her presence in Nicholas's life like her presence in all her plays: a tragedy only insofar as it fed his own. He didn't know her well enough to cast her as anything else. In all the photographs, she looked like nobody's mother.

Maram did not look like anyone's mother, either. As a kid he'd sometimes indulged in the fantasy that she'd marry Richard, tying herself legally to Nicholas forever and officially solidifying what he already thought of as their family unit, but he made the mistake of asking her once and she'd laughed at him.

"My relationship with your uncle succeeds because it's based on our love for the Library," she had told him. "Not our love for one another."

"You don't love him?"

They were having a rare afternoon out, just the two of them, at a cafe on the South Bank where Nicholas had spent most of his lunch staring around in wonder at all the chattering strangers. Now Maram set her fork down and regarded him solemnly.

"Do you want the grown-up answer," she said, "or an answer fit for a ten-year-old?"

Nicholas scoffed. What ten-year-old would choose the latter?

"I love Richard because he has never wanted me to be other than what I am," Maram said. "And that is a scholar. I'm dedicated first and foremost to the Library, to our books and to the preservation of our knowledge, and Richard loves this about me."

"So you love him because he loves you," said Nicholas, disappointed at the lack of romance in this reply.

"That doesn't sound like a good reason to love someone?"

Nicholas didn't know. He wondered if that was why he loved Richard, too; because Richard loved him, or at least came closer to loving him than anyone else in his life. Was that because Nicholas, like Maram, was an extension of the Library? Was the Library the only thing that held them together?

After that, he'd tried to put away his fantasies of family. Maram was a guardian, a friend, she would never be anything else. But the truth was that for quite a long time, if someone had come up to him and told him that for all these years, Maram had secretly been his mother, he'd have been ecstatic.

He would not have shrugged his shoulders and said, as Esther did, "Unlikely."

"Unlikely?" Nicholas repeated. "Esther, you look just like her."

Joanna said, her voice careful. "It does make sense."

"No, it doesn't," said Esther. "It doesn't tell us why she sent us here to Vermont, or why she told Collins to drop the wards, or what she wants from us. It doesn't tell us anything at all."

Nicholas was too agitated to stay sitting. He let his feet carry him to the far end of the room and then back. "You're wrong," he said. "It does explain a few things. As a thought exercise, let's say Maram is your mother and has been acting to keep you out of danger. That would certainly explain why she passed those tickets to you through the mirror: to get you off the research base and away from Tretheway. And it would explain why she's decided all of a sudden to go against the best interests of the institution she's been dedicated to for the past twenty-five years. You overstayed your time in Antarctica, the Scribe-seeking spell finally located you, and Maram had no choice but to act."

"She's not going against the Library's interests," Esther said, "she's playing right into them! She sent us here, *together,* and told Collins to drop the wards as soon as he could. She's made it easier for Richard to get us both in one place, not harder."

"But the Scribe-seeking spell is over for the year," Nicholas said. "Dropping the wards doesn't mean Richard will suddenly know where we are, not unless we stay for another entire year, waiting. He has no other way of tracking—"

The words dried up in his mouth, because across the room Joanna's face was suffused with fear. She was looking at him and shaking her head.

"Oh," he said. "Shit."

The book in the pantry. The book clearly emblazoned with the Library's tracking spell.

"I rest my case," said Esther. "So I propose we stop forcing sense out of a nonsensical situation, take that book, and throw it in the ocean."

"An ocean won't hurt it," said Joanna, "not while it's in progress."

"I could hurt it," Nicholas said. "So could Esther."

"No," said Collins. He'd moved in front of the living room doorway, his breadth crowding the space and his posture radiating a coiled, preparatory energy, like a predator about to spring. Nicholas sometimes forgot how large Collins was—how large he could make himself.

Esther stalked toward him. "What do you mean, no?"

"Do you have any idea," Collins said, "how many people the Library has had killed over the years? How many books they've bribed for and blackmailed for and straight-up stolen? We're talking centuries of this shit. A magical monopoly. Why do you think the two of you are the only Scribes left? The rest of you died writing the Library's spells. The Library doesn't want to 'preserve knowledge,' it just wants to preserve its own power, it wants to be the only game in town so everyone has to buy tickets and come watch." He turned to Nicholas. "I don't know what happened to your parents, but I'm willing to bet it wasn't—what'd your uncle tell you? A robbery gone wrong? Bullshit, Nicholas. That's bullshit. Your father died for his blood just like every other Scribe the Library's ever had. Just like you will."

Each one of Collins's words hit Nicholas like a blow, his ears ringing.

"I think Maram really does have a plan," Collins said. "I think she's sick of Richard's shit and ready to do something about it, finally, and I'm ready, too. I don't want to run, and I don't want to hurl anything into the ocean, I want to figure out what she wants us to do and see if we can execute it. She wanted you to know the wards were down and she said to find the thing—the thing Richard will use to find you. She's gotta be talking about that book. There's something there, we just have to figure it out. Please."

This last he said very softly, a direct appeal. Collins's eyes were steady and his expression so earnest Nicholas had to look away. Joanna was chewing her bottom lip, moving her long hair from shoulder to shoulder, her brow knitted. Esther was examining her fingernails as if bored with the whole thing.

"How much time do we have before the wards drop?" Nicholas asked Joanna.

"About two hours."

"So we give it two hours," Nicholas said, meeting Collins's gaze. "Two hours to think this through and decide if Maram's plan is intended to hurt us or help us."

"And what happens afterward?"

"You give me back my wards and we reset them," Joanna said.

"She said to let 'em drop," Collins said, though he hunched his shoulders apologetically. "I'm going to let 'em drop."

"Then we go," Esther said. "We destroy the book, leave this house, and we don't come back."

Joanna took a shuddering breath but didn't protest. Nicholas saw determination flash through her face and he had a sinking feeling that Joanna's own plans did not involve running. Even after everything she'd learned, she wouldn't leave the books or the house around them. He could see the truth of this in every line of her body and he knew Esther saw it, too.

"Thank you," Collins said. His posture changed, shoulders coming down, muscles relaxing, seeming instantly smaller. Nicholas wondered how he'd learned to do that, then wondered if he'd ever get a chance to find out, to actually get to know this person with whom he kept trusting his life.

"Will you go and get the book again?" Nicholas said to Joanna, and her nostrils flared as if she might protest, but then she nodded and turned to fetch it from the pantry. No one spoke until she came back and handed Nicholas the book, which he took with a cringing sense of revulsion, as if he might find it oozing with decay beneath his fingers. But it looked the same as ever, almost ordinary, softbound and neat. He turned to the first page and sat at the piano bench and thought about the draft he'd seen in Richard's study.

Flesh of my flesh.

Human remains—the remains of a Scribe—had bound the book. Whoever's life was being extended had been bound to a piece of that same body.

He thought of Richard's study itself, curios glimmering from every corner: stuffed birds, mummified bats, clay animals, all of them probably attached to spells. He thought about how Richard never got sick, how he'd only ever hired bodyguards for Nicholas and Maram, never for himself. And he thought of that portrait of the surgeon behind Richard's desk, his ancestor, founder of the Library. Alike to Richard in nearly all aspects except for those cold eyes glittering from behind spectacles. He thought about how he'd never seen a photograph of Richard as a young man, how he'd always looked exactly as he did now: fiftyish, handsome, the gray at his temples never encroaching further.

He thought again about the portrait. About the Library's first Scribe, the surgeon's own sister, and that single femur in the ivory frame. *Bone of my bone.*

He had assumed Richard wanted to find Esther so he could force Nicholas to use the draft in the binder, force Nicholas to drain Esther's blood and slice up her body and write a spell that would let Richard live forever.

What else had he misunderstood?

The other three had begun talking in low voices as he read, but he didn't wait for a pause. He spoke over them.

"It's Richard's life."

Three faces swiveled toward him.

"Richard's life," he repeated, holding the book gingerly. "I'm certain of it. He doesn't seem to age, he never gets ill . . ." He was shaking as he spoke, freezing cold even so close to the hot belly of the woodstove. "I think he's been around for a long time. I think maybe he was the person who started the Library."

Joanna put her hands to her mouth, glancing at her sister, whose eyelid twitched infinitesimally though she was otherwise still. Nicholas held his breath. He didn't know if he could bear being challenged on this, didn't know if he had the energy to argue something he knew instinctually, as sure as he'd been when he realized Esther was a Scribe. He prepared to launch a logical defense.

Collins said, "Yeah. That sounds pretty much on par with the level of fucked-up we've been dealing with."

Nicholas looked at him gratefully, but Esther said, "Even if that's true, it's just another complication, another question."

"No," said Nicholas. "No, it's not a question. It's an answer."

No matter how he turned it over in his mind, there was only one reason he could think that Maram might have sent both him and Esther—her daughter, a Scribe—to this house in the middle of nowhere. Only one reason she had sent him to Richard's study and forced him to confront the truth of Richard's cruelty, then twisted her way in convoluted circles around the impositions of her NDA to direct their attention to this book, Richard's book, Richard's life.

The book had been written by two Scribes. Two Scribes were needed to destroy it. But there was a safeguard written into the spell, a protection that was also a loophole.

Only mine own blood can end me.

One of the Scribes had to be Nicholas.

Esther was leaning toward him now, lifting the book from his hands, and he let her. He had no strength to hold on.

29

The memory came back to Esther as soon as her fingers touched the darkly oiled cover of Richard's book. She remembered where she had seen it before.

Her father crouched in front of her saying, "Can you rip this up? We're just trying something out."

The strangeness of feeling paper that wouldn't tear, how its flimsiness felt impossible, the frustration of failure and Abe's disappointed gaze. She'd held a match to it, thrown it into the woodstove, submerged it under soapy water in the sink. No matter what she'd done to it, the book remained intact.

"What if I'm wrong?" Nicholas was saying. "What if Esther and I destroy the book and it wasn't Richard's after all, it's some innocent soul who'll drop dead in the middle of Sunday dinner with their family, what if—"

"Innocent soul?" Collins said. "Nobody who got their hands on that particular book could be innocent."

"Who are we to pass that judgment?"

Nicholas's agitation was understandable, Esther thought. She'd probably be agitated, too, if she thought she might have to kill someone she knew, even if he'd done to her what Nicholas's uncle had done to him. Not that Esther had any uncles that she knew of. She wondered, while trying very hard not to, if Maram had brothers, and if Isabel had brothers, and if those imaginary brothers were in fact the same people.

Her whole childhood she'd devoured stories of children with dead and missing mothers, often easier to find than stories of children whose mothers were alive and well. The absence of a mother was a promise of adventure; mothers made things too safe, too comforting. Children with mothers didn't need to look outside their homes for affirmation of their supremacy in someone's story. They didn't need to write their own protagonism.

Esther remembered Cecily complaining about this when they'd watched *The Little Mermaid, Cinderella,* and *Snow White,* offended by the lack of loving birth mothers and the prevalence of monstrous stepmothers. She'd squeezed Esther tight and smeared her cheek with red kisses and said, "This evil stepmother loves you very much." But despite Cecily's love, which Esther had never doubted, she had already identified within herself the same motherless quality that drove Ariel to shore, Cinderella to the ball, Snow White into the forest. Her motherlessness was intrinsic to her sense of self, and her sense of self was all she'd had these many years alone.

What would it mean if her mother was alive? Not only alive, but aware of Esther and watching out for her, passing notes through magic mirrors and protecting her from afar, her own fairy godmother. What would it mean if her mother had not died, but left her?

Esther sat in an armchair with Richard's book in her hands and carefully erected a set of partitions in her mind—a little room where these thoughts could careen around as quickly as they liked, slamming against the walls, throwing themselves to the floor, temper-tantruming for attention they would not get unless Esther opened the door. There was no time to open the door. The door could wait. She turned the key firmly in the lock.

"Quit talking yourself out of this," Collins was saying to Nicholas.

Nicholas slumped back against the piano. "Maybe I want to talk myself out of it," he said. "Maybe I'm not prepared to star in a Shakespearian tragedy and murder my uncle."

"If you're talking about Hamlet, he didn't murder his uncle—that's the whole point," Collins said. "He couldn't make up his mind and everyone died because of it."

"He kills him in the third act!"

"Well, what the fuck act is this, then?"

Esther stood. She was still holding the book and subtly adjusted her grip, arranging her fingers just so before reaching out to Nicholas. "Here," she said, "I don't want to touch this anymore."

Still glaring at Collins, Nicholas reached out to take it. Esther waited until she could see his fingers tighten around the cover, his grip secure, and then she *pulled*.

Instinctively Nicholas pulled back, a tug-of-war that stopped when he caught on and dropped the book, furious.

"Esther!" Joanna said. She sounded impressed.

"You," Nicholas stuttered, "you—you—you were tricking me into killing someone!"

"Yes," Esther said, looking at the book, still unruffled and intact in her hands. "And it should have worked. We pulled hard enough to at least tear a page or two, but look, the paper's not even wrinkled."

Nicholas's outrage could still be seen on his face, but it was subsiding in favor of curiosity. "Odd," he said, taking it to see for himself. "You're right."

"Should we try again?"

He looked at her sharply, but then seemed, all at once, to deflate. He rested his free hand against the wall, steadying himself. "Yes. Let's try again."

Nicholas held the book open while Esther attempted to tear out an untearable page, and then they switched, Esther gripping the cover as Nicholas yanked on the fragile old paper with all his strength. Then they each held one wing to rend it apart like a wishbone. They tried to see if it would burn in the fire. They ran it under hot water in the kitchen sink.

Nothing, nothing, nothing. It was just as fruitless as Esther remembered from when she'd tried to destroy it for Abe.

By the time they took the book out of the sink, their hands dripping but the book bone-dry, Nicholas appeared exhausted and ill and Esther didn't feel much better than he looked.

"It's no use," Nicholas said, slouched at the kitchen table over a cup of nettle tea he wasn't drinking. "I should have known. We won't be able to destroy the book until we destroy whatever object he's attached his life to, which is almost definitely the bone in the portrait frame. Maram would know that—she's too clever not to, which means the whole theory is worthless. She wouldn't send us across an ocean to do something when she knows we'd fail."

"Thirty-five minutes until the wards drop," Joanna said, as if everyone present had not also been staring at the clocks.

"I give up," Nicholas said, and laid his head down on the table.

But Esther did not have the luxury of surrender. She knew her sister would not leave the house unless Esther knocked her out and dragged her, which wasn't out of the question but also certainly wouldn't go far in repairing a relationship they'd only just begun to mend.

"Collins, are you sure she said the wards absolutely had to drop? Because if she only wanted to bring our attention to the book, she's done that, and we can put the wards up."

"No," Collins said, "she was very clear. The wards come down."

Joanna had fallen into a chair beside Esther, and Esther reached out to touch her arm. "Jo, you know these wards better than any of us," she said. "Aside from Richard tracking that book, what else will happen when they drop?"

"Everyone who's ever known about the house will suddenly remember where it is," said Joanna. "They'll be able to find it again. As far as I know, Mom is the only person in that category, but we've established that I don't actually know very much."

"Okay," Esther said, lining this information up in her mind. "What else?"

Nicholas and Collins were both giving Joanna their full attention now and she shrank back a little beneath the pressure. But she said, "Anyone would be able to see the driveway and the house itself." She made a wry face. "The electrical company will probably notice a houseful of power being siphoned off the line. Phones and the internet will start working, and any kind of communication spell like water-scrying or mirror magic would work from the outside as well as the inside."

"So the mirror upstairs," Esther said slowly. "If the wards drop, then whoever's on the other end would be able to send things through, as well as receive them. Is that what you're saying?"

"Yes," said Joanna, and jerked her head up to meet Esther's eyes. "Oh."

"Oh what?" said Collins.

Nicholas said, "You think Maram's on the other side of the mirror."

"I think it's very possible," said Esther.

"But if that's so, she can only receive. She can't pass anything back," Nicholas said. "Until the wards are dropped."

"*Oh,*" said Collins.

30

Esther helped Joanna drag some of the junk into the hallway so they could all crowd into her old bedroom, then she perched on the bed with Nicholas and Sir Kiwi while Collins sat in a spindly backed wooden chair. Joanna sat cross-legged on the floor in front of the closet door, which was ajar just enough that she could keep an eye on the mirror inside. The wards would fall in two minutes. They hadn't yet discussed how long they would wait beyond that.

"We can't expect immediate action," Collins said. "For one thing, it's midnight in England, there's a decent chance Maram's asleep. So let's not start freaking out if seven o'clock hits and nothing happens immediately, all right?"

"One minute," said Nicholas.

Joanna dropped her head into her hands, and Esther saw that she was trembling. "These wards haven't dropped in thirty years," she murmured. "For thirty years we've been completely protected and now? What am I doing?"

"Being brave," said Collins.

"Ten seconds," said Nicholas. Joanna groaned and curled into herself as if her stomach hurt.

"Now," said Nicholas.

An instant later both Collins and Joanna were wincing, ducking their heads as if against a blast of noise, and Collins rotated his jaw like he was un-stopping his ears.

"Ow," he said.

Joanna was ashen and when she spoke, her voice shook. "They're down."

Joanna wasn't the only one who had been raised beneath these wards. Esther, too, had stood at Abe's knee and watched him set them, night after night. She'd listened at eight years old when he'd explained that of his two daughters only Joanna would ever read the spell, only Joanna could learn to keep their home safe; and at eighteen she'd listened to him tell her that the only way the wards would continue to protect her family was if she, Esther, was not under them. The wards had broken up her parents' marriage. The wards had tied her sister to this house. The wards had forced Esther to run for ten long years.

She knew what this cost Joanna. The agony was clear on her face, her mouth crumpled, her eyes squeezed shut, and she felt Joanna's pain like a pain in one of her own limbs.

But Esther was glad the wards were down.

Even in their short reacquaintance she had seen that Joanna could not go on in this lonely, unchanging life any more than Esther could have stayed in her own lonely tectonic one.

"Nothing's happening," Joanna said, kneeling before the mirror like she was about to pray.

"It's been no time at all," Nicholas said. "Collins is right, we'll have to wait."

"But for how long?"

"Even if this is a trap and Richard's right now commandeering a jet to fly here and kill us all, it'll take five hours at least," said Nicholas. "There's no spell in the Library that can transport a person magically across the Atlantic Ocean."

Esther stood, slapping her hands on her thighs, and Joanna jumped.

"I'll make tea," Esther said.

"I should take the dog out," Nicholas said, but he remained seated, arms on his knees, slouched forward. Esther was aware that all of them were in various states of dishevelment, but looking at Nicholas she was impressed once again by how successfully a five-hundred-dollar shirt could compensate for blood loss, stress, and exhaustion. As long as she didn't linger on his face, he looked elegantly tousled instead of the pan-fried mess Esther knew herself to resemble. If all this ended—when all this ended—she was going to allow herself a few "investment" pieces. Maybe a really nice cashmere sweater.

She indulged in these shallow thoughts like dark chocolate, nibbling their edges and letting them melt on her tongue, inconsequential. She thought about cashmere sweaters, fine leather shoes, silk underwear so thin you could feel someone's breath through it.

In the kitchen she put the water on and then, waiting for it to boil, she went into the living room. She'd stashed her duffel bag in a corner behind the couch and hauled it out, then sat on the couch beside it. When she unzipped it, she caught a whiff of her bedroom at the research base, all stale air and lemony detergent and a hint of Pearl's lavender shampoo, and her throat clenched. She kept digging through her bag.

She'd kept the note Maram had sent through the mirror and wrapped it in a thick wool sock along with the plastic vial of blood. With care she unwrapped both note and vial and set them on the coffee table. Then she pulled out *La Ruta Nos Aportó* and opened it to the title page, where her mother had written "Remember: the path provides the natural next step."

She looked at the note from the mirror and at the label on the vial: "This is the path. It will provide the natural next step." She looked again at the nearly identical words on the inside of the novel. Then back at the note. She compared the two, charting the climb of her own heartbeat.

The handwriting was very, very similar.

So similar it might arguably be the same hand.

How had she not clocked this before? She took a shaky breath. A floorboard creaked above her, and she felt a rush of gratitude that the others were all upstairs so she could steal some privacy to let herself, for one split second, believe. She traced her fingers over her mother's handwriting in the novel. There was a chance that when she went back upstairs, another note would be sitting on the floor of her old bedroom in this very same handwriting. A chance that on the other side of the mirror, a woman who looked like her was waiting.

The kettle began to whistle. Esther slipped the note and vial of blood into her pocket and went to make tea.

When she got upstairs, balancing mugs in one hand and a teapot in the other, the tension in the room was so taut she nearly turned around and went right back out. Nicholas was sitting on the bed with his feet planted on the floor and his gaze planted on the mirror, and Collins was pacing back and forth. Joanna was still kneeling in front of the closet.

"Jo, help me with these cups," Esther said, and for a while they were occupied with pouring, passing, sipping, wincing, blowing across the steaming surface of the water, sipping, wincing again.

"Been thirty-three minutes," Nicholas said. "But who's counting? Not I. I'm having a tea party, apparently."

"We don't need to sit in this room all night," Esther said. "Let's go downstairs and put on a record or something."

"Maybe only one of us should stay in the house and the rest should pack up and go," Joanna said.

Esther did not like this suggestion in the slightest and began to say so, but a sudden change in Joanna's face stopped her.

Her sister's eyes were fixed on the mirror, her lips parting in a little O, and Esther was on her feet before she knew what she was doing, hot tea spilling over the sides of her mug and down her fingers, but the heat felt far away, unimportant. She heard Nicholas suck in a breath as Joanna reached forward and pulled the closet door further open, so they could all clearly see what Esther had already seen: a piece of paper floating down from the mirror.

In its wake the glass seethed and settled, and the paper fluttered down before coming to rest on the floor. Joanna reached out and plucked it up, then stood and went to hand it to Nicholas. Esther saw that her fingers were shaking so badly she nearly dropped it.

"You look," she said to Nicholas. "I can't."

Esther willed herself patient as Nicholas cleared his throat and began to read aloud.

"We are on our way out of the house," he read. "The Library will soon be empty. Remember: the path provides the natural next step."

Goosebumps broke out on Esther's arms.

"That's it?" Nicholas said, flipping the paper over. "That's what we've been waiting for?"

"They're on their way," Joanna said, standing. "Richard knows where we are. Is she warning us to run?"

"But what of the last bit?" Nicholas said. "*The path provides the natural next step.* What path? What step?"

"The Library will soon be empty," Collins read over Nicholas's shoulder. "So what? What does she want us to do, hop on a plane, rent a car, get to the Library, break into Richard's office, and smash everything before someone comes after us?"

"Hmm," said Nicholas. "Maybe?"

To Esther their talk was noise, buzzing and meaningless. She touched her collarbone, where her tattoo lay inked beneath her sweater—a palindrome. A sentence that could be put through a mirror and come out unchanged. She took the plastic vial of blood and Maram's mirror-note from her pocket and held them in her hands, thinking about the novel she'd been translating in her spare time for years. In Gil's world, women found themselves in mirrors: they became hypnotized and stared into their own eyes until they recognized themselves, and once they did, the mirror ceased to be a trap and became instead a doorway. An escape route. A path.

If a mirror was a path, then the natural next step was *through* it.

Esther thought of Abe's poor, doomed groundhogs. She thought of Trev's finger mangled black and unnatural. She thought of the horror she'd felt when her own hand, covered in Trev's blood, had seemed to brush the mirror's surface, how she'd snatched it back expecting pain but found the skin unmarked.

Esther and Nicholas were untouched by ordinary spells the way shadows ceased to exist in a pitch-dark room, because darkness couldn't add to darkness. Richard's Scribe-seeking spell needed Nicholas's eye in order to see Esther, because only magic could see magic. Nicholas and Esther *were* magic. It treated them as a part of itself.

If Maram was on the other side of this mirror, if she had activated the spell, then her blood was necessary to pass things through. Hers or Cecily's, but Cecily's blood wasn't here.

Esther looked at the vial she'd taken from her duffel bag, filled with red. Maram's might be.

She went over to the mirror and tapped the glass: it was solid and unyielding. Carefully she unscrewed the cap of the vial and poured out a scant drop of the liquid inside, letting it fall onto her palm and smear red across her skin. She put a hand to the glass again, expecting resistance or pain or pins and needles or anything, any kind of sensation, but she felt nothing. Her fingers went through the glass like it was air. She snatched her hand back, her pulse skyrocketing.

"Esther," Joanna said. "What are you doing?"

Esther ignored her. She gripped the mirror's frame with both hands and took a huge breath, like she was about to jump into deep water. Then, before anyone could stop her, before she could change her mind, she plunged her face through the silvery surface of the mirror. Behind her, she heard Joanna scream.

She'd squeezed her eyes shut but when no pain came, she opened them. Before her was a stately room, empty, with a four-poster bed, dark oil paintings on the walls, and a beautiful blue rug, then she felt hands grabbing at her body and pulling her back, and a second later the stately room disappeared and she was looking at the mirror in the closet again, its surface rippling slightly.

Joanna, who'd grabbed her around the waist to haul her back, spun her around and searched her face with terrified eyes. But when she saw no damage, her expression changed from terror to incredulity.

"We can go through the mirror," Esther said. "Nicholas and I. We can go to the Library while it's empty and find whatever object Richard's tied himself to, and destroy it."

31

Nicholas had been the only Scribe for so long that it had not occurred to him there was anything he might not know about his own powers. He'd read all his father's notes and every book in the Library at least twice over, not to mention the thousands of pages Maram had found and collated from the notebooks of other Scribes, some of whom had been dead a century, some a millennium. Maram had traveled all over the world seeking this knowledge, purchasing it for enormous sums of money from museums and private archives, or bartering for it, or stealing it. Probably even killing for it. All so she could bring it home to Nicholas.

So he had thought.

Such an error of thinking, to believe himself the expert because he was the one with the power. Such an error of thinking to believe he had power in the first place. Everything he knew about writing books had been filtered through Maram. All this time, it was she who'd been the expert.

Amazing that even after the events of the past week, Nicholas still had the capacity for surprise.

Stepping through the mirror was like no physical experience he'd ever had. It was like swimming if the water were made of treacle and also of outer space, sweet and airless and tugging and infinite, and dark in a way that wasn't a binary to light but rather a different state entirely, complete unto itself. The body of the darkness was sound, which was sensation: countless wings brushing against one another, countless blades of golden grass moving in an endless wind, every distant highway ever heard. Nicholas's mind and body were still fully his, which made things even more peculiar, because his brain, limbs, nerves, everything was working to make rational human sense of something that had no senses.

It was terrible and incredible and if he'd had time, he would've started to panic—but he'd taken a step and the step ended. As his foot landed on the other side of the frame, the roaring darkness was gone, and he was in the world again. First his head, then his other foot came out of the mirror, and finally he was standing in Maram's bedroom, as naturally as if he'd gone through a door.

He put a hand to his jacket to check the inner pocket where Richard's book was tucked and a second later, he watched, fascinated, as Esther came through the glass. It was like watching someone emerge perfectly dry out of a vertical pool, and his head swam at the sight.

"Bizarre" was Esther's assessment of the experience. She tightened her curly ponytail and flicked her eyes around the room. Nicholas followed her gaze: the four-poster mahogany bed, the enormous Louis XV armoire, the silk carpet. He remembered lying on that carpet on one of the rare occasions Maram had granted him entry when he was a child, staying quiet so she wouldn't regret inviting him in.

Her bedroom door was locked from the outside and he fumbled with the three inside locks until he found the correct configuration of bolts, Esther hovering behind him, her wish to take over tangible. Finally, the door clicked open. He pushed it very slowly in case any domestic staff were nearby, but Maram's antechamber was as empty as her bedroom and Esther followed him through it into the hallway.

After Esther's revelation, they had waited an hour or so to ensure that Maram's assurances would be true, that she and Richard would indeed have left the house, and the Library would be empty. It had been nine o'clock in Vermont and was two in the morning here in England, the halls lit low, the huge windows black and nearly as reflective as the mirror they'd just come through. The marble floors shone under the light of the wall sconces.

"People really live here?" Esther whispered. "*You* really live here?"

Nicholas looked around for the source of her wonder. It was true that compared to Esther's shabby childhood home the Library was palatial, but recent understanding had so warped his memories that his eye, too, had changed. He'd spent the majority of his life in this house and until recently had felt he'd known it in the same alert, instinctive way he knew his own body; knew its coldest stones and softest sofas, knew the best place to find midafternoon sun, knew which rooms the staff cleaned at which hours and which rooms were rarely cleaned at all, knew every hallway, every painting. Turning a corner was like bending an elbow. Opening a door like blinking an eye.

Or it had been.

Now Nicholas felt he'd stepped through that looking glass and emerged into a parallel world. Physically everything was as he remembered, but his perception had changed so irrevocably that the physical surroundings themselves appeared altered. The height of the soaring ceilings felt cruel rather than grand, built to a scale not meant for human comfort, and the carpets sat rich and bright over the floor like they were hiding stains.

"It's like a museum," Esther said.

"Yes, and like a museum, you mustn't touch," Nicholas said, and Esther set down the thousand-year-old vase she'd picked up off its stand. Then, checking himself, he said, "Actually, touch away."

"Because fuck them?" Esther said, picking up the vase again and turning it in her hands.

"Fuck them," Nicholas confirmed. "I'd say we ought to smash it ceremonially, but it hasn't done anything wrong. Unfair to punish it for the Library's sins."

"Plus, it's really pretty."

"'Tis. Come on."

It was unaccountably strange to walk these halls feeling like a fugitive and he had to forcibly shake off the skulking slouch to his shoulders. It was too late at night for anyone to be about, but if anyone did see him, he wanted to look as natural as he always had, master of the domain, not to be questioned or bothered. He had no idea what Maram and Richard had told the staff about his disappearance; probably they'd been told nothing at all.

The two passed through the portrait gallery on the stairs and Esther slowed, examining all the austere, shadowed faces staring down at her. She pointed. "This looks like you."

"Well spotted," he said. "That was my father."

"And this woman?"

"My mother." He glanced around nervously.

"Do you think your uncle killed them?"

Nicholas swallowed. "Probably. Now come on."

They were headed to the Library, to the secret passage that led to Richard's study, though it was unclear how, exactly, they were going to get through the bookshelf, seeing as neither of them could read the spell.

When Nicholas had explained this conundrum earlier, back at Joanna's house, Esther had suggested ripping the bookshelf out of the wall.

"It's covered in books!" Nicholas had said, aghast at the suggestion.

"We can take the books out."

"And then what?" Nicholas said, working himself up. "Pile them on the floor? These are priceless volumes, irreplaceable, they—"

"The floor's not made of lava," Esther said. "They'll be fine."

"Worse comes to worse," Collins had put in, "you can go down and wake up Sofie, she'll read the spell for you. She's a good egg, I trust her."

"Who's Sofie?"

"Jesus, really? Sofie. She works in the kitchen. Probably baked literally every piece of bread you've ever shoved in your mouth."

"Oh, right, yes, Sofie," Nicholas said.

"You still have no idea who I'm talking about."

No, because Nicholas had always been discouraged from fraternizing with the staff, but he didn't think it would go over terribly well if he announced that.

But it turned out they did not need Sofie after all.

Esther and Nicholas reached the end of the hall where the Library's enormous electronic doors loomed, and Esther watched with interest as Nicholas put his eye to the scanner. They both winced as the loud whirring gears turned and the doors moaned open, but no one appeared in the hallway to investigate and soon enough they'd made their way inside and shut the doors behind them.

Nicholas started moving forward immediately and then noticed Esther wasn't following. When he looked back, he found her staring up at the soaring filigreed ceiling, the maze of shelves, the enormous windows draped in luxurious curtains.

"These can't all be . . ."

"Spell books? Yes."

Esther shook her head. "I wish Joanna could see this. She'd lose her mind."

"Maybe someday she'll visit," Nicholas said lightly, though he had trouble envisioning a future in which he was allowed to do anything so mundane as invite people to his home. He did not know what it would mean for his life or for the Library if this plan worked and Richard was . . . out of the picture, to put it delicately, which was the only way Nicholas felt capable of putting it. He'd always assumed the house and the books within it were deeded to him, but he realized now it was equally, if not more likely, that in the event of Richard's death, they'd be left to Maram.

Or perhaps there was no will in the first place. After all, it seemed Richard did not ever expect to die.

Nicholas was so distracted by his own looping thoughts that he took a wrong turn in the stacks and had to double back. When finally he did lead Esther below the oak-beamed ceiling of the section that had once been the chapel, and began to mount the dais, he had to work to understand what he was seeing.

The outline of the bookshelf and the spines of the books upon it were already hazy and insubstantial, and behind the vague mist of them he could see the stone wall and the wood of the secret door.

Nicholas flung out an arm and Esther thumped against it. "What?" she said, then noticed the shelf. "Oh! Problem solved?"

"Shh," Nicholas hissed. It was the only noise he could manage. His voice felt frozen in his throat and his lungs felt suddenly weak, wheezing for air that wouldn't come, the spell's placard looming in his mind's eye.

Duration: Max six minutes per reading.

Which meant someone had read this spell in the past six minutes. Someone had been here. Someone was *here*.

Slowly, very slowly, he began to turn around, eyes skimming the shelves for a hint of Richard's gray hair or a flicker of Maram's silk blouse, ears straining for the sound of breath, footsteps on the carpet, the creak of a door—anything. Esther, picking up on his tension, was perfectly still at his side. The tall shelves gleamed beneath their brass lights, the humidifying system hummed distantly, the books sat in motionless rows, and the red wingback chairs on either side of Seshat's display case hadn't moved. But the display case itself . . .

Nicholas sucked in a breath.

The hinged front of the case was hanging open ever so slightly, and when Nicholas crept forward, he saw that the limestone slab was off-center on its metal stand, and there was a dark smear in one corner that he didn't remember ever seeing before. But the most jarring—and anachronistic—change was the yellow Post-it stuck over Seshat's carved face.

It read, *Until 3:54 a.m.*

All at once, Nicholas understood. He let out a sigh of pure relief and turned to where Esther was still standing stock-still, one foot on the dais step.

"It's all right," he told her, unsticking the Post-it. "Maram read the spell for us before she left."

She'd read two spells, in fact. One was the spell to fade the bookcase.

The other was the four-thousand-year-old companion spell, priceless and rare and prized, which she had read to keep the way open for them.

When Nicholas spoke again, he did so around a lump in his throat. "Come on," he said, reaching for the doorknob.

"It's all right?" Esther said.

"It's all right." He slipped into the darkness of the passageway. Esther close behind. He took one squinting step up and a bright little light came on over his shoulder. When he glanced back, he found Esther holding a tiny flashlight.

"Where on earth did you get that?"

"Collins said we'd need it."

For some reason this smoothed the last of Nicholas's ruffled nerves and he moved up the stairs feeling distinctly calmer. Esther said, "Secret passageways, English country houses, malevolent old men. When I was a kid, this is what I thought magic should be like. Not hidden away in a basement, being used only to keep hiding itself."

"And? Is this everything you dreamed of?"

Esther let out a sound that, under different circumstances, might have been laughter. "Um, it's scarier in practice."

"You didn't dream about someone wanting to skin you alive and turn you into a book?"

"Weirdly, no."

They reached the narrow wooden hall at the top of the stairs and Esther beamed her meager light over Nicholas's shoulder. It lit a few feet in front of them and then was swallowed by the dark. "How long is it?"

"A few minutes' walk, I think." He trailed one hand along the wall as they moved forward. "I've only done it once."

"How many other secret passages are in this place?"

"Honestly, I don't know. There are a few I'm familiar with from the staff kitchen—one goes to the banqueting hall. But they're not secret so much as discreet." His middle finger caught on a snag in the wood and he snatched his hand from the wall, wincing. "Passages like this, though, truly hidden? Could be hundreds. Could be none. No one told me either way."

"But you got along with him, with Richard?" Esther said, and when Nicholas didn't respond right away, "I'm still trying to get a handle on the nature of your relationship."

"So am I," Nicholas said.

He couldn't let himself focus on anything other than action, because if he began to consider the implication, he might not be able to do what he'd ostensibly come here to do. Implication would lead to questions like: Would it be murder, the act that Nicholas had committed himself to committing? He wished, briefly but entirely, that he could see Richard again, give him a chance to explain himself before Nicholas made a choice he couldn't go back from.

"Could you pick up the pace a smidge?" Esther said, poking him in the back. "Walking this slow makes me nervous."

He'd done what he'd just decided not to do and started thinking.

"Sorry," he said.

"You're literally dragging your feet," she said. "Is it figurative, too?"

That made him smile despite his nerves. "I suppose it is."

"You're okay to keep going, though? To do this?"

"Yes," he said, and was glad that his voice sounded much firmer than his wobbling resolve. Maybe he could convince himself as well as Esther.

His vision seemed to be adjusting to the dark, the wooden walls of the passage growing clearer. Then he became aware that it wasn't his vision but actual light. They were at the end of the hallway, the wall suddenly visible in front of them, the trapdoor at their feet outlined with light. When Nicholas reached down to open it, the staircase below was illuminated.

Maram again, preparing their way?

He and Esther stood at the top of the stairs, both extremely still and quiet, listening, waiting. The silence grew around them, the narrow walls holding it like pressure building in a bottle, no sound but Nicholas's heart in his ears and Esther's breath at his shoulder. When they started down, their movements were painstaking and quiet, their feet barely audible on the steps.

The door opened easily beneath Nicholas's hand and swung inward without a sound, and they stepped from the stairwell into that mirror-glimmered room. This time the glass reflected only Esther and Nicholas, many iterations of them, all looking shadowy and tired—though Nicholas's vanity flickered to life at how tall he appeared compared to the very small woman at his side. The vain thought made him feel almost like himself for a moment. Whatever victory looked like, he hoped it allowed for pockets of comfortable shallowness. The forced introspection of the past week had unmoored him.

Esther paused in front of one of the mirrors and crouched, fingers hovering above the floor, and Nicholas saw there was still a faint bloodstain on the carpet. "Is this where Trev came through?" she asked, voice barely above a whisper.

"Yes."

"He wasn't going to kill me after all, was he?" Esther said. "He was going to shove me through the mirror and let Richard kill me while you wrote a book with my blood."

"Very probably."

She stood and turned to him, eyes glinting in the low light, looking suddenly like the person he'd watched take down an armed man twice her size. "Would you have done it?" she said. "Taken my blood and done whatever Richard told you to, no questions asked?"

"I like to think I would've asked at least *one* question," Nicholas said, rummaging around for some indignation.

"But you'd have done it, in the end."

"I don't know," he said, feeling so tired, suddenly, that he nearly sat down. Instead, he leaned against a mirrorless patch of wall. "Richard and Maram, they always had explanations, good ones, sound and rational. Even if things felt . . . wrong . . . I didn't see an alternative that was right."

Esther folded her arms and stared at the mirror through which Tretheway's crumpled, broken body had come. Nicholas waited, feeling miserable and uncertain. Maybe he should apologize for the version of himself that would've accepted the loss of her life and filled a pen with her blood. But how exactly did one apologize for theoretical monstrosity? He wasn't even good at apologizing for things he *had* done.

"Well," said Esther. "Thank you."

That gave him pause. "For what?"

"You haven't had many choices," she said. "And now that you do, you're choosing to help me. Which I appreciate."

"Oh." He could feel heat come into his face. "I'm helping myself just as much."

"You could turn me over to your uncle and resume your life of fine footwear and blissful ignorance."

Nicholas looked down. "I'm honestly delighted you noticed the quality of my footwear. They're custom made, these boots."

"Thank you," Esther said again.

You're welcome did not feel like a response he could give. He moved toward the door of Richard's study with a rush of nerves that was a poor substitute for energy but would have to do. He didn't hesitate in front of the doorway, or at least not physically, though he steeled himself for the sight of his eye still floating in its jar. His body felt like it was moving faster than his mind, which was probably for the best, and he let it carry him, his hand on the doorknob, lungs filling with air, feet moving as his brain scrambled to catch up. Richard's life, and the end of it, a turn of the knob away.

Nicholas turned the knob.

The study was dark, all the lights off. He took a few steps, hand groping along the wall for the light switch, then stopped. Esther stumbled into him, fingers closing around his arm.

"What?" she said.

Nicholas couldn't say what. A feeling: a prickle across his skin like a change in temperature, a barometric shift in the air. Even as his fingers found the switch and the overhead came on, he was flinching away from what he might find.

Richard and Maram, their eyes narrowed in the sudden light.

At his side, Nicholas heard Esther's intake of breath, but his own lungs had entirely ceased to function. He couldn't breathe, couldn't blink, could only stand frozen and staring. Maram was seated in a high-backed chair by Richard's desk and Richard was on his feet beside her, one hand resting possessively on her shoulder. In that tall chair, with tall Richard at her side, surrounded by the towering shelves packed with relics and curiosities, Maram appeared very small. Nicholas looked to her wrists, to her ankles— was she tied?—but she didn't appear to be restrained in any visible way.

"You see?" Maram said. She was speaking to Richard and seemed to be smiling, or at least her mouth was curved up. She didn't even glance at Esther. "I told you they'd come."

"You did," Richard said, nodding, with the quiet, pleased expression Nicholas had always longed to find turned on him. "I suppose I'll have to forgive you for your scheming, after all."

Esther's fingers were tight around Nicholas's arm. His vision was wavering in and out of focus, the study's many details blurring and then sharpening with brutal clarity, a tumult of random images: Maram's hands folded calmly in her lap, the crushed red of a velvet box, the stuffed monkey's endless black stare from its perch on an upper shelf, the dull curve of a clay amphora, the shine of the glass jar where his eye still sat suspended.

The glint of metal in Richard's hand as he moved away from Maram and toward Nicholas and Esther, his long legs eating the space between them so quickly that Nicholas didn't realize what was happening until it happened.

Richard was holding a gun.

At Nicholas's side Esther went completely silent and still. Her fast breath stopped. She let go of Nicholas's arm. The barrel was pointed directly at her head.

32

Collins was drinking. Joanna might even add "heavily." He'd had three beers in the past thirty minutes and had left her alone on the porch to go inside and get another one. But when he came back outside again, he was empty-handed.

"It wasn't helping," he said in explanation, thumping back down on the step beside her and rubbing his hands vigorously through his hair. "I'm still stressed the hell out."

He'd dragged Joanna away from her panicked vigil at the mirror by suggesting her cat friend might be hungry, then had insisted on opening one of the little cans of Sir Kiwi's high-end dog food Nicholas had brought, muttering about the mercury content and high sodium of the tuna Joanna had been using. It was clear he needed a task, so she had let him find a can opener and pour it into the bowl, but so far, the cat had not shown its furry face. Probably because it had been offered dog food.

"The cold is calming me down, though," said Joanna. "You were right to come outdoors."

Agitation had overheated her to the point where the sweat on her brow was only just beginning to dry in the chilly breeze.

"They'll be all right," Collins said. "Maram knows what she's doing. She wouldn't have gone through all this convoluted shit if she didn't think it would work."

He'd been repeating variations on these sentences since Esther and Nicholas had vanished through the mirror and Joanna hadn't yet figured out a reply. In part because she wasn't certain she believed him, and in part because she wasn't certain how to talk to him now that the other two had gone. She'd never spent so much time alone with an adult person her own age before, much less an adult man, much less an adult man she found attractive. She took a deep breath, pulling her jacket more tightly around her body and glancing sideways at him. In the golden porch light his lashes cast long, sooty shadows on his cheeks, and he was chewing on his lower lip in a way that made her want to stomp her foot. The sight was, at least, a good distraction from Joanna's fear.

"How did you end up involved in all this, anyway?" she said. "I mean books in general, not only the Library."

Collins leaned down to dig a pebble from the dirt at his feet. It looked very pale in the porch light, like a shard of bone.

"My grandmother had a book," he said. He chucked the pebble into the yard and went for another one. "She passed it down to my mother, along with the ability to hear them. Ours was from the U.S., about 1900. It let you see through the eyes of the nearest bird. The ink was already pretty faded, but my mom let my sister and I each read it on our sixteenth birthdays. She drove us outside the city, so we'd have a chance to get something other than a pigeon."

"What was it like?"

Collins smiled out at the dark trees. "My birthday's in May and I flew in the body of a heron over the Assabet River. There was lilac blooming everywhere. I still dream about it."

"Can your sister hear magic, too?"

"Yeah, though she's more of a . . . like, a hobbyist. I was the one who went really wild for it. I went deep into the internet and found a bunch of message boards that eventually connected us to the Boston crew."

For Joanna the internet was a once-a-week, ten-minute obligation at the local library. Though she knew people used it to reach out, to make connections, it had never occurred to her that she herself could have used it like that or been one of those people.

She said, "Could you have told me any of that under your NDA?"

Collins watched another pebble soar across the yard and shook his head.

"It must feel good to be able to say it now," she said.

"It does." He dusted off his hands and let them hang between his knees. "You know, when I finally met other people who knew about this stuff, it felt like the whole world had cracked its lid on me."

"Was that a good thing or a bad thing?"

"For me, good," said Collins fervently. "Like light and air could finally get in. At least until the Library snatched me up, and even that hasn't been all bad. I've learned a hell of a lot."

"You and Nicholas seem to get along," Joanna ventured.

"Sure, aside from the fact that he's spoiled rotten and basically useless," Collins said. "Like his stupid little dog." He smiled as he said it, though, like he couldn't help himself.

She had to ask. "Are you and him . . ."

"Nah," said Collins, and glanced at her sidelong. "I, um. I prefer . . . long hair."

Joanna was glad for the low light and the fact that her own long hair was pulled over one shoulder, partially obscuring her face from him, because she could feel her cheeks flooding hot.

She tried to keep her tone light. "Why not grow yours out, then?"

"In high school it was to my shoulders," he said. "Dyed black. I was a wannabe goth. Painted my fingernails black, too." He held out a hand to let her imagine it, though she found herself imagining something else entirely.

"How did you go from wannabe goth to hired muscle?"

Collins moved his shoulders, halfway to a shrug but not quite. "I was already this size by the time I was like, fourteen," he said. "Kids in school kinda took that as a challenge, I guess. Guys were always coming at me. My mom got tired of seeing me with black eyes, so she put me in karate, and then I started boxing in high school, and once I turned eighteen, I started bouncing at nightclubs. Paid my way through college."

She felt a pang of envy. "You went to college? What did you study?"

"Hospitality," he said, already laughing at himself before he'd finished the word. "My aunt owned this shitty motel for a while, she talked me into it. But I was one class away from a minor in art history. That's more up your alley I bet, right?"

"Hospitality sounds nice," she said dubiously, though she had no idea how a person could study such a thing. Did he get pop-quizzed on how to take someone's coat?

"What would you have studied?" he said.

"English," she said immediately.

"What kind of stuff do you like to read? Besides spells, I mean."

"Anything, really," she said. Then, because the lid on her life had already been cracked and she may as well push it open further, she turned her face toward the light, looked him in the eye, and said, "Especially romance."

Collins didn't look away. "Oh yeah?"

"Yes."

"Tell me why."

She wanted to say something flirtatious, something about sex scenes, maybe. Instead she told a deeper truth. "Romance novels are about connection. About people who connect with one another against the odds— despite their differences, their flaws, their secrets. In a romance novel you never have to worry, you know everything will end happily."

"Unlike real life," Collins said. "In real life you have to worry."

"Exactly. That's why I used to prefer novels."

"Used to?"

"Now I'm not so sure."

He tilted his head. "I've spent the last six months under a silencing spell that basically ruled out any chance I had of connecting with another person," he said. "Take it from me. The real thing is worth all the worry in the world."

Something about his posture had changed, a subtle reorientation that sent every nerve in Joanna's body crackling to sudden, explosive attention. His gaze was fixed on her mouth. "Are you worried right now?" she said.

He leaned closer. "Yup."

The air vanished from her lungs. Collins's eyes were all black pupil, those spiky shadows trembling on his cheek, and he was closing the distance between them centimeter by centimeter, his movements agonizingly slow, like he was waiting for her to stop him. A distantly hysterical part of her wanted to laugh at this. *Stop* him?

When he finally kissed her, it was soft, tentative. For a second. Then she wound her arms around his neck and parted her lips beneath his and he hauled her in closer, his hands on her waist, the small of her back, tangled in her hair, and it wasn't soft at all. This was a kiss that had no relationship whatsoever to the toothy make outs she remembered from high school, this was a different action altogether; a time-stopping, full-body action that sent heat surging across Joanna's skin even as she shivered beneath Collins's touch. He kissed her searchingly, like she was a page he couldn't wait to turn, and the thrill of it was so good that for a moment she thought the loud churn of an engine was the sound of her own body, her long-dormant machinery coming to life with a growl and a bang. Then, more quickly than it had begun—too quickly—the kiss stopped.

"Collins," she protested, gripping the open flaps of his jacket, but his head had turned toward the driveway, and she realized that the engine she'd heard wasn't her body, after all.

"Someone's coming," Collins said.

Joanna hadn't thought her heart rate could rocket any higher, but it could. She felt dazed, all the blood from her brain redirected elsewhere, and she touched her tingling mouth in disbelief. "Is it Richard?"

"Can't be Richard himself, not enough time," Collins said. He put a hand on her knee and squeezed, then pushed himself to his feet, his back to her. He radiated tension. "But he could've sent someone ahead, he's got people in New York for sure, probably in Boston, too. Where's that rifle you had when we first showed up?"

Joanna leaped up to get it and paused. The car was coming nearer and as it did the sound of its engine resolved into familiarity. When she peered around Collins's shoulders to look again, she saw the bright blue of a chassis sparking in the light from the porch, and an answering spark of hope flared in her chest. She knew this car.

"Wait," she said. "I think it's my mother."

It was.

At the end of the driveway the engine barely died before Cecily was tumbling out of the front seat, her eyes wild, lips for once bare of their signature red. Collins was still blocking Joanna and Cecily ran toward him, throwing up her fists and slamming them against his chest as he stumbled backward, both hands flying up to try to block her blows without hurting her.

"Where is my daughter?" she screamed. "What did you do with my daughter?"

"I'm here!" Joanna said, hurling her body between them, catching a fist to her collarbone. "Mom, I'm right here!"

Cecily gripped her arms, looking from her to Collins with tear-stained confusion. "Joanna?"

"Yes, I'm okay!"

"Who is this *man*?"

The complicated answer was currently beyond her, so she said, "His name is Collins. Collins, this is my mother, Cecily."

"A pleasure," he said doubtfully.

"The wards are down," Cecily said, still holding tightly to Joanna, searching her face. "I was in bed, almost asleep, thinking of you, and suddenly I knew where your house was. I knew how to get here! I thought—oh, I don't know what I thought! The worst, the very worst. But you know they're down? You did it yourself?"

"Yes," Joanna said, because although she had not chosen it, she had let it happen.

"Then Richard will be coming," Cecily said. "He'll be coming to get his book."

Joanna stared at her. "How did you know about Richard?"

Cecily stared back. "How do *you*?"

"Joanna said you were under a Library silencing spell," Collins said. "You shouldn't even be able to say his name."

Cecily's mouth dropped open and she took a step backward, but a second later she'd composed herself. "My silencing spell is broken," she said, looking at Joanna. "That's what I asked for in that note, the one I put through the mirror. I consented to the spell twenty-three years ago to protect your sister, but I couldn't take it anymore. I knew if I wasn't able to tell you the truth, I'd lose you."

Every time Joanna had looked at her mother in recent memory, it had been through a veil of suspicion so thick that Cecily's true outline was blurred. Joanna didn't know the necessary motions to lift that veil completely: she'd been wearing it for too long to just pick up her hands and push it away.

"There's another silencing spell in your basement," Cecily said. "One that I once read to someone else; one that only I can break. I want to break it now. There's been enough silence to last a lifetime." She reached out and grabbed Joanna's hands, her grip steady. "Will you let me in, Joanna? Please?"

There were no more wards. Cecily could push Joanna aside and walk in as easily as she could walk into any house. But she was asking. She was giving Joanna the choice.

"Come in, then," Joanna said. "Come in and tell me the truth."

33

"Give me the book," Richard said to Nicholas. "I know you've brought it with you. I can hear it."

"Maram," Nicholas said, "what is this?"

Esther's entire sensory awareness was split in two. Half of her was focused on the extremely capable-looking pistol pointed directly at her head, and the other half was glued to the dark-haired woman at Richard's side. This was Maram, perched on the edge of an enormous wooden desk and holding her own gun loosely, even casually, in her lap. Her gaze on Nicholas, not even a flick of the eye in Esther's direction, and those thick eyebrows—not unlike Esther's own, Nicholas was right—furrowed in apology.

"I'm sorry, Nicholas," said Maram. "I didn't like tricking you, or Richard. But after this one"—she waved a hand at Esther, still not looking at her—"pushed Tretheway through the mirror instead of the other way around, as intended, well—desperate times."

"What?" said Nicholas. "But—you—you—"

Maram spoke over his stammering. "Did your friend not tell you what she did to poor Tretheway?"

"Horrible way to go," said Richard.

"But you sent someone to save Esther," Nicholas said, "in the Auckland airport, you went behind Richard's back."

"We both know your uncle can be a bit stubborn," Maram said. "He would never have agreed to any plan that involved letting you out of the house, running around the world on your own. Would you have, darling?"

"Probably not," Richard said, rueful and fond.

Esther was barely listening to their words. She was staring at Maram, searching her features for the similarities Nicholas had seen. The eyebrows were alike, yes, and the shape of the face, but that wasn't enough to hang a theory on, and certainly not enough for them to have risked their lives on a guess. Only in the sudden, adrenaline-fueled clarity of the present did she realize how clouded her thinking had been mere minutes in the past. Her skepticism had been unfeigned, but it hadn't come from disbelief—it had come, as her skepticism so often did, from hope. She had wanted to believe what Nicholas had told her: that her mother was alive, had been alive, and was working to protect her.

But even if this person had given birth to her, which perhaps she had, Maram was not her mother. And the only person protecting Esther had been, as always, Esther.

"The book, Nicholas," Richard said, beckoning from the other end of the gun. "Or this bullet goes straight into your new friend's head."

He had such a pleasant-looking face that his words seemed even more awful by comparison. Behind him, over the desk, was the portrait Nicholas had described: a stern-faced Richard in a bloodstained apron, bone saw in hand, bone frame surrounding.

"You wouldn't kill her," said Nicholas. "You need her alive."

"Yes," Richard agreed. "But the state of her mind is inconsequential as long as her body is still breathing. I was once a surgeon, you know." With his free hand he tapped his own head. "I daresay I could inflict maximum damage without loss of life. If you could call it life, what she'd be left with. Is that what you want for her?"

Nicholas turned his own head from left to right—not shaking it, but looking around, looking for an answer. His eyes met Esther's and she felt as desolate as he looked. She'd had the chance to run, again, as she'd run so many times before, but instead she'd come with him here, into this trap. She could tell he wanted her to speak, to say something, but she couldn't imagine what she could say. If she opened her mouth, it would be to scream.

"There are people outside this door," Richard said, watching Nicholas cast his hopeless gaze around the room. "And in the Library itself, waiting by the passageway you took to get here. They have their orders. Please, let's not make this messy. Give me the book."

"First," Nicholas said, "why don't you give me answers."

Richard looked at him with a pitying smile. "You're not exactly in a position to bargain."

"Oh, let him ask his questions," Maram said. To Esther's ear her accent was British, but so clipped and perfect it sounded almost practiced. "We don't want to lose you, Nicholas. I know I speak for both Richard and myself when I say that our affection for you is entirely real."

"That's true." Richard nodded. "And it always has been. This doesn't change how we feel about you."

"How *you* feel about *me*?" Nicholas said.

"It's natural you'll need some time to adjust," said Maram, "to sort out your new understanding of things, but—"

"You staged my kidnapping and carved my eye out of my head," said Nicholas. "Is that what you mean by *things*?"

Richard winced. "You think I enjoyed that? My god, it was one of the worst days of my life."

Nicholas let out a hoarse, astonished laugh. "Am I even a person to you? Was my father? Or are we tools, like your scalpels and blood bags?"

"Of course you're a person," said Richard. "Everything I've done, I've done for our family, our legacy. For the Library."

"Our family," Nicholas said. "How old are you? You're not my uncle. Are we even related?"

Richard's kind eyes grew sad. "Yes," he said. "I admit it hurts to hear you even question it. My sister was a Scribe. You and your father are both descended from her line."

Esther didn't mean to speak, but her mind was spinning through the generations, tallying the numbers, and squaring them with what Nicholas had told her. "The bloodline spell," she said. "Was that you?"

Richard tensed at her voice, then visibly forced himself to relax. He steadied his gun at her head. "Nicholas told you about that, did he? You're quite right. The spell was my design—my sister wrote the actual book."

"With whose blood?" Nicholas said. "Whose body?"

Richard waved his free hand dismissively. "There were a lot more Scribes in those days."

Esther was still watching Maram. She couldn't help herself. Despite everything, despite the gun pointed at her head and the one dangling from Maram's fingers, despite the fact that Maram seemed barely to notice she was there, some treacherous part of her brain was still cataloging: the shape of the fingers, the curl of the nostrils, the wide forehead, the rosy undertone of her skin, which was a few shades darker than Esther's but if mixed with Abe's . . .

Esther blew out a hard breath, frustration mingling with fear and turning to anger. She had a gun in her face, and meanwhile the silly, dreaming child in her head was trying to splice two mismatched fibers together, waiting for a spark that might never come, instead of looking for the right wires, the real connections.

But the child spoke again. "What's in this for you?" Esther asked Maram, because she wanted to know and she wanted Maram to look at her, just once.

Maram turned back toward Richard, as if asking permission to reply.

Richard nodded. "No harm in telling them."

It was Nicholas who answered though, his voice nearly unrecognizable, mangled with rage. He said, "He's going to write a new spell for you. Isn't he? He's going to make you live forever."

"For a long, long time, anyway," Maram said. She smiled, wide and satisfied. "Yes."

"She's the only person I've ever met who loves the Library as much as I do," said Richard. "It's an enormous responsibility, taking care of all of this. I couldn't admit how hard it was to do alone until Maram came along and I realized I didn't have to. You can't imagine how lonely it's been, all these years. Seeing my family and loved ones die, one by one, leaving me to carry this all on my own shoulders."

"Responsibility," Nicholas spat. "Invented. No one asked our family to do this."

They spoke but Esther wasn't listening. She was still staring at Maram and Maram was still looking fixedly at Richard. Too fixedly? Was she avoiding Esther's gaze entirely? That was a tell itself, wasn't it?

And because Esther was watching, she was the only one to see Maram's face change.

Her expression had been attentive, composed, but suddenly her eyes went wide and her hands flew to her throat, her mouth opening as her cheeks went dark with blood and a rattling hiss leaked from her parted lips, like a slashed tire. She curled over, gasping for air, but just as Richard broke off midsentence and glanced at her with concern, she sucked in an enormous, rib-rattling breath, and sat up so straight she looked as if she'd been electrocuted.

"Are you all right?" Richard said, his composure giving way to such clear anxiety that Esther almost felt sorry for him.

"Ah," Maram rasped. One of her hands was still curled loosely around the base of her throat, but she held the other up in a gesture of placation. "I—swallowed—and it went down the wrong way. I'm all right now." She took a careful breath. "Eyes on the target, darling."

Richard turned his gaze back to Esther and Nicholas and made a visible effort to relax. "You can understand why I'm a little on edge," he said, almost like he was excusing himself. "It would be a brutal irony for her to die now."

"I wish you would," Nicholas said to Maram, but without conviction. The rage had bled from his voice and he sounded more exhausted than anything. Esther, on the other hand, was aflame with energy. She was still seeing Maram's face as she choked on nothing, the way her eyes had flown open, still hearing that hiss of breath and then the full-lunged suck of air. She'd seen a similar face that morning, had heard a similar hiss and gasp. Collins, right when the silencing spell had lifted.

"What a thing to say, Nicholas." Richard's tone was reproachful, the practiced echo of a thousand chastisements. "You've known this girl, what, a few days? Meanwhile Maram's been here, caring for you, your whole life. You don't actually want her to die."

"I don't actually want anyone to die," Nicholas said. "I want you to stop this madness and let Esther go and let Maram live a normal life and die an old lady, like a human being."

"Maybe we could strike a deal," Richard said. "Esther lives for a few more years, enough to bear you a couple children and see if any are born with your talent, and then—"

"Stop," Nicholas said, raising his hands as if to clap them over his ears. "Jesus Christ, stop."

Richard laughed, not without affection. "I didn't think that would be to your taste."

Maram rose from her chair and went to stand at Richard's side. Like Nicholas she looked expensive, her silk blouse perfectly tailored to her body and her skin expertly made up, her hair chignoned and shining.

"Maybe it will help you understand me," Maram said, "if you think of the Library as one of my children. Everything I've done to bring you here today has been to protect my child."

At Esther's side, Nicholas stiffened slightly, the ears of his attention pricking. She herself was suddenly finding it difficult to breathe.

"Nicholas of all people knows that I'm not what you might call maternal," said Maram, and Richard chuckled his agreement. "But like it or not, I'm still a mother. And as a mother, if you think someone might point a gun at your child . . ." Maram shrugged. "You take the necessary steps to protect her. You do your best to make certain any threat is a harmless buzz, and any possible wound is nothing worse than a sting."

Richard glanced at her, his brow creasing.

"I imagine," Maram continued, "that being a mother is like being on a path. And the path brings you to the natural next step."

Esther stepped forward. Richard whipped his gaze from Maram and said, "Don't move."

Esther took another step. She felt Nicholas reach out and clasp her wrist with his cold fingers and she shook him off.

"Enough," Richard said. "Nicholas, give me the book."

"Nicholas, don't," Esther said, and took another step. The gun was about four feet from her head now, with Richard another two feet behind it.

"Nicholas has done quite a lot to protect you," Richard said to her. "Do you really want him to see me do this? His nightmares are bad enough."

Esther glanced to Maram and for the first time, she found Maram looking back. Their eyes met, a shock like a live wire, and Maram gave her the tiniest of nods—but not tiny enough. Richard caught the movement out of the corner of his eye and said, "What is—"

But Esther didn't give him time to finish. She launched herself at him, taking those four feet between them in one leap, and Nicholas's shout of horror was drowned out by the explosion of the gun.

34

Aside from the vampire that had drained her father's blood, there was only one other book in Joanna's collection that had been in progress for as long as she'd known it. It was bound in a neat natural leather, and she'd often wondered about the spell that was ongoing between its pages, wondered who'd first read it and what had become of them.

Now she knew.

In the basement, she and Collins had watched as Cecily pricked her finger, pressed her blood to the last page of the leather book, and broke the silencing spell she'd read over two decades before. Joanna had heard the slight shift of sound as the spell ended, and even after they'd closed the door on the collection and climbed the stairs, she thought she could still sense the changed hum of the books below her.

Sir Kiwi was sitting in the hall waiting for them and leaped up as they came back in through the basement door, luxurious tail wagging. Cecily bent to pet her, her hand trembling slightly. Now that the shock of seeing Cecily was wearing off, Joanna realized her mother was wearing nothing more than slippers, black leggings, and the Beatles' *Revolver* T-shirt she had probably gone to sleep in, and her bare arms were goosebumped from the cold. Joanna ducked away down the front hall to the closet, returned with a thick wool sweater that had once belonged to Abe.

"Here," she said to her mother. "You can wear this."

Cecily held the sweater in her hands, shivering, though she didn't move to put it on. She traced a finger over the black pattern woven into the cream background. "This jacket is older than you are," she said. "I bought it for your father when we lived in Mexico City."

Joanna had already turned to follow Collins and Sir Kiwi to the kitchen, but at these words she stopped. "How is that possible? You and dad met after he came here."

"No," Cecily said. "That was the story we decided to tell you girls. But really, we met in Mexico City. When your father was still with Isabel."

Her voice, which was calm and steady, did not match her impossible words. A chill swept across Joanna's skin. "What? What are you saying?"

Cecily fit her arms into the sweater and pulled it tight across her body. "Let's sit down."

The kitchen lights were on, and everything felt too bright, from the shine of the hanging copper pans to the reflective glint of the fridge to the bare lines of Cecily's resolute face. Joanna turned off the overhead, dimming the room from a glare to a glow. Now they were lit only by the hanging lamp above the stove, its light soft from a grease-blurred bulb. Cecily sat at the kitchen table and Joanna sat across from her.

Collins held up the kettle and, putting his degree to good use, said, "Tea?"

Both Cecily and Joanna shook their heads, but Collins filled the kettle anyway, then leaned against the countertop with Sir Kiwi at his feet, glaring at Joanna. Even in their short acquaintance, she had come to recognize this as his worried face, and she tried to smile at him, but could feel it was a failure. His glare intensified.

Cecily was looking at him, her expression baffled. "Who exactly did you say—" Cecily started. Joanna cut her off.

"You said you came here to tell me the truth." She took a postural lesson from Collins and squared her shoulders, set her jaw. "So tell it."

It seemed for a second that her mother might protest, but then Cecily nodded. She smoothed her hands against the table like she was rolling out a map, then closed her eyes. She inhaled long and deep before opening them again.

"This all begins," she said, "with Isabel."

ISABEL HAD ALWAYS BEEN AMBITIOUS. SHE WAS BORN IN MEXICO CITY to a Zapotec mother and a half-Spanish father and raised in the family bookstore. The bookstore was a relic of the colonial fortune her paternal side had managed to mostly squander, and it had been started by her paternal grandparents as a passion project in the early thirties—intended at that time not for income, but to raise their social capital among the writers and artists whose presence they courted at their dinner table. It was from Isabel's paternal grandmother, the Mexican socialite and sometimes-writer Alejandra Gil, that her parents had inherited not only the bookstore but also what was then one of the largest collections of magical books in North America; and it was from this same grandmother that Isabel had inherited the ability to hear magic.

She must have inherited her ambition from one of her grandparents as well, because her parents themselves had none of their daughter's ferocious drive. By the time Isabel was born, her family's generational wealth lay squarely in two courts: connections, and books. Her parents, who'd maintained their expensive habits long after they could afford them, were only too keen to capitalize on the first and sell off the latter, to Isabel's dismay. From a young age she'd been convinced that her family's books held answers to the questions that had occupied the human mind for as long as it could think, answers she believed might be found in the mechanism that allowed these books to be written in the first place.

Was the power channeled from without, or did it come from within? Was it God, or Gods, or spirits, or demons? The miracles described in so many religious texts, were they in fact the product of powerful books, or had books been written in emulation of miracles?

Whatever the power was, wherever it came from, it spoke to her. As a little girl she'd imagined herself like Juana de Arco, chosen by a holy voice to lead and protect, and as she grew older she was more practical but no less dedicated. How could she study the texts and protect them if her parents kept selling them off?

It was Isabel who devoted herself to maintaining her parents' back-room collection, Isabel who traveled around first the city and later the country making contacts, asking questions, hunting down leads on new merchandise. She learned to appraise and to price. She read every book in the collection so many times she knew them by heart, and understood the patterns of repetition and intricacies of phrasing that their pages seemed to demand. Through study she began to know the world well enough to understand that she wanted it to know her.

She tried unsuccessfully to convince her parents to change to a lending model—like a kind of library, she kept saying, so they could make smaller but ongoing gains instead of a large onetime profit. That way they'd be able to keep all the books instead of letting them fall through their fingers, the numbers of the once-impressive collection slowly dwindling as they were sold off one by one. But her parents refused. Too much hassle when it was so easy to simply sell a book whenever they'd spent the funds from the last one.

At the time that Isabel was coming of age in the late seventies, the five largest book communities in the world were centered in Mexico City, Istanbul, Tokyo, Manhattan, and, most notably to Isabel, London.

London was notable because of the rumors.

Isabel had heard them from the book sellers and collectors she'd been seeking out since she was old enough to know how: rumors about a certain organization and a smiling man in a suit who was paying handsomely for entire collections. Rumors that if you refused him, he'd find a way to take them anyway and loan them back to you at exorbitant prices. These rumors were repeated in ominous tones of warning, but far from being warned off, Isabel was intrigued. The organization sounded like the very thing she herself had sought to build from her parents' store.

And then she heard the other rumors, and her intrigue solidified to intention.

These were the rumors that someone in London was not only collecting but producing. For nearly unpayable prices, it seemed a person could commission a specific book, a specific spell, which meant that somebody out there was actively writing the magic that Isabel had spent her entire life so far endeavoring to understand.

To her it was clear that all these rumors were describing the same organization and perhaps the same person: the smiling man in the suit. Whoever he was, Isabel wanted to know him. So she set her sights on England, attained it, and arrived at Oxford for her doctorate in theology with a suitcase full of her parents' most valuable stock. Quickly she established herself in the relevant circles and let it be known that she had a small but impressive collection she was willing to sell in its entirety, including the crown jewel: a fifteen-page volume of rechargeable wards, small and ancient and powerful.

It took two years for Richard to make contact.

By this time, she was known professionally as Maram Ebla, and it was to Maram Ebla that Richard addressed his letter of introduction. She'd chosen Maram because of a family predisposition toward palindromes, and the surname as a tribute to the ancient library of Ebla, which was often called the oldest library in the world. To herself, however, she was still Isabel.

Isabel had heard that the man in the suit was handsome, but she'd also heard that he was in his fifties, which to a woman in her twenties seemed abstractly old. So when Richard appeared at the door of her flat, stooping a little in the low-ceilinged hallway and smiling down at her with tender, cunning eyes, she was startled to find that not only was he attractive, but she was attracted to him.

In no uncertain terms, she told him she was seeking not compensation for her collection, but employment. More than employment, really. A livelihood. A life in the Library, among the books she so loved, as close to the source of the magic as she could get. By the end of their first visit Richard had made her a deal. He would give her a seven-year trial period in which she'd finish her degree and move back to Mexico City to work as the Library's representative in North America, traveling the continent and using her connections to locate private collections and persuade the owners to sell. She would send whatever books she acquired to the Library via a set of spells that would allow her to pass things through a mirror. This was also how she and Richard would stay in communication, by sending notes back and forth through space.

If Richard was suitably impressed at the end of seven years, Isabel would surrender her parents' collection to him and he would invite her into the Library, show her the secrets at the heart of the commissions, and make her an offer of full-time employment.

As a preliminary show of loyalty, she gave him the codex of wards, though she didn't mention that it had a twin, which stayed safely locked-up in her flat. Secrets were currency and Isabel intended to stay rich.

Richard paged through the wards with a critical eye. It was true they were far stronger than the wards the Library currently employed, he told her, but their strength would block the mirror spells he used to communicate with his global employees, like Isabel herself. He pocketed them anyway. He told her he thought he could amend the spell to allow the mirror magic to pass through—an offhand comment that took her breath away with what it implied. Amending spells was as good as writing them.

This was the knowledge she'd been seeking all her life.

Seven years could not pass quickly enough.

Isabel completed her degree and graduated from Oxford and moved back home, ostensibly to help out in her parents' shop but really to expand her list of connections and to make certain that the only books her parents sold were to collectors Isabel knew, so she could later buy—or take—the books back with the Library's support. She traveled to New York and Chicago and Los Angeles and read the mirror spell in her hotel rooms, pushing books through to a place she'd never been but held always in her mind, a candle to light the way.

Everything went almost exactly as planned, until she met Abe.

He'd come to Mexico City on her invitation, a fellow collector with whom she hoped to make a deal, like so many of the deals she'd made in the past three years she'd been working for the Library. The deal was this: Abe's knowledge would become her knowledge, his books would become Library books, and the Library's money would line his pockets.

But instead, Isabel found in Abe what she'd found also in Richard: someone as passionate about books as she herself, someone who believed that her capacity for hearing magic was a higher calling, a calling Abe shared. He, too, was dedicated to preserving the books; he, too, wanted to study and protect them.

Isabel was already half in love with Richard, but since their first meeting at her London flat she had neither seen nor spoken to him. They communicated solely through the notes they traded through spelled mirrors, and in the face of Abe's solid, earnest presence and his clear interest in her, Richard's appeal was shadowy, harder to recall. She and Abe began sleeping together and when she became unexpectedly pregnant, he proposed.

Isabel refused. She hadn't told Abe about her promise to Richard and to the Library, but she did so now. There were a little over three years left in her trial period and if Richard offered her a job at the end of that time, she fully intended to take it—regardless of Abe, and regardless of the baby he badly wanted.

Isabel did not want a child. But both she and Abe were from magical families; both she and Abe were committed, in their separate ways, to carrying on their magical lineage. Any child they had together would almost certainly be born with the gift they themselves had been born with, the ability to hear magic and to carry on the family work. It was this argument that convinced Isabel to keep the baby.

Isabel never told Richard she was pregnant and did not tell him when Esther was born, wary of saying anything that might jeopardize her chances of receiving the job offer that was still her ultimate goal. She figured she'd disclose her daughter only if and when she officially went to work for the Library, and had grand visions of toting Esther along with her, training her from childhood just as Isabel had trained herself.

As for Abe, he believed—because he wanted to believe—that having a child would change Isabel's priorities, that as soon as she saw her daughter's face, all her dreams of the Library would fade like mist in the tidal swell of maternal love.

This did not happen.

Isabel was impatient with nearly every aspect of parenting an infant, and impatient, too, with Abe's wariness about her continued involvement with the Library. What had seemed kindred ideals were already proving to diverge in some irreconcilable ways. It was true that Abe shared her interest in preserving the books, but unlike Isabel he had no interest in making a profit off them, and he deeply distrusted the Library's monopolistic business model. He wanted to keep expanding and protecting her family's collection in secret and maintain the storefront of ordinary books as their actual revenue stream.

By the time Esther was a year old, Abe and Isabel had ended their romantic relationship, and Abe, who'd already been doing the lion's share of the caretaking, took Esther with him when he moved out of their shared apartment. Isabel was on collection trips most of the week and saw her daughter on weekends, and it was she who suggested hiring a nanny: a friend of hers tangentially involved in the book scene, a young Belgian woman who adored Esther.

This was Cecily.

All three of them had already noticed—with great dismay and disappointment on Isabel's part and some uneasiness on Abe and Cecily's—that spells seemed to have no effect on Esther whatsoever. Cecily had a book that set an impassable perimeter and she used it one night in the living room, intending it to keep Esther safely inside a square of carpet while she cooked dinner, and not ten minutes after she'd set it, Esther crawled through the kitchen doorway. Abe and Isabel tested the baby with other books and found she could smash vases that had been spelled unbreakable and seemed impervious to any glamour they tried to place upon her. None of them were certain what to make of this.

Another year went by, during which Abe's mother—widowed for over a decade—passed away and left him their family home in Vermont. Abe and Cecily were together, Esther was almost three, and Cecily was six months pregnant, when Isabel's seven-year trial period ended and Richard formally invited her to England.

Finally, the time had come. Isabel was being offered the thing she still wanted most in the entire world: an invitation to the Library and all its secrets. Despite Abe's disbelieving protests, she left immediately, as she had always told him she would. With nothing to keep them in Mexico City, Abe and Cecily moved to Vermont, to the big old house at the foot of a mountain, and Joanna was born a few months later.

It would be two more years before they saw or heard from Isabel again.

Then, late one night, when both Esther and Joanna were fast asleep, she showed up on their doorstep. She had flown to New York on a work trip and, unbeknownst to Richard, rented a car and made the eight-hour drive from the city. She wasn't there to visit. She was there to tell Abe and Cecily what she'd learned in the past two years at the Library. She'd learned, finally, how they wrote new books.

She had learned about Scribes.

Not only that, she'd met one—a young man named John, who was missing an eye and had recently fathered a child. A child whom no magic could touch.

A child like Esther.

At first, Isabel had been ecstatic to understand that, far from being magic-less, her own daughter had the very power Isabel had structured her entire life around discovering. She could not help noticing, however, that John didn't seem happy to have produced a child with this power. In fact, both he and his wife seemed grim. More than grim, really. They seemed terrified.

Isabel took a calculated risk and confessed to the new father that she, too, was the parent of a Scribe. She hoped exposing her own vulnerability would encourage John to confide in her, to tell her the truth of his fear, and the gamble paid off. He told her that Scribes were not only Richard's most valuable commodity—they were also his biggest threat. Hundreds of years ago, he'd bound his life to a book and to the bone of a Scribe, his sister, and would live for as long as both book and bone remained whole. Only two Scribes could end the spell, one of whom had to be of Richard's bloodline, like John and his son.

Because of this, Richard decided it was in his best interest that no two Scribes ever live free at the same time. To this end, he'd commissioned a spell to seek them out, to hunt them down and either kill or capture them, ensuring that the only Scribe would be under his control. This spell required the eye of a mature, living Scribe. Written in the mid-1800s, "maturity" was specified as thirteen years of age, and John had lost his own eye to this spell at age thirteen, as had the Scribe before him. So the fate of his son—and Isabel's daughter—was at best to lose an eye and live the rest of their life in luxurious captivity, and at worst, to die. Probably soon. Three Scribes alive were two too many.

Isabel's consolation was that the seeking-spell could only be initiated once every twelve months on the anniversary of its first activation, for twenty-four hours, and Richard had gotten complacent in the last few years, letting the November date pass without reading it. He'd been searching all John's life without ever finding another and was starting to believe John was the last of his kind. The arrival of John's child had changed that. This year, Richard planned to set the spell in motion once again. This year— if John was still alive, if the spell was still active—he would find Esther.

Richard had agreed to take John and his wife on a rare trip to Scotland to see her family, and John told Isabel they were planning to use the opportunity to attempt an escape. The seeking spell wouldn't be able to pinpoint them if they kept moving, he told her, so each year on November 2, he and his family would keep moving for twenty-four hours. Isabel, who never missed a beat, made her own plan. She arranged to go to New

York the day after Richard and the Scribe left for Scotland and to come home a day before they were to return, careful to let Richard believe that her trip and its convenient scheduling was his idea.

She was also careful—ruthlessly careful—to make sure that Richard got a tip-off about John's escape plan. To protect Esther, she needed the seeking spell deactivated. She needed John dead.

Once in Vermont, she explained all this to a horrified Abe and Cecily, and then laid out her plan. She had a safeguard against the day the infant Scribe would turn thirteen, when Richard would inevitably reactivate the spell and follow it to Esther. The plan was this: in Vermont, she gave Abe and Cecily two books. One was the codex of wards that was twin to the ones now used by the Library, except these wards hadn't been amended, so they'd block any outside communication spells. The other book was one half of a two-way mirror spell.

Abe and Cecily would enchant one of their mirrors in Vermont to connect with Isabel's mirror in the Library. Meanwhile, Isabel would go back to England and immediately steal Richard's life-book from his study, then send it to Abe and Cecily through the glass. The Scribe and his wife were attempting an escape at the same time, after all, and she knew that when Richard returned from Scotland to find the book gone, he was likely to blame the book's disappearance on them. The second the life-book passed from England into Vermont, Abe and Cecily would read the warding spell and hide themselves and his book completely from view, forever. Thus, when Richard tried to find Esther someday, they would have a bargaining chip against him. They'd have collateral.

There was one final step to the plan.

To circumvent the truth spell Richard was sure to use on all his employees when he discovered his book was missing, Cecily would read Isabel a silencing spell, so even under magical compulsion she wouldn't speak of what she'd done. Isabel, in turn, would read the same spell to Cecily and Abe.

Then, bound by silence, they would part ways, and Isabel Gil would disappear forever.

CECILY'S VOICE WAS HOARSE BY THE TIME SHE'D FINISHED SPEAKING, despite the tea Collins had succeeded in pressing on her, and Sir Kiwi had ended up on her lap. Joanna was staring at a deep scuff on the kitchen table. Esther had made it with a fork when she was five, intent on carving her initials.

"But why would you tell us Isabel was dead?" Joanna asked. "Why would you let Esther believe that?"

"Legally, it was true," said Cecily. "Isabel left her entire life behind when she joined the Library, including her name. She falsified the death records. We didn't want Esther to ever go looking."

"And you wanted us to be afraid," Joanna said.

Cecily's hand stilled on Sir Kiwi's soft fur. "Yes. But for good reason. Richard is an incredibly dangerous man, you know that now."

"I don't know if there's ever a good reason to terrify children," Joanna said. Her mind was already working overtime to process the onslaught of information and she didn't want to ask it to process feelings, too, so she pushed them down, her anger, hurt, grief. Eventually they would bob to the surface and she would have to face them.

Collins spoke up from his cross-legged position on the tiled floor. "If Richard's book was supposed to be collateral," he said, "how come you didn't use that when Maram told you the Scribe-seeking spell was in effect? Esther was, what, eighteen? Why'd you send her away if you had the book all along?"

"I wanted to use it," Cecily said. "That's why I wanted to burn the wards—so Richard would know we had it, so he would come, so we could make a deal and Esther could stay with us. But Abe, he didn't think it would work. When Isabel made contact to tell us the seeking spell had been reactivated, she told us also that the book didn't matter after all, it was essentially indestructible, and we'd never truly be able to end Richard's life with it. She said the important thing was to make certain that Esther kept moving once a year. That was how we'd keep her safe.

"But Isabel and I used to be friends, remember, and I knew she was in love with Richard—then, and still. It seemed clear she was lying about the book to protect him. I thought your father was being cowardly." She turned toward Joanna. "And regardless of Richard, regardless of everything, I wanted the wards down because I wanted to get you out of the trap we'd built for you."

Joanna put her head in her hands. She couldn't look at her mother's face right now, anguished and guilty and suddenly old in the stove's greasy light, as if the conversation had aged her ten years.

"I'm sorry, baby," Cecily said, her voice thick. "This wasn't the life I wanted for you, or for Esther."

A sudden loud scratching sound echoed down the hall and through the kitchen, and they all jumped.

"What is that?" Cecily said, Sir Kiwi's ears pricking, and Collins started to climb to his feet.

"The cat," Joanna said. "He's hungry." She stood from the table, glad for a reason to walk away for a minute. "Give me a second."

She went down the hallway, letting herself breathe, struggling to keep her thoughts straight and opening the door on autopilot. She was so distracted that she could scarcely process what had come in along with a gust of chilly air.

The cat.

He had walked into the house, past her legs, without even glancing up, as if he'd done it a hundred times, and she stared after him, dumbfounded, as he sauntered toward the kitchen. Despite everything that was happening, despite what her mother had just told her, she found herself smiling. This had to be a sign, didn't it? A sign that everything would be all right?

She heard Collins say, "Oh, hey, kitty cat!" Then, "What'd you do with Joanna?"

"Jo?" Her mother called.

She shut the door again and rested her forehead against it for a breath, then turned and followed the cat. She found him crouched on the linoleum next to Collins though not quite within arm's reach, his ears flat, staring across the room at Sir Kiwi, who was whining excitedly and straining against the hold Cecily had on her.

"So Isabel," she said to her mother. "Maram. She's been protecting Esther. That's what all this was for."

Cecily readjusted her grip on Sir Kiwi, staring at the cat. "Your father was madly in love with Isabel," she said. "Even after we got together, I think he believed she might come to her senses and return to him, to Esther. And when that never happened . . . I don't think he ever trusted her again, not on any real level. He thought she wanted to keep Esther a secret from Richard not just to protect her, but also because it gave her power over him. He thought Esther was another card in Isabel's deck, to be pulled when the time was right."

"You trust her, though," Collins said. To Joanna, it sounded like a question. "You think she's on our side."

Cecily shook her head. "Isabel's loyalty has always been to the Library."

"But not anymore, right?" Joanna could hear the smallness of her own voice and she tried again, louder, stronger. "She wanted to finish what she started when she gave you that book. She wants to keep Esther safe."

Cecily looked up. Her face was bloodless, her eyes hooded and wet. She said, "I don't know what she wants."

35

It was true, what Richard had said. Nicholas's nightmares were bad enough.

He did not need to add the feeling of Esther pulling her arm from his grasp, or the way Richard's face hardened as his finger bent around the trigger. He didn't need the memory of that unmistakable crack, the collision of firing pin and powder, the acrid scent of an explosion, didn't ever need to relive the way he felt as he watched Esther pitch forward, his own knees barely holding him up, his heart a clenched fist as he watched her body fall.

And like so many nightmares, this one wasn't making logical sense.

Instead of keeling over onto the ground, Esther's body kept moving through the air—forward, not down. As if she wasn't falling at all, but leaping. Nicholas's ears were buzzing in the aftermath of the gunshot, a buzz that grew louder and louder, and maybe this wasn't a nightmare after all but a dream, because there were bees in the air, fat droning honeybees the size of bullets. One of them whirred past Nicholas's eye, black legs laden with pollen, and behind it, Esther's body was colliding with Richard's.

Maram had spelled Richard's gun just as she'd spelled Collins's. The bullets were useless.

Richard let out an inarticulate roar as the propulsion of Esther's low tackle sent him staggering backward into his desk, papers flying as his arms swept the desktop for vain purchase. There was no use, he was going down. He hit the ground with a jarring thud as Maram leaped away from him and behind the desk.

"Nicholas," she shouted, "Nicholas, the portrait, the frame!"

Nicholas was exhausted. His brain was foggy with lack of sleep, his red blood cells were far from replenished, and though Esther had not actually been shot his body was still reacting as if she had, shocked and shaking. But even the confusion of the past few minutes had not managed to erase years of following Maram's orders, and he acted on instinct, moving without quite having decided to.

He vaulted toward the portrait as Richard backhanded Esther away and struggled to his feet, but she wrapped her arms around his legs, dragging behind him as he lurched forward. He tried to kick her off. She clung on, and he fell back to his knees as Nicholas barely skirted his grasp and got behind the desk. Maram was standing below that bloodstained painting, one hand hovering over the canvas, her face a mask of urgency.

"It's covered in protective spells," she said, "I can't touch it."

Nicholas grabbed at the frame and pulled, but the painting was anchored to the wall and barely gave beneath his scrabbling fingers. Behind him he heard Esther grunt in pain, and when he turned, he saw that Richard had fought free of Esther's attempts to keep him on the ground and was lurching to his feet. Esther was on her hands and knees, maybe dazed from the blow that had opened the dripping red cut above her eye, and Nicholas had a nonsensical shock of incredulity that Richard would waste a Scribe's blood like that. Then he heard a click and felt the nudge of cold steel against his hand.

Maram was handing him her gun.

"Shoot it," she said. "Shoot the bone."

Nicholas, who'd been under armed guard all his life, had been around many guns yet never held one, much less shot one. But he didn't have time to doubt himself. Richard was behind the desk now and bowling into Maram, who was much smaller than he was, and unlike Esther had neither years of training nor any real strength to speak of. Richard held her tight against his chest, almost as if they were embracing, her arms pinned to her side.

"Why are you doing this?" he said. His voice was anguished but his eyes had never looked more like the eyes of the man in the portrait: cold, glittering, fathomless. He hadn't seen the gun Nicholas was levering to hold against the yellowed femur bone at the base of the frame, his fingers curling around the grip.

"I'm sorry," Maram gasped. "I have to do what's best for—"

"For who?" Richard slammed her against the wall, her head connecting with a hollow thud. "For Nicholas? For this girl? Not for yourself—you could've lived forever with me but instead you chose *this*, and why? For whom?"

Maram's hands came up though she wasn't struggling anymore. She was touching Richard's face, her fingers on his furious mouth. "For the books," she said. "For the future of magic."

Richard raised a hand to hit her again, and Nicholas pressed the barrel to the center of the femur where it was thinnest. He pulled the trigger.

The shot was so loud it drowned out other sensations, blurring the recoil pain in Nicholas's hand and turning Maram and Richard and Esther into figures in a pantomime, all face and silent gesture: Richard's hand completing its arc against the side of Maram's head, Maram staggering to one side beneath the blow, Esther climbing to her feet. Nicholas blinked hard, trying to clear his eye and head, and looked at what he'd done.

Under the barrel of the gun, the yellowed bone was cracked in two.

His ears were ringing from the sound of the gunshot but even so, he could hear the sound Richard was making: a high keening wail like an animal in pain. Nicholas turned from the portrait to find his uncle stumbling back from Maram, one hand going to the desk to hold himself up, his bloodied teeth bared in a grimace. Maram was doubled over, reeling from the recent blow, and suddenly Esther was at Nicholas's elbow, her hands pushing into his jacket, patting at him. Her lower lip was split and her face was frantic, hair tangled, all her usual composure shattered like the bone frame.

"Nicholas," she panted, "hurry, Nicholas, the book," and he understood what she wanted. He could not let himself look back at his uncle, who had both hands on the desk and was barely keeping to his feet, head hanging. Nicholas pulled the book from his jacket pocket and gripped one half of it, Esther's hands closing around the other side.

Abe and Joanna took good care of their collection. Nicholas had noticed this in the basement—the archival temperature and humidity, the glass cases to keep the dust away, the leather covers supple. Nicholas knew from his own experience, both with books and with the many fine leather boots he made sure were oiled every few months, that cared-for leather lasted a long time and was exceedingly difficult to tear with one's bare hands. Even leather made from the delicate hide of a human could be tanned into resiliency and, with the proper regimen of care, kept pliable and tough and unrippable.

But this book gave way beneath Nicholas and Esther's hands like it had been waiting for its bone counterpart to shatter, so it, too, could come apart. The pages fell from the spine like a butterfly with its wings sundered, and the leather cover tore so easily that Nicholas and Esther both fell back as the book came apart between them, paper floating down. As the first page hit the ground, so did Richard.

Richard fell to his knees and curled forward, his salt-and-pepper hair turning ash-gray, then bone-white, thinning across a scalp that was pink, then mottled, then sepia and taut across his skull. On some vestigial instinct of love Nicholas turned from Esther and went to his knees beside him, not close enough to touch, and Richard turned his face toward him.

This was the nightmare.

Those familiar features, those gentle eyes, that smiling mouth, all of it twisted in agony, and beneath the agony, a disbelief so pure it was almost innocent. Richard's face began to collapse like a bad squash, his skin aging before Nicholas's sight, wrinkling in folds and then tightening around his cheekbones and jaw as his eyes went rheumy and jaundiced. They sank into the dark hollows of their sockets and his lips skinned back from his teeth, still tinged red with blood, his gums swelling and receding until his mouth was all long yellow tooth and panting purple tongue. He was making a hideous sound, like he was breathing with lungs made of glass, and he reached for Nicholas with fingers that were clawed and gnarled and tipped with broken fingernails, his wrists like twigs as his flesh lost all moisture and adhered to the bone.

Then he slumped over, eyes and mouth still open and gaping, a mummy in a beautiful suit.

"Are you all right?" Nicholas heard Esther asking Maram.

Richard's twisted hand was inches from Nicholas's knee. Nicholas stared at it. It was unrecognizable as having belonged to a human who'd been alive only seconds before. Was it anger that had made Richard reach out in his last moments? An urge to strike? Or had it been something else? One final, fruitless attempt at connection?

"You understood," Maram said to Esther. "About the bullets. I hoped one of you would. You understood everything."

"Yes," Esther said.

There was a silence. Richard's hand began to swim in Nicholas's vision. "And you understood, too," Maram said, "about . . . about the relationship you and I share?"

If Nicholas had been in any state to laugh, he might have. He'd never heard Maram sound so awkward, so unsure. But he could barely hold his head upright on his neck, much less find the energy to smile. The part of him that had grown up seeking comfort in Richard's kind face wanted to grip the warped inhuman fingers of his uncle's hand and find a spell that would bring Richard back to life so he could explain himself, so he could tell Nicholas it was all a misunderstanding and Nicholas could beg his forgiveness and Richard could give it.

"I'd like to hear you say it clearly," said Esther.

Maram cleared her throat, regaining a little of her officiousness. "Well, I'm, that is, I don't feel I can quite use the word 'mother,' given our circumstances, but it's true that I'm the person who gave birth to you."

"Thanks for that," said Esther.

Black was encroaching on Nicholas's vision, a dizzying tunnel he let himself keel into. He put his head down on his knees and felt the very tip of Richard's curled dead fingers touch his hair, almost a caress, and for a moment he let himself pretend. But then Esther's living fingers touched his shoulder, so warm and solid that they brushed all pretense away and Nicholas understood, with mingled grief and triumph, that this was real.

36

Clouds looked different from above. They peaked and valleyed like a landscape, their hollows purple with unshed water, summits blazing white and pink in the last flares of the evening sun. Knolls and mesas went wispy at the edges, trailing off into the blue sky like smoke and breaking the illusion of solidity that almost made it seem the plane could put its wheels down and land.

Esther touched Joanna's hand where it lay on the armrest between them.

"Jo," she said, in a way that made Joanna suspect it wasn't the first time she'd said it.

"Hmm?" said Joanna, forehead still pressed to the window.

"I said, do you want a drink?"

Finally, Joanna turned. Spots of light danced in her vision and the interior of the plane looked yellowed, cramped and drab compared to what lay outside. Both Esther and a flight attendant were staring at her. Esther had a glass of something pale and fizzy sitting on her folded-down tray.

"Coffee," Joanna said to Esther, and when her sister gestured to the waiting flight attendant, readdressed her request. "Coffee. Please. With milk."

The attendant handed her a mug and pushed the cart another aisle down. Joanna took a sip.

"Blech," she said. "This is awful."

"Oh yeah?" Esther said and poked one of Joanna's dimples. "Why do you look so happy, then?"

Joanna batted her hand away though she couldn't stop smiling. "Turns out I like flying."

"Turns out I do, too, when it's first class." Esther stretched her legs appreciatively. "Don't tell Nicholas I said that."

Esther had not wanted to use the Library's money for anything, much less luxury plane tickets. It was literally blood money, she'd argued, but Nicholas had eventually talked her around by making her count the zeros in the various bank statements Maram had signed over to him. The accounts hadn't been transferred until days after they'd destroyed Richard's book—at which point Maram had already been long gone.

She had vanished in the thirty-odd minutes it had taken for Nicholas, who'd come back to Vermont with Esther after ending Richard's life, to realize that he shouldn't have left her alone in the Library. His first fear was that she would end the mirror spell and sever the link between the two houses, trapping him in Vermont, but she'd left the spell intact. Nicholas had gotten back through the mirror without a problem and found a manila envelope sitting on Maram's empty bed.

There was a note, too. It was as cryptic as Joanna had come to expect from her sister's mother.

Dear Nicholas and Esther, I have always wanted what was best for the Library. I have also always wanted, in my own way, what was best for you. It has become apparent that I myself am neither. What am I best for, then? I aim to find out. There is much to learn, still, about everything.

The envelope held documents Nicholas would need as the new de facto head of the Library: the deed to the house, information on the Library accounts that were now under Nicholas's name, instructions on how to find the paperwork and health insurance information for all Library employees. When Nicholas combed the collection, he found she had taken several books with her, including an invisibility glamour, a spell to let her walk through walls, and the bullets-to-bees spell. If the expiration date had not ended with Richard's life, they could have tracked her, but as it stood, she was untraceable. She'd already proven how easily she could obtain false passports.

"Thanks again for coming with me," Joanna said to her sister, dumping a paper sachet of sugar into her vile coffee. "Considering . . . you know." Considering her sister did not need a plane to get to England.

"Of course," said Esther. "I wouldn't let you fly alone your first time."

Since the two Scribes had returned to Vermont through the mirror several months ago, both of them had been constantly back and forth across the continents, and the room in Joanna's house that had once been Esther's bedroom and then a junk room was now looking very much like an extension of the Library.

"A satellite branch," Nicholas had said recently, looking around at the books carefully propped on shelves, the desk Collins had helped Joanna carry up the stairs, the new dehumidifier humming away in one corner.

For the past several weeks, Nicholas had been working near-tirelessly on a text for the spell Joanna was now flying across the world to read; a spell Joanna herself had helped write.

When Nicholas had first begun asking her advice, popping through the mirror to yell for her to come and look at a certain sentence, or asking what she thought about using dandelion over comfrey, she'd been suspicious he was condescending to her, letting her feel involved despite the fact that she was stuck on one side of the mirror while he and her sister could waltz across the Atlantic with a single step.

But when she'd put her new cell phone to use and shared her doubts with Collins, who was also bound by the laws of physics and thus most likely to sympathize, he'd laughed at her. "Nicholas is not that well-socialized," he said. "If he's asking for your help, it's because he wants your help, not because he wants to make you feel good."

The more she offered her opinion, the more Nicholas asked for it, until eventually he'd shifted his writing office almost entirely to Vermont. Joanna was especially pleased because this meant Esther, too, was around more often, fidgeting in a chair or pacing the room as Nicholas narrated the decisions he and Joanna were making on the draft. Nicholas was teaching Esther how to write magic, though he was the first to admit that a spell as difficult as the one they were attempting wasn't an ideal primer.

"Soon as this book's finished, we'll start you on proper lessons," Nicholas said, and his voice grew bitter. "Lessons designed by an expert."

He was taking Maram's disappearance very hard. Much harder than Esther seemed to be, though it was always hard to tell with her.

"Obviously there's a lot I want to know," Esther said. "But I'm not sure I want to cozy up to someone who's basically spent most of her adult life as a creepy henchwoman."

"That's Dr. Creepy Henchwoman, to you," Nicholas had answered, rather miserably.

Joanna supposed it made sense Nicholas was struggling more; regardless of blood ties, it was clear Nicholas had seen Maram as family—the only family he had left after Richard, and gone the same night he'd lost his uncle. He had tried unsuccessfully to hide his hurt and had not bothered to hide his anger. But Esther's sanguinity on the subject came partially from the final object in the envelope: a small, silver hand-mirror marked with blood.

"Clearly she plans to be in touch," Esther said. "We just have to be patient."

"Patience is not one of the virtues I've cultivated," Nicholas said, fixing his hair in the hand-mirror.

"Too busy with modesty," observed Collins.

Only days later did Esther tell Joanna that she'd had time alone with Maram (Isabel? No one was sure how to think of her) before coming back through the mirror. All her life she'd had questions, but she forgot most of them the instant Maram looked at her, those eyebrows raised expectantly.

"Go on," Maram had said. "Ask."

"The novel," Esther said. It was the first thing that had come to mind. "By Alejandra Gil. Why is it so important to you?"

Maram had looked surprised, as if that wasn't the question she'd expected. "My grandmother wrote it," she said. Then added, "Your great-grandmother. She was a writer . . . and I suppose, as a Scribe, you're a writer, too, in your way. Writing is in your blood, right along with magic. But really it was the title that made an impression on me as a girl. I always thought it suggested, on some palindromic level, that it's the steps themselves that make a path, instead of the other way round. We are creating even as we believe we are following."

Esther pulled down the neck of her sweater and exposed the first few words that were inked across her skin, and she saw the moment Maram realized what they said. For the first time, real emotion moved across her face, her mouth trembling before it smoothed out again. "I like that," she said.

"What was the name of your parents' bookstore?" Esther asked.

Maram touched a hand to the collar of her silk blouse. There was a distant quality to her expression, a boat receding from the shoreline. "Los Libros de Luz Azul."

Esther turned this over on her tongue, *Blue Light Books,* then smiled. "Luz Azul."

Maram, who'd given herself a name that could be read in a mirror, smiled back. "Our family loved palindromes. They're an old magic, you know."

"What happened to the store?" Esther swallowed her pride and admitted, "I looked for it."

"It's still there," Maram said, "though in a rather different form. Someday, I'll tell you that story."

Esther decided to take this as a promise. "One last question," she said. "For now."

"Go on."

"What did you think I would ask you?"

"Oh," Maram said. Her gaze lingered on Esther's face, perhaps doing what Esther had done when she'd first seen Maram standing in Richard's study: searching for signs of herself. "I thought you'd ask if I regret doing what I did."

Esther did not know which act Maram meant. Did she regret leaving her daughter all those years ago, or betraying the Library she'd left her for? But she rose to the bait and said, "Do you?"

At that, Maram reached out and brushed the back of her hand against Esther's. It was a strange piece of contact, intimate even in its oddness, and Esther shivered. "I don't know yet," Maram said, and Nicholas came back into the room.

IT WAS COLLINS WHO PICKED JOANNA AND ESTHER UP AT HEATHROW, idling curbside in a huge black Lexus with tinted windows. He had the window rolled down despite the cold and the sight of his face in profile made Joanna's stomach flip with nerves.

They hadn't really had a chance to talk since their kiss on the front porch, over two months ago now. Or rather, they hadn't talked about the kiss itself. They'd spoken of plenty else, some of it logistical and some of it personal, trading stories through phone calls and text messages and once, disastrously, a video call in which Joanna couldn't get the sound to work. Collins had left a few days after Esther and Nicholas had come back through the mirror; first to return the car to his friends in Boston and make his explanations to them and to his sister, then on a flight back to the Library in order to take over the Library's ward-setting and to open up one end of a different mirror spell that used his and Joanna's blood, so they didn't have to rely on Maram's and Cecily's. Also because Nicholas had absolutely no idea how to run a household and it was already starting to mutiny under his inept captaincy. Unlike Collins, the rest of the Library staff had been hired by more or less legitimate means and reacted with understandable dismay when Nicholas had magnanimously decreed them all "free to go."

"They're not indentured servants, dumbass," Collins had said. "They're your paid employees and they think you just fired them. Plus, what were you planning to do, cook your own dinner? Dust your own chandeliers? Ha!"

Collins had, somewhat clumsily, invited Joanna to come with him, but she had declined. She wasn't ready yet to leave her home and her father's memory, which still clung to her like a hand on her shoulder, sometimes comforting, sometimes grasping. Nicholas had decided to maintain the Library wards for the time being, but Joanna hadn't put her own back up since the night Collins had stolen them. He'd hidden them out in the forest, wrapped in a plastic bag and shoved down into the damp, moldering hollow of a tree, and though he'd given them back to her, she hadn't used them again. She felt exposed without their protection, like a door left open, but she kept thinking about what Collins had said about cracking the lid of his world, about the light coming in. So far, the only bad thing that'd happened was she'd had to officially connect her house to the electrical grid, though she'd left that particular task to Esther, since it was her field, after all.

Cecily, of course, was overjoyed. She'd dissolved into tears as soon as Esther had stepped through the mirror and hadn't really stopped crying for days. At first Esther had been her usual composed self; she'd seen Cecily sitting there in her old bedroom and said, "Hi, Mom," in a perfectly neutral voice, as if greeting her mother after an absence of minutes, not years. But when Cecily touched her, it was as if something in her broke. Her face lost all its pent-up control, shattering around the fault lines of a decade, and she began to sob into her mother's shoulder.

"Oh, my little baby," Cecily said, stroking her curling hair. "It's okay. It's okay. You're home."

"You lied to me," Esther sobbed. "You all lied to me."

"Yes," Cecily said, in those same soothing tones. "We did. I'm so sorry."

"Don't ever lie to me again."

"I won't. I promise I won't."

Despite the near-constant flow of tears, Cecily was so demonstrably overjoyed to have both her daughters in one place that she hugged and kissed Nicholas and Collins each time she saw them, as well. She was thrilled not only by Esther's presence, but by the fact that she could now roll down the driveway anytime she liked, Gretchen hanging her furry head out the window, car filled with Tupperwares of lasagna and salad and curry and all the other meals she'd been longing to bring her daughters for the past ten years. After the sixth time Esther went to bed behind a closed door and woke to find Cecily lovingly stroking her hair, she suggested they all have a chat about boundaries—"Psychological, not magical"—but it hadn't happened yet.

Cecily was in fact staying in the house for the two weeks Joanna would be gone, to feed the cat. Once he'd finally deigned to enter, it was as if he'd lived there all his life, and there wasn't a corner he hadn't shed into. For a while Joanna had used him as an excuse for why she couldn't visit the Library, but even she knew it was just that: an excuse.

The truth was, she was frightened.

She had never really been anywhere and never really done anything other than care for the books, had never really known anybody other than her family. Nor had she ever tried to let herself be known by others. She didn't know if she could.

Yet here she was. In England. Trying.

Esther spotted the Lexus right after Joanna had, but she was afflicted by none of Joanna's nerves and immediately shouted "Collins!" waving her arm like a traffic conductor. Joanna was wearing what she always wore—black jeans and her red wool coat (though she'd let her mother trim her hair), but she was worried somehow that she'd look different than she had that night on the porch, that she'd look different to Collins.

He didn't look the same to her. He looked better.

At the sound of Esther's voice, he jerked his head up and threw open the car door, and a second later Joanna found herself wrapped in a hug so tight she had to pound his back to get him to loosen his grip.

"Collins, let her breathe," Esther said.

"Sorry, sorry," Collins said, then shoved Joanna away so he could hold her at arm's length and stare at her, grinning madly, before he reeled her back in. She was grinning, too, a smile she hid against the soft crinkle of his puffy black jacket. He had poured on a too-sweet cologne that made the back of her throat itch, but she didn't mind one bit. By the time he let her go, her nerves were calmed, and excitement had taken their place.

He hugged Esther, too, who only came up to his armpit and was so swallowed by his embrace that only her legs were visible, then he led them to the car and flung open the doors for them to get in.

"No luggage, right?" he said, and they shook their heads. Joanna had put her suitcase through the mirror in Vermont rather than checking it, so she was unencumbered by luggage aside from a small leather backpack she'd gotten years ago at an estate sale.

She knew people drove on the other side of the road here but still it felt wrong to climb into what she thought of as the driver's seat, Collins behind the wheel to her right. She palmed the dashboard nervously as he pulled out into the line of Heathrow traffic.

"Nice car," Esther said from the back. She was sitting all the way on the edge of the middle seat, practically between Collins and Joanna.

"Buckle up," said Collins. "We got about an hour and a half drive." He was still grinning, and he slammed on his turn signal with far more force than necessary. "Welcome to Ye Olde Merry England. How was baby's first plane ride?"

"I loved it," said Joanna. "They kept giving us snacks. Here, I brought you a souvenir." She dug around in her backpack and came up with a plastic-wrapped brownie, which she dropped into Collins's waiting palm.

"First class is wild," said Esther, as Collins ripped into the package with his teeth and spat a piece of plastic off his tongue. "The seats are—"

She broke off abruptly, and Joanna swiveled in her seat to find her sister staring down at her cell phone, her face completely still, her shoulders slightly hunched as if against a blow. Alarm clanged through Joanna's body.

"What?" Collins said, eyes flicking from the highway to the rearview mirror and back.

"Pearl called," Esther said.

Joanna let out her breath. "Isn't that good?"

"I don't know yet."

"Did she leave a message?"

"No." Esther put a hand to her throat and closed her eyes. "She must have read the book."

Esther had agonized for days over which book to send to the research base, which book to send to give Pearl proof of magic. It had to be romantic, but not cheesy; amazing, but not disquieting; beautiful, but not frighteningly so. She'd had finally settled on a Library book Nicholas had offered, which made any nearby plant sprout clusters of golden berries that rang like bells, and mailed the book with specific instructions that Pearl should go to the greenhouse, prick her finger, and read without stopping until she believed.

Joanna knew it wasn't only magic that Esther was asking Pearl to believe in.

Suddenly, the phone in Esther's hand let out a long, low trill, and everyone in the car jumped.

"Oh my god," Esther said, her voice quavery, her face ashen. "It's Pearl. It's a video call. What do I do?"

Collins punched on the car radio and tossed a cable from the console into the back seat. "Put her on speaker!"

"Fuck off," Esther said, throwing the cable back, then she sat up straight, squared her shoulders and pulled her hair out of its ponytail. "How do I look?"

"Magical," said Joanna.

Esther swiped her thumb across the phone screen and said, "Hello?"

There was no sound in the car but the swish of the tires on the highway, and Joanna's heart began to plummet . . . until, audible even from the weak phone speaker, there came the round chime of fruiting bells. Esther held a hand over her mouth, her eyes filling with tears, and a woman's voice said, "This is absolutely mad. The tomatoes are *ringing*, Esther."

Collins said loudly, "She's *Australian*?"

Esther was wiping her eyes and beaming down at her phone. "They'll stop eventually," she said. "Oh my god, Pearl. I am so happy to see your face."

"This doesn't quite make up for ditching me in Antarctica with memory loss and a broken arm," said Pearl, "but it's an excellent step forward."

"What's the next step?" Esther said.

"Twenty-four hours of in-person explanation and a spell to make me a concert-level pianist."

Esther raised an eyebrow at Joanna, who shook her head. "We don't have anything like that yet," said Esther, "but I'll work on it."

"Wait, where are you? Are you with someone?"

"I'm in England, in a car with my sister."

Collins made an offended noise through his mouthful of brownie.

"Show me!" said Pearl.

Esther turned the phone around and Joanna found herself face-to-face with a pretty, tear-streaked blond girl in Carhartt overalls. She waved tentatively.

"Aww, you look like Esther," said Pearl.

"Thank you!"

Esther turned the phone back around and said, "I'm taking you off video, okay?" and the chiming of the bells was gone. Esther raised the phone to her ear, scrunched herself up in a corner of the back seat as if that would afford her more privacy, and said in a low voice, "I've missed you so much."

Collins, exhibiting rare tact, turned on the radio, and warm cello filled the car as Esther murmured to Pearl. "This okay?" he said. "You can find a pop station if you want. Isn't that what you like?"

"I think my pop sensibilities are a little dated," said Joanna. "This is nice."

"We'll do London later this week," Collins said, waving his hand in the direction Joanna supposed was the city. "Nicholas has a whole tourist thing planned out, Tower of London, the Soane Museum, Westminster Abbey, basically a bunch of freaky haunted shit he thinks you'll like. And maybe we could, I don't know, eat dinner. I mean, have dinner. Go *out* to dinner. You and me. If you want."

"Yes, please," Joanna said. She was struck by the bubbling urge to laugh, so she did, and Collins's hands relaxed on the wheel.

"Nicholas gave me a credit card," said Collins. "He told me to take you somewhere really fancy."

"I don't need fancy."

"No one needs fancy, but maybe you want it. Also, on this side of the pond, *fancy* means you're into someone." He darted a sideways glance at her. "You probably know that from all your romance novels, huh."

"Yes," she said. "But books can only teach you so much."

THEY SPED THROUGH FIELDS LIGHTLY WHITENED WITH SNOW, SOME OF them dotted with bright russet cows, not so different from Vermont in some ways except far fewer trees and no mountains. After a while, Collins rolled the car to a stop on the empty road and Joanna looked around, confused. There were wintery rolling fields as far as her eye could see, not even a farmhouse to break up the monotony of land and sky. The narrow country road stretched out before them and vanished over a distant hill.

"You ready?" Collins said, looking at her. "We'll add your blood to the wards soon as we get to the house so you won't have to go through this again."

With a start, Joanna realized what he meant. "We're here?"

"At the boundaries of the wards, yeah," he said. "The driveway's right there."

She squinted through her window, following his gesturing hand, but all she saw was grass, snow, brush. The more she attempted to focus the hazier her vision became, like Vaseline was being slowly smeared across her eyes, and her head began to pound dully. She'd never been on this side of the wards before.

"Can you see it?" she asked Esther, twisting in her seat, though she knew the answer. Esther nodded.

"I'll go fast," Collins said, and hung a left straight into the hedge.

Joanna braced, but it wasn't impact she felt: it was stomach-turning, brain-scrambling nausea, as if her head had swapped places with her feet and her organs were being impossibly rearranged under her skin, her heart sliding toward her kidneys, her lungs splitting apart and spinning down her arms. Everything was streaked dark and wet like her eyes had been rotated in their sockets and she heard herself moan, an animal sound from a throat that barely felt like her own, a throat that was burning with bile as she retched, trying in vain to locate herself within her own body as the world flipped and slithered around her.

Then, as abruptly as the chaos had begun, it stopped, and Joanna was aware of herself once again. She was folded over, the seat belt holding her up as she dangled over her knees, drool on her chin, hair in her eyes, Esther's hand gripping her shoulder.

"Ugh," Joanna managed. She dragged the back of her hand across her mouth and Esther, who was leaning into the front seat, smoothed the hair away from her face. Joanna hoped Collins wasn't looking.

"It's over," Esther said, her hand cool on Joanna's brow. "We're here. You okay?"

Joanna swallowed, testing herself for nausea, but it had retreated.

"That was an experience I'd like never to repeat," she said, and unbuckled her seat belt, looking out through the windshield. They were in what seemed to be a garage, somewhere windowless and dim and concrete. Another big black car was parked along one wall, identical to the one they sat in now. Collins had already hopped out and come around to open her door, offering her a hand out, which she took because she still felt a bit shaky.

The passage from the garage was so dark and musty that Joanna paused, disoriented, when Collins opened the door onto a white marble floor and ushered them into an enormous, gleaming room. Huge windows framed the countryside they'd just been driving through—the rolling hills, hedges like stitches on a quilt, a minnowy sky. In the distance, Joanna could see a still, dark lake and an old greenhouse, the glass broken, the inside a tangle of winter-dead vines.

A click-click of little nails on marble made her look up right as Sir Kiwi pranced into the room, Nicholas a few paces behind her wearing very blue shoes and very pressed trousers. Joanna had seen him just yesterday, but here in his grand home she felt suddenly shy, out of place. She crossed her arms as he came toward them and the grin he'd been wearing faded into sudden diffidence, as if her reserve was contagious.

"Hello," he said formally. "You made it."

"We did," she said. "Thank you for having me."

Tentatively he reached out like he was going to pat her shoulder, but seemed to change his mind halfway through and pulled her into a hug instead, wrapping his arms tightly around her. After a moment she hugged him back, feeling graceless and very pleased. Aside from Collins, she'd never been hugged by anyone outside her family, and certainly never by anyone who smelled this expensive, like a department store.

"Your sweater's soft," she said.

"I know," he said. "I can't believe you're standing here. Your first flight! How was it? Come on, I put your things in your room, I'll show you to it. Esther insisted you two share because she's frightened of the dark—"

"I'm not frightened of the dark, I'm frightened of your giant haunted murder house, thank you—"

"—But if you want your own space, we've got plenty of it, so just say the word. Are you hungry? Thirsty? Dinner's in an hour, but I thought maybe cocktails in the Winter Drawing Room first?"

"Nicholas," said Collins.

"What? The breakfast room instead?"

"No, no. No more rooms. Maybe let them sit down for a second before you talk their faces off."

"I've never had guests before," Nicholas said. "Excuse me if I'm a little overexcited. This is the ballroom, obviously, and there, that's the Winter Drawing Room. Ink-making kitchen to your right, staff kitchen farther down that hall. You two will be upstairs in the East Wing."

Joanna's neck was already starting to hurt from craning and staring; even the ceilings were elaborate, high and carved and limned in gold. The polished stone floors barely registered their feet, swallowing the sound, but as they ascended the curving staircase their steps began to echo faintly. And there was another sound making itself known, as well: a vast, churning hum.

Without meaning to, Joanna had slowed behind the other three, looking back the way they'd come. The Library's books were below her, she could feel them as clearly as she felt her own hands hanging by her sides. It was like standing over an enormous beehive, honeyed vibrations slowly dripping down her body, all her senses stroked by a hot wind, and she closed her eyes, overwhelmed.

"You get used to it," Collins said, close by. She opened her eyes again to find him waiting with her. "There are bedrooms on the top floor if it's too much for you."

"No," Joanna said quickly, because it wasn't a bad feeling, it was almost soothing, like fingers in her hair. "But I want to see them."

"Now?"

She nodded. Nicholas, who'd been listening from down the hall, doubled back, his steps quick and anticipatory. "Down," he said, though Joanna didn't need him to tell her that, nor to lead her back through the marble-floored hall and down a long hallway carpeted in robin's-egg blue and lined with massive oil paintings, all the way to an enormous metal door. She could have found this door with her eyes shut and her hands tied behind her back, following only that ocean of not-quite-sound, and when

Nicholas opened it with a whir of gears and swept an arm for her to enter first, she did so eagerly.

She stepped into a dream. Lights flickered on as she moved inside and the crystal chandelier above her flared to life, illuminating the ornate ceiling and curving walls, the heavy brocade drapes, richly patterned carpet, dark coruscating wood, velvet-cushioned chairs, shining bronze. And the books. Books on every single wall, shelf after towering glass-doored shelf arranged in twisting, mazy rows, books staring at her from every direction, behind glass doors, propped on stands, their covers facing out, neat placards at every base.

Joanna thought of her basement at home and the pride with which she'd always cared for her own meager collection: dusting their pages, memorizing their words, all the while believing she and Abe were unique in their purpose and chosen in their isolation. Abe had always known this place existed and still he had encouraged those beliefs. Was it to keep her safe, or to keep her stationary, or both? She would never be able to ask him.

At her elbow, Esther said quietly, "Are you thinking about Dad?"

Joanna turned to her, a lump in her throat. She nodded. "How did you know?"

"Because I think of him whenever I'm in here, too."

There were many conversations Joanna would never get to have with Abe, but just as many that she wanted to have with her sister, and even after several months of having Esther back in her life, it still felt like a miracle to think she might be able to. There was so much yet unsaid between them, so much they didn't know about one another, and so much time in which to learn. She leaned into her sister's shoulder and let the sturdy warmth of it ground her.

"What will you do with all of this?" she asked.

"That's a recent matter of debate," Nicholas said, and Esther let out a snort. "As the largest concentrated base of magical knowledge in the world," he continued, shooting Esther a sharp look, "I do think we have some responsibility to ensure it's properly archived and maintained. I have lots of money, I have a full staff, and the house is massive enough to hold a million guests—"

"Twenty-five guests," said Collins. "Thirty tops."

"—so, I was thinking, I don't know, maybe . . . a school?"

"Because the history of boarding schools is such a noble one," said Esther. "Not at all based on colonialism and assimilation."

"Esther wants us to pack up every book and ship it off to its country of origin," said Nicholas. "Personally, I think it might be difficult to get anything to, let's see, Prussia, or Ceylon, or Bengal, for example, and anyway, even places that still exist on a map need a mailing address— someone to be on the other end and receive the packages."

"That's why we need to make connections with more global magical communities," Esther said. "Collins is with me on this, aren't you, Collins?"

"I never said I was against more connections," Nicholas protested, as Collins and Esther shared a fist-bump.

Collins had been right, Joanna thought. She was getting used to the roar of the Library, letting the hum settle in her body and pump through her veins like blood. It already felt like a part of her.

THEY DID END UP HAVING COCKTAILS IN THE WINTER DRAWING ROOM, then dinner in a vast dining room Nicholas said hadn't been used in years. The four of them clustered at one end of the enormous table and Joanna tried not to apologize to the black-uniformed staff who came in and out, pouring wine, clearing plates, complaining in low tones to Collins about a broken pilot light and the poor timing of the next scheduled trip into town for groceries.

"It's been rather informal around here as of late," said Nicholas apologetically, as if Joanna knew the first thing about formality, or cared. "Collins doesn't have the hang of the whole boss thing yet."

"But you," said Collins, "you're a real alpha."

Nicholas had Sir Kiwi on his lap and was feeding her a piece of steak.

The food was very good, but Joanna was unable to eat much. She kept thinking about what would happen after dinner, when she would read the spell that she herself had helped write, powered by her own sister's blood.

This was, after all, the reason she was finally here.

The spell had taken many weeks for Nicholas to compose, in part because it was complicated, and in part because he had to regrow some red blood cells so he could lose them all over again in the service of writing it. The rest of the blood would be Esther's, which was why the spell had been so challenging: never before had Nicholas written a spell for two Scribes. He had sworn not to write a book for at least another year afterward, and for health reasons probably should not even have written this one, but he was adamant in his refusal to wait.

Joanna understood why. This spell was Nicholas's way of doing a small penance for the harm the Library had caused over the past centuries, much of it so tangled it was impossible to find the tip of the thread to start unraveling the ugly knot. But one wrong, at least, had a clear path to right.

It had been two centuries since Richard had cast the spell that confined all magic talent only to bloodlines. It might be years more before they'd know if this new spell worked. A whole new generation of people might have to be born before they'd know for sure if they'd succeeded in breaking Richard's inheritance spell.

Or maybe they themselves would lose their own magic, Collins and Joanna suddenly down to five senses, Esther and Nicholas's blood suddenly powerless. Maybe all their power would be siphoned away into other bodies, other lives, as random as it had been for the thousands of years before Richard had focused it into families. This was a risk they'd all agreed to take, and Joanna savored the hum of the Library, committing the sensation to memory in case she never heard it again.

Finally, the time came.

They gathered in the room that had once been Richard's office and was now a mess of broken glass, slashed canvas, and torn pages, the floor covered in the ruins of books and artifacts. Collins had told Joanna about watching Nicholas smash the jar that held his eye but he had not mentioned where the eye itself had ended up, and Joanna stood beneath the empty shelves and shuddered.

For a moment she had the urge to leave their newly written book and walk away from this place where so many terrible things had been done. She would climb into one of those big black cars, somehow drive herself out of the wards and back to the airport, and fly home to her old familiar mountains, the sky, the trees, the cat, the immutable walls she knew as well as she knew her own face.

"Are you ready?" Esther said.

Joanna looked down at her. Ten years had done their work and Esther was not the girl she'd known in childhood. There were already fragile lines starting at the corners of her eyes, bracketing her mouth, settling above her expressive brows, and Joanna found them so unbearably beautiful she had to turn away. She hadn't known if she would ever get to see this: her sister, grown. The changes in Esther's face felt like a gift.

Nicholas was sitting cross-legged on the bare desk, chin in hand, Collins to one side holding a small dish of powdered herbs, ready for his cue to step forward. Like Esther they were watching Joanna, waiting for her to take the next step.

Joanna put her hand in Esther's. Esther's touch was confident as she pressed the tip of a silver knife into Joanna's finger and the blood beaded up flower-bright on her skin, surface-tense with the urge to run. The thrum of magic filled the air: the endless sugar of a hot blue sky, the beat of a thousand gossamer wings, a wind that moved anything on earth that could be moved, which was everything.

Joanna opened the book.

ACKNOWLEDGMENTS

Welcome to the acknowledgments pages of a writer who loves acknowledgments pages. For you classy readers who prefer a short and punchy statement of gratitude, the tl;dr is THANK YOU, EVERYBODY!!! For those of you like me, i.e., nosy, read on for the answers to today's most pressing questions, such as the name of my agent, who my friends are, which institutions have given me money, and whether or not I will thank an illiterate animal (spoiler: I will).

To begin, the name of my agent is Claudia Ballard and she's magnificent. Claudia, I'm so grateful to you for sticking with me through years of drafts, disappointments, and a complete renunciation of the literary realism for which you originally signed me. Thank you for your keen editorial eye and your steadfast enthusiasm. Also from WME, thank you to Matilda Forbes Watson for thrilling cross-pond negotiations, Sanjana Seelam for West Coast finesse, Camille Morgan for tireless title brainstorming, and Caitlin Mahony for bringing this book to the wider world, and for an enthusiastic early read that buoyed my heart.

At William Morrow, thank you to my phenomenal editor Jessica Williams for your clear, creative vision of what the book was, and what it could be. Thank you also to Julia Elliott for plot witchery. Thank you to my excellent UK editors, Selina Walker at Century and Sam Bradbury at Del Rey—Nicholas's stately home would be in ruins without you.

Thank you to Melissa Vera at Salt & Sage Books for your kind, careful read; and to Ronkwahrhakónha Dube, thank you for the generous magic of your insight and questioning.

Thank you to Jacoby Smalls for Antarctic intel.

Thank you to my mother, Gail Mooney, for raising me in a home filled with books, and for giving me a love of language, travel, good deals and good times. To my father, Frederic Törzs, thank you for the generosity of your love and the absurdity of your humor. Thank you to my fun, funny, wise sister, Jesse Törzs. The first stories were for you; this story is for you; and every story until the end, for you.

Thank you to my stepmother, Niki; to my stepfather, Steve; and to my stepsisters, Ella, Sophie, and Tessa. I'm grateful you're family.

A heartfelt thank you to Douglas Capra, whose parting gift paid off my student loans and afforded me time to write. Dougie, you had excellent taste in books, and I can only hope you would have liked this one. We miss you always.

Thank you to my earliest readers: to Lesley Nneka Arimah for providing the impetus and encouragement to start this novel in the first place and to Abbey Mei Otis for subfreezing writing dates in my half-finished trailer.

Thank you to the Clarion West class of 2017, Team Eclipse: Shweta Adhyam, Elly Bangs, David Bruns, Mark Galarrita, Aliza (A.T.) Greenblatt, Iori Kusano, Patrick Lofgren, Robert Minto, Stephanie Malia Morris, Andrea Pawley, Joanne Lim-Pousard, Vina Jie-Min Prasad, and Gordon B. White. I am wildly grateful for and intensely proud of you. Thanks especially to Andrea Chapela, who wrote the Spanish original of the paragraph Esther translates in chapter 4, and who gave me a Zoom lecture on structure and POV that rocked this novel's world. And to Alexandra Manglis, Adam Shannon, and Izzy Wasserstein, thank you for every thread in our web of conversation. Your brilliance, humor, tenacity, and affection have improved my life and my writing immeasurably.

To Sally Franson, thank you for deep dives and undiluted joys. Thank you to Nicole Sara Simpkins, keeper of our myths and memories. Thank you to Eric Andersen for making the house a home, and thank you also to Nate White, Gabriela Farias, Dr. Aaron Mallory, and Ashton Kulesa for keeping me from loneliness even in the depths of COVID-19 quarantine and the isolation of writing a novel.

Thank you to my therapist, Heather Smith. I know it's your job to listen to me, but you're really good at your job.

Thank you to Joanna Newsom for going on tour in the fall of 2019.

Thank you to Lauren Joslin for shaping my early imagination.

Thank you to the Minnesota State Arts Board, the Minnesota Regional Arts Council, the Loft, the Jerome Foundation, the McKnight Foundation, Norwescon, and the National Endowment for the Arts for financial support over the years. Thank you to the Norton Island residency for jump-starting this stalling book after the hard summer of 2020 and to the Lighthouse Works Fellowship, where I stole Daphne's last name (thanks, Daphne) and wrote "the end" to the sound of the tides.

Thank you to my writing professors at the University of Montana, especially to Debra Magpie Earling for your encouragement of all things witchy. Thank you to my Clarion West instructors. Thank you to Peter Bognanni for support, first as your student and now as your colleague. Also at Macalester, thank you to Mark Mazullo for good food and even better conversation, and thank you to Matt Burgess who once solved the plot by asking me, "Who's keeping secrets from whom?"

Thank you to Igor, cat of my heart and soul, for setting the aesthetic.

Lastly, thank you to everyone who may read, work on, or otherwise help this book after I turn in my acknowledgments. I appreciate each one of you immensely.